E. M. FORSTER was born in 1879 and educated at King's College, Cambridge. His first novel, WHERE ANGELS FEAR TO TREAD, was published in 1905 and was followed in 1907 by THE LONGEST JOURNEY. Later came A ROOM WITH A VIEW in 1908 and HOWARDS END in 1910. In 1914 he completed MAURICE but it was not published until 1971. Such publication was delayed by the novel's homosexual theme. In 1924, the brilliant A PASSAGE TO INDIA, based on Forster's firsthand observation of Indian life, appeared. His other works include collections of short stories and essays, a volume of criticism, a libretto for Benjamin Britten's opera BILLY BUDD, a filmscript, and a study of Virginia Woolf. In 1953, Forster was awarded membership in the Order of Companions of Honor by Queen Elizabeth II. On his ninetieth birthday in 1969, he received the Order of Merit. A year later on June 7 he died in Coventry, England.

THE
LIFE TO COME

AND
OTHER SHORT STORIES

E. M. FORSTER

 A BARD BOOK/PUBLISHED BY AVON BOOKS

AVON BOOKS
A division of
The Hearst Corporation
959 Eighth Avenue
New York, New York 10019

First Bard Printing, December, 1976
Second Printing

Contents

Introduction

On his death in June 1970 E. M. Forster left behind, at King's College, Cambridge, England, a considerable corpus of unpublished literary work, complete and incomplete, and in a wide range of genres: novels (*Maurice*, published in 1971, and two substantial fragments), stories, plays, poems, essays, talks—to say nothing of letters, diaries and notebooks. Since, in addition, a significant proportion of his published work had never appeared in volume form, and since several of his books were out of print or would shortly need reprinting, the moment seemed ripe for a new and, as nearly as possible, complete edition. This was published in London by Edward Arnold as the Abinger Edition of E. M. Forster.

The present volume, which corresponds to volume 8 of the Abinger Edition, contains, by intention at least, all Forster's surviving stories which are complete and which were not included in *The Celestial Omnibus* (1911) or *The Eternal Moment* (1928). They span six decades—from, probably, 1903 to 1958, with some revision as late as 1962—and represent every phase of Forster's career as a writer. Only two have previously been published: "Albergo Empedocle", which appeared in *Temple Bar* in December 1903,[1] and—included here for good measure—the composite "Three Courses and a Dessert", which was spread over the four issues of *Wine and Food* for 1944.

How is it that nearly half the extant stories by a

[1] And is reprinted in *Albergo Empedocle and Other Writings*, edited by George H. Thomson (New York, Liveright, 1971).

writer of Forster's stature remained unpublished during his lifetime? To answer that question it is convenient to divide the unpublished stories into two groups. The stories in the first group, which consists of "Ansell", "The Purple Envelope", "The Helping Hand" and "The Rock", are of an earlier vintage than those in the second, as well as being sharply differentiated from them in subject-matter; and it is on a chronological basis that they are placed, in this volume, with "Albergo Empedocle", the first of Forster's stories to achieve publication. Of "Albergo Empedocle" itself little need be said. In 1958 Forster told Wilfred Stone that he did not consider it "good enough" for reprinting;[2] but in 1910 he had included it—in preference even to "The Road from Colonus" as well as to "The Story of the Siren"—among the stories which he initially submitted to Sidgwick & Jackson alongside "The Celestial Omnibus".[3] Stone considers it "a better tale than some that Forster felt were good enough to reprint",[4] a judgement with which I concur.

Of the unpublished stories, those in the first group are all very early indeed, having been written, probably, within the limits of 1903 and early 1906—at a time, that is, when E. M. Forster was by no means a name for editors to conjure with. His first novel, *Where Angels Fear to Tread,* was not published until October 1905 (on what he regarded as poor terms), and like most young writers he received a fair number of rejection slips: a diary entry at the end of 1904, for example, records that " 'Gemistus Pletho' and 'The Story of the Siren' have gone the rounds and failed". The essay and story in question both, in point of fact, found subsequent homes (the latter not till 1920, when it appeared

---

[2] Wilfred Stone, *The Cave and the Mountain: A Study of E. M. Forster* (Stanford and London, Stanford University Press and Oxford University Press, 1966), pp. 129, 407.

[3] Frank Sidgwick, letter to Forster, 1 July 1910 (Bodleian Library, Sidgwick & Jackson papers, vol. 8, no. 149).

[4] Stone, *op. cit.,* p. 144.

as a Hogarth Press booklet); but at this stage Forster was easily discouraged—"Independent [Review] going smash, no one else takes my things," he laments in December 1904—and other rejected stories seem to have been consigned at an early stage to the bottom drawer, and to have stayed there. Although only one of these four stories survives in typescript rather than manuscript, both "The Purple Envelope" and "The Rock" are known to have been rejected by at least one editor, and a similar fate probably attended "The Helping Hand".

However that may be, the four stories, though comparatively lightweight, are far from negligible. The best, as it happens, is also probably the earliest. The handwriting of "Ansell" suggests a date around 1902 or 1903; and the latter year was specified by Forster in conversation with William Plomer, who read and admired the story in 1945. The eponymous hero is not the intellectual of *The Longest Journey,* but a garden boy—to ignore his carefully chronicled series of promotions—whose relationship with the narrator echoes Forster's own childhood friendship, as described in *Marianne Thornton* and fictionalized in *Maurice,* with a garden boy of that name. It is possible that Forster never intended "Ansell", as it stands, for publication. Any such aim must surely, in any case, have been abandoned by early 1904, since a diary entry of 4 March records the rejection by *Temple Bar* of "The Story of the Siren"—into whose opening paragraph "Ansell" 's central statement (that there are higher values than academic ones) and climactic incident (the disastrous loss of some notes for a thesis) have been absorbed. It is worth comparing the descent, in "Ansell", of the Greek optative book-box into a nameless river—

About halfway down it hit a projecting rock, opened like a water-lily, and rained its sweetness upon the deep. Most of the books were heavy and plunged like meteors through the trees into the river. One or two of the smaller ones roosted coyly for a minute on the branches before they too slipped through and disappeared. . . . Liddell and Scott's Greek Lexicon remains open on the ledge where the box split. In dry weather an invisible person rapidly turns over the leaves . . .

—with that, in "The Story of the Siren", of the Deist Controversy notebook into the Mediterranean:

It dived, like a piece of black slate, but opened soon, disclosing leaves of pale green, which quivered into blue. Now it had vanished, now it was a piece of magical india-rubber stretching out to infinity, now it was a book again, but bigger than the book of all knowledge. It grew more fantastic as it reached the bottom, where a puff of sand welcomed it and obscured it from view. But it reappeared, quite sane though a little tremulous, lying decently open on its back, while unseen fingers fidgeted among its leaves.

Each passage shows Forster's imaginative handling of tragi-comic incident at its best; of the two stories as a whole, "Ansell", with its witty surface and beautifully modulated tone of underlying melancholy, is the more homogeneous and coherent, perhaps the more subtle and profound.

Falling books—this time the works of Maeterlinck recur in "The Purple Envelope"; it will take the death of Leonard Bast in *Howards End* to exhaust their symbolic possibilities. Not quite flawless like "Ansell", though more immediately striking, "The Purple Envelope" may owe its origin to a story Forster heard and recorded in his diary on 8 December 1903, about a man who "breathed his friend's name on a mirror and couldn't rub it out". The incident of the shared pipe also has its real-life counterpart, in an encounter with a shepherd recorded on 12 September 1904 and mentioned in the 1960 Introduction to *The Longest Journey;* while yet another diary entry of this period— "Only the sportsman who is killing something leads the perfect life of the open air"—reads like a blueprint for young Howard, who "loved to take life, as all those do who are really in touch with nature". On 1 January 1905, in a letter to R. C. Trevelyan, Forster refers to

> my unfinished ghost story, which I destine for Temple Bar.[5] An old man—a very nice one too— has committed, from high motives, a crime; you mustn't mind what. Justice, so obviously immanent in our daily life, compels him to reveal it in pieces: I mean that *he* is in pieces: falls into them when he goes to sleep. His head is shot one night by mistake for a wild duck, and when they call him in the morning he is dead, and no traces are ever found of the murderer. . . . But I somehow think I am too refined to write a ghost story.

The letter is followed, three days later, by a postcard:

> I want to say to you that I have just transformed "The Purple Envelope" into something comparatively respectable, which will probably be refused by Temple Bar.

It was indeed; and five years later it was among the stories weeded out by Sidgwick & Jackson. A tale of real tension, it may have irritated precisely by its "respectability", its teasing failure to deliver the expected

---

[5] Why *Temple Bar,* which had taken nothing from Forster since "Albergo Empedocle", whereas the *Independent Review* had by now published or accepted four of his stories and three of his essays? In *The Longest Journey* Rickie is told by the editor of the *Holborn,* "Write a really good ghost story and we'd take it at once"; and it seems likely that Forster had been offered a similar incentive by *Temple Bar.*

supernatural goods (or to label the natural brand that has replaced them); or it may have puzzled by its moral ambivalence—the quality that was to fool D. H. Lawrence into thinking Forster had made "a nearly deadly mistake glorifying those *business* people in *Howards End*".[6] The aphorisms on "sportsmen" quoted above were not, of course, Forster's last word on the subject—"we know," he writes ironically in *Anonymity,* "that if a man shoots an albatross he is not a criminal but a sportsman, and that if he stuffs the albatross afterwards he becomes a naturalist also." Nevertheless, in "The Purple Envelope" the mindless Howard is presented as "a kind comfortable youth, singularly free from envy and uncharitableness"; while a catalogue of his later shortcomings, culminating in the bland statement that "such a man is neither a comfort to the aged nor an example to the young", is at once offset by the narrator's stepping forward to add: "But I stop with him whenever I get the chance." Conversely, Howard's humanitarian uncle, however "nice" in Forster's original schema, emerges as a priggish, pompous fraud.

"The Helping Hand", which at the end of 1904 Forster felt "might be worked up and published", is a much slighter affair, almost unique within Forster's fiction in hardly even hinting at any values more universal or less worldly-wise than the inadvisability, when plagiarized, of squealing too soon. A cluster of names dropped by Forster in recording a visit to the Poldo-Pezzoli Gallery on 21 October 1901 is almost identical with a cluster from the story, and strongly suggests for the one variable the equation: "Giovanni da Empoli" = Antonio Pollaiuolo. Possibly, indeed, we have here a *conte à clef:* for although the first monograph on Pollaiuolo, by one Maud Cruttwell, was not published until 1907 he features prominently—and often in the context of disputed

---

[6] *The Letters of D. H. Lawrence,* edited by Aldous Huxley (London, Heinemann, 1932), p. 552.

attributions—in her 1904 volume on Verrocchio in the same series. There are other indications that Maud Cruttwell may have sat for Forster as Lady Anstey— perhaps in Florence, where she lived and where Forster, whose "Lucy" fragments suggest a quizzical familiarity with the reattribution industry, spent some time in 1901; she may even have held forth in his presence on Pol- laiuolo's date of birth, thus enabling him to predict cor- rectly "a long note saying why not in" 1426 (1429 in the story).

For the composition of "The Rock" we have Forster's own wry account in his Introduction to *The Collected Short Stories*. After describing the process of "sitting down on the theme as if it were an anthill" which oc- curred with "The Story of a Panic" near Ravello in 1902, and with "The Road from Colonus" in Greece the following year, he continues:

> And I did it, or rather tried it on, a third time, in Cornwall, at the Gurnard's Head. Here, just in the same way, a story met me, and, since the Panic and Colonus had both been published and ad- mired, I embraced it as a masterpiece. . . . As the theme swarmed over me, I put my hand into my purse, drew out a golden sovereign—they existed then—and inserted it into a collecting box of the Royal Lifeboat Institution which had been erected upon the Gurnard's Head for such situations as this. I could well afford it. I was bound to make the money over and again. . . . The Rock was the title of this ill-fated effort. It was a complete flop. Not an editor would look at it. My inspiration had been genuine but worthless, like so much inspira- tion, and I have never sat down on a theme since.

For all that, the central idea *is* a good and a strong one; it is the realization that has failed. The visit to Cornwall was probably one made in February and March 1906, a date that tallies well with the hand in which the story is written.

An interval of some sixteen years separates the two groups of unpublished stories. Those in the later group are peculiarly hard to date with any precision, since most of them were evidently the subject of extensive intermittent tinkering, while some, as we shall see, may have been completely rewritten. In substance and in their extant form, however, they were written in the following years:

The Life to Come: 1922
Dr Woolacott: 1927
Arthur Snatchfold: 1928
The Classical Annex: 1930–31
What Does It Matter?: probably the 1930s
The Obelisk: 1939
The Torque: 1958 at the latest
The Other Boat: 1957–8

Seven out of eight, that is, were written after the publication of *A Passage to India,* when any editor who rejected a story by E. M. Forster would have done so only for the very reason that deterred him from offering them, and caused *Maurice* to remain unpublished for fifty-seven years: their homosexual content.

They are, however, markedly different from *Maurice,* as well as from each other. Moreover, whereas Forster never wavered in regarding the novel as a serious work of art as well as a declaration of faith, his estimate of some, at least, of the stories was subject to violent fluctuations. Thus his diary for 8 April 1922 reads:

Have this moment burnt my indecent writings or as many as the fire will take. Not a moral repentance, but the belief that they clogged me artistically. They were written not to express myself but to excite myself, and when first—15 years back? —I began them, I had a feeling that I was doing something positively dangerous to my career as a

novelist. I am not ashamed of them. . . . It is just
that they were a wrong channel for my pen.

Yet only three months later he records in a letter to
Florence Barger the completion of

> a short story ["The Life to Come"] which is . . .
> violent and wholly unpublishable, and I do not yet
> know whether it is good. I may show it to Goldie,
> but there is more sensuality in my composition
> than in his, and it might distress him.

The reference to Goldsworthy Lowes Dickinson, the
man above all others whose esteem Forster treasured,
is significant. In 1913 Dickinson's "disgust" at a "Rab-
elaisian" story of Forster's had shaken him so severely
as to retard work on *Maurice*. "How dependent on
approval!" is Forster's rueful diary comment; and, although in the event the high-minded Dickinson approved of the high-minded *Maurice*, Forster doubtless
took even greater care thereafter not to expose himself
again to disapproval, from Dickinson or anyone else.

Fewer people, certainly, knew about the short stories
than knew about *Maurice*, and fewer still were privi-
leged to see them, or to hear Forster reading them
aloud. William Plomer, having read one story and not
cared for it, was never shown another. Siegfried Sassoon
saw and appears to have liked "The Life to Come", as
did Forrest Reid and—to Forster's particular gratifica-
tion—that "relentless judge of the emotional",[7] Lytton
Strachey. T. E. Lawrence, on the other hand, laughed
at it—a reaction that puzzles me as much as it puzzled
Forster—and was perhaps lucky, three years later, to be
shown "Dr Woolacott". This, by way of contrast, he
considered "the most powerful thing I ever read . . .
more charged with the real high explosive than anything I've ever met yet";[8] and Forrest Reid, again,

---

[7] Letter to Sassoon, 20 December 1923.
[8] Letter to Forster, 27 October 1927.

liked "Dr Woolacott". In the early 1930s a number of the stories were seen by Christopher Isherwood; but their most regular readers at the time of their composition were probably Forster's close friends Joe Ackerley and Jack ("Sebastian") Sprott. Ackerley was also selected, some time during the 1960s, to help Forster execute "a grand review" of the stories, in which, to Sprott's "rage", they "destroyed several they thought not good enough to survive". [9] Among the victims, probably, of this second "purgation" were "a jokey thing" about "a girl who thought that two young men were always fighting when in fact they were making love", [10] and another story to which Forster refers in a diary entry of 16 July 1964:

> Suddenly remembered a short story I tore up a couple of years ago like a fool, called Adventure Week where 8 bored boys have to go into camp and are tricked by the only clever one into a delicious disaster. It was so gay and warm. . . . It was a craftsman['s] dissatisfaction that destroyed it.

Not a moral repentance . . . a craftsman's dissatisfaction—one cannot doubt that the words are sincere; and yet something more seems needed to account for these introverted *autos-da-fé*, or for the conflicting resolutions "The Torque to be torn up" and "to prepare The Torque for non-publication". [11] "The Other Boat" contains a notable distinction between "tribal" and "personal" color prejudices; and it would be surprising if the sexual prejudices of the tribe left the creator of *Maurice*, even in full maturity, totally unscathed. There are plenty of indications that they did not, and that con-

---

[9] Letter from Sprott to the editor, 25 August 1971.
[10] Letter from Isherwood to the editor, 28 November 1971.
[11] The first injunction (30 December 1958) appears to have been ignored, the second (9 October 1962) to have involved mainly the production of an incomplete typescript.

siderable tensions were involved. Did the stories provide a release from the tensions, or did they exacerbate them? And were they art or, as Forster believed in April 1922, a distraction from art?

In the letter to myself which I have already quoted, Professor Sprott answered these two questions, in effect, with a guarded affirmative: the homosexual stories were "an amusement certainly; perhaps a relief in various senses, including the fact that he could still write stories". The implication is that, though the 1922 holocaust may conceivably have been a necessary price for the completion of *A Passage to India,* thereafter there was no real dilemma: as far as fiction went, it was unpublishable "sexy stories" (Forster's own phrase) or nothing. This view receives strong support from the written evidence:

> Having sat for an hour in vain trying to write a play, will analyse causes of my sterility. . . . 2. Weariness of the only subject that I both can and may treat—the love of men for women & vice versa. (Diary, 16 June 1911.)

> I shall never write another novel after it [*A Passage to India*]—my patience with ordinary people has given out. But I shall go on writing. I don't feel any decline in my "powers". (Letter to Siegfried Sassoon, 1 August 1923.)

> I want to love a strong young man of the lower classes and be loved by him and even hurt by him. That is my ticket, and then I have wanted to write respectable novels. . . . (Personal memorandum, 1935.)

> I should have been a more famous writer if I had written or rather published more, but sex has prevented the latter. (Diary, 31 December 1964.)

Given Forster's deep inner honesty and artistic integrity, his gradual acceptance of himself as a homosexual made the decision to abandon the writing of fiction for publication heroic but almost inevitable. Perhaps we should even regard *A Passage to India,* gratefully, as a magnificent rearguard action, initiated before the turning-point came with *Maurice,* and completed with the aid of a theme that relegated sex to a minor role. To cavil at Forster's subsequent "silence" is to forget, *inter alia,* some of the most perceptive and scintillating essays in the English language. Those who love his memory will surely rejoice to know that from time to time "he could still write stories", whether extant or otherwise, whether good, bad or indifferent.

How good *are* these stories? Where sexual themes are concerned, critical responses are notoriously subject to distortion by personal—or tribal—prejudices;[12] and not every reader will find it easy to assess coolly a group of stories in which buggery is an almost unvarying feature, accompanied in most cases by a greater or lesser degree of violence. For better or worse, however, the actual physical encounters are described briefly and, by the standards of today, with circumspection, not to say circumlocution: "a muscle thickened up out of gold" is perhaps the most explicit sexual statement in the book. In this and in little else they resemble *Maurice;* they are free alike from the latter's didacticism and from the sentimentality that so many reviewers recognized, while noticing, apparently, few of the many incidental felicities.

If Forster wrote these stories "not to express myself but to excite myself"— the distinction is perhaps a little too neat and simple—they have all, in varying degrees, transcended their origin. Though no two have quite the same flavour, they fall roughly into two categories: those where Forster seems to be cocking a more

12 From Forster's diary, 25 October 1910: "To work out:— The sexual bias in literary criticism. . . . What sort of person would the critic prefer to sleep with, in fact."

or less cheerful snook at the heterosexual world in general and certain selected targets—women, the Church, pedantic schoolmasters, town councillors—in particular; and those in which some of his profoundest concerns— love, death, truth, social and racial differences—find powerful and sombre expression. P. N. Furbank believes that Forster himself "made a clear distinction in his mind between the facetious and the serious homosexual stories",[13] and that only the former caused him misgivings. If Furbank is right, his "facetious" (my "cheerful snook") category must have included all the stories that Forster destroyed; of those that survive (or rose phoenix-like from the flames), "The Obelisk", "What Does It Matter?" and "The Classical Annex" fall into this first category, "The Life to Come", "Dr Woolacott", "Arthur Snatchfold" and "The Other Boat" into the second. Somewhere between the two subgroups lies "The Torque", an interesting but uneven piece which, though complete, had probably not reached its final form. It is characterized by a strong sense of history and, intermittently, a grave stylized beauty all its own; but the ending is perfunctory, and the preceding rape-fantasy is perhaps the worst bit of writing in the book. (It is interesting to note from the manuscript variants that in these stories as elsewhere—the Marabar Caves episode, for example—it was always the scenes of violent action that gave Forster most trouble.)

The first sub-group need not detain us long. They are lively and amusing, the gaiety only occasionally degenerates into perkiness or "facetiousness", and they will be enjoyed by those for whom good clean fun is not irretrievably compromised by an infusion of dirt. Nor are they entirely frivolous: in its somewhat music-hall or comic-postcard way, "The Obelisk" is an unbowdlerized version of that famous "call to the blood and to the relaxed will", the nude bathing scene in *A Room with a*

[13] Letter to the editor, 27 November 1971.

View. There is a sharp edge, too, to the Ruritanian extravaganza "What Does It Matter?"—to which the subtitle "A Morality" has not been added for nothing.

The second sub-group, however, constitutes an altogether weightier body of work. I have already quoted T. E. Lawrence's remarkable encomium of "Dr Woolacott"; and, although the story's fascination for T.E. tells us more, perhaps, about his powerfully developed death-wish than about its own intrinsic quality, it is certainly a strange and haunting tale, reminiscent of "The Point of It" both in its evocation of the twilight boundary between life and death and in its exaltation of ecstasy-in-death over mediocre and joyless life. More completely satisfactory, perhaps, is "Arthur Snatchfold": the horrors of a vapid, pointless, sham-rural weekend in uncongenial company are deftly evoked— enough to drive anyone to a roll in the bracken with the milkman; there is a memorable vignette, etched in acid, of a less successful, more unlikable Henry Wilcox; and the final clubroom scene, tense and genuinely poignant, is a minor triumph of craftsmanship *à la* Maupassant.

The remaining two pieces in this sub-group show Forster at the height of his powers, with a tragic grandeur unequalled in his stories, and unsurpassed even in *A Passage to India.* (It is perhaps significant that each is concerned with an East–West encounter.) The title-story—the one admired by Sassoon, Strachey and Forrest Reid but mocked by T. E. Lawrence—began, as Forster told Sassoon, "with a purely obscene fancy of a missionary in difficulties".[14] Thence it developed, via one of Forster's best malicious jokes (the conversion of Vithobai to a "love of Christ" that he has totally misunderstood), into a powerful, bitter and beautifully proportioned four-act drama of passion and hypocrisy, played out by the native chieftain and the missionary to a bleakly ritualized offstage chorus of spiritual and commercial oppressors. This story embodied what Forster

---

[14] Letter to Sassoon, 1 August 1923.

described as "a great deal of sorrow and passion that I have myself experienced"[15] and came, with "Dr Woolacott", "more from my heart than anything else I have been able to turn [out]".[16] When we recall that the novels which meant most to Forster were *The Longest Journey* and *Maurice*, the sternness with which deep emotional experience has here been transmuted into high, austere art is indeed striking.

Equal in achievement is "The Other Boat", which in the course of composition underwent an even more radical change than did "The Life to Come". The first section, written probably around 1913, was intended as the opening of a novel which at an early stage got bogged down and abandoned. In 1948, indeed, this chapter was published in *The Listener*[17] as "Entrance to an Unwritten Novel"; and when, nearly a decade later, Forster decided to use it as the opening of a story with a homosexual twist he headed the continuation "Exit from an Unwritten Novel". In marked contrast with "The Life to Come", with its succession of taut, dramatic little scenes separated by long intervals of time, almost the entire action of "The Other Boat" takes place within a single night, in a cramped cabin on a P. and O. liner. The sexual play is here exceptionally well realized; no fantasy coupling but a totally convincing relationship between two characters drawn as sharply, and with as sure an ear for the particular tone of voice, as any in Forster's work. (The letter beginning "Hullo the Mater!" is a tiny masterpiece in itself.) Very remarkable, too, and most original in conception, is the long post-coital conversation, with its mixture of tenderness, scheming and mutual incomprehension, its subtle shifts of mood that lead to disaster. And the grim

15 *Ibid.*

16 Letter to Forrest Reid, 8 September 1927; the last word is actually "it."

17 23 December 1948, pp. 975–6; reprinted in *New York Times Book Review*, 6 February 1949, pp. 3, 31 as "Cocoanut & Co.: Entrance to an Abandoned Novel".

irony of the concluding paragraph forms a worthy finale to Forster's fiction.

The last item in this volume—"Three Courses and a Dessert: Being a New and Gastronomic Version of the Old Game of Consequences"—may well have been the latest, if not in execution, at least in origin. In any case, departure from a chronological order that is at best partly conjectural seems justified both by its multiple authorship and by its particular character: though comfortably the longest story in the volume, it is essentially a post-prandial frolic *à quatre*. The idea seems to have sprung, towards the end of 1943, from the brain of André Simon, founder and for many years editor of *Wine and Food*. Christopher Dilke, who at that time diversified his military duties by writing regularly for the magazine, was invited to set the scene and provide the First Course. This was read by Simon

> with such pleasure that I find it difficult to believe that it runs to as much as 5,000 words. It is just what I had hoped for and it leaves the reader in the right state of expectancy, to say nothing of the headache to the next three.

The identity of "the next three" was as yet undetermined. Geoffrey McNeill-Moss is known to have been approached, as may have been Horace Annesley Vachell, Louis Golding, G. B. Stern and (for the Dessert) Charles Morgan, all of whose names were mooted by Simon in the letter just quoted; while Forster, some two months later, was in turn recommending J. H. Simpson, alias John Hampson. Forster himself, though in 1941 he had contributed to *Wine and Food* a morsel entitled "You Sausage!", seems to have been an afterthought on Simon's part, and Dilke's contribution to have been in proof before Forster was approached. His letter of acceptance—presented by Simon to Dilke with the suggestion that after reading it he may "require an outsize

in hats"—is one of the few extant letters from Forster
to an editor, and is worth quoting at length:

> I should like to have a shot at the fish. I felt at first
> I couldn't attempt it, but found the first instalment
> so fresh and stimulating. I have never read any-
> thing by Christopher Dilke before. How good he
> is! I certainly shan't reach his level of action and
> ingeniousness, and I doubt whether your other con-
> tributors will reach it either. My criticism of him—
> as an installer—is that he has made too much
> happen. With the bombers over the soup, one can
> only save the other courses by constantly prevari-
> cating.
>
> I don't expect to be able to turn out a contribu-
> tion of that length. How short may it permissibly
> be? And I may have to consult you over culinary
> details. . . . But I must read the proof again. I am
> keeping it, by the way, as I shall [want?] to refer
> to it constantly. (Letter to Simon, 28 January
> 1944.)

Forster's contribution certainly involves less "action
and ingeniousness" than Dilke's, or that of A. E. Coppard which follows. Still, if we bear in mind Elizabeth
Bowen's dictum that "speech is what the characters *do
to each other*",[18] there is action enough, including a
characteristic sudden death employed to uncharacter-
istic ends. At the same time, and without impairing
unity of tone, Forster has contrived to give free rein to
his own unrivalled irony and grasp of social nuance. If
he admired Dilke's opening he must also, as an insouci-
ant self-mocker, have relished the joke at his expense
with which, on the last page, James Laver cuts through
a knot of Gordian proportions. The entire team, indeed,
clearly enjoyed its romp in pre-Bond land, and has

---

[18] *Collected Impressions* (London, Longman, 1950), p. 255.

played the game with zest and skill, if not always in strict accordance with the rules.

Of the twelve unpublished stories, only one ("The Purple Envelope") exists in a form with which Forster was satisfied to the point of submission to an editor. (The opening pages of "The Other Boat" constitute, as we have seen, another partial exception.) Of the remainder, many are in a physical state—untidy manuscript, heavily corrected typescript, a mixture of the two —in which no editor or publisher would normally accept copy from a living author. The handwriting is often —and over the years increasingly—difficult to decipher; many of the corrections are imperfectly or ambiguously made; some of the typescripts are full of obvious uncorrected errors, and suspicions that other, less obvious ones exist are reinforced by Forster's evident and inveterate carelessness as a reader of typescripts and proofs.

Much more problematic, about half the stories are extant, in part or in whole, in two or more versions. To establish a text of "The Other Boat", for example, it is necessary to adjudicate between the rival claims of (*a*) a complete typescript of 45 pages, with corrections effected by various means; (*b*) a carbon copy of (*a*), with a slightly different set of corrections; (*c*) a set of autograph directives for corrections to be made either to (*a/b*) or to an earlier typescript; (*d*) the version of the opening pages published in 1948 as "Entrance to an Unwritten Novel"; (*e, f* and *g*) a total of five autograph sheets differing considerably from the three corresponding passages in (*a*); and (*h*) two typewritten sheets differing considerably from the corresponding passage in both (*a*) and, in so far as they overlap, (*g*). Even this account errs on the side of over-simplification.

My aim—that of most textual editors—is to present a text corresponding, substantively, to Forster's *latest intentions,* in so far as they can be determined. Both the italicized words are crucial. *Intentions,* not the way they have been carried out: obvious typing errors, for example, have been corrected, and where, in a much-rewritten sentence, words have been added in the wrong place, or too many or too few deleted, I have tried to reconstruct the successive process involved and to restore sense out of nonsense. *Latest* intentions: although *one* of the criteria for identifying these has been the assumption that changes are more likely to be for the better (in my own fallible judgement) than for the worse, where the consensus of evidence points to a particular reading as being the later I have adopted it even if the earlier reading strikes me as unquestionably superior. In one such case (page 206) the discrepancy is so startling that I have recorded the earlier version in a footnote.

With this single exception, I have kept textual matters within the confines of these paragraphs and a few notes at the end of the volume. The notes—one or two of which are expository rather than textual—record all substantive editorial emendations and interpolations, other than manifest errors which admit of only one possible correct reading; where a lacuna seems to have occurred—see, for example, page 111 and the note on page 254—I have endeavoured to fill it as simply and functionally as possible. Unless otherwise specified, then, every word in this book is Forster's, even if some were in his mind rather than on the paper that survived him, and even if one cannot be certain that he would finally have preferred all of them to their rivals.

One last point about spelling, punctuation, capitalization and word-division. Although, like most good writers, Forster achieved some subtle effects with these resources, and although he was greatly upset by some punctuation changes which "beast Jenks" of the *Independent Review* made to "The Story of a Panic",[19] it is

---

[19] On the assumption that the points at issue are indicated by the differences in punctuation between the periodical and volume versions, Jenks appears to have been a fussy over-punctuator, with a particular addiction to the semi-colon. Forster's outburst occurs in a diary entry of 7 August 1904.

clear that in general he was exceedingly slapdash over such matters; again and again, to give only one example, he forgets to close his quotations. I have therefore felt at liberty, provided no nuance was involved, to make such alterations as seemed desirable for reasons of consistency or ease in reading.

It remains for me to thank a number of people for their help and encouragement. I am profoundly grateful, in the first instance, to Forster's literary executors—the late Professor W. J. H. Sprott and the Provost and Fellows of King's College, Cambridge—for setting me, as general editor of this edition, the most congenial (and challenging) task that I could ever have wished for. The kindness, as well as trust, which they showed me from the outset has been exemplified by many people at King's, that friendly and hospitable college to which Forster extended for more than seventy years his gratitude, affection and loyalty. I am particularly indebted to the Vice-Provost, Dr Donald Parry; to the Librarian, Dr A. N. L. Munby, and all members of his staff; to Mr George Rylands, who since Professor Sprott's untimely death in September 1971 has kept an alert and benevolent eye on the project; to Mr. P. N. Furbank, Forster's biographer, for endless patience and generosity in answering questions and giving me access to his files; and to Miss Elizabeth Ellem, now Archivist of Churchill College, Cambridge, whose splendid earlier work in sorting and listing the Forster archive at King's lightened my task immeasurably. The expert knowledge of both Mr Furbank and Miss Ellem has more than once kept me from going astray; for any editorial aberrations that remain I alone am responsible.

My debt to all these people, as also to the indispensable London Library, will extend far beyond the confines of the present volume, and I hope that they will regard the thanks expressed here as coextensive with my work on the Abinger Edition; if in subsequent volumes my statement of gratitude takes a more summary form it will not be because the gratitude itself is wearing thin. On the present occasion I owe especial thanks to Mr Christopher Dilke, Mr James Laver, C.B.E., A. D. Peters & Co. (representing the A. E. Coppard estate) and the Wine and Food Society for permission to reprint the relevant sections of "Three Courses and a Dessert"; to Messrs Dilke and Laver also for allowing me to ransack their memories over a luncheon happily unmarred by air-raids or assassinations; and to Mr Dilke, further, for lending me a number of pertinent letters and allowing me to quote from them. I am grateful also to Mr George Sassoon for permission to quote from Forster's letters to Siegfried Sassoon. For their courtesy and helpfulness in answering inquiries, and in several cases reading and commenting on this Introduction, I would like to thank Mr Robert Buckingham, Mr Christopher Isherwood, Mr William Plomer, Mr William Roerick and Mr Patrick Wilkinson; valuable suggestions for improving the editorial matter were made also by Mr J. G. Bell, Mr Andrew Best, Mrs William Blake, Mr. T. S. Matthews, Miss Patricia Parkin, Professor Wilfred Stone and Professor George H. Thomson. The acknowledgement of my deepest and most lasting debt of all—that to my wife—may perhaps be allowed to conclude this Introduction to a volume by a writer for whom, after all, personal relationships were the supreme and ultimate value.

OLIVER STALLYBRASS

Ansell

"It's a cruel box," said the porter, who, beguiled by its moderate size, had hoisted it onto his shoulder and then hastily dumped it back on the platform. "The weight's cruel. That'll need a barrow." He went and fetched one, and wheeled the box and the bag across the line.

"That's packed very close."

"Yes," I replied; "it's books."

"Books!" he echoed in an injured voice, for I had incautiously displayed twopence and twopence alone in the palm of my hand. "I don't hold with books in the country. What you want is recr'ation and h'air and h'exercise." He cast a searching glance at my stooping shoulders and bounced away with the barrow, calling out, "Just hurry and open the back of the cart. You've got a libr'y this journey, I can tell you."

A large-boned person got up from the front seat, and as he turned to pull out the pin and drag the seat forward I saw that it was Ansell. I hesitated a moment as to what would be the proper thing to do, and then held out my hand, which he grasped in a vice and swung from side to side like a scythe. That long handshake is a wonderful thing; it may merely mean shyness, but it can also denote reproach, forgiveness or intense affection. In this case I took it as punishment for snobbishness, for it left my fingers squeezed together like macaroni and my hand the colour of old parchment.

Ansell had not lost his simple manner, and apologized with total freedom from self-consciousness for being himself in a tweed suit and the "muck cart" with Josiah, instead of Charles in livery with the landau and the pair of bays, who had all gone with the ladies to a flower show at Poppyfield. He then took up the book-box and heaved it with precision into the back. The cart immediately tilted at a miserable angle, and the shafts plucked Josiah heavily and rose into the air. It was better when he and the bag got in in front, but we both have long legs and were terribly cramped with the seat pushed so far forward.

My visits to the Hall had not been frequent, but they had been lengthy, and had allowed me to make Ansell's acquaintance. The first had been when I was fourteen and he was garden and stable boy. We were thrown at one another by my cousin, who thought it nice I should have a companion, and in a few days were on the most intimate footing. We scraped out a hole in the side of the large straw stack, and made it into a house, where we stored apples and gooseberries and "Kola" lemonade, which we got cheap from Ansell's aunt in the village. We made birdlime from a recipe in *The Boy's Own Book,* and caught Mrs Perill's prize bantam chickens in it. The sound of our whoops and shrieks as we jumped with abandon on one another's hats penetrated even into the smoking-room, where my father was arguing with my cousin as to the respective merits of Eton and Winchester as a school for me. The noise exasperated them. My cousin was aghast at the friendship he had created. No work was done in the garden and very little in the stable. Ansell was always called off by Master Edward. And my father did not like my entire separation from rational companions and pursuits. I had suddenly stopped reading and no longer cared to discuss with him the fortunes of the Punic War or the course of Aeneas from Troy. The result was an intervention of the powers. I and Ansell were only to play together once a week, and then it was to be something sensible—cricket or bat, trap and ball—not senseless bear-gardening. And then I went away and to school.

I came again when I was eighteen. Ansell was now sole gardener and only occasional stable boy. I had just

got a scholarship at Cambridge, and was resting after
my labours. But I had forgotten how to rest, and preferred reading to outdoor amusements. Ansell once or
twice suggested taking me shooting or teaching me to
swim, but I refused, partly because I now found him
such a dull companion, partly because I did not shine
at outdoor pursuits, having been exempted at school by
a doctor's certificate and thus fallen behind in the athletic race. I was very sensitive on this point, and knew
that Ansell would laugh at my incompetencies, and this
I could not bear. So we remained on very friendly terms
but saw one another little.

Now I met him again. The deficiencies of eighteen
were accentuated at twenty-three, but I had also gained
the armour of the grown-up person, which can ward off
the lesser shafts of disapproval and ridicule. We were
now so very different that comparison was painless and
even interesting. I was writing a dissertation on the
Greek optative for a Fellowship, and Ansell was now
gamekeeper to the small shooting my cousin had recently purchased, and only occasional gardener and
groom.

I began to put him at his ease.

"How you've grown, Ansell!"

"Aye, Master Ed—sir; and how *you've* grown."

"Josiah doesn't seem to alter, though."

"No, Josiah doesn't alter."

"Do you remember what times we used to have: the
birdlime."

"Oh aye, the birdlime."

"And the plum tree with the branch you broke."

"Oh aye, that there branch. It's broke now."

We were feeding on the past, and I knew that we
could not live by that alone. So I went on to inquire
after our common acquaintances, he replying in a chant,
"Oh, he's very well—Oh, she's very well—Oh, he went
come this two year."

Dead silence ensued, which was well enough for Ansell, to whom it merely meant that neither of us had any

more to say. But to educated people silence matters: it is a token of stupidity and lack of invention. I racked my brains for some remark that would serve to keep my self-respect, but could find none. Ansell remained motionless, staring in front of him at Josiah's ears. He too was thinking, as the sequel proved, but felt under no obligation to speak till the thought was ripe, whereas unless I speak I cannot go on thinking.

At last it came. He tossed his head at the back of the cart and said: "Them books."

Grammarians have a theory—I know it to my cost—that the original case is not the nominative but the accusative. It is so pure and colourless that it does not even make a statement. It merely says: "Them books." So Ansell's remark was not meant as a criticism, but merely signified the topic which he would like to hear me discuss.

I did not shrink. I knew he would not sympathize, but I did not mind that now. After six years of a student's life I was perfectly inured to attacks upon my implements. I had heard books attacked for their bulk, their weight, their fragility, their similarity, their contradictiousness, their uselessness, their effect upon the figure, their drain upon the pocket, and also for their contents. People who read Wordsworth quoted "One impulse from a vernal wood", and people who read Ecclesiastes quoted "Of making many books". And at the last I heard them unmoved, and was unmoved too at the slope of my shoulders and the curve of my back and the contraction of my chest. All good work must wear out some muscles, and though the Greek optative wears out more than most it is none the less good work.

The dissertation was to be sent in within a month. I had only just begun to write it out, but had my notes all prepared—editions interleaved and annotated, and pages of cross-references and criticisms of rival theories. The optative does not admit of very flowing treatment, and I had plenty of time to dump my remarks down and get them typewritten. My cousin had invited me to stay

with him, and I had refused on the score of work. But
on his renewing the invitation and offering the library,
for which he had just bought an *Encyclopaedia Britannica,* for my exclusive use, I accepted, though I had
to bring my own books, since neither the encyclopaedia
nor the Hundred Best Books which balanced it would
quite suit my purpose.

There they all were in the box behind: the seeds and
the fruit of my career—chiefly the seeds, to judge by
the weight.

In response to Ansell's remark I rapidly sketched my
past, leaving out its numerous triumphs with becoming,
though superfluous, modesty. I then explained the reason for the particular books: how I was engaged in
writing about the grammar that was spoken by the
Greeks in ancient times, and how, if what I had written
was considered better than what had been written about
the *Consolato del Mare* or Euclidean Space or the Respiratory Organs of Snakes—titles of the rival dissertations—I should then receive eighty pounds a year and
rooms in college and a free meal every evening, and be
allowed to impart my knowledge to others.

He seemed more clownish than I expected, for there
was another long pause. At last he raised his head and
said:

"Well, of course I hope you'll succeed."

"Thanks very much." It was not often I met with
goodwill where there was no sympathy, and I made the
most of it, for sympathy was so rare—extinct almost,
since my father died. Another silence ensued, during
which I calculated Ansell's chest measurement—we
were about the same at fourteen—and then tried to console myself by calculating his brain capacity. It was a
close evening, and rain was impending. We were about
halfway now, where the road goes up the river ravine
in a ledge that has been cut in the rock. Far below us,
almost shrouded in trees, ran the river. An open wooden
fence guarded us from the precipice.

Just where the ravine is steepest, Josiah began to dance.

"Steady, there, steady," said Ansell. "It's those clegs again. Steady, steady, stead—" Bang. Josiah had backed the cart against the wooden railing. He drew forward, calculated his distance and backed again. Bang. And crack, for the fence was giving. He drew forward again.

"Jump out, Master Edward," cried Ansell. "I daren't loose the reins, for you daren't hold 'em."

Indeed I was perfectly numb and incapable with terror. I could not move. I could only wonder whether we should all strike the river at the same time, and whether it would be at the same place. The box, Ansell, me, Josiah? Or would Josiah pass us on the way and come in with the box? And the box was behind me, so I should fall on it . . . bound with iron at the corners.

Bang! and a long crack this time, for the fence was reeling backwards. Something slipped from the cart into the abyss, and I concluded it was me. Then that it was Ansell, who was gone. But no. He had got out before the concussion, and had taken advantage of the recoil to haul Josiah forward and just save us from going over the edge. Josiah had kicked him on the shin and he had torn the armholes out of his new suit, but we were safe.

It then struck me that what had gone was the box. A great deal was crowded into that half-second, for I was just in time to see the conclusion of its fall. About half-way down it hit a projecting rock, opened like a water-lily, and rained its sweetness upon the deep. Most of the books were heavy and plunged like meteors through the trees into the river. One or two of the smaller ones roosted coyly for a minute on the branches before they too slipped through and disappeared. Then I heard the voice of Ansell, who had removed the cleg and soothed the horse.

"Them books saved us. They went at the very moment. I felt 'em tugging us over the edge. Get out now—get out and hold Josiah. When I put the seat back again we'll be a deal more comfortable."

"Ansell!" I said.

"Oh, I'm all right, Master Edward."

I felt ashamed, for I had not been going to ask after his health. After a decent interval I said, "Shall we be able to get the books and papers back?"

"Oh, I dessay we shall one or two. But the river's swift, and few shallows, and the rain's coming. We may try tomorrow."

"You know it means—it means that I've failed if I lose those books?"

"Aye?" said Ansell. "Well, there's other things but books."

"It means—well, it's as if you had to lose your leg."

"I never have lost my leg and I don't want to," said Ansell, not to be moved from questions of fact.

"Well, you're right. Hypothetics is a poor study: the science of what might have happened but did not. The optative is sometimes used in hypothetical sentences, which is an odd coincidence."

I felt that only brilliant conversation would save me from insanity, and knew that Ansell would not find me out if I borrowed the brilliant remarks of others. I might have recited *A Hundred Gems of Humor* from end to end, and he would not have found me out. I sparkled a few minutes to myself, and then had to stop. Suicide seemed the only course, when Ansell began to talk. Like the chorus in the Greek tragedy which breaks into song when human misery and sordid passions are at their fullest, he began right away from the all-pervading subject, and kept away from it too, which is more than can be said for a chorus. The weight of books which kept him down or, to be more accurate, up, had fallen into the river, and now he was at his own level and could speak of the things that he cared for.

He began by a description of the new shooting: how it ran up the Carlham woods right into the heart of the hills and took in a bit of the great east moor. There were plenty of grouse there, and black game. The air was so pure that you felt like a different person and so clear

that you could see the sea. The valleys were so thick
with rabbits that not even—not anybody could miss
them. Then I heard of the new barn and the cowhouse
and the plan for supplying the house from the river
direct, which had worked so well till Miss Flora had
found an eel in her bath, and the arrogance of Charles
and the sour temper of the cook, which meant a match,
for they was born to plague each other, and the necessity for a new lightning-conductor, and the probable
profits of his aunt and the probability of his inheriting
them, and finally he burst into a description of the great
landslip in the upper burn which had turned an arid
waste of rocks and pebbles into a deep bathing-pool,
always full to the brim with clear brown water, always
shaded from the sun, always sheltered from the wind.

It did not soothe me, any more than the praises of
Athens soothed the jealousy of Medea, but I was conscious of the artistic effect, and that was something.

If I met with one sign of true sympathy, I think I
should break down. But fortunately I do not. The utmost
anyone will venture is that they are "sorry for my disappointment, but now I shall be able to have a *real*
holiday". To do them justice, they have been very kind.

"I suppose you've got it all in your head all right,"
said my cousin. "When you know a thing you know a
thing." But when he realized I had not, he at once
countermanded the projected shooting-party for the
morrow and ordered a grand search for the debris. All
the night I lay awake listening to the rain, but the
morning was fine, and the whole establishment turned
out with implements to their taste, and took their lunch
with them.

As Ansell predicted, we got "one or two"—even
more. He himself dived pertinaciously into the pool below the road, and fished up the cover of an Aristotle,
half a volume of discarded notes, and *Elizabeth and
her German Garden,* which I was bringing as a present
for Flora. We sent word down stream, and the miller

from Doublebois sent up two or three that had come down in the wheel. But of the unfinished dissertation and the essential notes there was not a sign. They had all gone out to sea in the spate, together with the bulk of the books. The household was hopeful, seeing that the salvage filled a fair-sized basket, and a person so clever as Mr Edward would be sure to be able to find something in it to write about, but I knew that my career was closed. If I met with one sign of sympathy I should break down.

But Ansell has appropriated me, and I have no time to think of the future. I cannot fend him off. I have a bruise on my shoulder from shooting and a cut on the foot from bathing, and the pony has rubbed my knee raw against a wall. And we talk—goodness knows what of: I cannot remember afterwards, but I know that an allusion to the box of books is a recognized witticism.

Liddell and Scott's Greek Lexicon remains open on the ledge where the box split. In dry weather an invisible person rapidly turns over the leaves, hurrying from one word to another. But in the damp his ardour flags. There is something rather poetical in the idea of this unembodied searcher after knowledge, and I would write a Greek epigram on him, but I am forgetting the words.

Whenever we pass the place Ansell looks over and says "Them books!" and laughs, and I laugh too as heartily as he, for I have not yet realized what has happened.

Albergo Empedocle

The last letter I had from Harold was from Naples.

We've just come back from Pompeii (he wrote).
On the whole it's decidedly no go and very tiring.
What with the smells and the beggars and the mosquitoes we're rather off Naples altogether, and
we've changed our plans and are going to Sicily.
The guidebooks say you can run through it in no
time; only four places you have to go to, and very
little in them. That suits us to a T. Pompeii and
the awful Museum here have fairly killed us—
except of course Mildred, and perhaps Sir Edwin.

Now why don't you come too? I know you're
keen on Sicily, and we all would like it. You would
be able to spread yourself no end with your archaeology. For once in my life I should have to
listen while you jaw. You'd enjoy discussing temples, gods, etc., with Mildred. She's taught me a
lot, but of course it's no fun for her, talking to us.
Send a wire; I'll stand the cost. Start at once and
we'll wait for you. The Peaslakes say the same,
especially Mildred.

My not sleeping at night, and my headaches are
all right now, thanks very much. As for the blues,
I haven't had any since I've been engaged, and
don't intend to. So don't worry any more.

Yours,
Harold

Dear Tommy, if you aren't an utter fool you'll
let me pay your ticket out.

I did not go. I could just have managed it, but Sicily was then a very sacred name to me, and the thought of running through it in no time, even with Harold, deterred me. I went afterwards, and as I am well acquainted with all who went then, and have had circumstantial information of all that happened, I think that my account of the affair will be as intelligible as anyone's.

I am conceited enough to think that, if I had gone, the man I love most in the world would not now be in an asylum.

1

The Peaslake party was most harmonious in its composition. Four out of the five were Peaslakes, which partly accounted for the success, but the fifth, Harold, seemed to have been created to go with them. They had started from England soon after his engagement to Mildred Peaslake, and had been flying over Europe for two months. At first they were a little ashamed of their rapidity, but the delight of continual custom-house examinations soon seized them, and they had hardly learned what "Come in" and "Hot water, please" were in one language, before they crossed the frontier and had to learn them in another.

But, as Harold truly said, "People say we don't see things properly, and are globe-trotters, and all that, but after all one travels to enjoy oneself, and no one can say that we aren't having a ripping time."

Every party, to be really harmonious, must have a physical and an intellectual centre. Harold provided one, Mildred the other. He settled whether a mountain had to be climbed or a walk taken, and it was his fists that were clenched when a porter was insolent, or a cabman tried to overcharge. Mildred, on the other hand, was the fount of information. It was she who generally held the Baedeker and explained it. She had been expecting her continental scramble for several years, and had read a fair amount of books for it, which a good memory often enabled her to reproduce.

But they all agreed that she was no dry encyclopaedia. Her appetite for facts was balanced by her reverence for imagination.

"It is imagination," she would say, "that makes the past live again. It sets the centuries at naught."

"Rather!" was the invariable reply of Harold, who was notoriously deficient in it. Recreating the past was apt to give him a headache, and his thoughts obstinately returned to the unromantic present, which he found quite satisfactory. He was fairly rich, fairly healthy, very much in love, very fond of life, and he was content to worship in Mildred those higher qualities which he did not possess himself.

These two between them practically ran the party, and both Sir Edwin and Lady Peaslake were glad that the weight of settling or explaining anything should be lifted off their shoulders. Sir Edwin sometimes held the Baedeker, but his real function was the keeping of a diary in which he put down the places they went to, the people they met, and the times of the trains. Lady Peaslake's department was packing, hotels, and the purchasing of presents for a large circle of acquaintance. As for Lilian, Mildred's sister, whatever pleased other people pleased her. Altogether it was a most delightful party.

They were, however, just a little subdued and quiet during that journey from Palermo to Girgenti. They had done Palermo in even less time than Baedeker had allowed for it, and such audacity must tell on the most robust of tourists. Furthermore they had made an early start, as they had to get to Girgenti for lunch, do the temples in the afternoon, and go on the next morning to Syracuse.

It was no wonder that Lady Peaslake was too weary to look out of the window, and that Harold yawned when Mildred explained at some length how it was that a Greek temple came to be built out of Greece.

"Poor boy! You're tired," she said, without bitterness, and without surprise.

Harold blushed at his impoliteness.

"We really do too much," said Lady Peaslake. "I never bought that Sicilian cart for Mrs Popham. It would have been the very thing. She will have something out of the way. If a thing's at all ordinary she will hardly say thank you. Harold, would you try at Girgenti? Mind you beat them down. Four francs is the outside."

"Certainly, Lady Peaslake." His method of purchasing for her was to pay whatever was asked, and to make good the difference out of his own pocket.

"Girgenti will produce more than Sicilian carts," said Mildred, smoothing down the pages of the guidebook. "In Greek times it was the second city of the island, wasn't it? It was famous for the ability, wealth and luxury of its inhabitants. You remember, Harold, it was called Acragas."

"Acragas, Acragas," chanted Harold, striving to rescue one word from the chaos. The effort was too much for him, and he gave another yawn.

"Really, Harold!" said Mildred, laughing. "You're very much exhausted."

"I've scarcely slept for three nights," he replied in rather an aggrieved voice.

"Oh, my dear boy! I'm very sorry. I had no idea."

"Why did not you tell me?" said Sir Edwin. "We would have started later. Yes, I see you do look tired."

"It's so queer. It's ever since I've been in Sicily. Perhaps Girgenti will be better."

"Have you never slept since Naples?"

"Oh, I did sleep for an hour or so last night. But that was because I used my dodge."

"Dodge!" said Sir Edwin. "What ever do you mean?"

"You know it, don't you? You pretend you're someone else, and then you go asleep in no time."

"Indeed I do not know it," said Sir Edwin emphatically.

Mildred's curiosity was aroused. She had never heard Harold say anything unexpected before, and she was determined to question him.

"How extremely interesting! How very interesting! I don't know it either. Who do you imagine yourself to be?"

"Oh, no one—anyone. I just say to myself, 'That's someone lying awake. Why doesn't he go to sleep if he's tired?' Then he—I mean I—do, and it's all right."

"But that is a very wonderful thing. Why didn't you do it all three nights?"

"Well, to tell the truth," said Harold, rather confused, "I promised Tommy I'd never do it again. You see, I used to do it, not only when I couldn't sleep, but also when I was in the blues about something—or nothing—as one is, I don't know why. It doesn't get rid of them, but it kind of makes me so strong that I don't care for them—I can't explain. One morning Tommy came to see me, and I never knew him till he shook me. Naturally he was horribly sick, and made me promise never to do it again."

"And why have you done it again?" said Sir Edwin.

"Well, I did hold out two nights. But last night I was so dead tired, I couldn't think what I wanted to—of course you understand that; it's rather beastly. All the night I had to keep saying, '*I*'m lying awake, *I*'m lying awake, *I*'m lying awake,' and it got more and more difficult. And when it was almost time to get up I made a slip and said, 'He's lying awake'—and then off I went."

"How very, very interesting," said Mildred, and Lilian cried that it was a simply splendid idea, and that she should try it next time she had the toothache.

"Indeed, Lilian," said her mother, "I beg you'll do no such thing."

"No, indeed," said Sir Edwin, who was looking grave. "Harold, your friend was quite right. It is never safe to play tricks with the brain. I must say I'm astonished: you of all people!"

"Yes," said Harold, looking at a very substantial hand. "I'm such a stodgy person. It is odd. It isn't brain or imagination or anything like that. I simply pretend."

"It is imagination," said Mildred in a low determined voice.

"Whatever it is, it must stop," said Sir Edwin. "It's a dangerous habit. You must break yourself of it before it is fully formed."

"Yes. I promised Tommy. I shall try again tonight," said Harold, with a pitiful little sigh of fatigue.

"I'll arrange to have a room communicating with yours. If you can't sleep tonight, call me."

"Thanks very much, I'm sure not to do it if you're near. It only works when one's alone. Tommy stopped it by taking rooms in the same house, which was decent of him."

The conversation had woken them up. The girls were quiet, Lilian being awed, and Mildred being rather annoyed with her parents for their want of sympathy with imagination. She felt that Harold had so little, that unless it was nourished it would disappear. She crossed over to him, and managed to say in a low voice:

"You please me very much. I had no idea you were like this before. We live in a world of mystery."

Harold smiled complacently at the praise, and being sure that he could not say anything sensible held his tongue. Mildred at once began to turn his newly found powers to the appreciation of Girgenti.

"Think," she said, "of the famous men who visited her in her prime. Pindar, Aeschylus, Plato—and as for Empedocles, of course he was born there."

"Oh!"

"The disciple, you know, of Pythagoras, who believed in the transmigration of souls."

"Oh!"

"It's a beautiful idea, isn't it, that the soul should have several lives."

"But, Mildred darling," said the gentle voice of Lady Peaslake, "we know that it is not so."

"Oh, I didn't mean that, mamma. I only said it was a beautiful idea."

"But not a true one, darling."

"No."

Their voices had sunk into that respectful monotone which is always considered suitable when the soul is under discussion. They all looked awkward and ill at ease. Sir Edwin played tunes on his waistcoat buttons, and Harold blew into the bowl of his pipe. Mildred, a little confused at her temerity, passed on to the terrible sack of Acragas by the Romans. Whereat their faces relaxed, and they regained their accustomed spirits.

"But what are dates?" said Mildred. "What are facts, or even names of persons? They carry one a very little way. In a place like this one must simply feel."

"Rather," said Harold, trying to fix his attention.

"You must throw yourself into a past age if you want to appreciate it thoroughly. Today you must imagine you are a Greek."

"Really, Mildred," said Sir Edwin, "you're almost too fanciful."

"No, father, I'm not. Harold understands. He must forget all these modern horrors of railways and Cook's tours, and think that he's living over two thousand years ago, among palaces and temples. He must think and feel and act like a Greek. It's the only way. He must—well, he must *be* a Greek."

"The sea! The sea!" interrupted Harold. "How absolutely ripping! I swear I'll put in a bathe!"

"Oh, you incorrigible boy!" said Mildred, joining in the laugh at the failure of her own scheme. "Show me the sea, then."

They were still far away from it, for they had hardly crossed the watershed of the island. It was the country of the mines, barren and immense, absolutely destitute of grass or trees, producing nothing but cakes of sallow sulphur, which were stacked on the platform of every wayside station. Human beings were scanty, and they were stunted and dry, mere withered vestiges of men. And far below at the bottom of the yellow waste was the moving living sea, which embraced Sicily when she was green and delicate and young, and embraces her now, when she is brown and withered and dying.

"I see something more interesting than the sea," said Mildred. "I see Girgenti."

She pointed to a little ridge of brown hill far beneath them, on the summit of which a few gray buildings were huddled together.

"Oh, what a dreadful place!" cried poor Lady Peaslake. "How uncomfortable we are going to be!"

"Oh dearest mother, it's only for one night. What are a few drawbacks, when we are going to see temples! Temples, Greek temples! Doesn't the word make you thrill?"

"Well, no, dear, it doesn't. I should have thought the Pesto ones would have been enough. These can't be very different."

"I consider you are a recreant party," said Mildred in a sprightly voice. "First it's Harold, now it's you. I'm the only worthy one among you. Today I mean to be a Greek. What hotel do we go to?"

Lady Peaslake produced her notebook and said: "Grand Hôtel des Temples. Recommended by Mr Dimbleby. Ask for a back room, as those have the view."

But at the Girgenti railway station, the man from the Temples told them that his hotel was full, and Mildred, catching sight of the modest omnibus of the Albergo Empedocle, suggested that they should go there, because it sounded so typical.

"You remember what the doctrine of Empedocles was, Harold?"

The wretched Harold had forgotten.

Sir Edwin was meanwhile being gently urged into the omnibus by the man from the Empedocle.

"We know nothing about it, absolutely nothing. Are you—have you clean beds?"

The man from the Empedocle raised his eyes and hands to heaven, so ecstatic was his remembrance of the purity of the blankets, the spotlessness of the sheets. At last words came, and he said, "The beds of the Empedocle! They are celestial. One spends one night there, and one remembers it for ever!"

2

Sir Edwin and Lady Peaslake were sitting in the Temple of Juno Lacinia and leaning back on a Doric column— which is a form of architecture neither comfortable as a cushion nor adequate as a parasol. They were as cross as it was possible for good-tempered people to be. Their lunch at the dirty hotel had disagreed with them, and the wine that was included with it had made them heavy. The drive to the temples had joggled them up and one of the horses had fallen down. They had been worried to buy flowers, figs, shells, sulphur crystals, and new-laid antiquities, they had been pestered by the beggars and bitten by the fleas. Had they been Sicilian-born they would have known what was the matter, and lying down on the grass, on the flowers, on the road, on the temple steps—on anything, would have sunk at once into that marvellous midday sleep which is fed by light and warmth and air. But being northern-born they did not know—nor could they have slept if they had.

"Where on earth are Harold and Mildred?" asked Lady Peaslake. She did not want to know, but she was restless with fatigue.

"I can't think why we couldn't all keep together," said Sir Edwin.

"You see, papa," said Lilian, "Mildred wants to see the temples that have tumbled down as well as these, and Harold is taking her."

"He's a poor guide," said Sir Edwin. "Really, Lilian, I begin to think that Harold is rather stupid. Of course I'm very fond of him, he's a thoroughly nice fellow,

honest as the day, and he's good-looking and well-made
—I value all that extremely—but after all brains are
something. He is so slow—so lamentably slow—at
catching one's meaning."

"But, father dear," replied Lilian, who was devoted
to Harold, "he's tired."

"I am tired, too, but I can keep my wits about me.
He seems in a dream; when the horse fell he never at-
tempted to get down and sit on its head. It might have
kicked us to pieces. He's as helpless as a baby with
beggars. He's too idle to walk properly; three times he
trod on my toes, and he fell up the temple steps and
broke your camera. He's blind, he's deaf—I may say
he's dumb, too. Now this is pure stupidity, and I believe
that stupidity can be cured just like anything else, if you
make the effort."

Lilian continued the defence, and repeated that he
had hardly slept for three nights.

"Ridiculous. Why can't he sleep? It's stupidity again.
An effort is needed—that is all. He can cure it if he
chooses."

"He does know how to cure it," said Lilian, "but you
thought—and so did he—that—"

She produced an explosion of ill-temper in her father,
which was quite unprecedented.

"I'm very much annoyed with him. He has no right
to play tricks with his brain. And what's more I am
annoyed with Mildred, too."

"Oh, father!"

"She encourages him in his silliness—makes him
think he's clever. I'm extremely annoyed, and I shall
speak to them both, as soon as I get the opportunity."

Lilian was surprised and pained. Her father had never
blamed anyone so strongly before. She did not know—
indeed, he did not know himself—that neither the in-
digestion nor the heat, nor the beggars, nor the fleas,
were the real cause of his irritation. He was annoyed
because he failed to understand.

Mildred he could pardon; she had merely been indiscreet, and as she had gone in for being clever when quite a child such things were to be expected from her. Besides, he shrewdly guessed that, although she might sometimes indulge in fancies, yet when it came to action she could be trusted to behave in a thoroughly conventional manner. Thank heaven! she was seldom guilty of confusing books with life.

But Harold did not escape so easily, for Sir Edwin absolutely failed to understand him, for the first time. Hitherto he had believed that he understood him perfectly. Harold's character was so simple; it consisted of little more than two things, the power to love and the desire for truth, and Sir Edwin, like many a wise thinker, concluded that what was not complicated could not be mysterious. Similarly, because Harold's intellect did not devote itself to the acquisition of facts or to the elaboration of emotions, he had concluded that he was stupid. But now, just because he could send himself to sleep by an unexplained device, he spied a mystery in him, and was aggrieved.

He was right. There was a mystery, and a great one. Yet it was trivial and unimportant in comparison with the power to love and the desire for truth—things which he saw daily, and, because he had seen daily, ignored.

His meditations took shape, and he flung this challenge at the unknown: "I'll have no queerness in a son-in-law!" He was sitting in a Doric temple with a sea of gold and purple flowers tossing over its ruins, and his eyes looked out to the moving, living sea of blue. But his ears caught neither the echo of the past nor the cry of the present, for he was suddenly paralysed with the fear that after all he had not done so well for his daughter as he hoped.

Meanwhile, Mildred, at the other end of the line of temples, was concentrated on the echoes of the past. Harold was even more inattentive to them than usual. He was very sleepy, and would only say that the flowers were rather jolly and that the sea looked in prime condition if only one could try it. To the magnificence and pathos of the ruined Temple of Zeus he was quite dead. He only valued it as a chair.

"Suppose you go back and rest in the carriage?" said Mildred, with a shade of irritation in her voice.

He shook his head and sat yawning at the sea, thinking how wonderfully the water would fizz up over his body and how marvellously cold would be the pale blue pools among the rocks. Mildred endeavoured to recall him to higher pleasures by reading out of her Baedeker.

She turned round to explain something and he was gone.

At first she thought it was a mild practical joke, such as they did not disdain to play on each other; then that he had changed his mind and gone back to the carriage. But the custodian at the gate said that no one had gone out, and she returned to search the ruins.

The Temple of Zeus—the third greatest temple of the Greek world—has been overthrown by an earthquake, and now resembles a ruined mountain rather than a ruined building. There is a well-made path, which makes a circuit over the mass, and is amply sufficient for all rational tourists. Those who wish to see more have to go mountaineering over gigantic columns and pilasters, and squeeze their way through passes of cut stone.

Harold was not on the path, and Mildred was naturally annoyed. Few things are more vexatious for a young lady than to go out with an escort and return without. It argues remissness on her own part quite as much as on that of her swain.

Having told the custodian to stop Harold if he tried to come out, she began a systematic hunt. She saw an enormous block of stone from which she would get a good view of the chaos, and, wading through the gold and purple flowers that separated her from it, scrambled up.

On its further side were two fallen columns, lying close together, and the space that separated them had been silted up and covered with flowers. On it, as on a bed, lay Harold, fast asleep, his cheek pressed against the hot stone of one of the columns, and his breath swaying a little blue iris that had rooted in one of its cracks.

The indignant Mildred was about to wake him but, seeing the dark line that still showed beneath his eyes, stayed her voice. Besides, he looked so picturesque, and she herself, sitting on the stone watching him, must look picturesque, too. She knew that there was no one to look at her, but from her mind the idea of a spectator was never absent for a moment. It was the price she had paid for becoming cultivated.

Sleep has little in common with death, to which men have compared it. Harold's limbs lay in utter relaxation, but he was tingling with life, glorying in the bounty of the earth and the warmth of the sun, and the little blue flower bent and fluttered like a tree in a gale. The light beat upon his eyelids and the grass leaves tickled his hair, but he slept on, and the lines faded out of his face as he grasped the greatest gift that the animal life can offer. And Mildred watched him, thinking what a picture might be made of the scene.

Then her meditation changed. "What a wonderful thing is sleep! How I would like to know what is passing through his brain as he lies there. He looks so peaceful and happy. Poor boy! When he is awake he often looks worried. I think it is because he can't follow the conversation, though I try to make it simple, don't I? Yet some things he sees quite quickly. And I'm sure he has lots of imagination, if only he would let it come out. At all events I love him very much, and I believe I shall love him more, for it seems to me that there will be more in him than I expected."

She suddenly remembered his "dodge" for going to sleep, and her interest and her agitation increased.

"Perhaps, even now, he imagines himself to be someone else. What a marvellous idea! What will he say if he wakes? How mysterious everything is if only one could realize it. Harold, of all people, who seemed so ordinary—though, of course, I love him. But I am going to love him more."

She longed to reach him in his sleep, to guide the course of his dreams, to tell him that she approved of him and loved him. She had read of such a thing. In accordance with the advice of the modern spiritualistic novel she pressed her hands on her temples and made a mental effort. At the end of five minutes she had a slight headache and had effected nothing. He had not moved, he had not even sighed in his sleep, and the little blue flower still bent and fluttered, bent and fluttered in the regular onslaught of his breath.

The awakening, when it did come, found her thoughts unprepared. They had wandered to earthly things, as thoughts will do at times. At the supreme moment, she was wondering whether her stockings would last till she got back to England. And Harold, all unobserved, had woken up, and the little blue flower had quivered and was still. He had woken up because he was no longer tired, woken up to find himself in the midst of beautiful flowers, beautiful columns, beautiful sunshine, with Mildred, whom he loved, sitting by him. Life at that moment was too delicious for him to speak.

Mildred saw all the romance melting away; he looked so natural and so happy; there was nothing mysterious about him after all. She waited for him to speak.

Ten minutes passed, and still he had not spoken. His eyes were fixed steadily upon her, and she became nervous and uncomfortable. Why would he not speak? She determined to break the silence herself, and at last, in a tremulous voice, called him by his name.

The result was overwhelming, for his answer surpassed all that her wildest flights of fancy had imagined, and fulfilled beyond all dreaming her cravings for the unimagined and the unseen.

He said, "I've lived here before."

Mildred was choking. She could not reply.

He was quite calm. "I always knew it," he said, "but

it was too far down in me. Now that I've slept here it is at the top. I've lived here before."

"Oh, Harold!" she gasped.

"Mildred!" he cried, in sudden agitation, "are you going to believe it—that I have lived before—lived such a wonderful life—I can't remember it yet—lived it here? It's no good answering to please me."

Mildred did not hesitate a moment. She was carried away by the magnificence of the idea, the glory of the scene and the earnest beauty of his eyes, and in an ecstasy of rapture she cried, "I do believe."

"Yes," said Harold, "you do. If you hadn't believed now you never would have. I wonder what would have happened to me."

"More, more!" cried Mildred, who was beginning to find her words. "How could you smile? How could you be so calm? O marvellous idea! That your soul has lived before! I should run about, shriek, sing. Marvellous! Overwhelming! How can you be so calm? The mystery! And the poetry, oh, the poetry! How can you support it? Oh, speak again!"

"I don't see any poetry," said Harold. "It just has happened, that's all. I lived here before."

"You are a Greek! You have been a Greek! Oh, why do you not die when you remember it?"

"Why should I? I might have died if you hadn't believed me. It's nothing to remember."

"Aren't you shattered, exhausted?"

"No: I'm awfully fit. I know that you must have believed me now or never. Remembering has made me so strong. I see myself to the bottom now."

"Marvellous! Marvellous!" she repeated.

He leapt up onto the stone beside her. "You've believed me. That's the only thing that's marvellous. The rest's nothing." He flung his arms round her, and embraced her—an embrace very different from the decorous peck by which he had marked the commencement of their engagement. Mildred, clinging to him, murmured "I do believe you," and they gazed without flinching into each other's eyes.

Harold broke the silence, saying, "How very happy life is going to be."

But Mildred was still wrapped in the glamour of the past.

"More! More!" she cried. "Tell me more! What was the city like—and the people in it? Who were you?"

"I don't remember yet—and it doesn't matter."

"Harold, keep nothing from me! I will not breathe a word. I will be silent as the grave."

"I shall keep nothing. As soon as I remember things, I will tell them. And why should you tell no one? There's nothing wrong."

"They would not believe."

"I shouldn't mind. I only minded about you."

"Still—I think it is best a secret. Will you agree?"

"Yes—for you may be right. It's nothing to do with the others. And it wouldn't interest them."

"And think—think hard who you were."

"I do just remember this—that I was a lot greater then than I am now. I'm greater now than I was this morning, I think—but then!"

"I knew it! I knew it from the first! I have known it always. You have been a king—a king! You ruled here when Greece was free!"

"Oh! I don't mean that—at least I don't remember it. And was I a Greek?"

"A Greek!" she stammered indignantly. "Of course you were a Greek, a Greek of Acragas."

"Oh, I daresay I was. Anyhow it doesn't matter. To be believed! Just fancy! You've believed me. You needn't have, but you did. How happy life is!"

He was in an ecstasy of happiness in which all time except the present had passed away. But Mildred had a tiny thrill of disappointment. She reverenced the past as well.

"What do you mean then, Harold, when you say you were greater?"

"I mean I was better, I saw better, heard better, thought better."

"Oh, I see," said Mildred, fingering her watch. Harold, in his most prosaic manner, said they must not keep the carriage waiting, and they regained the path.

The tide of rapture had begun to ebb away from Mildred. His generalities bored her. She longed for detail, vivid detail, that should make the dead past live. It was of no interest to her that he had once been greater.

"Don't you remember the temples?"

"No."

"Nor the people?"

"Not yet."

"Don't you at all recollect what century you lived in?"

"How on earth am I to know?" he laughed.

Mildred was silent. She had hoped he would have said the fifth B.C.—the period in which she was given to understand that the Greek race was at its prime. He could tell her nothing; he did not even seem interested, but began talking about Mrs Popham's present.

At last she thought of a question he might be able to answer. "Did you also love better?" she asked in a low voice.

"I loved very differently." He was holding back the brambles to prevent them from tearing her dress as he spoke. One of the thorns scratched him on the hand. "Yes, I loved better too," he continued, watching the little drops of blood swell out.

"What do you mean? Tell me more."

"I keep saying I don't know any more. It is fine to remember that you've been better than you are. You know, Mildred, I'm much more worth you than I've ever been before. I do believe I am fairly great."

"Oh!" said Mildred, who was getting bored.

They had reached the Temple of Concord, and he retrieved his tactlessness by saying, "After all I'm too happy to go back yet. I love you too much. Let's rest again."

They sat down on the temple steps, and at the end of ten minutes Mildred had forgotten all her little disappointments, and only remembered this mysterious sleep, and his marvellous awakening. Then, at the very height of her content, she felt, deep down within her, the growth of a new wonder.

"Harold, how is it you can remember?"

"The lid can't have been put on tight last time I was sent out."

"And that," she murmured, "might happen to anyone."

"I should think it has—to lots. They only want reminding."

"It might happen to me."

"Yes."

"I too," she said slowly, "have often not been able to sleep. Oh, Harold, is it possible?"

"What?"

"That I have lived before."

"Of course it is."

"Oh, Harold, I too may remember."

"I hope you will. It's wonderful to remember a life better than this one. I can't explain how happy it makes you: there's no need to try to worry. It'll come if it is coming."

"Oh, Harold! I am remembering!"

He grasped her hands crying, "Remember only what is good. Remember that you were greater than you are now! I would give my life to help you."

"You have helped me," she cried, quivering with excitement. "All fits together. I remember all. It is not the first time I have known you. We have met before. Oh, how often have I dimly felt it! I felt it when I watched you sleeping—but then I didn't understand. Our love is not new. Here in this very place when there was a great city full of gorgeous palaces and snow-white marble temples, full of poets and music, full of marvellous pictures, full of sculptures of which we can hardly dream, full of noble men and noble thoughts, bounded by the sapphire sea, covered by the azure sky, here in the wonderful youth of Greece did I speak to you and know you and love you. We walked through the marble streets, we led solemn sacrifices, I armed you for the battle, I welcomed you from the victory. The centuries have parted us, but not for ever. Harold, I too have lived at Acragas!"

Round the corner swept the Peaslakes' carriage, full of excited occupants. He had only time to whisper in her ear, "No, Mildred darling, you have not."

3

There was a dirty little sitting-room in the Albergo Empedocle, and Mildred was sitting there after dinner waiting for her father. He had met some friends at the temples, and he and she had agreed to pay them a visit. It was a cold night, and the room smelt of mustiness and lamp-oil. The only other occupant was a stiff-backed lady who had found a three-year-old number of *Home Chat*. Lady Peaslake, Lilian and Harold were all with Sir Edwin, hunting for the key of his Gladstone bag. Till it was found he could not go out with her, for all his clean collars were inside.

Mildred was thoroughly miserable. After long torture she had confessed to herself that she was self-deceived. She had never lived in Acragas. She remembered nothing. All her glowing description was pure imagination, the result of sentimental excitement. For instance, she had spoken of "snow-white marble temples". That was nonsense, sheer nonsense. She had seen the remains of those temples, and they were built of porous stone, not marble. And she remembered now that the Sicilian Greeks always covered their temples with coloured stucco. At first she had tried to thrust such objections away and to believe that she had found a truth to which archaeology must yield. But what pictures or music did she remember? When had she buckled on Harold's armour, and what was it like? Was it probable that they had led a sacrifice together? The visions, always misty, faded away. She had never lived in Acragas.

But that was only the beginning of her mortification. Harold had proved her wrong. He had seen that she was a shifty, shallow hypocrite. She had not dared to be alone with him since her exposure. She had never looked at him and had hardly spoken. He seemed cheerful, but what was he thinking? He would never forgive her.

Had she only realized that it is only hypocrites who cannot forgive hypocrisy, whereas those who search for truth are too conscious of the maze to be hard on others—then the bitter flow of her thoughts might have been stopped and the catastrophe averted. But it was not conceivable to her that he should forgive—or that she should accept forgiveness, for to her forgiveness meant triumph of one person over another.

So she went still further towards sorrow. She felt that Harold had scored off her, and she determined to make the score as little as she could. Was he really as sincere as he had seemed? Sincere he might be, but he might be self-deceived even as she was. That would explain all. He too had been moved by the beauty of the scene, by its wonderful associations. Worn out, he had fallen asleep, and, conscious perhaps that she was in a foolish sympathetic state, had indulged in a fit of imagination on awaking. She had fallen in with it, and they had encouraged each other to fresh deeds of folly. All was clear. And how was she to hide it from her father?

Each time she restated the question it took a more odious form. Even though she believed Harold had been as foolish as herself, she was still humiliated before him, for her folly had been revealed, and his had not. The last and worst thought pressed itself upon her. Was he really as simple as he seemed? Had he not been trying to deceive her? He had been so careful in speaking of his old life: would only say that he had been "greater", "better"—never gave one single detail by which archaeology might prove him wrong. It was very clever of him. He had never lost his head once. Jealous of her superior acquirements, he had determined to put her to ridicule. He had laid a cunning bait and she had swallowed it. How cleverly he had lured her on to make the effort of recollection! How patiently he had heard her rapturous speech, in order that he might prove her silly to the core! How diabolically worded was his retort—"No, Mildred darling, you have not lived at Acragas." It implied: "I will be kind to you and treat you well when you are my wife, but recollect that you are silly, emotional, hypocritical; that your pretensions to superiority are gone for ever; that I have proved you inferior to me, even as all women are inferior to all men. Dear Mildred, you are a fool!"

"Intolerable! Intolerable!" she gasped to herself. "If only I could expose him! I never dreamt it of him! I was never on my guard!"

Harold came quickly into the room, and she was at once upon the defensive. He told her that her father was ready and she got up to go, her ears aching in expectation of some taunt. It came—a very subtle one. She heard him say, "Kiss me before you go," and felt his hands grasp her elbows.

"No!" she said, shrinking from his touch, and frowning towards the stiff-backed lady, who sat a little stiffer.

"You'll have to," was his reply, and catching hold of her—he was very strong—he lifted her right above his head, and broke the feathers in her hat against the ceiling. He never completed his embrace, for she shrieked aloud, inarticulate with passion, and the voice of Sir Edwin was heard saying, "Come, come, Harold, my boy—come, come!"

He set her down, and white with rage she hissed at him, "I never thought I should live to find you both charlatan and cad," and left the room.

Had she stayed, she would have been gratified at the prompt effect of her rebuke. Harold stood where she left him, dumb with misery, and then, without further warning, began to cry. He cried without shame or restraint, not even turning his head or covering his face with his hands, but letting the tears run down his cheeks till they caught in his moustache, or dropped onto the floor. Sir Edwin, not unmoved, stood before him for a moment, stammering as he tried to think of something that should both rebuke and console.

But the world has forgotten what to say to men of twenty-four who cry. Sir Edwin followed his daughter, giving a despairing look at Lady Peaslake and Lilian as he departed.

Lady Peaslake took up the line of behaving as if nothing had happened, and began talking in a high voice about the events of the day. Harold did not attempt to leave the room, but still stood near the table, sobbing and gulping for breath.

Lilian, moved by a more human impulse, tremulously asked him why he cried, and at this point the stiff-backed lady, who had sat through everything, gathered up her skirts as if she had seen a beetle, and slipped from the room.

"I cry because I'm unhappy: because Mildred's angry with me."

"Er—er," said Lady Peaslake, "I'm sure that it would be Mildred's wish that you should stop."

"I thought at dinner," he gasped, "that she was not pleased. Why? Why? Nothing had happened. Nothing but happiness, I mean. The best way, I thought, of showing I love her is to kiss her, and that will make her understand again. You know, she understood everything."

"Oh yes," said Lady Peaslake. "Look," she added to divert him, "how do you like my new embroidery?"

"It's hideous—perfectly hideous!" was his vigorous reply.

"Well, here is a particular gentleman!" said good-natured Lady Peaslake. "Why, it's Liberty!"

"Frightful," said Harold. He had stopped crying. His

face was all twisted with pain, but such a form of expressing emotion is fairly suitable for men, and Lady Peaslake felt easier.

But he returned to Mildred. "She called me a cad and a charlatan."

"Oh, never mind!" said Lilian.

"I may be a cad. I never did quite see what a cad is, and no one ever quite explained to me. But a charlatan! Why did she call me a charlatan? I can't quite see what I've done."

He began to walk up and down the little room. Lady Peaslake gently suggested a stroll, but he took no notice and kept murmuring, "Charlatan."

"Why are pictures like this allowed?" he suddenly cried. He had stopped in front of a coloured print in which the martyrdom of St Agatha was depicted with all the fervour that incompetence could command.

"It's only a saint," said Lady Peaslake, placidly raising her head.

"How disgusting—and how ugly!"

"Yes, very. It's Roman Catholic."

He turned away, shuddering, and began his everlasting question—"Why did she call me a charlatan?"

Lady Peaslake felt compelled to say, "You see, Harold, you annoyed her, and when people are annoyed they will say anything. I know it by myself."

"But a charlatan! I know for certain that she understands me. Only this afternoon I told her—"

"Oh, yes," said Lady Peaslake.

"Told her that I had lived before—lived here over two thousand years ago, she thinks."

"Harold! My dear Harold! What nonsense are you talking?" Lady Peaslake had risen from her chair.

"Over two thousand years ago, when the place had another name."

"Good heavens; he is mad!"

"Mildred didn't think so. It's she who matters. Lilian, do you believe me?"

"No," faltered Lilian, edging towards the door.

He smiled, rather contemptuously.

"Now, Harold," said Lady Peaslake, "go and lie down, there's a good boy. You want rest. Mildred will call you charlatan with reason if you say such silly, such wicked things—good gracious me! He's fainting! Lilian! Water from the dining-room! Oh, what has happened? We were all so happy this morning."

The stiff-backed lady re-entered the room, accompanied by a thin little man with a black beard.

"Are you a doctor?" cried Lady Peaslake.

He was not, but he helped them to lay Harold on the sofa. He had not really fainted, for he was talking continually.

"You might have killed me," he said to Lady Peaslake, "you have said such an awful thing. You mean she thinks I never lived before. I know you're wrong, but it nearly kills me if you even say it. I have lived before—such a wonderful life. You will hear—Mildred will say it again. She won't like talking about it, but she'll say it if I want her to. That will save me from—from—from being a charlatan. Where is Mildred?"

"Hush" said the little man.

"I have lived before—I have lived before, haven't I? Do you believe me?"

"Yes," said the little man.

"You lie," said Harold. "Now I've only to see people and I can tell. Where is Mildred?"

"You must come to bed."

"I don't speak or move till she comes."

So he lay silent and motionless on the sofa, while they stood around him whispering.

Mildred returned in a very different mood. A few questions from her father, followed by a few grave words of rebuke, had brought her to a sober mind. She was terribly in fault; she had nourished Harold's insanity, first by encouraging it, then by rebuffing it. Sir Edwin severely blamed her disordered imagination, and bade her curb it; its effects might be disastrous, and he told her plainly that unless Harold entirely regained his normal condition he would not permit the marriage to take place. She acknowledged her fault, and returned determined to repair it; she was full of pity and contrition, but at the same time she was very matter-of-fact.

He heard them return and rushed to meet her, and she rushed to meet him. They met in the long passage, where it was too dark to see each other's faces.

"Harold," she said hurriedly, "I said two dreadful words to you. Will you forgive me?"

She tried to touch him, but he pushed her off with his arm, and said, "Come to the light."

The landlord appeared with a lamp. Harold took it and held it up to Mildred's face.

"Don't!" she said feebly.

"Harold!" called Lady Peaslake. "Come back!"

"Look at me!" said Harold.

"Don't!" said Mildred and shut her eyes.

"Open your eyes!"

She opened them, and saw his. Then she screamed and called out to her father: "Take him away! I'm frightened. He's mad! He's mad!"

Harold said quite calmly, "This is the end."

"Yes," said Sir Edwin, nervously taking the lamp, "now it's bed-time."

"If you think I'm mad," said Harold, "I am mad. That's all it means."

"Go to bed, Harold, to please me."

"Six people say I'm mad. Is there no one, no one, no one who understands?" He stumbled up the passage as if he were blind, and they heard him calling, "Tommy."

In the sitting-room he caught his foot in the carpet and fell. When they picked him up, he was murmuring: "Harold can't stand up against six. What is Harold? Harold. Harold. Harold. Who is Harold?"

"Stop him!" cried the little man. "That's bad! He mustn't do that."

They shook him and tried to overtalk him, but he still went on. "What is Harold? Six letters. H.A.R.O.L.D. Harold. Harold. Harold."

"He's fainted again!" cried Lady Peaslake. "Oh, what has happened?"

"It's a sunstroke," said Sir Edwin. "He caught it through sleeping in the sun this afternoon. Mildred has told me all about it."

They took him up and carried him to his room.

As they were undressing him, he revived, and began to talk in a curious, thick voice.

"I was the last to go off the sofa, wasn't I? I counted five go—the wisest first—and I counted ten kinds of wine for certain before I slipped. Your conjurers are poor—but I liked the looks of the flute-girl."

"Go away, dears," said Lady Peaslake. "It's no good our stopping."

"Yes, I liked the flute-girl; is the porter I gave you last week a success?"

"Yes," said the little man, whose cue it was always to agree.

"Well, he'd better help carry me home, I don't want to walk. Nothing elaborate, you know. Just four porters for the litter, and half a dozen to carry the lights. That won't put you out."

"I'm afraid you must stop here for the night."

"Very well, if you can't send me back. Oh, the wine! The wine! I have got a head."

"What is he saying?" asked Mildred through the door.

"Is that the flute-girl?" said Harold, raising an interested eye.

Sir Edwin laid hold of him, but he was quite passive, and did not attempt to move. He allowed himself to be undressed, but did not assist them, and when his pyjamas were handed to him he laughed feebly and asked what they were for.

"I want to look out the window." They took him to it, hoping that the fresh air would recall his wits, and held him tight in case he tried to leap out. There was no moon, and the expanse of trees and fields was dark and indistinguishable.

"There are no lights moving in the streets," said

Harold. "It must be very late. I forgot the windows were so high. How odd that there are no lights in the streets!"

"Yes, you're too late," said the little man. "You won't mind sleeping here. It's too far to go back."

"Too far—too far to go back," he murmured. "I am so sleepy, in this room I could sleep for ever. Too far—too far—oh, the wine!"

They put him into the bed, and he went off at once, and his breathing was calm and very regular.

"A sunstroke," whispered Sir Edwin. "Perhaps a good night's rest—I shall sit up."

But next morning Harold had forgotten how to put on his clothes, and when he tried to speak he could not pronounce his words.

4

They had a terrible scene with him at the Girgenti railway station next morning when the train came in. However, they got him onto it at last, and by the evening he was back at Palermo and had seen the English doctor. He was sent back to England with a keeper, by sea, while the Peaslakes returned by Naples, as soon as Mildred's health permitted.

Long before Harold reached the asylum his speech had become absolutely unintelligible; indeed, by the time he arrived at it, he hardly ever uttered a sound of any kind. His case attracted some attention, and some experiments were made, which proved that he was not unfamiliar with Greek dress, and had some knowledge of the alphabet.

But he was quite blank when spoken to, either in ancient or modern Greek, and when he was given a Greek book he did not know what to do with it, and began tearing out the pages.

On these grounds the doctors have concluded that Harold merely thinks he is a Greek, and that it is his mania to behave as he supposes that a Greek behaved, relying on such elementary knowledge as he acquired at school.

But I firmly believe that he has been a Greek—nay, that he is a Greek, drawn by recollection back into his previous life. He cannot understand our speech because we have lost his pronunciation. And if I could look at the matter dispassionately—which I cannot—I should only rejoice at what has happened. For the greater has replaced the less, and he is living the life he knew to be greater than the life he lived with us. And I also believe that if things had happened otherwise he might be living that greater life among us, instead of among friends of two thousand years ago, whose names we have never heard. That is why I shall never forgive Mildred Peaslake as long as I live.

Most certainly he is not unhappy. His own thoughts are sweet to him, and he looks out of the window hour after hour and sees things in the sky and sea that we have forgotten. But of his fellow men he seems utterly unconscious. He never speaks to us, nor hears us when we speak. He does not know that we exist.

So at least I thought till my last visit. I am the only one who still goes to see him; the others have given it up. Last time, when I entered the room, he got up and kissed me on the cheek. I think he knows that I understand him and love him: at all events it comforts me to think so.

The Purple Envelope

On the morning of his twenty-first birthday Howard shaved himself with particular care. He scraped his fat cheeks till they shone and smarted, he pursued an imaginary beard far down his neck, and then, taking hold of his small yellow moustache, he combed it and waxed it and pulled it till it was as straight as a ruler and as sharp as a needle.

"After all, I don't look such an ass," he thought. For he had a very proper wish to be handsome and terrible and manlike, now that he was a man. It was a cold morning, and the little shaving-glass became coated with his breath.

The inexorable, he read. Someone had traced those words upon the glass, and now they started out in clearness against the misty background. "Prosy beast!" thought Howard, recognizing the finger of some underhousemaid. He rubbed the glass clean, admired himself again, and then went to the open window to look at the view, which had always seemed to him the most beautiful in the world.

There was no garden on this side. The house looked straight into meadows, and beyond the meadows woods began, running uninterruptedly towards the sea. Somewhere in those woods was the river, and Howard fancied he could just make out the great pool, shining through a gray tangle of leafless trees. But what he liked best were the rabbits, who were hopping in the meadows by dozens, and even strolling along the gravel path. "Oh, it is a shame, it is!" he murmured wrathfully. For his uncle would allow no wild thing to be killed—not a rabbit, no, nor a hare, nor a pheasant, partridge, rook, sparrow or butterfly. And Howard loved to take life, as all those do who are really in touch with nature.

He was a kind comfortable youth, singularly free from envy and uncharitableness. But he did wish that he was coming of age here not as a guest but as an owner. What a shooting-party he would have had! A shooting-party and a dance. Whereas his uncle had provided a house full of elderly relatives, church, and a meeting of the Selborne Society.

"A piece of paper for you, dear boy," said his uncle as soon as he reached the dining-room.

The piece of paper was a cheque. It was adequate but not startling.

"And by your plate is a present."

Howard ran to his plate and undid a large parcel, which contained nothing better than the complete works of M. Maeterlinck.

"I hope you'll get to like the man," said Mr Sholton. "As far as kindness can be taught, it is taught by him."

"Thank you most awfully," said Howard. "I'm fairly sure to get to like him no end." He piled the volumes up like bricks, and felt that his moustache was already drooping. Then he received the other family presents— Watts's *Hope,* Watts's *Love and Death,* Botticelli's *Madonna of the Magnificat,* a sovereign-purse, a watch-chain, a tea-caddy, and *In Tune with the Infinite* by Mr Trine.

They all drew up to the food, but Mr Sholton had some more to say about Maeterlinck, and said it over a dish of cooling eggs.

"I particularly admire his conception of Justice. He believes that Justice dwells in each of us. When we do wrong it is because we are acting superficially, and contradicting our real self, who does the real deeds, and cannot err. And the inexorable—" He stopped suddenly and, much to Howard's relief, began to help the eggs.

"Inexorable!" murmured some ladies, liking the word. And the conversation went on in that strain of dreamy kindly culture which is so pleasant for those who have got it in their blood or who have not got anything else. It was the butler who broke the spell.

"Left for Mr Howard, sir, on the attainment of his majority, with good wishes for your happy birthday, Mr Howard, sir."

Howard gave a sharp cry of joy. The butler was carrying a gun.

"Who from?" asked Mr Sholton, frowning a little.

The gun had just been left, without any name, by a lady.

"Duck!" cried Howard, falling fiercely on his present and tearing it from its wrappings. "Take care!" screamed everyone, for he was sighting imaginary birds amongst the furniture. The works of Maeterlinck slipped one by one from the table onto the floor.

"What was the lady like?" asked Mr Sholton.

"I scarcely saw her," said the butler in an offended voice. "She was very pressed. She said she did not care how soon she got back. Those were her words. She was not a young lady, but at the same time she was not exactly old."

Howard gave a cry of astonishment. The gun was like no gun he had ever seen. Its bore, instead of being circular, was oval.

"I am sorry she would not come in," said Mr Sholton, who was always courteous. "Which way did she go?"

"The way of the woods," replied the butler, and retired.

"But what am I to do?" cried Howard plaintively. "I never saw such a gun. It wouldn't take anything. No one makes oval cartridges I ever heard of. Here's one, just one, come with it. But she should have sent a gross."

"Come, Howie!" said his uncle gently. "I dare say your friend will be writing. And you know how degenerate I am; however many cartridges you had, they would be useless to you here."

The other relatives exchanged glances. They deplored the growing brutality of the young man. They censured the ill-directed generosity of the middle-aged lady. They celebrated the wisdom, the unexpected wisdom, of old Mrs Sholton, who had at the last moment left the estate not to her grandson, but to her son. When Howard returned to the table he found favour neither with his aunt, the anti-vivisectionist, nor with Mr and Mrs Bellingham, vegetarian cousins, nor with Miss Bellingham (Sister Rose Edith)—and with his uncle least favour of all. It was unwise of him to talk so persistently of shooting and hunting and other forms of murder. Nor should he have left his uncle's present in a heap upon the floor. Mr Sholton was very thoughtful all the day, and had a walk with Mr Bellingham at the end of it.

"You really feel it my duty?" said Mr Bellingham, when the walk was over. "You put it that way?"

"I do," replied Mr Sholton. "You care for power as little as myself. But the things I love you love also; and the things I do—or rather don't do—I can trust you to omit them after me."

"It's hard luck on Howard," said Mr Bellingham, who was upright and sympathetic, like most of the Sholton stock. "Naturally he counts on the place coming to him."

"And so it ought, in the ordinary course of things. But did you ever know things to take an ordinary course? Look!" He pointed to the beautiful country by which the house was surrounded on every side. "All that's mine. Think of it as Howard's! Think of the vulgarity, the slaughter, the desecration of nature that would come after me. It's more like Paradise than anything I've ever known—and because he's my nephew is it to be made into Hell?"

Mr Bellingham could scarcely reply to this. "You are taking a most serious step," he said at last.

"Nothing," whispered Mr Sholton, "to the steps I have taken already." He left his cousin abruptly and did not refer to the subject again.

As for Howard, he managed to idle through his visit. For a day or two he tried to be more spiritual, and made a list of the fresh words in Maeterlinck and looked them up in the dictionary. But he was dreadfully bored; he might not do anything worth doing, he had had no presents worth having. No more cartridges had come for the silly gun, and there had been no letter. His uncle was not very pleasant, and always busy with papers, and as for his aunts they would catch him and make him stand for hours in the shrubbery, on the chance of seeing a long-tailed tit. They caught him one cold afternoon, and just as the tit came near he remembered something and exclaimed "The inexorable! That was the word!" and the tit was frightened and flew away.

"The inexorable!" Next morning, when he shaved, he breathed on the glass again to see if anything would happen. It was a little amusement for him. Nor was he disappointed. *Ring my own life* now stood out against the misty background.

"She is mad, that slavey," he meditated. " 'The inexorable; ring my own life'—whatever does she want to smear that on the glass for?" All day he had so little to think about that he thought about the writing. And that night he breathed on the glass before he went to bed. *Ring my own life* had disappeared. He wiped the glass clean, opened the bedroom window according to his custom, and slept the sleep at all events of the healthy.

Habits—so he had recently been told in church—are easily formed when we are young. And it was almost without thinking that he went straight to the shaving-glass as soon as he got up. It was fun to cloud the surface over, and suddenly to blot out the reflection of the room. The morning was very cold and he only had to open his mouth to steam like a boiling kettle.

"Rot!" he exclaimed stupidly.

One word, *Humanitarian,* was written across the glass.

Howard struck himself sharply on the chest. Then he went to the window, and there was the same tangible, commonplace world—the pearl-gray sky, the rabbits hopping, the sun coming through mists out of the sea.

When he felt quite awake he came back and breathed on the glass again.

There was the word, as plain as any rabbit, with clean sharp outlines, *Humanitarian*.

Someone had come in and written it during the night. He went to the door. As usual he had forgotten to lock it. Then he scuttled back to bed, for the housemaid was approaching with the hot water.

"Beastly cheek!" he murmured, wrathfully surveying the damsel as she moved about the room. He was loth to abandon first impressions, and took it as an extra proof of the housemaid's guilt that she could gaze without flinching on the fading word.

For the sake of something to say, he spoke of the matter at breakfast.

"No servant of mine would do such a thing," said Mr Sholton, flushing, "and for the matter of that no one in the house."

"Well, they won't get the chance again," said Howard. "I'll pretty well lock my door, I can tell you; it's lucky I didn't wake up, for I let out pretty hard when I'm frightened."

"Do you indeed?" said his uncle coldly. "It's my opinion, Howard, that you wrote these words yourself."

" 'Pon my honour I'm not having you on!" cried the young man.

"You must know by now that I trust you. My explanation is that you wrote those words in your sleep."

"Me sleepwalking?" he exclaimed. It was as bad as being told that he snored. "I'm not that sort."

"None the less it is my explanation." Mr Sholton felt very sour and dogmatic that morning. The episode was distasteful to him, and he could not tell why.

"Me write humanitarian! I can't even spell it."

"So I have often observed," was the reply. Howard went a little redder than usual.

The suave voice of Mrs Bellingham now intervened. "It is a probable explanation," she said, "but we must never forget the possibility of other agencies. Would you tell me, Howard, exactly the words you have found on your shaving-glass, from time to time?" As she spoke she took out a little green notebook.

"My dear, you could scarcely write to them yet," said her husband. "Their time is extraordinarily valuable."

"I am only collecting data," said Mrs Bellingham. "Data for the Psychical Research Society," she explained for Howard's benefit.

"The inexorable ring my own life humanitarian," he dictated, feeling an awful fool. The phrase was copied into Mrs Bellingham's book.

"Thank you, Howard," said she, smiling brightly. "We live in a world of mystery, and one has no right to neglect a possible clue."

That night Howard locked his door. He did not hold with people messing round when he was asleep.

According to agreement, he did not breathe on the shaving-glass when he woke up. He carried it carefully into the breakfast-room to perform the operation in public. The ladies gathered round him; the men were also interested, but restrained themselves till they saw which way the thing would turn.

Principles the pur

Mrs Bellingham gave a piercing scream, and the whole room was in an uproar.

"I locked my door," shouted Howard. "I tell you I locked my door. 'Principles the pur'? What's it mean? How's it here? Who the devil's been writing this time?"

"You yourself, my boy," said Mr Sholton. "In your sleep." He hated the shaving-glass more than ever.

Howard forgot himself. "Oh, drop that sleepwalking, I won't stand it."

"Oh Howie! Howie!" cried the aunts.

But Howard cherished his materialism. He would not have it questioned. In the midst of those hysterical anaemic people he stood wrathful and solid, declaring that he slept when he slept, and that when he was awake, as now, he was very much awake indeed.

"The words are fading," they yelled. "Howard! Breathe! Quick!"

"Oh, breathe yourself!" he retorted.

Mrs Bellingham breathed nervously. And for her also *Principles the pur* stood out upon the glass.

"We are on the verge of something great," she cried. "Tonight he will return, and write again!"

"I'm sorry for him if he does," said the young man. "I'm sorry for him if he does. If he's being funny he'll remember it."

"We do not like bluster here," said his uncle gently. "We are apt to consider it a sign of fear rather than of courage."

"But of course I'm afraid," he cried. "Who isn't?"

There was a pause. Then Mr Bellingham said: "To speak for myself and my wife, we are rather approaching the thing in a scientific spirit. The Society for Psychical—"

"Spooks!" interrupted Howard. "I knew we'd come to spooks. And I'd rather it was they than I. Who says I'm a beastly somnambulist?"

"Breakfast," said Mr Sholton. "Breakfast. Breakfast."

All through the meal Mrs Bellingham kept the shaving-glass by her plate and breathed on it at intervals, much to her host's annoyance. For Mr Sholton was a refined dreamy man, who liked spiritual things to be treated with reverence and grace. He did not believe in ghosts; there was something vulgar about them; they made too palpable a connection with the unseen. No spirit would descend from the empyrean to smear messages on a shaving-glass—the shaving-glass of a brain-less, squalid-souled youth.

"Howard!" she cried suddenly. " 'Principles' has a small p. There's a full stop after it. There's a capital T to 'The'. After 'pur' comes a hyphen. Tell me: what punctuation was there the other times?"

"I don't go in for stops," said Howard. He was cross, and, like his uncle, he could not eat. These people made him feel ill. He didn't care a hang about the "message"; what he wanted to know was who had come into his room. And it required all Mrs Bellingham's tact and enthusiasm to remind him of what he scarcely remembered. At last she was able to restore the inscriptions as follows: *The inexorable . . . [du] ring my own life, humanitarian principles. The pur-*

"Here's at all events some sense," she told them. "It's an odd way to split up 'during', but we have good authority for it." She smiled at Mr Sholton, who had his own theory on the division of words. "And, if I'm right, next time we shall have the other syllable of 'pur-'— 'purport' or 'purpose' most probably. A new sentence is beginning. We have only to read it off."

As soon as Howard could escape, he got his new gun and took it to show the keeper, a jolly, idle man who dated from the bloody reign of old Mrs Sholton. The keeper had often seen the gun before; indeed Howard took it every morning. But they were both simple folk, who valued repetition, and on this occasion, as on others, the following conversation took place:

"If I may venture, sir, this is but a poor present. I never seed a noval gun."

Howard (laughing immoderately): "A *noval* gun and a *novel* gun, eh? D'ye see? Noval—novel."

The keeper (holding his sides): "Not a hovel gun, sir; a *hoval* gun; made like a No."

This tangle had a great fascination for them. They entered again and again, till they were weak with mirth. Mr Sholton overheard them, and raised his hands to heaven. But for all that Howard was tranquil and confident when he returned to the house.

Mrs Bellingham greeted him mysteriously. "Howard, I am so sorry; we ought to stop the experiment; it worries Robert" (Mr Sholton). "He doesn't like it; he says it is a trap."

"Trap away!" said Howard. "I don't mind."

"It's a pity Robert feels this; for Sister Rose Edith has made a most brilliant and practical suggestion."

"It's nothing to do with my uncle. It's my show, and I am going through with it."

The ladies were delighted. They had done their duty by their host, and now Sister Rose Edith could speak.

"Let us obscure the glass with candle smoke," said she, "and if it should be Howard who touches it the traces will be found on his finger when he wakes."

So that evening Howard and the three Bellinghams met stealthily on the landing, and the shaving-glass was smoked over a flat candlestick. They felt they were being a little absurd, and had a sudden reaction. Mrs Bellingham giggled, and as for the Sister she turned quite skittish, and made a thumbmark in the top left-hand corner "pour encourager les autres".

Gravity returned to Howard when he entered his bedroom. He locked the door, placed the shaving-glass on the dressing-table as usual, and began his survey.

There was not anything remarkable about the room, nor had there ever been. It was just a square room, rather lofty, with a sash window and a door. To the right, in a similar but rather larger room, slept his uncle. To the left was the apartment of the Bellinghams. Overhead reposed the servants. Underneath was the private sitting-room of the aunts. Behind him ran the broad landing, from one end of the house to the other, and in front, out through the window, were the meadows, the woods and the sea. Thus, on every side, he was bounded by the familiar.

He flung up the window. It was snowing a little, and he could not see much. But he saw, for the first time, that close under the sill there ran a broad stringcourse. A man—if he was fool enough, or if he was a boy— might possibly swarm up the drainpipe to the right, and then do a horizontal bar along the stringcourse till he reached Howard's room.

"He shall have the chance," thought Howard, and left the window open. Then he turned the bed, so that he might sleep facing the light. He provided himself with a candle, matches and some heavy volumes of

Maeterlinck. And at the last moment he went to the cupboard and got out the gun. This was not at all right of him, and very dangerous besides. As he slipped in the solitary cartridge he said to himself, "I was only told never to have it loaded in the grounds; nothing was ever said about the house." To a mind such as his the argument seemed quite sound. "Self-defence too," he murmured, as he got into bed and laid the gun beside him.

He slept like a truthful man, and never turned once all night. It was rather cold when he woke up and no wonder, for there had been a good deal of snow, and some of the flakes had sailed into the room. What else had sailed in he did not discover. But more words had been traced upon the glass—traced by a finger. He looked at his own fingers. They were clean.

We are now coming to those scenes which are easier to imagine than to describe, and the scene at the breakfast table was one of them. Here was the blackened glass; here was the mark of Sister Rose Edith's thumb, and here below it had been written other words.

-ple envelope

And what had been written last time? *principles. The pur-* Mrs Bellingham shrieked wildly: "The purple envelope! The purple envelope! I said so. Our new sentence is beginning! Howard is chosen; the message is for him. Tonight— tonight—"

"Tonight," sang out Howard, "the glass shall be under my pillow." For he could be as brave as any animal.

"Dare you?" they cried. "You must not thwart the spirit; you must not anger it. We are on the edge of a secret. Leave the glass where it was before."

"Under my pillow, thank you, and the spirit shall touch me first!"

There was a gust of snow against the window, and one of the aunts screamed. "Oh, don't blaspheme," she sobbed. "Who knows what's around us? Something awful—something awful may come in any minute.

Where's Robert? Why's he so late? Why's it so dark? Oh, leave the thing alone!"

Mrs Bellingham kissed the old lady, who was not much of a personage, and comforted her. "It's research, dearest. Nothing was ever found without courage, and Howard is brave. Don't you want to hear this message to the end?"

The aunt continued to cry.

"It's out duty to inquire—to keep our minds open for Truth. We mustn't stagnate. Robert tells you that. Look! Here he comes; as well as ever." And as their host entered the room they greeted him with one great cry of:

"The Purple Envelope!"

Mr Sholton raised his hands to his ears, and then fell forward, without a word, upon the carpet.

They were silent at last. The thing was beginning to go to far.

Mr Sholton was carried back to his bed. In about half an hour he sent down a message that he was much better—practically well—and that he would like to see Howard alone.

He looked anything but practically well. He was still lying down, with the clothes drawn up to his chin, and his face was that of a man who has known unspeakable terror.

"Shut the door, Howie!" he chattered. "Please shut the door at once!"

The bedroom was horribly airless. Both the windows were tightly closed, and over the register of the grate there had recently been pasted a thick sheet of brown paper.

"Yes, the draughts!" said Mr Sholton, following his nephew's glance. "I put this collapse down to the draughts."

Howard would have put it down to sleeping in such an atmosphere. Why, even the mouseholes in the wainscot had been stopped with fresh plaster, and plastering had begun round the frames of the windows!

"Take a comfortable chair, dear boy," he continued. He was anxious to be friends with Howard. They had drifted apart ever since the arrival of that fatal gun.

"Oh, all right!" said Howard awkwardly. As his uncle delayed to speak he took a good stare at the furniture and pictures. "These must be worth pots," he observed at last.

Mr Sholton sighed. If Howard had been in a book he might have admired him as a smart little berserk hero. Unfortunately he was alive, and scarcely the person from whom to demand intelligence, sympathy or forgiveness. And Mr Sholton was demanding all three.

"Howard," he began, "you know that I have always tried to spread, during my own life, humanitarian principles." He interrupted himself with a strange cry of alarm. When he spoke again it was to say: "Reach me that drawer of papers. I want to put myself in your hands without comment."

Apparently the drawer belonged to a cabinet, though no cabinet was visible in the room. Mr Sholton had it placed by him, drew his left hand from under the bed-clothes, and began to rummage for what he wanted. Howard stared at the pictures again, and in an evil moment his eye fell on a tempera panel which hung in the centre of the wall. It had been painted in Umbria, by some scholar of Perugino, and seemed scarcely a thing of paint at all—rather some exhalation of green and tender blue, full of sweetest unreality. The Virgin —no woman, neither was she divine—knelt in aimless adoration to the Child, and on either side of her stood beautiful bloodless saints, who tottered piously, like the aspens which shadowed them. There are not many men who have such a picture in their bedroom, and each morning and evening, when Mr Sholton looked at it, he felt that his life had not entirely failed.

had put the thing rather well. After a pause, he tried the

"Well, she's not my idea of a tootsy!" said Howard, and clenched his criticism by a coarse and vapid jest. His uncle did not laugh. But he laughed himself, for he jest a second time. It sounded better than ever. This time Mr Sholton spoke.

"I can't find what I want, Howard. It doesn't matter."

"Oh, I'll grope. What is it?" The drawer was full of papers and packets, of all sizes and colours.

"What I want isn't here." And Mr Sholton laid his hand over the drawer.

"What was it you wanted?"

"Please do not trouble to look, or to stop here longer. I dare say you are anxious to pay your daily visit to the keeper."

"But hadn't you something to lay before me?" His uncle's manner had changed, and he could not think why.

"Nothing worth your notice," said Mr Sholton, lying most obviously. Howard's sleeve chanced to brush his hand. He could not keep back a cry of disgust.

"So long! I say"—he had stopped at the door—"did you know we smoked that glass last night, and this morning my fingers were clean? Clears *me,* doesn't it?"

"Do I suppose you couldn't wash your hands?" shouted Mr Sholton, in a sudden fit of terror and rage. "Couldn't you wash your hands?"

Howard's honesty was irregular, but well defined. He would sooner have killed himself than lied in this particular way. He turned with a good deal of dignity, and left the room.

He brooded over the trouble all day. Even to him it had become mysterious. Who had written those words? Why had his uncle fainted? What was hidden in that drawer? And his aunt—the one who was almost dotty —why would she continually cry? For a time he even forgot to think about his gun.

Night came at last—the night which was to solve something. The excitement began early: scarcely had he locked his door to undress when there was a tap upon it. A note from his uncle.

"Apologies, I hope," thought Howard. He was right.

"My dear boy: I am older than you are, and till last

week I was your guardian. You must believe, therefore, that I have my reasons when I ask you to do something strange. Tonight, when you go to bed, shut your window, and then smash that shaving-glass to pieces. You shall have a new one, and much more besides, if you will obey me. You are not a sleepwalker; I ought never to have said such a thing; I ask you to forgive me. I have never taken this affair as a joke. It is either nothing, or else it is incalculably grave. Once or twice in our lives we touch the corner of the unknown. Some people strive to touch it; they think it will be pleasant or exciting; like the Bellinghams. Howard, don't think that. Shut the window. Break the glass into little pieces."

Most men would have thought a little after such a letter. Howard was driven into action. He flung the window up to the top, hoping that his uncle would hear the rattle of it.

The snow came pouring in, and there was a bitter wind from the east. His teeth chattered as he retired, with his strange equipment—the loaded gun, which he laid beside him, and the shaving-glass, which he placed underneath his pillow. The candle blew out before he was quite settled, and at once his impudence deserted him. Had he remembered the matches? Had he put a good thick book on the chair? The shaving-glass slipped out, and it was as if a sheet of ice fell upon his neck. Soon his feet got cold, and as he chafed them together the bedclothes seemed heavier. It struck him that the snow must be drifting this way, right across the room. Though it was so dark, he could see it streaming towards him eternally, covering the floor, trimming the brass bedrail, soaking into the blankets. The flakes were small at first, and disappeared quickly; they only chilled his feet; but soon they began to form a white crust which stretched up to his knees. And they came larger —as large as peas, as large as blackberries. Every now and then he kicked upwards and sent some of the crust rustling onto the carpet. But still the bedclothes grew heavier, for the flakes were as large as lumps of sugar, and he could feel the weight of each as it fell. His feet and knees were paralysed; he could move them no longer; he could scarcely stretch his hand out to the gun, which chilled him like an icicle. The chairs and the dressing-table now began to appear out of the night in their ghostly coverings, and as to the carpet it must be ankle-deep. The flakes were as big as apples, and he was paralysed up to his thighs. He drew deep breaths, for he knew what was going to happen, and for the first time he realized the unacknowledged warmth of life.

"If only I was standing!" he said, and began to cry piteously. Through his tears the flakes were enormous and pounded upwards towards his heart. At last there came a flake greater than all the rest, which blocked up the whole window, and something was sitting across it, and as it broke upon him he screamed and lunged forward, and came on nothing but the blanket; which was perfectly dry.

When he lit the candle he saw that he had been asleep for several hours. "The thing's gone far enough," he thought, and sprang out of bed to shut the window. The carpet was not ankle-deep in snow, nor had any snow fallen on it at all. But the room was freezing, and as he pulled down the sash he thought that the air without felt more genial than the air within.

He turned to go back. By the side of his bed stood his uncle.

Now he understood the whole thing. Mr Sholton was the sleepwalker. And he had known it. He had come night after night along the stringcourse and written on the glass. He had found the black marks on his finger. Hence his faintness and his anger. Everything was explained now. And, if it had not been for the bad dream and the cold, Howard would have been tranquil and even amused. But he shuddered when his uncle groped under the pillow. If those fingers had touched him he would have died.

Mr Sholton had come just as he was, in pyjamas and

thick night-socks. His eyes were wide open, but he saw nothing, and though his mouth moved no sound came out of it. In the light of the candle he was even thinner and more spiritual than usual, and the finger with which he wrote upon the glass seemed half transparent. He did not wish to write; his face was distorted and his little chest heaved with inaudible sighs. When his task was over he moved away willingly and approached the window. The cold grew intolerable.

"Wake up!" said Howard hoarsely.

The figure stopped. It could hear him. Its features altered. Returning to the bed, it felt up and down amongst the clothes.

"That's all right," said Howard. "Wake up. Wake up."

He did not speak again. For he saw his uncle's face plainly, and it was transfigured with hate. At last things were simple. They were here to kill each other.

The young man was helpless from the first. He was only a cold frightened lump of flesh and blood, and there was nothing in him to oppose the power of the sleepwalker. A tiny net seemed to fall over him, and after it fell another. Slowly he was drawn towards the bed. He cursed his obstinacy. He cursed the Bellinghams and their fiendish experiments, and he cursed every breath his uncle should ever draw, every pleasure he should approach, every kind word he should ever utter. They were face to face now, with the bed between them. Howard snatched up the shaving-glass, and hurled it at the enemy. But he must have aimed badly, for the glass smashed on the opposite wall. The figure smiled. Another net fell over him, and he bent forward obediently to kiss the finger that beckoned him. His mouth was blistered with the cold. But ere they touched, his hands fell on the gun, and for a moment he was strong again. There was no time to sight. He fired straight into his uncle's body.

With the click of the trigger he awoke for good. He was alone, the candle was flickering out, the shaving-glass was smashed, the window was shut. But there was no explosion. The new gun had missed fire.

So he was a sleepwalker after all.

Then he did a thing which sounds like madness, but which really saved him from going mad. He dressed quickly and let himself out of the front door. After these two dreams he could endure the room no longer. For a whole hour he ran through the snowy glades of the woods and over the fields, till he was tired and warm. Then he fell into a loosened rick of hay and buried himself up to his chin, and was asleep at once, nor did he move or dream again.

When he woke the sky was pale green and the shadows on the snow were purple. The rick chanced to be above the house and he had an agreeable view of the smoking kitchen chimney. Woods too are beautiful in the early morning, and as he filled his pipe the sun rose clear out of the winter sea. Possibly there would be skating. As he felt for matches he came on the oval cartridge which he must have taken away from the room in his flight. He slit it open. It was full of rubbish.

"This unknown female is a rotter!" he observed. "Not one grain of powder in it. Just the kind of thing a woman would think funny. Why, if it hadn't been a dream I should have been done for. But Lord! How I hate him still! It's as if it wasn't a dream."

He threw the cartridge away. One of his uncle's shepherds came up the hill, and they spoke with precision of the weather. The pipe drew well, and it was still between his teeth when a rabbit hopped cheerfully towards him. "But I'll kill something," he thought, and waited till the creature ventured into the field. There he chased it skilfully, and by good luck ran it down and twisted its neck with pleasure. Now the poacher was ready for breakfast, and, having given the rabbit to the admiring shepherd, he swaggered away to the house.

The other guests had assembled, and, forgetting a most necessary toilet, he burst into their midst. "Sorry!" he cried, "but I have had a night and a half. It's all explained, I'm a sleepwalker after all! Bad dreams, bad cartridge, and the shaving-glass no more good either."

Then he saw that nearly everyone was crying.

"You break it to him," said one aunt, and the other replied, "No, dear, I can't, you."

"It is an apt comment," said Mr Bellingham slowly, "on the futility of our daily life. While we have been intent on useless inquiries into the other world, real tragedy has come upon us unheralded. My poor Howard! I don't know how to put it to you; I must simply say, without any attempt at preparation—that your uncle is dead."

"Dead?" said Howard politely. "I'm very sorry for that. But what of?"

"Suddenly, of something internal, during the night."

"A chill?" he cried, puzzled again.

"No, he complained of the cold yesterday, but the doctor says it was not a chill. Indeed the room this morning was suffocating. All the cracks and windows were plastered up. There was a little hole through the brown paper over the register, but that was really all."

"It was unlike him," said the ladies gently. "He used not to object to the air."

But Howard cared for nothing if it was not a chill. He was desperately hungry, and began to eye the food. "A curious collapse, the doctor says," whispered Mr Bellingham. "Thank God, he did not suffer, but it was as if something exploded inside him; all the sources of life have been deranged. This is what the doctor says. You, when you see him, would imagine no such thing. For he died with a quiet smile on his face, and his finger stretched out, as if to bless us."

He raised his voice a little for the last sentence, and again they paid the homage of tears for their kind departed friend, who would never take his seat at that table again.

"Bacon for anyone?" asked Howard. "Mrs Bellingham, some bacon?" He had slipped into his uncle's chair, and was lounging forward over the dish.

They looked at him in horror. He was covered with mud and hay, his eyes were still bloodshot, and in his face there was neither affection nor anger nor remorse, nor any spiritual quality but the hunger of the beasts who are said to perish.

In their common misery Mrs Bellingham found time to whisper to her husband, "Our young friend is a little premature!"

As for the purple envelope—where it was hidden, what exactly it contained, why it had not been destroyed—all this should have been stated clearly at the beginning of the story, and there is no point in stating it now. But when Mr. Sholton left the estate to his cousin he was giving away what had never been his. Howard now reigns over those woods and meadows, even as his grandmother desired. Power has made him dictatorial and noisy. He eats and drinks enormously, he quarrels with his neighbors, he is rude to his lady, he has not the slightest conception of the intellectual problems which underlie our daily life, nor of the spiritual problem which surrounds it. Such a man is neither a comfort to the aged nor an example to the young. But I stop with him whenever I get the chance.

"Oh, take away this beastly oval gun!" he said to me on the occasion of my last visit. "It's just the thing for you—smart, showy and absolutely useless."

He is quite right. I have a certain regard for the weapon, and I refused it, with thanks.

The Helping Hand

When Lady Anstey's book on Giovanni da Empoli was published, Mr Henderson found in it much that needed forgiveness. His friend did not write as charmingly as she talked: a horrid slime of culture oozed over her style, her criticisms were affected, her enthusiasms abominable. This he could have forgiven; but how could he forgive the subject-matter? The dear lady had appropriated, without acknowledgement, facts and theories for which he, and he alone, was responsible. He had studied Giovanni da Empoli for years, and the premature fruit of his labours now lay upon the breakfast table—a little apple-green book, four shillings net, being one of Messrs Angerstein's series of Pocket Painters.

Mrs Henderson, a devoted wife, was turning over the leaves with a smile upon her face, for she was pleased that the words of Lady Anstey had been printed on such heavy paper. She knew nothing of the shameful plagiarism, her interest in art being sympathetic rather than intelligent: she was always glad when her friends and her husband got on in it, just as she was glad when her son got on at school.

"What a long list of books she has read to write it!" she observed. "Did you know she could read German? And when did she go to Italy? Wasn't Empoli the place you made us go to—the dirty hotel where we had to hunt the chickens out of the bedroom window?"

"Yes," replied Mr Henderson, remembering with anguish the nights at Empoli which he had spent and Lady Anstey had not.

"Why did we go there? I've forgotten."

"I had things to look up in the archives." He held up the newspaper as a screen. •

"I think you look up too much. Here's Lady Anstey who a little time back knew no more about Italian art than I do, and yet look! I wish you'd write a little book like this. I'm sure you could do it."

"I haven't the knack of putting things brightly." He never said all he thought about the Pocket Painters and similar editions, believing that anything which induces people to look at pictures has its value.

"Yes: I dare say it's all superficial and wrong."

He answered with some animation, "What makes you think so?"

"Because I mistrust new theories—not that I should have known there was a theory. But she says there is one in the preface."

"Giovanni da Empoli," said Mr Henderson eagerly, "is one of the great puzzles of the Quattrocento. It is highly probable from internal and external evidence that many pictures attributed to other painters should be given to him."

"Cut your bread and butter, dear, do not bite it," said Mrs Henderson to their son.

"If we take one of the Pieros in the National Gallery, the portrait in the Poldi-Pezzoli at Milan, the so-called Baldovinetti at Naples, and the *cassoni* attributed to Pesellino, we notice in all a certain—"

" 'Empoli is a quaint old town not untinged with the modern spirit,' " interrupted their son, who was reading out of Lady Anstey's book in the nasal twang that is considered humorous by the young. " 'Here in 1409'— then a long note saying why not in 1429—"

"Exactly," said his father.

" '—in 1409 young Giovanni was born, here, when not on his travels, he lived, and here he died in 1473. Our painter never married. Of his six children four—' "

"Don't read at meals, dear," said his mother, taking the book. "This is a great surprise to me and a great pleasure. I never thought Lady Anstey had it in her."

No more she had. The book was the work of Mr Henderson. He had no one to blame but himself. Lady Anstey had said, "I want to write a book about Giovanni da Empoli: tell me everything you know," and he had told her, cautiously at first in barren statements, then, as he grew warm, infusing the facts with life, till at last the whole theory stood up before her delighted eyes. "Tell it me again," she said, for she was not quick at following, and he had told it her again and she had made notes of it, and he had placed his own notes at her disposal.

He reminded himself that facts are universal property, and it is no matter who gives them to the world. But ideas—should there not be some copyright in ideas? He had only meant to stimulate Lady Anstey, not to equip her. However, she had Virgil on her side, and Molière and Shakespeare, and all the ancient Greeks who had taken everything and said nothing to anybody, and splendid fellows they were.

She was perfectly open when they next met, greeting him with "And here is someone else to whom I owe more than I can say." For her book was a success, and Messrs Angerstein had asked her to do one on Botticelli.

"I'm so glad he's been of use," said Mrs Henderson, imagining herself to be engaged in conventional civilities. "I never knew he had studied the man." For Mr Henderson had decided to bear his burden in silence, and neither to his wife nor to anyone else did he give one hint of his mortification. He had in him something of the saint, and knew it would be wrong as well as undignified to repine.

"And now tell me all about Botticelli," said Lady Anstey. But Mr Henderson told very little about Botticelli. He regarded Lady Anstey with frozen admiration, almost with terror, as a being devoid of conscience and consciousness. They continued great friends, but he saw her as seldom as possible.

Her book, in spite of its popular form, made a considerable impression in artistic circles, and she was soon drawn into the congenial and lucrative atmosphere of controversy. In a fortunate hour Sir William Magnus disagreed with her, and a duel ensued, conducted with courtesy on his side and spirit on hers. Wisely refraining from venturing into new fields, she contented herself with repeating the statements she had made in her book. Mrs Henderson, who always followed anything personal, was able to write her a hearty letter of congratulation on her victory.

Mr Henderson did not write. The triumph of his theory gave him no pleasure, for it had triumphed in a mangled form. Lady Anstey had wielded it fairly well, but she had missed all the subtleties, she had spoiled the purity of its outline. Yet she had not spoiled it enough to justify his publishing it anew, under his own name.

He suffered a good deal, though he trained himself to laugh at the irony of the situation. He would like to have found someone to laugh with, but all his friends were embroiled on one side or the other, and he could not trust them to keep silent. As for his wife, she did not believe in irony. Meanwhile the book ran through several editions, and there was a rumour that the Powers that Be in the National Gallery were troubled, and meditated changing the label on the Piero della Francesca.

By the time Professor Rinaldi came to England, Mr Henderson was tired of laughing and needed sympathy. Rinaldi, whom Mrs Henderson called the Italian, was a man of great learning and artistic insight, who had become so disgusted with controversies over beauty that he had left Rome and retired to the curatorship of a small provincial gallery. There he lived, or as others said rotted, studying continually because he could not help it, but avowing his intention of never publishing again.

Here was a man to whom Mr Henderson could speak freely. They were old friends, and he determined to pay him a visit in London.

"Do," said Mrs Henderson, "and I will finish off the spring-cleaning."

Mr Henderson left on the Thursday, and Mrs Henderson turned out the dinning-room. On Friday she did the drawing-room. On Saturday she began at her husband's study, and came across a pasteboard box labelled Giovanni da Empoli.

Recognizing the name, she opened it and read on the top sheet inside: "Reasons for believing G. to be born in 1409." A strange impulse moved her, and she went for Lady Anstey's book. It gave identical reasons.

Then in one moment the loving wife became a student of art. All Saturday she sat with the book and the papers before her, and discovered that they coincided, not here and there but everywhere. The last paper in the box was a letter from Lady Anstey saying "Many thanks for loan of notes, which have been most acceptable."

All Sunday she thought over the revelation, all Monday and all Tuesday she acted on it. Mr Henderson returned on the Wednesday.

He was looking more cheerful than she had seen him for weeks. "The world is ruled by irony," he observed, and smiled, as if he found the rule easy to bear.

"And how is the Italian?" she asked, rather ill at ease.

"As fine as ever. 'A little less imagination in archaeology and a little more in art' was his advice to Sir William yesterday."

The word "art" gave her an opening, and she exclaimed, "Yes indeed! Yes indeed! Yes indeed!"

"Why this enthusiasm?"

"You dear thing!" she cried, embracing him; "you're too good to be alive!"

"What have I done?" he asked, looking grave.

"I've found you out—that you wrote Lady Anstey's book—that she took all your facts and ideas and never said a word. And all these months you've let her talk and become famous and make money. I do admire and love you for it—but do be glad I'm different!"

"What have you been doing?" he said sternly.

"Nothing rude—don't be cross. I only let it out in the course of conversation, or put it in a letter if I was writing one."

"And to whom have you written?"

"Oh, not to Lady Anstey: to Lady Magnus about the vacuum-cleaner, and one or two more. And yesterday I met the editor of the *Dudley* and he was horrified. Don't be angry—no, I don't mind if you are angry; it's simple justice I want; she shall *not* pick your brains and no one know; you *shall* have the credit for your own theory."

"Unfortunate," said Mr Henderson. "Professor Rinaldi has just proved to me that the theory in question is wrong, that the facts are wrong, that the book is wrong, that I am wrong. Unfortunate."

The Rock

We had been talking for some time, and she was so full of kindness and of insight that at last I ventured to ask about her husband.

"Did you ever question him? I hope so," she added, seeing that I hesitated.

"I went down to see him last month. We went for a sail."

"Did he charge you anything?"

"I did pay him a little."

"And I suppose you talked to the people?"

"The excitement is over. They resent him no longer. They— I won't say understand, for nobody could understand. But they have accepted him."

"I hoped for that," she said gravely. "They are simple and manly again, and he will be one of them. You saw the rock?"

"Oh yes. He showed me the rock."

On the north coast of Cornwall there is a promontory, high and fantastic, stretching for half a mile into the sea. In places it is crowned with broad boulders, in places its backbone is so narrow that one can see the water on either side, foaming against precipices that are polished black. Great moors are behind it, full of cairns and stone circles and the chimneys of deserted mines. Nearer at hand lies the farmers' country, a fertile strip that follows the indentations of the cliff. And close under the promontory itself is a little fishing village, so that many types of civilization, fruitful and fruitless, can be encompassed in a single gaze.

The rock of which she was speaking is hidden from all of them, for it lies very low in the water. It is some two hundred yards from the extreme point and resem-

bles a square brown desk, with a slope towards the
land. A wave will break on the high part, seethe down
the slope, and then be merged in the surrounding blue,
to break yet again at the foot of the promontory. One
day, during their holidays, he sailed too near this rock,
capsized, and was washed up onto it. There he lay,
face downwards, with the rising tide frothing over him.
She was up on the headland, and ran to the village for
help. A boat put out at once. They rowed manfully—
they were splendid fellows—and they reached him just
as his hands relaxed and he was sliding head foremost
into death. So much is known to all of us, and it was
the crisis of his life. But, in a story about his life, it is
not the crisis.

She began to speak, but waited a moment for the
maid to clear away the tea. In the waning light her
room seemed gentle and gray, and there hung about
it an odour (I do not write *"the* odour") of Roman
Catholicism, which is assuredly among the gracious
things of the world. It was the room of a woman who
had found time to be good to herself as well as to
others; who had brought forth fruit, spiritual and
temporal; who had borne a mysterious tragedy not
only with patience but actually with joy.

"When he got to land," she said, "he would not even
shake hands with them. He kept on saying, 'I don't
know what to do. I can't think. I shall come to you
again,' and they replied, 'Oh, that'll be all right, sir.'
You can imagine the scene, and it was not till the evening that I realized his difficulty. You—how much
would you give for your life?"

I stared blankly.

"I hope that you will never have to decide. May you
always have your life as a right. Most of us do. But
now and then a life is saved—as one might save a
vase from breaking—and then the proprietor must
think what it is worth."

"Is there not a tariff for rescue?" said I, inclined to
be irritable and dense.

"In calm weather—it was quite calm and they did not run the slightest danger—the tariff appears to be fifteen shillings a rescuer. For two pounds five my husband could have been clear of all obligation. We neither of us felt two pounds five enough. Next morning we left, full of promises. I think they still believed in us, but I am not sure."

She paused, and I ventured to say: "But a sum that was great to *them*—that was the point. The question is purely practical."

"So all our friends said. One suggested a hundred pounds, another the present of a new boat, another that, every Christmas, I should knit each man a comforter. You see, there are no such things as purely practical questions. Every question springs straight out of the infinite, and until you acknowledge that you will never answer it."

"Then what did *you* suggest?"

"I suggested that I should settle that bill myself, and never show him the receipt. But he refused and, I think, rightly. Nor do I know what I should have done."

"But what did those three men want?" I persisted. "You cannot drive me from it: that's the point."

"They would have accepted anything: they were in want of nothing. Until we tourists came they were happy and independent. We taught them the craving for money —money obtained by rowing half a mile upon the tranquil sea. The minister, with whom we corresponded, implored us to be quick. He said that the whole village was anxious and greedy, and that the men were posing as heroes. And there were we, finding the world more glorious every day, the air more delicate, music sweeter, birds, sky, the sun—everything transfigured because he had been saved. And our love—we had been married five years, but now it never seemed to have been love before. Can you tell me what these things are worth?"

I was silent. I told myself that this was fluid, unsubstantial stuff. But in my heart I knew that she and all that she said was a rock in the tideway.

"For a time he was merely interested. He was amused at the problem, and the sensations it aroused in him. But at last he only cared for the solution. He found it one evening in this little room, when a sunset, more glorious than today's, was flaming under the wych-elm. He asked me, as I ask you, what such things were worth, and gave the answer: 'Nothing; and nothing is my reward to the men who saved me.' I said: 'It is the only possible reward. But they will never understand it.' 'I shall make them understand it in time,' he told me, 'for my gift of nothing shall be all that I have in the world.' "

Again the story becomes common property. He sold up his goods—everything—every cherished trifle that he had—and gave the value of them to the poor. Some money was settled on her, and that he could not touch, but he gave away the rest. Then he went down to that village penniless and asked for charity from his rescuers.

His sufferings had been terrible. He drew out all their disappointment and pettiness and cruelty; she covered her face when she spoke of it. I was glad to tell her that this had passed: they had come to treat him as an idiot and then as a good fellow, and now he was working for one of them. As I moved from her room I said, "No one but you will ever understand it." But her eyes filled with tears and she cried: "Don't—don't praise me for that. For if I had not understood, he might be with us now."

This conversation taught me that some of us can meet reality on this side of the grave. I do not envy them. Such adventures may profit the disembodied soul, but as long as I have flesh and blood I pray that my grossness preserve me. Our lower nature has its dreams. Mine is of a certain farm, windy but fruitful, halfway between the deserted moorland and the uninhabitable sea. Hither, at rare intervals, she should descend and he ascend, to shatter their spiritual communion by one caress.

The Life to Come

1 *Night*

Love had been born somewhere in the forest, of what quality only the future could decide. Trivial or immortal, it had been born to two human bodies as a midnight cry. Impossible to tell whence the cry had come, so dark was the forest. Or into what worlds it would echo, so vast was the forest. Love had been born for good or evil, for a long life or a short.

There was hidden among the undergrowth of that wild region a small native hut. Here, after the cry had died away, a light was kindled. It shone upon the pagan limbs and the golden ruffled hair of a young man. He, calm and dignified, raised the wick of a lamp which had been beaten down flat, he smiled, lit it, and his surroundings trembled back into his sight. The hut lay against the roots of an aged tree, which undulated over its floor and surged at one place into a natural couch, a sort of throne, where the young man's quilt had been spread. A stream sang outside, a firefly relit its lamp also. A remote, a romantic spot . . . lovely, lovable . . . and then he caught sight of a book on the floor, and he dropped beside it with a dramatic moan as if it was a corpse and he the murderer. For the book in question was his Holy Bible. "Though I speak with the tongues of men and of angels, and have not—" A scarlet flower hid the next word, flowers were everywhere, even round his own neck. Losing his dignity, he sobbed "Oh, what have I done?" and not daring to answer the question he hurled the flowers through the door of the hut and the Bible after them, then rushed to retrieve the latter in an agony of grotesque remorse. All had fallen into the stream, all were carried away by the song. Darkness and beauty, darkness and beauty. "Only one end to this," he thought. And he scuttled back for his pistol. But the pistol was not with him, for he was negligent in his arrangements and had left it over with the servants at the further side of the great tree; and the servants, awoken from slumber, took alarm at his talk of firearms. In spite of all he could say, they concluded that an attack was impending from the neighbouring village, which had already proved unfriendly, and they implored their young master not to resist, but to hide in the brushwood until dawn and slip away as soon as the forest paths were visible. Contrary to his orders, they began packing, and next morning he was riding away from the enchanted hut, and descending the watershed into the next valley. Looking back at the huge and enigmatic masses of the trees, he prayed them to keep his unspeakable secret, to conceal it even from God, and he felt in his unhinged state that they had the power to do this, and that they were not ordinary trees.

When he reached the coast, the other missionaries there saw at once from his face that he had failed. Nor had they expected otherwise. The Roman Catholics, far more expert than themselves, had failed to convert Vithobai, the wildest, strongest, most stubborn of all the inland chiefs. And Paul Pinmay (for this was the young man's name) was at that time a very young man indeed, and had partly been sent in order that he might discover his own limitations. He was inclined to be impatient and headstrong, he knew little of the language and still less of native psychology, and indeed he disdained to study this last, declaring in his naïve way that human nature is the same all over the world. They heard his story with sympathy but without surprise. He related how on his arrival he had asked for an audience, which Vithobai had granted inside his ancestral stockade. There, dictionary in hand, he had put the case for Christ, and at the end Vithobai, not deigning to reply in person, had waved to a retainer and made him answer. The retainer had been duly refuted, but Vithobai remained impassive and unfriendly behind his amulets and robes. So he put the case a second time, and another retainer was put up against him, and the audience continued on these lines until he was so exhausted that he was fain to withdraw. Forbidden to sleep in the village, he was obliged to spend the night all alone in a miserable hut, while the servants kept careful watch before the entrance and reported that an attack might be expected at any moment. He had therefore judged it fitter to come away at sunrise. Such was his story—told in a mixture of missionary jargon and of slang—and towards the close he was looking at his colleagues through his long eyelashes to see whether they suspected anything.

"Do you advise a renewed attempt next week?" asked one of them, who was addicted to irony.

And another: "Your intention, I think, when you left us, was to get into touch with this unapproachable Vithobai personally, indeed you declared that you would not return until you had done so."

And a third: "But you must rest now, you look tired."

He was tired, but as soon as he lay down his secret stole out of its hiding-place beyond the mountains, and lay down by his side. And he recalled Vithobai, Vithobai the unapproachable, coming into his hut out of the darkness and smiling at him. Oh how delighted he had been! Oh how surprised! He had scarcely recognized the sardonic chief in this gracious and bare-limbed boy, whose only ornaments were scarlet flowers. Vithobai had laid all formality aside. "I have come secretly," were his first words. "I wish to hear more about this god whose name is Love." How his heart had leapt after his despondency of the day! "Come to Christ!" he had cried, and Vithobai had said, "Is that your name?" He explained No, his name was not Christ, although he had the fortune to be called Paul after a great apostle, and of course he was no god but a sinful man, chosen to call other sinners to the Mercy Seat. "What is Mercy? I wish to hear more," said Vithobai, and they sat down together upon the couch that was almost a throne. And he had opened the Bible at 1. Cor. 13, and had read and expounded the marvellous chapter, and spoke of the love of Christ and of our love for each other in Christ, very simply but more eloquently than ever before, while Vithobai said, "This is the first time I have heard such words, I like them," and drew closer, his body aglow and smelling sweetly of flowers. And he saw how intelligent the boy was and how handsome, and determining to win him there and then imprinted a kiss on his forehead and drew him to Abraham's bosom. And Vithobai had lain in it gladly—too gladly and too long—and had extinguished the lamp. And God alone saw them after that.

Yes, God saw and God sees. Go down into the depths of the woods and He beholds you, throw His Holy Book into the stream, and you destroy only print and paper, not the Word. Sooner or later, God calls every deed to the light. And so it was with Mr Pinmay. He began, though tardily, to meditate upon his sin. Each time he looked at it its aspect altered. At first he assumed that all the blame was his, because he should have set an example. But this was not the root of the matter, for Vithobai had shown no reluctance to be tempted. On the contrary . . . and it was his hand that beat down the light. And why had he stolen up from the village if not to tempt? . . . Yes, to tempt, to attack the new religion by corrupting its preacher, yes, yes, that was it, and his retainers celebrated his victory now in some cynical orgy. Young Mr Pinmay saw it all. He remembered all that he had heard of the antique power of evil in the country, the tales he had so smilingly dismissed as beneath a Christian's notice, the extraordinary uprushes of energy which certain natives were said to possess and occasionally to employ for unholy purposes. And having reached this point he found that he was able to pray; he confessed his defilement (the very name of which cannot be mentioned among Christians), he lamented that he had postponed, perhaps for a generation, the victory of the Church, and he condemned, with increasing severity, the arts of his seducer. On the last topic he became truly eloquent, he always found something more to say, and having begun by recommending the boy to mercy he ended by asking that he might be damned.

"But perhaps this is going too far," he thought, and perhaps it was, for just as he finished his prayers there was a noise as of horsemen below, and then all his colleagues came dashing into his room. They were in extreme excitement. Cried one: "News from the interior, news from the forest. Vithobai and the entire of his people have embraced Christianity." And the second: "Here we have the triumph of youth, oh it puts us to shame." While the third exclaimed alternately "Praise be to God!" and "I beg your pardon." They rejoiced one with another and rebuked their own hardness of heart and want of faith in the Gospel method, and they thought the more highly of young Pinmay because he was not elated by his success, on the contrary, he appeared to be disturbed, and fell upon his knees in prayer.

2 *Evening*

Mr Pinmay's trials, doubts and final triumphs are recorded in a special pamphlet, published by his Society and illustrated by woodcuts. There is a picture called "What it seemed to be", which shows a hostile and savage potentate threatening him; in another picture, called "What it really was!", a dusky youth in western clothes sits among a group of clergymen and ladies, looking like a waiter, and supported by underwaiters, who line the steps of a building labelled "School". Barnabas (for such was the name that the dusky youth received at his baptism)—Barnabas proved an exemplary convert. He made mistakes, and his theology was crude and erratic, but he never backslid, and he had authority with his own people, so that the missionaries had only to explain carefully what they wanted, and it was carried out. He evinced abundant zeal, and behind it a steadiness of purpose all too rare. No one, not even the Roman Catholics, could point to so solid a success.

Since Mr Pinmay was the sole cause of the victory, the new district naturally fell to his charge. Modest, like all sincere workers, he was reluctant to accept, refusing to go although the chief sent deputation after deputation to escort him, and only going in the end because he was commanded to do so by the Bishop. He was appointed for a term of ten years. As soon as he was installed, he set to work energetically—indeed, his methods provoked criticism, although they were fully justified by their fruits. He who had been wont to lay such stress on the Gospel teaching, on love, kindness, and personal influence, he who had preached that the Kingdom of Heaven is intimacy and emotion, now reacted with violence and treated the new converts and even Barnabas himself with the gloomy severity of the Old Law. He who had ignored the subject of native psychology now became an expert therein, and often spoke more like a disillusioned official than a missionary. He would say: "These people are so unlike ourselves that I much doubt whether they have really accepted Christ. They are pleasant enough when they meet us, yet probably spread all manner of ill-natured gossip when our backs are turned. I cannot wholly trust them." He paid no respect to local customs, suspecting them all to be evil, he undermined the tribal organization, and—most risky of all—he appointed a number of native catechists of low type from the tribe in the adjoining valley. Trouble was expected, for this was an ancient and proud people, but their spirit seemed broken, or Barnabas broke it where necessary. At the end of the ten years the Church was to know no more docile sons.

Yet Mr Pinmay had his anxious moments.

His first meeting with Barnabas was the worst of them.

He had managed to postpone it until the day of his installation by the Bishop, and of the general baptism. The ceremonies were over, and the whole tribe, headed by their chief, had filed past the portable font and been signed on the forehead with the cross of Christ. Mistaking the nature of the rite, they were disposed to gaiety. Barnabas laid his outer garment aside, and running up to the group of missionaries like any young man of his people said, "My brother in Christ, oh come quickly," and stroked Mr Pinmay's flushed face, and tried to kiss his forehead and golden hair.

Mr Pinmay disengaged himself and said in a trembling voice: "In the first place send your people each to his home."

The order was given and obeyed.

"In the second place, let no one come before me again until he is decently clad," he continued, more firmly.

"My brother, like you?"

The missionary was now wearing a suit of ducks with shirt, vest, pants and cholera belt, also sun-helmet, starched collar, blue tie spotted with white, socks, and brown boots. "Yes, like me," he said. "And in the third place are you decently clad yourself, Barnabas?"

The chief was wearing but little. A cincture of bright silks supported his dagger and floated in the fresh wind when he ran. He had silver armlets, and a silver necklet, closed by a falcon's head which nestled against his throat. His eyes flashed like a demon, for he was unaccustomed to rebuke, but he submitted and vanished into his stockade.

The suspense of the last few weeks had quite altered Mr Pinmay's character. He was no longer an open-hearted Christian knight but a hypocrite whom a false step would destroy. The retreat of Barnabas relieved him. He saw that he had gained an ascendancy over the chief which it was politic to develop. Barnabas respected him, and would not willingly do harm—had even an affection for him, loathsome as the idea might seem. All this was to the good. But he must strike a second blow. That evening he went in person to the stockade, taking with him two colleagues who had recently arrived and knew nothing of the language.

The chief received them in soiled European clothes —in the interval he had summoned one of the traders who accompanied the baptismal party. He had mastered his anger, and speaking courteously he said: "Christ awaits us in my inner chamber."

Mr Pinmay had thought out his line of action. He dared not explain the hideous error, nor call upon his fellow sinner to repent; the chief must remain in a state of damnation for a time, for a new church depended on it. His reply to the unholy suggestion was "Not yet".

"Why not yet?" said the other, his beautiful eyes filling with tears. "God orders me to love you now."

"He orders me to refrain."

"How can that be, when God *is* Love?"

"I have served him the longer and I know."

"But this is my palace and I am a great chief."

"God is greater than all chiefs."

"As it was in your hut let it here be. Dismiss your companions and the gate will be barred behind them, and we close out the light. My body and the breath in it are yours. Draw me again to your bosom. I give myself, I, Vithobai the King."

"Not yet," repeated Mr Pinmay, covering his eyes with his hand.

"My beloved, I give myself . . . take me . . . I give you my kingdom." And he fell prone.

"Arise, Barnabas. . . . We do not want your kingdom. We have only come to teach you to rule it rightly. And do not speak of what happened in the hut. Never mention the hut, the word hut, the thought, either to me or to anyone. It is my wish and my command."

"Never?"

"Never."

"Come, my gods, come back to me," he cried, leaping up and wrenching at his clothes. "What do I gain by leaving you?"

"No, no, no!" prevaricated Mr Pinmay. "I said Never speak, not that I would never come."

The boy was reassured. He said: "Yes. I misunderstood. You do come to Christ, but not yet. I must wait. For how long?"

"Until I call you. Meanwhile obey all my orders, whether given directly or through others."

"Very well, my brother. Until you call me."

"And do not call me your brother."

"Very well."

"Or seek my company." Turning to the other missionaries, he said, "Now let us go." He was glad he had brought companions with him, for his repentance was still insecure. The sun was setting, the inner chamber garlanded, the stockade deserted, the boy wild with passion, weeping as if his heart had broken. They might have been so happy together in their sin and no one but God need have known.

3 Day

The next crisis that Mr Pinmay had to face was far less serious, yet it shocked him more, because he was unprepared for it. The occasion was five years later, just before his own marriage. The cause of Christ had progressed greatly in the interval. Dancing had been put down, industry encouraged, inaccurate notions as to the nature of religion had disappeared, nor in spite of espionage had he discovered much secret immorality. He was marrying one of the medical missionaries, a lady who shared his ideals, and whose brother had a mining concession above the village.

As he leant over the veranda, meditating with pleasure on the approaching change in his life, a smart European dog cart drove up, and Barnabas scrambled out of it to pay his congratulations. The chief had developed into an affable and rather weedy Christian with a good knowledge of English. He likewise was about to be married—his bride a native catechist from the adjoining valley, a girl inferior to him by birth, but the missionaries had selected her.

Congratulations were exchanged.

Mr Pinmay's repentance was now permanent, and his conscience so robust that he could meet the chief with ease and transact business with him in private, when occasion required it. The brown hand, lying dead for an instant in his own, awoke no reminiscences of sin.

Wriggling rather awkwardly inside his clothes, Barnabas said with a smile: "Will you take me a short drive in your dog-cart, Mr Pinmay?"

Mr Pinmay replied that he had no dog-cart.

"Excuse me, sir, you have. It stands below. It, and the horse, are my wedding gift to you."

The missionary had long desired a horse and cart, and he accepted them without waiting to ask God's blessing. "You should not have given me such an expensive present," he remarked. For the chief was no longer wealthy; in the sudden advent of civilization he had chanced to lose much of his land.

"My reward is enough if we go one drive, sir."

As a rule he did not choose to be seen pleasuring with a native—it undermined his authority—but this was a special occasion. They moved briskly through the village, Barnabas driving to show the paces of the horse, and presently turned to the woods or to what remained of them; there was a tolerable road, made by the timber-fellers, which wound uphill towards a grove. The scene was uninteresting, and pervaded by a whitish light that seemed to penetrate every recess. They spoke of local affairs.

"How much of the timber is earmarked for the mines?" inquired Mr Pinmay, in the course of the conversation.

"An increasing amount as the galleries extend deeper into the mountain. I am told that the heat down there is now so great that the miners work unclad. Are they to be fined for this?"

"No. It is impossible to be strict about mines. They constitute a special case."

"I understand. I am also told that disease among them increases."

"It does, but then so do our hospitals."

"I do not understand."

"Can't you grasp, Barnabas, that under God's permission certain evils attend civilization, but that if men do God's will the remedies for the evils keep pace? Five years ago you had not a single hospital in this valley."

"Nor any disease. I understand. Then all my people were strong."

"There was abundant disease," corrected the missionary. "Vice and superstition, to mention no others. And intertribal war. Could you have married a lady from another valley five years ago?"

"No. Even as a concubine she would have disgraced me."

"All concubines are a disgrace."

"I understand. In regard to this marriage, sir, there is, however, a promise that you made me once."

"About the mining concession, of course? Exactly. Yes, I never thought you were treated fairly there. I will certainly approach my future brother-in-law to get you some compensation. But you ought to have been more careful at the time. You signed your rights away without consulting me. I am always willing to be consulted."

"It is not the mining concession," said Barnabas pa-

tiently; although a good steward for the Church, he
had grown careless where his own affairs were concerned. "It is quite another promise." He seemed to be
choosing his words. Speaking slowly and without any
appearance of emotion, he said at last: "Come to
Christ."

"Come to Him indeed," said Mr Pinmay in slightly
reproving tones for he was not accustomed to receive
such an invitation from a spiritual inferior.

Barnabas paused again, then said: "In the hut."

"What hut?" He had forgotten.

"The hut with the Mercy Seat."

Shocked and angry, he exclaimed: "Barnabas, Barnabas, this is disgraceful. I forbad you ever to mention
this subject."

At that moment the horse drew up at the entrance of
the grove. Civilization tapped and clinked behind them,
under a garish sun. The road ended, and a path where
two could walk abreast continued into the delicate gray
and purple recesses of the trees. Tepid, impersonal, as
if he still discussed public affairs, the young man said:
"Let us both be entirely reasonable, sir. God continues
to order me to love you. It is my life, whatever else I
seem to do. My body and the breath in it are still
yours, though you wither them up with this waiting.
Come into the last forest, before it is cut down, and I
will be kind, and all may end well. But it is now five
years since you first said Not yet."

"It is, and now I say Never."

"This time you say Never?"

"I do."

Without replying, Barnabas handed him the reins,
and then jerked himself out of the cart. It was a most
uncanny movement, which seemed to proceed direct
from the will. He scarcely used his hands or rose to his
feet before jumping. But his soul uncoiled like a spring,
and thrust the cart violently away from it against the
ground. Mr Pinmay had heard of such contortions, but
never witnessed them; they were startling, they were

disgusting. And the descent was equally sinister. Barnabas lay helpless as if the evil uprush had suddenly
failed. "Are you ill?" asked the clergyman.

"No."

"Then what ails you?"

"No."

"Do you repent of your words?"

"No."

"Then you must be punished. As the head of the
community you are bound to set an example. You are
fined one hundred pounds for backsliding."

"No." Then as if to himself he said: "First the grapes
of my body are pressed. Then I am silenced. Now I
am punished. Night, evening and a day. What remains?"

What should remain? The remark was meaningless.
Mr Pinmay drove back alone, rather thoughtful. He
would certainly have to return the horse and cart—
they had been intended as a bribe—and the hundred
pounds must be collected by one of his subordinates.
He wished that the whole unsavoury business had not
been raked up into the light just before his wedding.
Its senselessness alarmed him.

4   *Morning*

The concluding five years of Mr Pinmay's ministry were
less satisfactory than their predecessors. His marriage
was happy, his difficulties few, nothing tangible opposed
him, but he was haunted by the scene outside the grove.
Could it signify that he himself had not been pardoned?
Did God, in His mystery, demand from him that he
should cleanse his brother's soul before his own could
be accepted? The dark erotic perversion that the chief
mistook for Christianity—who had implanted it? He
had put this question from him in the press of his
earlier dangers, but it intruded itself now that he was
safe. Day after day he heard the cold voice of the
somewhat scraggy and unattractive native inviting him

to sin, or saw the leap from the cart that suggested a dislocated soul. He turned to the Christianity of the valley, but he found no consolation there. He had implanted that too: not in sin, but in reaction against sin, and so its fruits were as bitter. If Barnabas distorted Christ, the valley ignored Him. It was hard, it lacked personality and beauty and emotion and all that Paul Pinmay had admired in his youth. It could produce catechists and organizers, but never a saint. What was the cause of the failure? The hut, the hut. In the concluding years of his stay, he ordered it to be pulled down.

He seldom met Barnabas now. There was no necessity for it, since the chief's usefulness decreased as the community developed and new men pushed their way to the top. Though still helpful when applied to, he lost all capacity for initiative. He moved from his old stockaded enclosure with its memories of independence, and occupied a lofty but small modern house at the top of the village, suitable to his straitened circumstances. Here he and his wife and their children (one more every eleven months) lived in the semi-European style. Sometimes he worked in the garden, although menial labour was regarded as degrading, and he was assiduous at prayer meetings, where he frequented the back row. The missionaries called him a true Christian when they called him anything, and congratulated themselves that witchcraft had no rallying-point; he had served their purpose, he began to pass from their talk. Only Mr Pinmay watched him furtively and wondered where his old energies had gone. He would have preferred an outburst to this corrupt acquiescence; he knew now that he could deal with outbursts. He even felt weaker himself, as if the same curse infected them both, and this though he had again and again confessed his own share of the sin to God, and had acquired a natural loathing for it in consequence of his marriage.

He could not really feel much sorrow when he learned that the unfortunate fellow was dying.

Consumption was the cause. One of the imported workers had started an epidemic, and Mr and Mrs Pinmay were busied up to the moment of their own departure, negotiating an extension to the cemetery. They expected to leave the valley before Barnabas did, but during the last week he made, so to speak, a spurt, as if he would outstrip them. His was a very rapid case. He put up no fight. His heart seemed broken. They had little time to devote to individuals, so wide was the scope of their work, still they hurried over to see him one morning, hearing that he had had a fresh haemorrhage, and was not likely to survive the day. "Poor fellow, poor lad, he was an important factor ten years back—times change," murmured Mr Pinmay as he pushed the Holy Communion under the seat of the dog-cart—Barnabas's own cart, as it happened, for Mrs Pinmay, knowing nothing of the incident, had acquired it cheaply at a sale a couple of years back. As he drove it briskly up through the village Mr Pinmay's heart grew lighter, and he thanked God for permitting Barnabas, since die we must, to pass away at this particular moment; he would not have liked to leave him behind, festering, equivocal, and perhaps acquiring some sinister power.

When they arrived, Mrs Barnabas told them that her husband was still alive, and, she thought, conscious, but in such darkness of spirit that he would not open his eyes or speak. He had been carried up onto the roof, on account of the heat in his room, and his gestures had indicated that he would be left alone. "But he must not be left alone," said Mr Pinmay. "We must watch with him through this dark hour. I will prepare him in the first place." He climbed the staircase that led through a trapdoor onto the roof. In the shadow of the parapet lay the dying man, coughing gently, and stark naked.

"Vithobai!" he cried in amazement.

He opened his eyes and said: "Who calls me?"

"You must have some covering, Barnabas," said Mr

Pinmay fussily. He looked round, but there was nothing on the roof except a curious skein of blue flowers threaded round a knife. He took them up. But the other said, "Do not lay those upon me yet," and he refrained, remembering that blue is the colour of despair in that valley, just as red is the colour of love. "I'll get you a shawl," he continued. "Why, you are not lying upon a mattress, even."

"It is my own roof. Or I thought it was until now. My wife and household respected my wishes. They laid me here because it is not the custom of my ancestors to die in a bed."

"Mrs Barnabas should have known better. You cannot possibly lie on hard asphalt."

"I have found that I can."

"Vithobai, Vithobai," he cried, more upset than he expected.

"Who calls me?"

"You are not going back to your old false gods?"

"Oh no. So near to the end of my life, why should I make any change? These flowers are only a custom, and they comfort me."

"There is only one comforter. . . ." He glanced around the roof, then fell upon his knees. He could save a soul without danger to himself at last. "Come to Christ," he said, "but not in the way that you suppose. The time has come for me to explain. You and I once sinned together, yes, you and your missionary whom you so reverence. You and I must now repent together, yes, such is God's law." And confusedly, and with many changes of emotion and shiftings of his point of view and reservations, he explained the nature of what had happened ten years ago and its present consequences.

The other made a painful effort to follow, but his eyes kept closing. "What is all this talk?" he said at last. "And why do you wait until I am ill and you old?"

"I waited until I could forgive you and ask your forgiveness. It is the hour of your atonement and mine.

Put away all despair, forget those wicked flowers. Let us repent and leave the rest to God."

"I repent, I do not repent . . ." he wailed.

"Hush! Think what you say."

"I forgive you, I do not forgive, both are the same. I am good I am evil I am pure I am foul, I am this or that, I am Barnabas, I am Vithobai. What difference does it make now? It is my deeds that await me, and I have no strength left to add to them. No strength, no time. I lie here empty, but you fill me up with thoughts, and then press me to speak them that you may have words to remember afterwards. . . . But it is deeds, deeds that count, O my lost brother. Mine are this little house instead of my old great one, this valley which other men own, this cough that kills me, those bastards that continue my race; and that deed in the hut, which you say caused all, and which now you call joy, now sin. How can I remember which it was after all these years, and what difference if I could? It was a deed, it has gone before me with the others to be judged."

"Vithobai," he pleaded, distressed because he himself had been called old.

"Who calls me the third time?"

"Kiss me."

"My mouth is down here."

"Kiss my forehead—no more—as a sign that I am forgiven. Do not misunderstand me this time . . . in perfect purity . . . the holy salutation of Christ. And then say with me: Our Father which art in Heaven, hallowed be Thy name. . . ."

"My mouth is down here," he repeated wearily.

Mr Pinmay feared to venture the kiss lest Satan took an advantage. He longed to do something human before he had the sinking man carried down to receive the Holy Communion, but he had forgotten how. "You have forgiven me, my poor fellow," he worried on. "If you do not, how can I continue my vocation, or hope for the forgiveness of God?"

The lips moved.

"If you forgive me, move your lips once more, as a sign."

He became rigid, he was dying.

"You do still love me?"

"My breast is down here."

"In Christ, I mean." And uncertain of what he ought to do he laid his head hesitatingly upon the poor skeleton. Vithobai shivered, then looked at him with surprise, pity, affection, disdain, with all, but with little of any, for his spirit had mainly departed, and only the ghosts of its activities remained. He was a little pleased. He raised a hand painfully, and stroked the scanty hair, golden no longer. He whispered, "Too late," but he smiled a little.

"It is never too late," said Mr Pinmay, permitting a slow encircling movement of the body, the last it would ever accomplish. "God's mercy is infinite, and endureth for ever and ever. He will give us other opportunities. We have erred in this life but it will not be so in the life to come."

The dying man seemed to find comfort at last. "The life to come," he whispered, but more distinctly. "I had forgotten it. You are sure it is coming?"

"Even your old false religion was sure of that."

"And we shall meet in it, you and I?" he asked, with a tender yet reverent caress.

"Assuredly, if we keep God's commandments."

"Shall we know one another again?"

"Yes, with all spiritual knowledge."

"And will there be love?"

"In the real and true sense, there will."

"Real and true love! Ah, that would be joyful." His voice gained strength, his eyes had an austere beauty as he embraced his friend, parted from him so long by the accidents of earth. Soon God would wipe away all tears. "The life to come," he shouted. "Life, life, eternal life. Wait for me in it." And he stabbed the missionary through the heart.

The jerk the knife gave brought his own fate hurry-

ing upon him. He had scarcely the strength to push
the body onto the asphalt or to spread the skein of blue
flowers. But he survived for a moment longer, and it
was the most exquisite he had ever known. For love was
conquered at last and he was again a king, he had sent
a messenger before him to announce his arrival in the
life to come, as a great chief should. "I served you for
ten years," he thought, "and your yoke was hard, but
mine will be harder and you shall serve me now for
ever and ever." He dragged himself up, he looked over
the parapet. Below him were a horse and cart, beyond,
the valley which he had once ruled, the site of the hut,
the ruins of his old stockade, the schools, the hospital,
the cemetery, the stacks of timber, the polluted stream,
all that he had been used to regard as signs of his disgrace. But they signified nothing this morning, they were
flying like mist, and beneath them, solid and eternal,
stretched the kingdom of the dead. He rejoiced as in
boyhood, he was expected there now. Mounting on the
corpse, he climbed higher, raised his arms over his head,
sunlit, naked, victorious, leaving all disease and humiliation behind him, and he swooped like a falcon from
the parapet in pursuit of the terrified shade.

Dr Woolacott

For this, from stiller seats we came
                                    CYMBELINE V. iv

1

People, several of them, crossing the park. . . .

Clesant said to himself, "There is no reason I should
not live for years now that I have given up the violin,"
and leant back with the knowledge that he had faced
a fact. From where he lay, he could see a little of the
garden and a little of the park, a little of the fields and
the river, and hear a little of the tennis; a little of everything was what was good for him, and what Dr Woolacott had prescribed. Every few weeks he must expect
a relapse, and he would never be able to travel or marry
or manage the estates, still there, he didn't want to
much, he didn't much want to do anything. An electric
bell connected him with the house, the strong beautiful
slightly alarming house where his father had died, still
there, not so very alarming, not so bad lying out in the
tepid sun and watching the colourless shapeless country
people. . . .

No, there was no reason he should not live for years.

"In 1990, why even 2000 is possible, I am young,"
he thought. Then he frowned, for Dr Woolacott was
bound to be dead by 2000, and the treatment might not
be continued intelligently. The anxiety made his head
ache, the trees and grass turned black or crimson, and
he nearly rang his bell. Soothed by the advancing figures, he desisted. Looking for mushrooms apparently,
they soothed him because of their inadequacy. No mush-

87

rooms grew in the park. He felt friendly and called out in his gentle voice, "Come here."

"Oh aye," came the answer.

"I'm the squire, I want you a moment, it's all right."

Set in motion, the answerer climbed over the park fence. Clesant had not intended him to do this, and fearful of being bored said: "You'll find no mushrooms here, but they'll give you a drink or anything else you fancy up at the house."

"Sir, the squire, did you say?"

"Yes; I pass for the squire."

"The one who's sick?"

"Yes, that one."

"I'm sorry."

"Thank you, thanks," said the boy, pleased by the unexpected scrap of sympathy.

"Sir . . ."

"All right, what is it?" he smiled encouragingly.

"Sick of what illness?"

Clesant hesitated. As a rule he resented that question, but this morning it pleased him, it was as if he too had been detected by friendly eyes zigzagging in search of a treasure which did not exist. He replied: "Of being myself perhaps! Well, what they call functional. Nothing organic. I can't possibly die, but my heart makes my nerves go wrong, my nerves my digestion, then my head aches, so I can't sleep, which affects my heart, and round we go again. However, I'm better this morning."

"When shall you be well?"

He gave the contemptuous laugh of the chronic invalid. "Well? That's a very different question. It depends. It depends on a good many things. On how carefully I live. I must avoid all excitement, I must never get tired, I mustn't be——" He was going to say "mustn't be intimate with people," but it was no use employing expressions which would be meaningless to a farmworker, and such the man appeared to be, so he changed it to "I must do as Dr Woolacott tells me."

"Oh, Woolacott . . ."

"Of course you know him, everyone round here does, marvellous doctor."

"Yes, I know Woolacott."

Clesant looked up, intrigued by something positive in the tone of the voice.

"Woolacott, Woolacott, so I must be getting on." Not quite as he had come, he vaulted over the park palings, paused, repeated "Woolacott" and walked rapidly after his companions, who had almost disappeared.

A servant now answered the bell. It had failed to ring the first time, which would have been annoying had the visitor proved tedious. The little incident was over now, and nothing else disturbed the peace of the morning. The park, the garden, the sounds from the tennis, all reassumed their due proportions, but it seemed to Clesant that they were pleasanter and more significant than they had been, that the colours of the grass and the shapes of the trees had beauty, that the sun wandered with a purpose through the sky, that the little clouds, wafted by westerly airs, were moving against the course of doom and fate, and were inviting him to follow them.

2

Continuance of convalescence . . . tea in the gun-room. The gun-room, a grand place in the old squire's time, much energy had flowed through it, intellectual and bodily. Now the bookcases were locked, the trophies between them desolate, the tall shallow cupboard designed for fishing-rods and concealed in the wainscoting contained only medicine-bottles and air cushions. Still, it was Clesant's nearest approach to normality, for the rest of his household had tea in the gun-room. There was innocuous talk as they flitted out and in, pursuing their affairs like birds, and troubling him only with the external glint of their plumage. He knew nothing about them, although they were his guardians and familiars; even their sex left no impression on his mind. Throned on the pedestal of a sofa, he heard them speak of their wishes and plans, and give one another to understand that they had passionate impulses, while he barricaded himself in the circle of his thoughts.

He was thinking about music.

Was it quite out of the question that he should take up the violin again? He felt better, the morning in the garden had started him upon a good road, a refreshing sleep had followed. Now a languorous yearning filled him, which might not the violin satisfy? The effect might be the contrary, the yearning might turn to pain, yet even pain seemed unlikely in this kindly house, this house which had not always been kindly, yet surely this afternoon it was accepting him.

A stranger entered his consciousness—a young man in good if somewhat provincial clothes, with a pleasant and resolute expression upon his face. People always were coming into the house on some business or other, and then going out of it. He stopped in the middle of the room, evidently a little shy. No one spoke to him for the reason that no one remained: they had all gone away while Clesant followed his meditations. Obliged to exert himself for a moment, Clesant said: "I'm sorry —I expect you're wanting one of the others."

He smiled and twiddled his cap.

"I'm afraid I mustn't entertain you myself. I'm something of an invalid, and this is my first day up. I suffer from one of those wretched functional troubles—fortunately nothing organic."

Smiling more broadly, he remarked: "Oh aye."

Clesant clutched at his heart, jumped up, sat down, burst out laughing. It was that farm-worker who had been crossing the park.

"Thought I'd surprise you, thought I'd give you a turn," he cried gaily. "I've come for that drink you promised."

Clesant couldn't speak for laughing, the whole room seemed to join in, it was a tremendous joke.

"I was around in my working-kit when you invited me this morning, so I thought after I'd washed myself up a bit and had a shave my proper course was to call and explain," he continued more seriously. There was something fresh and rough in his voice which caught at the boy's heart.

"But who on earth are you, who are you working for?"

"For you."

"Oh nonsense, don't be silly."

" 'Tisn't nonsense, I'm not silly, I'm one of your farm-hands. Rather an unusual one, if you like. Still, I've been working here for the last three months, ask your bailiff if I haven't. But I say—I've kept thinking about you—how are you?"

"Better—because I saw you this morning!"

"That's fine. Now you've seen me this afternoon you'll be well."

But this last remark was flippant, and the visitor through making it lost more than the ground he had gained. It reminded Clesant that he had been guilty of laughter and of rapid movement, and he replied in reproving tones: "To be well and to be better are very different. I'm afraid one can't get well from one's self. Excuse me if we don't talk any more. It's so bad for my heart." He closed his eyes. He opened them again immediately. He had had, during that instant of twilight, a curious and pleasurable sensation. However, there was the young man still over at the further side of the room. He was smiling. He was attractive—fresh as a daisy, strong as a horse. His shyness had gone.

"Thanks for that tea, a treat," he said, lighting a cigarette. "Now for who I am. I'm a farmer—or rather, going to be a farmer. I'm only an agricultural labourer now—exactly what you took me for this morning. I wasn't dressing up or posing with that broad talk. It's come natural to say 'Oh aye', especially when startled."

"Did I startle you?"

"Yes, you weren't in my mind."

"I thought you were looking for mushrooms."

"So I was. We all do when we're shifting across, and when there's a market we sell them. I've been living with that sort all the summer, your regular hands, temporaries like myself, tramps, sharing their work, thinking their thoughts when they have any." He paused. "I like them."

"Do they like you?"

"Oh well. . . ." He laughed, drew a ring off his finger, laid it on the palm of his hand, looked at it for a moment, put it on again. All his gestures were definite and a trifle unusual. "I've no pride anyway, nor any reason to have. I only have my health, and I didn't always have that. I've known what it is to be an invalid, though no one guesses it now." He looked across gently at Clesant. He seemed to say: "Come to me, and you shall be as happy as I am and as strong." He gave a short account of his life. He dealt in facts, very much so when they arrived—and the tale he unfolded was high-spirited and a trifle romantic here and there, but in no way remarkable. Aged twenty-two, he was the son of an engineer at Wolverhampton, his two brothers were also engineers, but he himself had always taken after his mother's family, and preferred country life. All his holidays on a farm. The war. After which he took up agriculture seriously, and went through a course at Cirencester. The course terminated last spring, he had done well, his people were about to invest money in him, but he himself felt "too scientific" after it all. He was determined to "get down into the manure" and feel people instead of thinking about them. "Later on it's too late." So off he went and roughed it, with a few decent clothes in a suitcase, and now and then, just for the fun of the thing, he took them out and dressed up. He described the estate, how decent the bailiff was, how sorry people seemed to be about the squire's illness, how he himself got a certain amount of time off, practically any evening. Extinguishing his cigarette, he put back what was left of it into his case for future use, laid a hand upon either knee, smiled.

There was a silence. Clesant could not think of anything to say, and began to tremble.

"Oh, my name—"

"Oh yes, of course, what's your name?"

"Let me write it down, my address too. Both my Wolverhampton address I'll give you, also where I'm lodging here, so if ever—got a pencil?"

"Yes."

"Don't get up."

He came over and sat on the sofa; his weight sent a tremor, the warmth and sweetness of his body began casting nets.

"And now we've no paper."

"Never mind," said Clesant, his heart beating violently.

"Talking's better, isn't it?"

"Yes."

"Or even not talking." His hand came nearer, his eyes danced round the room, which began to fill with a golden haze. He beckoned, and Clesant moved into his arms. Clesant had often been proud of his disease but never, never of his body, it had never occurred to him that he could provoke desire. The sudden revelation shattered him, he fell from his pedestal, but not alone, there was someone to cling to, broad shoulders, a sunburnt throat, lips that parted as they touched him to murmur—"And to hell with Woolacott."

Woolacott! He had completely forgotten the doctor's existence. Woolacott! The word crashed between them and exploded with a sober light, and he saw in the light of the years that had passed and would come how ridiculously he was behaving. To hell with Woolacott, indeed! What an idea! His charming new friend must be mad. He started, recoiled, and exclaimed: "What ever made you say that?"

The other did not reply. He looked rather foolish,

and he too recoiled, and leant back in the opposite
corner of the sofa, wiping his forehead. At last he said:
"He's not a good doctor."

"Why, he's our family doctor, he's everyone's doctor round here!"

"I didn't mean to be rude—it slipped out. I just had
to say it, it must have sounded curious."

"Oh, all right then," said the boy, willing enough to
be mollified. But the radiance had passed and no effort
of theirs could recall it.

The young man took out his unfinished cigarette, and
raised it towards his lips. He was evidently a good deal
worried. "Perhaps I'd better explain what I meant," he
said.

"As you like, it doesn't matter."

"Got a match?"

"I'm afraid I haven't."

He went for one to the further side of the room, and
sat down there again. Then he began: "I'm perfectly
straight—I'm not trying to work in some friend of my
own as your doctor. I only can't bear to think of this
particular one coming to your house—this grand house
—you so rich and important at the first sight and yet
so awfully undefended and deceived." His voice faltered. "No, we won't talk it over. You're right. We've
found each other, nothing else matters, it's a chance in
a million we've found each other. I'd do anything for
you, I'd die if I could for you, and there's this one thing
you must do straight away for me: sack Woolacott."

"Tell me what you've got against him instead of talking sentimentally."

He hardened at once. "Sentimental, was I? All right,
what I've got against Woolacott is that he never makes
anyone well, which seems a defect in a doctor. I may be
wrong."

"Yes, you're wrong," said Clesant; the mere repetition of the doctor's name was steadying him. "I've been
under him for years."

"So I should think."

"Of course, I'm different, I'm not well, it's not natural for me to be well, I'm not a fair test, but other people—"

"Which other people?"

The names of Dr Woolacott's successful cases escaped him for the moment. They filled the centre of his mind, yet the moment he looked at them they disappeared.

"Quite so," said the other. "Woolacott," he kept on saying. "Woolacott! I've my eye on him. What's life after twenty-five? Impotent, blind, paralytic. What's life before it unless you're fit? Woolacott! Even the poor can't escape. The crying, the limping, the nagging, the medicine-bottles, the running sores—in the cottages too; kind Dr Woolacott won't let them stop. . . . You think I'm mad, but it's not your own thought you're thinking: Woolacott stuck it ready diseased in your mind."

Clesant sighed. He looked at the arms, now folded hard against each other, and longed to feel them around him. He had only to say, "Very well, I'll change doctors," and immediately. . . . But he never hesitated. Life until 1990 or 2000 retained the prior claim. "He keeps people alive," he persisted.

"Alive for what?"

"And there's always the marvellously unselfish work he did during the war."

"Did he not. I saw him doing it."

"Oh—it was in France you knew him?"

"Was it not. He was at his marvellously unselfish work night and day, and not a single man he touched ever got well. Woolacott dosed, Woolacott inoculated, Woolacott operated, Woolacott spoke a kind word even, and there they were and here they are."

"Were you in hospital yourself?"

"Oh aye, a shell. This hand—ring and all mashed and twisted, the head—hair's thick enough on it now, but brain stuck out then, so did my guts, I was a butcher's shop. A perfect case for Woolacott. Up he came with his 'Let me patch you up, do let me just patch you up,' oh, patience itself and all that, but I took his measure, I was only a boy then, but I refused."

"Can one refuse in a military hospital?"

"You can refuse anywhere."

"I hadn't realized you'd been wounded. Are you all right now?"

"Yes, thanks," and he resumed his grievances. The pleasant purple-gray suit, the big well-made shoes and soft white collar, all suggested a sensible country lad on his holiday, perhaps on courtship—farm-hand or farmer, countrified anyway. Yet with them went this wretched war-obsession, this desire to be revenged on a man who had never wronged him and must have forgotten his existence. "He is stronger than I am," he said angrily. "He can fight alone, I can't. My great disadvantage— never could fight alone. I counted on you to help, but you prefer to let me down, you pretended at first you'd join up with me—you're no good."

"Look here, you'll have to be going. So much talk is fatal for me, I simply mustn't get overtired. I've already far exceeded my allowance, and anyhow I can't enter into this sort of thing. Can you find your own way out, or shall I ring this bell?" For inserted into the fabric of the sofa was an electric bell.

"I'll go. I know where I'm not wanted. Don't you worry, you'll never see me again." And he slapped his cap onto his head and swung to the door. The normal life of the house entered the gun-room as he opened it —servants, inmates, talking in the passages, in the hall outside. It disconcerted him, he came back with a complete change of manner, and before ever he spoke Clesant had the sense of an incredible catastrophe moving up towards them both.

"Is there another way out?" he inquired anxiously.

"No, of course not. Go out the way you came in."

"I didn't tell you, but the fact is I'm in trouble."

"How dare you, I mustn't be upset, this is the kind of thing that makes me ill," he wailed.

"I can't meet those people—they've heard of something I did out in France."

"What was it?"

"I can't tell you."

In the sinister silence, Clesant's heart resumed its violent beating, and though the door was now closed voices could be heard through it. They were coming. The stranger rushed at the window and tried to climb out. He plunged about, soiling his freshness, and whimpering, "Hide me."

"There's nowhere."

"There must be . . ."

"Only that cupboard," said Clesant in a voice not his own.

"I can't find it," he gasped, thumping stupidly on the panelling.

"Do it for me. Open it. They're coming."

Clesant dragged himself up and across the floor, he opened the cupboard, and the man bundled in and hid, and that was how it ended.

Yes, that's how it ends, that's what comes of being kind to handsome strangers and wanting to touch them. Aware of all his weaknesses, Dr Woolacott had warned him against this one. He crawled back to the sofa, where a pain stabbed him through the heart and another struck between the eye. He was going to be ill.

The voices came nearer, and with the cunning of a sufferer he decided what he must do. He must betray his late friend and pretend to have trapped him on purpose in the cupboard, cry "Open it. . . ."

The voices entered. They spoke of the sounds of a violin. A violin had apparently been heard playing in the great house for the last half-hour, and no one could find out where it was. Playing all sorts of music, gay, grave and passionate. But never completing a theme. Always breaking off. A beautiful instrument. Yet so unsatisfying . . . leaving the hearers much sadder than if it had never performed. What was the use (someone asked) of music like that? Better silence absolute than this aimless

disturbance of our peace. The discussion broke off, his
distress had been observed, and like a familiar refrain
rose up "Telephone, nurse, doctor . . ." Yes, it was
coming again—the illness, merely functional, the heart
had affected the nerves, the muscles, the brain. He
groaned, shrieked, but love died last; as he writhed in
convulsions he cried: "Don't go to the cupboard, no
one's there."

So they went to it. And no one was there. It was as it
had always been since his father's death—shallow, tidy,
a few medicine-bottles on the upper shelf, a few cushions stored on the lower.

3

Collapse. . . . He fell back into the apparatus of decay
without further disaster, and in a few hours any other
machinery for life became unreal. It always was like
this, increasingly like this, when he was ill. Discomfort
and pain brought their compensation, because they were
so superbly organized. His bedroom, the anteroom
where the night-nurse sat, the bathroom and tiny kitch-
en, throbbed like a nerve in the corner of the great
house, and elsewhere normal life proceeded, people pursued their avocations in channels which did not disturb
him.

Delirium. . . . The nurse kept coming in, she performed medical incantations and took notes against the
doctor's arrival. She did not make him better, he grew
worse, but disease knows its harmonies as well as health,
and through its soft advances now rang the promise,
"You shall live to grow old."

"I did something wrong, tell me, what was it?" It
made him happy to abase himself before his disease, nor
was this colloquy their first.

"Intimacy," the disease replied.

"I remember. . . . Do not punish me this once, let me
live and I will be careful. Oh, save me from him."

"No—from yourself. Not from him. He does not exist. He is an illusion, whom you created in the garden because you wanted to feel you were attractive."

"I know I am not attractive, I will never excite myself again, but he does exist, I think."

"No."

"He may be death, but he does exist."

"No. He never came into the gun-room. You only wished that he would. He never sat down on the sofa by your side and made love. You handed a pencil, but he never took it, you fell into his arms, but they were not there, it has all been a daydream of the kind forbidden. And when the others came in and opened the cupboard: your muscular and intelligent farm-hand, your saviour from Wolverhampton in his Sunday suit—was he there?"

"No, he was not," the boy sobbed.

"No, he was not," came an echo, "but perhaps I am here."

The disease began to crouch and gurgle. There was the sound of a struggle, a spewing sound, a fall. Clesant, not greatly frightened, sat up and peered into the chaos. The nightmare passed, he felt better. Something survived from it, an echo that said "Here, here". And, he not dissenting, bare feet seemed to walk to the little table by his side, and hollow, filled with the dark, a shell of nakedness bent towards him and sighed "Here".

Clesant declined to reply.

"Here is the end, unless you. . . ." Then silence. Then, as if emitted by a machine, the syllables "Oh aye".

Clesant, after thought, put out his hand and touched the bell.

"I put her to sleep as I passed her, this is my hour, I can do that much. . . ." He seemed to gather strength from any recognition of his presence, and to say, "Tell my story for me, explain how I got here, pour life into me and I shall live as before when our bodies touched." He sighed. "Come home with me now, perhaps it is a farm. I have just enough power. Come away with me for an evening to my earthly lodging, easily managed by a . . . the . . . such a visit would be love. Ah, that was the word—love—why they pursued me and still know I am in the house; love was the word they cannot endure, I have remembered it at last."

Then Clesant spoke, sighing in his turn. "I don't even know what is real, so how can I know what is love? Unless it is excitement, and of that I am afraid. Do not love me, whatever you are; at all events this is my life and no one shall disturb it; a little sleep followed by a little pain."

And his speech evoked strength. More powerfully the other answered now, giving instances and arguments, throwing into sentences the glow they had borne during daylight. Clesant was drawn into a struggle, but whether to reach or elude the hovering presence he did not know. There was always a barrier either way, always his own nature. He began calling for people to come, and the adversary, waxing lovely and powerful, struck them dead before they could waken and help. His household perished, the whole earth was thinning, one instant more, and he would be alone with his ghost—and then through the walls of the house he saw the lights of a car rushing across the park.

It was Dr Woolacott at last.

Instantly the spell broke, the dead revived, and went downstairs to receive life's universal lord; and he—he was left with a human being who had somehow trespassed and been caught, and blundered over the furniture in the dark, bruising his defenceless body, and whispering, "Hide me."

And Clesant took pity on him again, and lifted the clothes of the bed, and they hid.

Voices approached, a great company, Dr Woolacott leading his army. They touched, their limbs intertwined, they gripped and grew mad with delight, yet through it all sounded the tramp of that army.

"They are coming."

"They will part us."

"Clesant, shall I take you away from all this?"

"Have you still the power?"

"Yes, until Woolacott sees me."

"Oh, what is your name?"

"I have none."

"Where is your home?"

"Woolacott calls it the grave."

"Shall I be with you in it?"

"I can promise you that. We shall be together for ever and ever, we shall never be ill, and never grow old."

"Take me."

They entwined more closely, their lips touched never to part, and then something gashed him where life had concentrated, and Dr Woolacott, arriving too late, found him dead on the floor.

The doctor examined the room carefully. It presented its usual appearance, yet it reminded him of another place. Dimly, from France, came the vision of a hospital ward, dimly the sound of his own voice saying to a mutilated recruit, "Do let me patch you up, oh but you must just let me patch you up. . . ."

Arthur Snatchfold

1

Conway (Sir Richard Conway) woke early, and went to the window to have a look at the Trevor Donaldsons' garden. Too green. A flight of mossy steps led up from the drive to a turfed amphitheatre. This contained a number of trees of the lead-pencil persuasion, and a number of flower-beds, profuse with herbaceous promises which would certainly not be fulfilled that weekend. The summer was heavy-leaved and at a moment between flowerings, and the gardener, though evidently expensive, had been caught bending. Bounding the amphitheatre was a high yew hedge, an imposing background had there been any foreground, and behind the hedge a heavy wood shut the sky out. Of course what was wanted was colour. Delphinium, salvia, red-hot-poker, zinnias, tobacco-plant, anything. Leaning out of the baronial casement, Conway considered this, while he waited for his tea. He was not an artist, nor a philosopher, but he liked exercising his mind when he had nothing else to do, as on this Sunday morning, this country morning, with so much ahead to be eaten, and so little to be said.

The visit, like the view, threatened monotony. Dinner had been dull. His own spruce gray head, gleaming in the mirrors, really seemed the brightest object about. Trevor Donaldson's head was mangy, Mrs Donaldson's combed up into bastions of iron. He did not get unduly fussed at the prospect of boredom. He was a man of experience with plenty of resources and plenty of armour, and he was a decent human being too. The Don-

102

aldsons were his inferiors—they had not travelled or read or gone in for sport or love, they were merely his business allies, linked to him by a common interest in aluminium. Still, he must try to make things nice, since they had been so good as to invite him down. "But it's not so easy to make things nice for us business people," he reflected, as he listened to the chonk of a blackbird, the clink of a milk-can, and the distant self-communings of an electric pump. "We're not stupid or uncultivated, we can use our minds when required, we can go to concerts when we're not too tired, we've invested—even Trevor Donaldson has—in the sense of humour. But I'm afraid we don't get much pleasure out of it all. No. Pleasure's been left out of our packet." Business occupied him increasingly since his wife's death. He brought an active mind to bear on it, and was quickly becoming rich.

He looked at the dull costly garden. It improved. A man had come into it from the back of the yew hedge. He had on a canary-coloured shirt, and the effect was exactly right. The whole scene blazed. *That* was what the place wanted—not a flower-bed, but a man, who advanced with a confident tread down the amphitheatre, and as he came nearer Conway saw that besides being proper to the colour scheme he was a very proper youth. His shoulders were broad, his face sensuous and open, his eyes, screwed up against the light, promised good temper. One arm shot out at an angle, the other supported a milk-can. "Good morning, nice morning," he called, and he sounded happy.

"Good morning, nice morning," he called back. The man continued at a steady pace, turned left, and disappeared in the direction of the servants' entrance, where an outburst of laughter welcomed him.

Conway hoped he might return by the same route, and waited. "That is a nice-looking fellow, I do like the way he holds himself, and probably no nonsense about him," he thought. But the vision had departed, the sunlight stopped, the garden turned stodgy and green again, and the maid came in with his tea. She said, "I'm sorry to be late, we were waiting for the milk, sir." The man had not called him sir, and the omission flattered him. "Good morning, sir" would have been the more natural salutation to an elderly stranger, a wealthy customer's guest. But the vigorous voice had shouted "Good morning, nice morning," as if they were equals.

Where had he gone off to now, he and his voice? To finish his round, welcomed at house after house, and then for a bathe perhaps, his shirt golden on the grass beside him. Ruddy brown to the waist he would show now. . . . What was his name? Was he a local? Sir Richard put these questions to himself as he dressed, but not vehemently. He was not a sentimentalist, there was no danger of him being shattered for the day. He would have liked to meet the vision again, and spend the whole of Sunday with it, giving it a slap-up lunch at the hotel, hiring a car, which they would drive alternately, treating it to the pictures in the neighbouring town, and returning with it, after one drink too much, through dusky lanes. But that was sheer nonsense, even if the vision had been agreeable to the programme. He was staying with the Trevor Donaldsons; and he must not repay their hospitality by moping. Dressed in a cheerful gray, he ran downstairs to the breakfast-room. Mrs Donaldson was already there, and she asked him how his daughters were getting on at their school.

Then his host followed, rubbing his hands together, and saying "Aha, aha!" and when they had eaten they went into the other garden, the one which sloped towards the water, and started talking business. They had not intended to do this, but there was also of their company a Mr Clifford Clarke, and when Trevor Donaldson, Clifford Clarke and Richard Conway got together it was impossible that aluminium should escape. Their voices deepened, their heads nodded or shook as they recalled vast sums that had been lost through unsound investments or misapplied advice. Conway found himself the most intelligent of the three, the quickest at taking a point, the strongest at following an argument. The moments passed, the blackbird chonk-chonked unheeded, unnoticed was the failure of the gardener to produce anything but tightly furled geraniums, unnoticed the ladies on the lawn, who wanted to get some golf. At last the hostess called, "Trevor! Is this a holiday or isn't it?" and they stopped, feeling rather ashamed. The cars came round, and soon they were five miles away, on the course, taking their turn in a queue of fellow merrymakers. Conway was good at golf, and got what excitement he could from it, but as soon as the ball flew off he was aware of a slight sinking feeling. This occupied them till lunch. After coffee they walked down to the water, and played with the dogs—Mrs Donaldson bred Sealyhams. Several neighbours came to tea, and now the animation rested with Donaldson, for he fancied himself as a country magnate, and wanted to show how well he was settling into the part. There was a good deal of talk about local conditions, women's institutes, education through discipline, and poaching. Conway found all this quite nonsensical and unreal. People who are not feudal should not play at feudalism, and all magistrates (this he said aloud) ought to be trained and ought to be paid. Since he was well-bred, he said it in a form which did not give offence. Thus the day wore away, and they filled in the interval before dinner by driving to see a ruined monastery. What on earth had they got to do with a monastery? Nothing at all. Nothing at all. He caught sight of Clifford Clarke looking mournfully at a rose-window, and he got the feeling that they were all of them looking for something which was not there, that there was an empty chair at the table, a card missing from the bridge-pack, a ball lost in the gorse, a stitch dropped in the shirt; that the chief guest had not come. On their way out they passed through the village, on their way back a cinema, which was giving a Wild West stunt. They returned through darkling lanes. They did not say, "Thank you! What a delightful day!" That would be saved up for tomorrow morning, and for the

final gratitude of departure. Every word would be
needed then. "I *have* enjoyed myself, *I have,* absolutely
marvellous!" the women would chant, and the men
would grunt, as if moved beyond words, and the host
and hostess would cry, "Oh but come again, then, come
again." Into the void the little unmemorable visit would
fall, like a leaf it would fall upon similar leaves, but
Conway wondered whether it hadn't been, so to speak,
specially negative, out of the way unflowering, whether
a champion, one bare arm at an angle, hadn't carried
away to the servants' quarters some refreshment which
was badly needed in the smoking-room.

"Well, perhaps we shall see, we may yet find out," he
thought, as he went up to bed, carrying with him his
raincoat.

For he was not one to give in and grumble. He believed in pleasure; he had a free mind and an active
body, and he knew that pleasure cannot be won without
courage and coolness. The Donaldsons were all very
well, but they were not the whole of his life. His daughters
were all very well, but the same held good of them. The
female sex was all very well and he was addicted to it,
but permitted himself an occasional deviation. He set his
alarm watch for an hour slightly earlier than the hour at
which he had woken in the morning, and he put it under
his pillow, and he fell asleep looking quite young.

Seven o'clock tinkled. He glanced into the passage,
then put on his raincoat and thick slippers, and went to
the window.

It was a silent sunless morning, and seemed earlier
than it actually was. The green of the garden and of the
trees was filmed with gray, as if it wanted wiping. Presently the electric pump started. He looked at his watch
again, slipped down the stairs, out of the house, across
the amphitheatre and through the yew hedge. He did not
run, in case he was seen and had to explain. He moved
at the maximum pace possible for a gentleman, known
to be an original, who fancies an early stroll in his pyjamas. "I thought I'd have a look at your formal garden,

there wouldn't have been time after breakfast" would
have been the line. He had of course looked at it the day
before, also at the wood. The wood lay before him now,
and the sun was just tipping into it. There were two
paths through the bracken, a broad and a narrow. He
waited until he heard the milk-can approaching down
the narrow path. Then he moved quickly, and they met,
well out of sight of the Donaldsonian demesne.

"Hullo!" he called in his easy out-of-doors voice; he
had several voices, and knew by instinct which was
wanted.

"Hullo! Somebody's out early!"

"You're early yourself."

"Me? Whor'd the milk be if I worn't?" the milkman
grinned, throwing his head back and coming to a stand-
still. Seen at close quarters he was coarse, very much of
the people and of the thick-fingered earth; a hundred
years ago his type was trodden into the mud, now it
burst and flowered and didn't care a damn.

"You're the morning delivery, eh?"

"Looks like it." He evidently proposed to be facetious—the clumsy fun which can be so delightful when it
falls from the proper lips. "I'm not the evening delivery
anyway, and I'm not the butcher nor the grocer, nor'm I
the coals."

"Live around here?"

"Maybe. Maybe I don't. Maybe I flop about in them
planes."

"You live around here, I bet."

"What if I do?"

"If you do you do. And if I don't I don't."

This fatuous retort was a success, and was greeted
with doubled-up laughter. "If you don't you don't! Ho,
you're a funny one! There's a thing to say! If you don't
you don't! Walking about in yer night things, too, you'll
ketch a cold you will, that'll be the end of you! Stopping
back in the 'otel, I suppose?"

"No. Donaldson's. You saw me there yesterday."

"Oh, Donaldson's, that's it. You was the old granfa' at the upstairs window."

"Old granfa' indeed. . . . I'll granfa' you," and he tweaked at the impudent nose. It dodged, it seemed used to this sort of thing. There was probably nothing the lad wouldn't consent to if properly handled, partly out of mischief, partly to oblige. "Oh, by the way . . ." and he felt the shirt as if interested in the quality of its material. "What was I going to say?" and he gave the zip at the throat a downward pull. Much slid into view. "Oh, I know—when's this round of yours over?"

" 'Bout eleven. Why?"

"Why not?"

" 'Bout eleven *at night*. Ha ha. Got yer there. Eleven at night. What you want to arst all them questions for? We're strangers, aren't we?"

"How old are you?"

"Ninety, same as yourself."

"What's your address?"

"There you go on! Hi! I like that. Arstin questions after I tell you No."

"Got a girl? Ever heard of a pint? Ever heard of two?"

"Go on. Get out." But he suffered his forearm to be worked between massaging fingers, and he set down his milk-can. He was amused. He was charmed. He was hooked, and a touch would land him.

"You look like a boy who looks all right," the elder man breathed.

"Oh, *stop* it. . . . All right, I'll go with you."

Conway was entranced. Thus, exactly thus, should the smaller pleasures of life be approached. They understood one another with a precision impossible for lovers. He laid his face on the warm skin over the clavicle, hands nudged him behind, and presently the sensation for which he had planned so cleverly was over. It was part of the past. It had fallen like a flower upon similar flowers.

He heard "You all right?" It was over there too, part

of a different past. They were lying deeper in the wood, where the fern was highest. He did not reply, for it was pleasant to lie stretched thus and to gaze up through bracken fronds at the distant treetops and the pale blue sky, and feel the exquisite pleasure fade.

"That was what you wanted, wasn't it?" Propped on his elbows the young man looked down anxiously. All his roughness and pertness had gone, and he only wanted to know whether he had been a success.

"Yes. . . . Lovely."

"Lovely? You say lovely?" he beamed, prodding gently with his stomach.

"Nice boy, nice shirt, nice everything."

"That a fact?"

Conway guessed that he was vain, the better sort often are, and laid on the flattery thick to please him, praised his comeliness, his thrusting thrashing strength; there was plenty to praise. He liked to do this and to see the broad face grinning and feel the heavy body on him. There was no cynicism in the flattery, he was genuinely admiring and gratified.

"So you enjoyed that?"

"Who wouldn't?"

"Pity you didn't tell me yesterday."

"I didn't know how to."

"I'd a met you down where I have my swim. You could 'elped me strip, you'd like that. Still, we mustn't grumble." He gave Conway a hand and pulled him up, and brushed and tidied the raincoat like an old friend. "We could get seven years for this, couldn't we?"

"Not seven years, still we'd get something nasty. Madness, isn't it? What can it matter to anyone else if you and I don't mind?"

"Oh, I suppose they've to occupy themselves with somethink or other," and he took up the milk-can to go on.

"Half a minute, boy—do take this and get yourself some trifle with it." He produced a note which he had brought on the chance.

"I didn't do it fer that."

"I know you didn't."

"Naow, we was each as bad as the other. . . . Naow . . . keep yer money."

"I'd be pleased if you would take it. I expect I'm better off than you and it might come in useful. To take out your girl, say, or towards your next new suit. However, please yourself, of course."

"Can you honestly afford it?"

"Honestly."

"Well, I'll find a way to spend it, no doubt. People don't always behave as nice as you, you know."

Conway could have returned the compliment. The affair had been trivial and crude, and yet they both had behaved perfectly. They would never meet again, and they did not exchange names. After a hearty handshake, the young man swung away down the path, the sunlight and shadow rushing over his back. He did not turn round, but his arm, jerking sideways to balance him, waved an acceptable farewell. The green flowed over his brightness, the path bent, he disappeared. Back he went to his own life, and through the quiet of the morning his laugh could be heard as he whooped at the maids.

Conway waited for a few moments, as arranged, and then he went back too. His luck held. He met no one, either in the amphitheatre garden or on the stairs, and after he had been in his room for a minute the maid arrived with his early tea. "I'm sorry the milk was late again, sir," she said. He enjoyed it, bathed and shaved and dressed himself for town. It was the figure of a superior city-man which was reflected in the mirror as he tripped downstairs. The car came round after breakfast to take him to the station, and he was completely sincere when he told the Trevor Donaldsons that he had had an out-of-the-way pleasant weekend. They believed him, and their faces grew brighter. "Come again then, come by all means again," they cried as he slid off. In the train he read the papers rather less than usual and smiled to himself rather more. It was so pleasant to have been completely right over a stranger, even down to little details like the texture of the skin. It flattered his vanity. It increased his sense of power.

2

He did not see Trevor Donaldson again for some weeks. Then they met in London at his club, for a business talk and a spot of lunch. Circumstances which they could not control had rendered them less friendly. Owing to regrouping in the financial world, their interests were now opposed, and if one of them stood to make money out of aluminium the other stood to lose. So the talk had been cautious. Donaldson, the weaker man, felt tired and worried after it. He had not, to his knowledge, made a mistake, but he might have slipped unwittingly, and be poorer, and have to give up his county state. He looked at his host with hostility and wished he could harm him. Sir Richard was aware of this, but felt no hostility in return. For one thing, he was going to win, for another, hating never interested him. This was probably the last occasion on which they would foregather socially; but he exercised his usual charm. He wanted, too, to find out during lunch how far Donaldson was aware of his own danger. Clifford Clarke (who was allied with him) had failed to do this.

After adjourning to the cloakroom and washing their hands at adjacent basins, they sat opposite each other at a little table. Down the long room sat other pairs of elderly men, eating, drinking, talking quietly, instructing the waiters. Inquiries were exchanged about Mrs Donaldson and the young Miss Conways, and there were some humorous references to golf. Then Donaldson said, with a change in his voice: "Golf's all you say, and the great advantage of it in these days is that you get it practically anywhere. I used to think our course was good, for a little country course, but it is far below the average. This is somewhat of a disappointment to us both, since we settled down there specially for the golf. The fact is, the country is not at all what it seems when first you go there."

"So I've always heard."

"My wife likes it, of course, she has her Sealyhams, she has her flowers, she has her local charities—though in these days one's not supposed to speak of 'charity'. I don't know why. I should have thought it was a good word, charity. She runs the Women's Institute, so far as it consents to be run, but Conway, Conway, you'd never believe how offhand the village women are in these days. They don't elect Mrs Donaldson president yearly as a matter of course. She takes turn and turn with cottagers."

"Oh, that's the spirit of the age, of course. One's always running into it in some form or other. For instance, I don't get nearly the deference I did from my clerks."

"But better work from them, no doubt," said Donaldson gloomily.

"No. But probably they're better men."

"Well, perhaps the ladies at the Women's Institute are becoming better women. But my wife doubts it. Of course our village is particularly unfortunate, owing to that deplorable hotel. It has had such a bad influence. We had an extraordinary case before us on the Bench recently, connected with it."

"That hotel did look too flash—it would attract the wrong crowd."

"I've also had bother bother bother with the Rural District Council over the removal of tins, and another bother—a really maddening one—over a right of way through the church meadows. That almost made me lose my patience. And I really sometimes wonder whether I've been sensible in digging myself in the country, and trying to make myself useful in local affairs. There is no gratitude. There is no warmth of welcome."

"I quite believe it, Donaldson, and I know I'd never have a country place myself, even if the scenery is as pleasant as yours is, and even if I could afford it. I make

do with a service flat in town, and I retain a small fur-
nished cottage for my girls' holidays, and when they
leave school I shall partly take them and partly send
them abroad. I don't believe in undiluted England, nice
as are sometimes the English. Shall we go up and have
coffee?"

He ran up the staircase briskly, for he had found out
what he wanted to know: Donaldson was feeling poor.
He stuck him in a low leathern armchair, and had a look
at him as he closed his eyes. That was it: he felt he
couldn't afford his "little place", and was running it
down, so that no one should be surprised when he gave
it up. Meanwhile, there was one point in the conversation it amused him to take up now that business was
finished with: the reference to that "extraordinary case"
connected with the local hotel.

Donaldson opened his eyes when asked, and they had
gone prawn-like. "Oh, that was a case, it was a really
really," he said. "I knew such things existed, of course,
but I assumed in my innocence they were confined to
Piccadilly. However, it has all been traced back to the
hotel, the proprietress has had a thorough fright, and I
don't think there will be any trouble in the future. Indecency between males."

"Oh, good Lord!" said Sir Richard coolly. "Black or
white?"

"White, please, it's an awful nuisance, but I can't take
black coffee now, although I greatly prefer it. You see,
some of the hotel guests—there was a bar, and some of
the villagers used to go in there after cricket because
they thought it smarter than that charming old thatched
pub by the church—you remember that old thatched
pub. Villagers are terrific snobs, that's one of the disappointing discoveries one makes. The bar got a bad
reputation of a certain type, especially at weekends,
someone complained to the police, a watch was set, and
the result was this quite extraordinary case. . . . Really,
really, I wouldn't have believed it. A *little* milk, please,

Conway, if I may, just a little; I'm not allowed to take
my coffee black."

"So sorry. Have a liqueur."

"No, no thanks, I'm not allowed that even, especially
after lunch."

"Come on, do—I will if you will. Waiter, can we have
two double cognacs?"

"He hasn't heard you. Don't bother."

Conway had not wanted the waiter to hear him, he
had wanted an excuse to be out of the room and have a
minute alone. He was suddenly worried in case that
milkman had got into a scrape. He had scarcely thought
about him since—he had a very full life, and it included
an intrigue with a cultivated woman, which was gradually ripening—but nobody could have been more decent
and honest, or more physically attractive in a particular
way. It had been a charming little adventure, and a remarkably lively one. And their parting had been perfect.
Wretched if the lad had come to grief! Enough to make
one cry. He offered up a sort of prayer, ordered the
cognacs, and rejoined Donaldson with his usual brisk-
ness. He put on the Renaissance armour that suited him
so well, and "How did the hotel case end?" he asked.

"We committed him for trial."

"Oh! As bad as that?"

"Well, we thought so. Actually a gang of about half a
dozen were involved, but we only caught one of them.
His mother, if you please, is president of the Women's
Institute, and hasn't had the decency to resign! I tell
you, Conway, these people aren't the same flesh and
blood as oneself. One pretends they are, but they aren't.
And what with this disillusionment, and what with the
right of way, I've a good mind to clear out next year,
and leave the so-called country to stew in its own juice.
It's utterly corrupt. This man made an awfully bad impression on the Bench and we didn't feel that six
months, which is the maximum we are allowed to im-
pose, was adequate to the offence. And it was all so
revoltingly commercial—his only motive was money."

Conway felt relieved; it couldn't be his own friend, for anyone less grasping. . .

"And another unpleasant feature—at least for me— is that he had the habit of taking his clients into my grounds."

"How most vexatious for you!"

"It suited his convenience, and of what else should he think? I have a little wood—you didn't see it—which stretches up to the hotel, so he could easily bring people in. A path my wife was particularly fond of—a mass of bluebells in springtime—it was there they were caught. You may well imagine this has helped to put me off the place."

"Who caught them?" he asked, holding his glass up to the light; their cognacs had arrived.

"Our local bobby. For we do possess that extraordinary rarity, a policeman who keeps his eyes open. He sometimes commits errors of judgement—he did on this occasion—but he's certainly observant, and as he was coming down one of the other paths, a public one, he saw a bright yellow shirt through the bracken—upsa! Take care!"

"Upsa!" were some drops of brandy, which Conway had spilt. Alas, alas, there could be no doubt about it. He felt deeply distressed, and rather guilty. The young man must have decided after their successful encounter to use the wood as a rendez-vous. It was a cruel stupid world, and he was countenancing it more than he should. Wretched, wretched, to think of that good-tempered, harmless chap being bruised and ruined . . . the whole thing so unnecessary—betrayed by the shirt he was so proud of. . . . Conway was not often moved, but this time he felt much regret and compassion.

"Well, he recognized that shirt at once. He had particular reasons for keeping a watch on its wearer. And he got him, he got him. But he lost the other man. He didn't charge them straight away, as he ought to have done. I think he was genuinely startled and could scarcely believe his eyes. For one thing, it was so early in the morning—barely seven o'clock."

"A strange hour!" said Conway, and put his glass down, and folded his hands on his knee.

"He caught sight of them as they were getting up after committing the indecency, also he saw money pass, but instead of rushing in there and then he made an elaborate and totally unnecessary plan for interrupting the youth on the further side of my house, and of course he could have got him any time, any time. A stupid error of judgement. A great pity. He never arrested him until 7.45."

"Was there then sufficient evidence for an arrest?"

"There was abundant evidence of a medical character, if you follow me—what a case, oh, what a case!— also there was the money on him, which clinched his guilt!"

"Mayn't the money have been in connection with his round?"

"No. It was a note, and he only had small change in connection with his round. We established that from his employer. But how ever did you guess he was on a round?"

"You told me," said Conway, who never became flustered when he made a slip. "You mentioned that he had a milk round and that the mother was connected with some local organization which Mrs Donaldson takes an interest in."

"Yes, yes, the Women's Institute. Well, having fixed all that up, our policeman then went on to the hotel, but it was far too late by that time, some of the guests were breakfasting, others had left, he couldn't go round cross-questioning everyone, and no one corresponded to the description of the person whom he saw being hauled up out of the fern."

"What was the description?"

"An old man in pyjamas and a mackintosh—our Chairman was awfully anxious to get hold of him—oh, you remember our Chairman, Ernest Dray, you met him at my little place. He's determined to stamp this sort of thing out, once and for all. Hullo, it's past three, I must be getting back to my grindstone. Many thanks for lunch. I don't know why I've discoursed on this somewhat unsavoury topic. I'd have done better to consult you about the right of way."

"You must another time. I did look up the subject once."

"How about a spot of lunch with me this day week?" said Donaldson, remembering their business feud, and becoming uneasily jolly.

"This day week? Now can I? No, I can't. I've promised this day week to go and see my little girls. Not that they're little any longer. Time flies, doesn't it? We're none of us younger."

"Sad but true," said Donaldson, heaving himself out of the deep leather chair. Similar chairs, empty or filled with similar men, receded down the room, and far away a small fire smoked under a heavy mantelpiece. "But aren't you going to drink your cognac? It's excellent cognac."

"I suddenly took against it—I do indulge in caprices." Getting up, he felt faint, the blood rushed to his head and he thought he was going to fall. "Tell me," he said, taking his enemy's arm and conducting him to the door, "this old man in the mackintosh—how was it the fellow you caught never put you on his track?"

"He tried to."

"Oh, did he?"

"Yes indeed, and he was all the more anxious to do so, because we made it clear that he would be let off if he helped us to make the major arrest. But all he could say was what we knew already—that it was someone from the hotel."

"Oh, he said that, did he? From the hotel."

"Said it again and again. Scarcely said anything else, indeed almost went into a sort of fit. There he stood with his head thrown back and his eyes shut, barking at us, 'Th'otel. Keep to th'otel. I tell you he come from th'otel.' We advised him not to get so excited, whereupon he became insolent, which did him no good with Ernest Dray, as you may well imagine, and called the Bench a row of interfering bastards. He was instantly removed from the court and as he went he shouted back at us—you'll never credit this—that if he and the old grandfather didn't mind it why should anyone else. We talked the case over carefully and came to the conclusion it must go to Assizes."

"What was his name?"

"But we don't know, I tell you, we never caught him."

"I mean the name of the one you did catch, the village boy."

"Arthur Snatchfold."

They had reached the top of the club staircase. Conway saw the reflection of his face once more in a mirror, and it was the face of an old man. He pushed Trevor Donaldson off abruptly, and went back to sit down by his liqueur-glass. He was safe, safe, he could go forward with his career as planned. But waves of shame came over him. Oh for prayer!—but whom had he to pray to, and what about? He saw that little things can turn into great ones, and he did not want greatness. He was not up to it. For a moment he considered giving himself up and standing his trial, however what possible good would that do? He would ruin himself and his daughters, he would delight his enemies, and he would not save his saviour. He recalled his clever manoeuvres for a little fun, and the good-humoured response, the mischievous face, the obliging body. It had all seemed so trivial. Taking a notebook from his pocket, he wrote down the name of his lover, yes, his lover who was going to prison to save him, in order that he might not forget it. Arthur Snatchfold. He had only heard the name once, and he would never hear it again.

The Obelisk

Ernest was an elementary schoolmaster, and very very small; it was like marrying a doll, Hilda sometimes thought, and one with glass eyes too. She was larger herself: tall enough to make them look funny as they walked down the esplanade, but not tall enough to look dignified when she was alone. She cherished aspirations; none would have guessed it from her stumpy exterior. She yearned for a trip in a Rolls Royce with a sheikh, but one cannot have everything or anything like it, one cannot even always be young. It is better to have a home of one's own than to always be a typist. Hilda did not talk quite as she should, and her husband had not scrupled to correct her. She had never forgotten—it was such a small thing, yet she could not forget it—she had never forgotten that night on their honeymoon when she had said something ungrammatical about the relative position of their limbs.

He was now asking her to decide whether they should sit in the shelter or walk to the obelisk. There was time to do one or the other before the bus went, but not to do both.

"Sit down will be best," she replied. But as soon as they were in the shelter, looking at the undersized and undercoloured sea, she wished she had chosen the obelisk. "Where is it? What's it for? Who's it to?" she asked.

"I don't know to whom it was erected—to some local worthy, one presumes. As regards its situation, it stands above the town in the direction of the landslip."

"Would *you* like to go to it?"

"I can't honestly say that I should. My shoes are somewhat tight."

"Yes, I suppose we're best where we are and then some tea. Do you know how far off it is?"

"I can't say that I do."

"It may be quite near. Perhaps you could ask these people." She lowered her voice, not to be overheard by the people in question: two sailors who were seated on the other side of the glass screen.

"I don't think I could well do that," said Ernest timidly; a martinet at home and at school, he was terrified of anything unfamiliar.

"Why not?"

"They won't know."

"They might."

"There is no naval station here, Hilda, they are merely visitors like ourselves, no ships are ever stationed at a small watering-place." He breathed on his pince-nez, and placed it between himself and the sea.

"Shall I ask them?"

"Certainly, if you wish to do so."

Hilda opened her mouth to speak to the sailors, but no sound came out of it. "You ask, it seems better," she whispered.

"I don't wish to ask, I shall not ask, I have told you my reasons already, and if you are incapable of following them I really can do no more."

"Oh, all right, dear, don't get in such a fuss, it doesn't matter, I'm sure I don't want to go to your obelisk."

"Why, in that case, do you want to inquire how to get there? And why 'my' obelisk? I was not aware that I possessed one."

She felt cross—Ernest did tie one up so—and determined to speak to the sailors to prove her independence. She had noticed them as she sat down, one of them particularly. "Please excuse me," she began. They were laughing at something, and did not hear her. "Please could you kindly tell us—" No reply. She got up and said to her husband, "Oh, let's go, I hate this place."

"Certainly, certainly," said he, and they moved off down the esplanade in an offended silence. Hilda, who had been in the wrong, soon felt ashamed of herself. What on earth had made her behave like that, she wondered; it had been almost a quarrel, and all about nothing. She determined never to mention the beastly obelisk again.

This was not to be, for it appeared on a noticeboard, "To the Obelisk and Landslip", and an arrow pointed to a gap in the crumbly cliffs. She would have marched by, but Ernest stopped. "I think I should—I think I *should* like to go if you don't object," he said, in a voice that was intended to be conciliatory. "I could talk to the class about it on Monday. I am very short of material."

Turning back, she looked at the shelter where they had sat. She could see the long dark legs of the sailors sticking out of it; the esplanade was almost deserted otherwise. "No, of course I shouldn't mind," she said.

"Excellent, excellent, admirable." He led the way. The sea, such as it was, disappeared, and they began climbing a muddly sort of gorge—not romantic, though she tried to pretend it was so. Rocks of no great size overhung them, a stream dripped through mud. The weather was stuffy and an aeroplane could be heard being sick in the distance. Hilda took a stern line with herself; whatever they did this afternoon, she wanted to be doing something else. How nice Ernest was really! How genuine! How sincere! If only his forehead wasn't quite so bulgy, and had a little more hair hanging over it, if his shoes weren't quite so small and yellow, if he had eyes like a hawk and an aquiline nose and a sinewy sunburnt throat . . . no, no, that was asking too much, she must keep within bounds, she must not hope for a sinewy throat, or for reckless arms to clasp her beyond redemption. . . . That came of going to those cinemas . . .

"It's ever so lovely here, don't you think," she exclaimed, as they rounded a corner and saw a quantity of unripe blackberries.

"I should scarcely describe it in those terms."

"I'm ever so glad we didn't stick in that awful shelter."

"What makes you keep on saying 'ever so'?"

"Oh, I'm sorry. Did I? Ever so what oughtn't I to have said?"

"No, no, you are getting it wrong. 'Ever so what' is not the question, but 'ever so' itself. The phrase is never needed. I can't think why it has become so popular. It is spreading into circles where one would not expect to hear it. Curious. You try to form a sentence in which 'ever so' is not redundant."

She tried, but her thoughts went off to that disastrous night when he had pulled her up in much the same way, and had made her feel worthless, and had humiliated her, and had afterwards tried to caress her, and she couldn't stand it. That had been his fault, but it was her fault if she minded now, she wanted to be really educated, and here he was helping her. Penitent, she looked at his pink and pear-shaped face, slightly beaded with sweat and topped by too small a hat, and determined to improve her grammar and to really love him.

There was a scrambling noise behind, and the two sailors came rushing up the path like monkeys.

"What do these fellows want here? I don't like this," cried Ernest.

Stopping dead short, they smiled, showing dazzling teeth. One of them—not the one she had noticed—said, "We right for the Oboblisk, chum?"

Ernest was nervous. The place was deserted, the path narrow, and he wouldn't anywhere have been easy with people whose bodies were so different from his own. He replied with more than his usual primness: "Obelisk. The notice on the esplanade says 'To the Obelisk and Landslip'. I fear I can tell you no more."

"Call it the Ob and be done, eh!"

"Thank you, sir, thank you, and thank you, madam," said the other sailor. He was a much better type—an educated voice and a gallant bearing, and when Hilda stood aside to let them stride past he saluted her. "Excuse us, sir," he called back, as if the path and indeed the whole gorge was Ernest's private property. "Sorry to trouble you, but we thought we'd go a walk, make the most of our brief time on shore, sir, you know."

"A sensible thing to do," said Ernest, who was recovering from his alarm, and liked being called sir.

"Just a little change, anyhow. Got a fag on you, Tiny?"

The other sailor fumbled in his jumper. "Fergot 'em again," he replied.

"Well, of all the . . ."

"Ferget me own what d'ye call 'em next."

"Nice person to go out with, isn't he, sir? Promised to bring along a packet, then lets us both down!"

"Have one of mine if it comes to that," said Ernest.

"No, sir, I won't do that, but it's very good of you all the same."

"Oh, come along, my man, take one."

"No, sir; I don't cadge."

"Oh!" said Ernest, rather taken aback.

"Do have one, my husband has plenty."

"No, thank you, madam, I'd rather not." He had pride and a will, and a throb of pleasure went through her, pleasure mixed with despair. She felt him looking at her, and turned away to inspect the blackberries. In a moment he would go on, dart up the path with his companion, and disappear as it were into heaven.

"What about you?" said Ernest to the sailor so strangely called Tiny.

Tiny had no such scruples. He thrust out his huge paw with a grin and grunt. "Her" sailor shook his head and looked a little disdainful. "There's nothing Tiny wouldn't say no to, is there, Tiny?" he remarked.

"Tiny's a sensible fellow," said Ernest. The sailors, by their civil yet cheerful demeanour, had quite reassured him. He now dominated the situation, and behaved as if he was conducting an open-air class for older boys.

"Come along, Tiny." He stretched up a match to the expectant lips.

"Thanks ever so," Tiny responded.

Hilda let out a cackle. It was "ever so", the forbidden phrase. The sailors laughed too, as did Ernest. He had become unusually genial. He astonished her by saying, "Oh, Hilda, I'm so sorry, here I am smoking and I never asked you whether you would smoke too." It was the first time he had invited her to smoke in public. She declined, thinking he was testing her, but he asked her again and she took one.

"I'm ever so—I'm very sorry."

"That's quite all right, dear, might I have a match?"

"Her" sailor whipped a box out of his breast. Tiny, equally polite, blew on the tip of his cigarette and held it towards her. She felt flustered, enmeshed in blue arms, dazzled by rose-red and sunburnt flesh, intoxicated by strength, saltiness, the unknown. When she escaped it was to her husband. Her sailor still held out the lighted match which she had used. "Sir, may I change my mind and have one of your cigarettes after all?" he said coolly.

"Of course, of course, come along all and sundry."

He took one, used the lighted match on it, then blew the match out and placed it in his breast. The match they had shared—there it lay . . . close to him, hidden in him, safe. . . . He looked at her, touched his jumper, smiled a little and looked away, puffing his cigarette. At that moment the sun blazed out and it turned into a nice afternoon.

She looked away too. There was something dangerous about the man, something of the bird of prey. He had marked her down for his fell purpose, she must be careful like any other heroine. If only he wasn't so handsome, so out-of-the-way handsome. "Who's saying no, Stan, now?" his companion guffawed. So his name was Stan. . . . Stanley perhaps. What had led such a man to join the Navy? Perhaps some trouble at home.

"Stan's sensible, don't you tease Stan," piped Ernest.

They proceeded in a safe enough formation towards the obelisk, the two sailors in front, she behind Tiny's buttocks, from which she had nothing to fear. Gradually the order altered—Ernest's fault. He was elated with his success, and kept on pestering the men with questions about their work. Tiny fell back to deal with them, but was ill-informed. So "Stan" joined them, and she went on ahead. It was nicer than she expected—everyone good-tempered, including her husband. But she still wished she had not come.

"It's a funny thing, a day on shore," said the easy silky voice. He had stolen up behind her—no scrambling this time. She turned, and his eyes moved up and down her body.

"How do you mean, funny? I don't understand."

"You hardly know what to do with yourself. You're let out of prison, as it were, the discipline stops, you find a shipmate who happens to be on leave too, you go off with him, although you have nothing in common, he wants to go to the pictures, so you go, he thinks he'd like a walk, so you go, he asks the way of strangers, with the result that you inflict yourself on them too. It's a funny life, the Navy. You're never alone, you're never independent. I don't like tacking on to people, the way that youngster I'm with does. I've told him of it before, but he turns everything into a joke."

"Why is he called Tiny?"

"Merely because he's so large. Another joke. You know the kind of thing, and how weary one gets of it. Still, life's not a bed of roses anywhere, I suppose."

"No, it isn't, it isn't."

She ought not to have made such a remark, and she was glad when he ignored it and went on: "And I've got to be called Stan although my name's really Stanhope."

"Stanhope?"

"It was my mother's family name. We came from Cheshire. However, all that's over, and I'm Stan." There was a tinge of melancholy in his voice which made it fatally attractive. For all his gaiety, he had suffered, suffered. . . . When she threw away her cigarette he did the same, and he gently touched his breast.

This frightened Hilda. She didn't want any nonsense, and she suggested that they should wait for her husband. He obeyed, and turned his profile to her as they waited. He looked even finer that way than full-face; the brow was so noble, the nose and the chin so firm, the lips so tender, the head poised so beautifully upon the sinewy neck, the colouring lovelier than imagination can depict. Here, however, was Ernest, coming round the corner like a cheerful ant. He held Tiny's cap in his hand, and was questioning him on the subject of his naval costume.

"Are we going on any further?" she called.

"I think so. Why not?"

"It seems turning out rather a climb."

"We have plenty of time, abundance of time, before the bus goes."

"Yes, but we must be keeping these gentlemen back, you and I walk so slowly."

"I was not aware of walking slowly. You in a hurry, Stan?" he called familiarly.

"Not the least, not in the very least, sir, thank you."

"You, Tiny?"

"Hurry for what?"

"Do you want to go on and leave us?"

Grateful to Hilda for calling him a gentleman, he beamed up at her and said, "What's 'is name, please?" —pointing to Ernest as if he were some rare animal and could not answer questions.

"My husband—his name's Ernest."

"Think his Trilby'd fit me?" His hand shot out to pull it off, but he was checked by a quiet word of reproof from Stanhope. Ernest scuttled back a step. "Chum, I won't hurt you, chum, chuck chuck, chum, chum," as if feeding chicken.

"Certain people always go too far, they spoil things,

it's a pity," Stanhope remarked to her as they continued their walk.

How right he was—though for the moment Tiny had entertained her, also she got a wicked pleasure when Ernest's cowardice got exposed. She smiled, and felt clever herself, not realizing that Stanhope now walked behind her, which was exactly what she had not meant to happen. "My husband and him seem getting on quite nicely," she said.

"Tiny's always ready to play the fool, day in, day out. I'm afraid I don't understand it. Something wrong with me, I suppose."

"One gets rather tired of anything that's always the same, I think."

He offered no opinion, and they walked on for five minutes without saying anything. The path was well marked and not steep, and many pretty flowers, both yellow and pink, grew between the stones. Glimpses of the sea appeared, dancing blue, the aeroplane turned into a gull. The interval separating the two sailors gradually increased. "What made you join the Navy?" she said suddenly.

He told her—it was fascinating. He was of good family—she had guessed as much!—but wanted to see the world. He had left a soft job in an office when he was eighteen. He told her the name of the office. She happened to have heard of it in her typist days, and was instantly possessed by a feeling of security. Of course she was safe with him—ridiculous. He reeled off the names of ports, known and unknown. He was not very young when you were close to him, but Hilda did not like very young men, they were not distinguished, and her dream was distinction. These well-marked features, this hair, raven-black against the snowy line of the cap, yet flecked at the temples with gray, suited her best, oh and those eyes, cruel eyes, kind eyes, kind, cruel, oh! they burnt into your shoulders, if you turned and faced them it was worse. And she so dumpy! She tried to steady herself by her modesty, which was considerable, and well-grounded. And a batch of people came down-hill and passed them—it was only an extension of the esplanade. "No, Hilda, no one like this is going to bother to seduce you," she told herself.

"I suppose I can't persuade you," he said. He took out of his jumper a cigarette-case, and opened it.

"But I thought you hadn't got any cigarettes," she cried.

He snapped the case up, put it back, and said, "Caught!"

"What do you mean? Why ever did you ask for one when you had all those?"

"I decline to answer that question," he smiled.

"I want to know. You must answer. Tell me! Oh, go on! Do tell me."

"No, I won't."

"Oh, you're horrid."

"Am I? Why?" The ravine had got wilder, almost beautiful. The path climbed above thick bushes and little trees. She knew they ought to wait again for Ernest, but her limbs drove her on. She repeated: "You must tell me. I insist." He drove her more rapidly before him. Then he said, "Very well, but promise not to be angry."

"I'm angry with you already."

"Then I may as well tell. I pretended I'd no cigarettes on the chance of your husband offering me one."

"But why? You said no when he did."

"It wasn't a cigarette that I wanted. And now I suppose you're angry. I didn't want to go on, and it was my only chance of stopping. So I asked Tiny for one. I knew he'd be out of them, he always is. I wanted some excuse to keep with your party, because I wanted to—" He took the extinguished match from his pocket. "Better throw this away now, hadn't I? Or you'll be angry again."

"I'm not angry, but don't start being silly, please."

"There are worse things than silliness."

Hilda didn't speak. Her knees were trembling, her heart thumping, but she hurried on. Whether he threw the match away or not she did not know. After a pause he said in quite a different voice: "I've done quite enough talking, you know. Now you talk."

"I've nothing to say," she said, her voice breaking. "Nothing ever happens to me, nothing will, I . . . I do feel so odd." He seemed to tug her this way and that. If only he wasn't so lovely! His hand touched her. Almost without her knowing, he guided her off the path, and got her down among the bushes.

Once there, she was lost. Under pretext of comforting he came closer. He persuaded her to sit down. She put her hand to his jersey to thrust him off, and it slid up to his throat. He was so gentle as well as so strong, that was the trouble, she did not know which way to resist him, and those eyes, appealing, devouring, appealing. He constrained her to lie down. A little slope of grass, scarcely bigger than a couch, was the scene of her inadequate resistance; beyond the dark blue of his shoulders she could see the blue of the sea, all around were thick thorny bushes covered with flowers, and she let him do what he wanted.

"Keep still," he whispered. "They're passing."

From the path came the sound of feet.

"Don't talk just yet." He continued to hold her, his chin raised, listening. "They're gone now, but talk quietly. It's all right. He won't know. I'll fix up a story. Don't you worry. Don't you cry."

"It's your fault, you made me . . ."

He laughed gently, not denying it. He raised her up, his arms slanting across her back unexpectedly kind. He let her say whatever she wanted to, as long as she did not say it too loud, and now and then he stroked her hair. She accused him, she exalted Ernest, repeating, "I'm not what you think I am at all." All he said was "That's all right," or "You shan't come into any trouble, I swear it, I swear it, and you mustn't cry," or "I play tricks—yes. But I never let a woman down. Look at me. Do as I tell you! Look at me, Hilda."

She obeyed. Her head fell on his shoulder, and she

gave him a kiss. For the first time in her life she felt worthy. Her humiliation slipped from her, never to return. She had pleased him.

"Stanhope . . ."

"Yes, I know."

"What do you know?"

"I'm waiting until it's absolutely safe. Yes."

He held her against him for a time, then laid her again on the grass. She was consciously deceiving her husband, and it was heaven. She took the lead, ordered the mysterious stranger, the film-star, the sheikh, what to do, she was, for one moment, a queen, and he her slave. They came out of the depths together, confederates. He helped her up, then respectfully turned away. She hated grossness, and nothing he did jarred.

When they were back on the path, he laid his plans. "Hilda, it's no use going on to the Obelisk," he said, "it's too late, they're in front of us and we shall meet them coming down. He'll want to know how they passed us without seeing us, and if you've an explanation of that I've not. No. We shall have to go back and wait for them on the esplanade."

She patted her hair—she had good hair.

"Make up some story when they arrive. Muddle them. We shall never muddle them if we meet them face to face on this path. You leave it to me—I'll confuse them in no time."

"But how?" she said dubiously, as they started the long descent.

"I shall see when I see them. That's how I always work."

"Don't you think it would be better if you hid here, and I went down alone? Our bus leaves before very long, then you'll be safe."

He shook his head, and showed his teeth, scorning her gaily. "No, no, I'm better at telling stories than you, I don't trust you. Take your orders from me, don't ask questions, and it'll be all right. I swear it will. We shall pull through."

Yes, he was wonderful. She would have this gallantry to look back upon, especially at night. She could think of Ernest quite kindly, she'd be able to put up with him when he made his little wrong remarks or did his other little wrong things. She'd her dream, and what people said was false and what the Pictures said was true: it was worth it, worth being clasped once in the right arms, though you never had them round you again. She had got what she longed for, and it was what she longed for, not a smack in the face, not a sell. . . . She had always yearned for a lover who would be nice *afterwards*—not turn away like a satisfied brute, as handsome men are supposed to do. Stanhope was—what do you call it . . . a gentleman, a knight in armour, a real sport. . . . O for words. Her eyes filled with happy tears of happiness.

Swinging ahead of her onto the esplanade, he gave her his final instructions. "Take your line from me, remember we've done nothing we shouldn't, remember it's going to be much easier than you think, and don't lose your head. Simpler to say than to do, all the same don't do it, and if you can't think of anything else to do look surprised. Our first job is to sit down quietly on the esplanade and wait."

But they were not to wait. As they came out of the gap in the cliffs, they saw Ernest on a bench, and Tiny leaning on the esplanade railings observing the sea. Ernest jumped up all a bunch of nerves, crying, "Hilda, Hilda, where have you been? Why weren't you at the Obelisk? We looked and looked for you there, we hunted all the way back—"

Before she could answer, indeed before he had finished, Stanhope launched a violent counter-attack. "What happened to you, sir? We got to the Obelisk and waited, then we've been shouting and calling all the way back. The lady's been so worried—she thought an accident had happened. Are you all right, sir?" He bayed on, full-chested, magnificent, plausible, asking questions and allowing no time for their reply.

"Hilda, impossible, you couldn't have been, or I should have seen you."

"There we were, sir, we had a good look at the view and waited for you, and then came down. It was not meeting you on the way back that puzzled us so."

"Hilda, were you really . . ."

By now she had had her cue, and she heard her voice a long way off saying in fairly convincing tones, "Oh yes, we got up to the Obelisk."

And he believed, or three-quarters believed her. How shocking, but what a respite! It was the first lie she had ever told him, and it was unlikely she would ever tell him a worse. She felt very odd—not ashamed, but so queer, and Stanhope went on with his bluffing. The wind raised his dark forelock and his collar. He looked the very flower of the British Navy as he lied and lied. "I can't understand it," he repeated. "It's a relief to know nothing's wrong, but not to run into you as we came down . . . I don't understand it, I'm what you may call stumped, well, I'm damned."

"I'm puzzled equally, but there is nothing to be gained by a prolonged discussion. Hilda, shall we go to our bus?"

"I don't want you to go until you feel satisfied," said she. A false step; she realized as much as soon as she had spoken.

"Not satisfied? I am perfectly satisfied. With what have I to be dissatisfied? I only fail to grasp how I failed to find you when I reached the monument."

Hilda dared not go away with him with things as they were. She didn't know how to work out the details of the lie, it was in too much of a lump. Alarmed, she took refuge in crossness. "You've got to grasp it some time or other, you may as well now," she snapped. Her lover looked at her anxiously.

"Well, be that as that may be, we must go."

"What's your explanation, Tiny?" called Stanhope, in his splendid authoritative way, to create a diversion.

Tiny cocked up one heel and replied not.

"He can scarcely solve a problem which baffles the three of us, and it is so strange that you were ahead of us on the path going up, yet a good ten minutes behind us coming down," enunciated Ernest.

"Come along, Tiny, you've a tongue in your head, haven't you, mate? I'm asking you a question. Don't stand there like a stuck pig."

"Ber-yutiful view," said Tiny, turning round and extending his huge blue arms right and left along the railings of the esplanade. "You was showing the lady the Ob, perhaps."

"Of course we inspected the monument. You know that. You haven't answered my question."

" 'Ope you showed it 'er properly while you was about it, Stan. Don't do to keep a thing like that all to yourself, you know. Ern, why they call that an ob?"

"Obelisk, obelisk," winced Ernest, and was evidently more anxious to go.

"You said it, obblepiss."

"I said nothing of the sort."

"You said it, obblepiss." The giant was grinning amiably, and seemed totally unaware that anything had gone wrong. But how different sailors are! How unattractive, in Tiny's case, was the sun-reddened throat and the line of broad shoulders against the sea! He was terribly common, really, and ought not to be answering people back. "Anyone ever seed a bigger one?" he inquired. No one replied, and how should they to so foolish a question? "Stands up, don't it?" he continued. No one spoke. "No wonder they call that a needle, for wouldn't that just prick."

"Stop that infernal talk at once," exploded Stanhope, and he seemed needlessly vexed, but oh, how handsome he looked, and how his dark eyes flashed; she was glad to see him angry and to have this extra memory.

"Stan, Stan, what's the matter, Stan?"

"If you speak again I'll brain you."

"Ever seed a bigger one—a bigger obolokist, I mean. That's all I said. Because I 'ave. Killopatra's Needle's bigger. Well? Well? What you all staring at me for? What you think I was going to say? Eh? Oh, look at little Ern, ain't he just blushing. Oh, look at Stan. Lady, look at 'em."

Hilda did observe that the two older men were going most extraordinary colours, her lover purplish, her husband rose-pink. And she did not like the tone of the conversation herself, she scarcely knew why, and feared something awkward might come out if it went on much longer. "We must go, or we shall miss that bus," she announced. "We shall never clear up why we never met, and it isn't of the least importance. Ernest, do come along, dear."

Ernest muttered that he was willing, and the episode ended. Goodbyes were said, by Tiny tempestuously. Plunging across the esplanade, he seized the unfortunate schoolmaster's arm, and whirled it around like a windmill. "Goo bye, Ern, take care of yerself, pleased to have met yer, termater face and all," he bawled.

"Pleased to have met you both," said Ernest with restraint.

"Ju-jitsu . . . now as yer neck snaps . . ."

Hilda and Stanhope profited by this noisy nonsense to say their farewells. They would not have dared otherwise. The touch of his hand was cool and dry, but he was nearly worn out, and it trembled. It had not been easy for him, returning her unreproached and unsuspected to her husband, fighting for her, using stratagem after stratagem, following hopeless hints. . . . The perfect knight! The gangster lover who really cares, who knows . . . "My darling . . . thank you for everything for ever," she breathed. He dared not reply, but his lips moved, and he slipped his left hand into his breast. She knew what he meant: the match was there, the symbol of their love. He would never forget her. She had lived. She was saved.

What a contrast to the other—so boisterous, so common, so thoroughly unattractive! It was strange to think of them in the same uniform, strange to look down the esplanade and see them getting more and more like one another as the distance increased. The actual parting had gone off easily. Ernest had produced his cigarettes again. "Have one more, both of you, before you repair to your boat," he called. The powerfully made sailors stooped, the lean distinguished fingers and the battered clumsy ones helped themselves again to his bounty. Perky, he had lit up himself, and now he was strutting away with his good little wife on his arm.

Of course the first few minutes alone with him were awful. Still, she drew strength from the fact that she had deceived him so completely. And somehow she did not despise him, she did not despise him at all. He seemed nicer than usual, and she was pleased when he started to said one thing, she another, while the cloud of her past discuss the relative advantages of gas and electricity. He said one thing, she another, while the cloud of her past swept gloriously out to sea. Home and its details had a new freshness. Even when the night came, she should feel differently and not mind.

They reached the bus-stop with several minutes to spare. There was a picture-postcard kiosk, and she had a good idea: she would buy a postcard of the Obelisk, so that if the topic came up again she would know what it looked like.

There was an excellent selection, and she soon visualized it from several points of view. Though not as tall as Cleopatra's Needle, it boasted a respectable height. One of the cards showed the inscription "Erected in 1879 to the memory of Alfred Judge, one-time Mayor". She memorized this, for Ernest often mentioned inscriptions, but she actually bought a card which brought in some of its surroundings. The monument was nobly placed. It stood on a tongue of rock overlooking the landslip.

"Well, you won't have seen that today! Will you?" said the woman in the kiosk as she took payment.

Hilda thought she would fall to the ground. "Oh gracious, what ever do you mean?" she gasped.

"It's not there to be seen."

"But that's the Obelisk. It says so."

"It says so, but it's not there. It fell down last week. During all that rain. It's fallen right over into the land-slip upside-down, the tip of it's gone in ever so far, rather laughable, though I suppose it'll be a loss to the town."

"Ah, there it is," said her husband, coming up and taking the postcard out of her hand. "Yes, it gives quite a good idea of it, doesn't it? I'll have one displaying the inscription."

Then the bus swept up and took them away. Hilda sank into a seat nearly fainting. Depth beneath depth seemed to open. For if she couldn't have seen the Obelisk he couldn't have seen it either, if she had dawdled on the way up he must have dawdled too, if she was lying he must be lying, if she and a sailor—she stopped her thoughts, for they were becoming meaningless. She peeped at her husband, who was on the other side of the coach, studying the postcard. He looked handsomer than usual, and happier, and his lips were parted in a natural smile.

What Does It Matter?
A Morality

Before the civil war, Pottibakia was a normal member of the Comity of Nations. She erected tariff walls, broke treaties, persecuted minorities, obstructed at conferences unless she was convinced there was no danger of a satisfactory solution; then she strained every nerve in the cause of peace. She had an unknown warrior, a national salvo, commemorative postage-stamps, a characteristic peasantry, arterial roads; her emblem was a bee on a bonnet, her uniform plum-gray. In all this she was in line with her neighbours, and her capital city could easily be mistaken for Bucharest or Warsaw, and often was. Her president (for she was a republic) was Dr Bonifaz Schpiltz; Count Waghaghren (for she retained her aristocracy) being head of the police, and Mme Sonia Rodoconduco being Dr Schpiltz's mistress (for he was only human).

Could it be this liaison which heralded the amazing change—a change which has led to the complete isolation of a sovereign state? Presidents so often have mistresses, it is part of the constitution they have inherited from Paris, and Dr Schpiltz was an ideal president, with a long thin brown beard flecked with gray, and a small protuberant stomach. Mme Rodoconduco, as an actress and a bad one, also filled her part. She was extravagant, high-minded and hysterical, and kept Bopp (for thus all the ladies called him) on tenterhooks lest she did anything temperamental. She lived in a lovely villa on the shores of Lake Lago.

Now Count Waghaghren desired the President's

downfall, and what the Count desired always came about, for he was powerful and unscrupulous. He desired it for certain reasons of *haute politique* which have been obscured by subsequent events—perhaps he was a royalist, perhaps a traitor or patriot, perhaps he was an emissary of that sinister worldwide Blue Elk organization which is said to hold its sessions in the Azores. It is hopeless to inquire. Enough that he decided, as part of his scheme, to sow dissension between husband and wife. Mme Schpiltz's relatives were financiers, and a scandal was likely to start fluctuations on the exchange.

His plot was easily laid. He forged a letter from Mme Rodoconduco to Mme Schpiltz, inviting her to visit the lovely Villa Lago at a certain hour upon a certain day, he intercepted the reply of Mme Schpiltz accepting the invitation, and he arranged that the President and his mistress should be found in a compromising position at the moment of her call. All worked to perfection. The gendarme outside the villa omitted (under instructions) the national salvo when the President's wife drove up, the servants (bribed) conducted her as if by mistake to the Aphrodite bedroom, and there she found her husband in a pair of peach-blush pyjamas supported by Mme Rodoconduco in a lilac negligée.

Mme Rodoconduco went into hysterics, hoping they would gain her the upper hand. She shrieked and raved, while Count Waghaghren's microphone concealed under the lace pillows transmitted every tremor to his private cabinet. The President also played up. At first he pretended he was not there, then he rebuked his wife for interfering and his mistress for licentiousness, whereas he—he was a man, with a morality of his own. "I am a man, ha ha!" and he tried folding his arms. Smack! He got one over the ear from Mme Rodoconduco for that. All was going perfectly except for the lack of cooperation on the part of Mme Schpiltz, who had started on entering the room and had said "Bopp Bopp Bopp", but had then said no more. She watched the lovers without animosity and without amusement, occasionally showing concern when they struck one another but not caring to intervene. When there was a pause she said rather shyly, "Madame—madame, j'ai faim," and since the only reply was a stare she added, "Vous m'avez invitée pour le goûter, n'est-ce-pas?"

"Certainly not, out of my house!" shrieked Mme Rodoconduco, but seeing a genuine look of disappointment on her visitor's face she said, "Oh, very well, if you must eat you must."

The servants now took Mme Schpiltz into another apartment, where *goûter* for two was already in evidence. She fell upon it, and Mme Rodoconduco followed her and sulkily did the honours. No allusion was made to the Aphrodite bedroom, the President had slipped away, and though the hostess was very nervous and therefore very rude she became easier in the presence of so much apathy, and they chatted on subjects of intellectual interest for quite a time.

The Count was unaccustomed to incidents without consequence and expected one lady or the other to come round to him in tears, or it might be the President himself asking him, as man to man, for advice in a little private difficulty. Then they would have fallen into his toils. But nothing happened. A few more officials and lackeys were in the know, but that was all. He must devise some other means of starting the ball rolling.

It may be remembered that there was a gendarme on duty that afternoon outside the Villa Lago. He, in the course of his usual dossier, reported that the President winked at him before driving away.

"Did you wink back?"

"Oh no, sir."

The Count docked him a week's pay, and an order went out to all ranks that when the President of the Republic winked at them they were to wink back.

The order had no effect because it was based on a misconception. It is true that the President had winked as he drove away, but only because some dust blew in his eye. His thoughts were with the ladies at their *goûter,* not of gendarmes at all. Defeated by the subsequent steadiness of his gaze, Count Waghaghren reissued the order in a more drastic form: all ranks were to wink without waiting. This again had no effect. We do not see what we do not seek, and Dr Schpiltz, though a stickler for uniforms, was oblivious to all that passes inside them. It was his wife who enlightened him. "Oh Bopp, how the poor policemen's eyes do twitch," she remarked at a review. His attention once drawn he observed that a twitch seemed to have become part of the national salvo. He did not like innovations about which he had not been consulted, and was about to issue a memorandum, when he noticed that the twitch was accompanied in some cases with a roguish smile. This put him on the right track. He had seen the same combination on the faces of little milliners and modistes of easy virtue, and he came to the only possible conclusion: the police were giving him the glad eye.

This called for a reprimand. But before drafting it he waited to make sure. There was no hurry—he could play cat and mouse if he liked, and he did get amusement at watching the forces of law and order playing futile tricks. He never winked back, oh no, he was always impassive and correct, besides, "I am a man, aha, no danger in that quarter for *me!*" and he pulled at his thin brown beard. His drives through his capital city became more vivid, and he began to contrast the methods of superior and subordinate ranks. The way in which a peasant lad, fresh inside his uniform, would be half afraid to move his eyelid, and yet move it as if he could have moved much more, was indescribably droll. He became more and more entertained by his discovery, which not even his wife shared now, for she had a mind like a sieve and completely forgot the whole matter.

One day he happened to take a short constitutional in the Victory Park. This splendid park is a favourite resort of Pottibakians of all types, and it was his duty, as first citizen in the state, to walk there now and then.

"Look," the people would say, "there is the President walking round the bandstand! He is holding a newspaper in his hand, just as if he were you or me! Marvellous!" But it was in a quieter part of the park that he suddenly encountered an incredibly good-looking mounted gendarme, and before he could stop himself had winked back. The man, who was very young, smiled charmingly, and pretended to have trouble with his horse. This led to a short conversation. There was not time for much, since the Bessarabian Minister was expected, but it included some presidential patting of the horse's neck, and a slight leaning forward on the part of its rider. "Mirko, Your Excellency, Mirko Bolnovitch. Yes." Which was all very well, but where? Not in the park, for God's sake, and he could not risk more tension with his wife. It is the pride of the Republic to house its president in prehistoric discomfort, and No. 100, Browning Street does not even possess a tradesman's entrance. The parlour is on the left of the door, the schoolroom on the right, and Mme Schpiltz or the young ladies see everyone who comes in. Not there, nor indeed anywhere. He withdrew hurriedly.

After his interview with the Bessarabian Minister he received a letter from Mme Rodoconduco. They had scarcely met since she boxed his ears, but it was tacitly understood that they were not to break. She wrote now on the deepest of black-edged paper, to make him part of the death of her brother, a realistic novelist to whom she was greatly attached. She must instantly repair to his estate, in case her nephews took a wrong view of the will. This, and the funeral, would detain her for at least a week, but as soon as she got back she much hoped to see her Bopp, and to apologize for her unfortunate warmth. On the whole not a bad letter. The woman wanted money—still, he had faced that long ago. She spoke of good taste and restraint—oh that she possessed them to the extent Mme Schpiltz did!—and she implied that though her mourning would be in good taste it could not be restrained. A *ménage à trois:* is it impossible when all three are rather exceptional? Finally she asked him a favour. All the servants at the Villa Lago had been dismissed owing to their treachery, and she wanted someone to keep an eye on the new set in her absence. Would he be so very good as to pay a surprise visit one afternoon—Friday, say?

He replied pleasantly, condoled, enclosed a cheque, said he would look in at the villa next Friday at 3.0 on the pretext of having a bathe, hoped too for the possibilities of a *ménage à trois*. She replied to this from her family estate. His note had caught her just before starting, she said, she was deeply appreciative, also for the enclosure, though the loss of a brother could never be repaired, and if only Mme Schpiltz could feel it possible to receive her some time. . . . Then she spoke of the grief of the tenantry and the conduct of her nephews, correct hitherto, the arrangements in the little upland church, the hearse, the wreaths of Alpine flowers. . . .

The Bessarabian affair still occupying him, he thought no more of Friday till his secretary reminded him. Then, punctually at 3.0, he drove up to the deserted villa. By chance his gendarme friend from the park was on guard. He had hardly given him a thought from that moment to this, but now it was as if he had been thinking of him all the time. He wanted to greet him, but it was impossible with the new major-domo bowing and inquiring whether he had done right in Madame la Baronne's absence to cover the sconces with brown holland. Turning away, he inspected the villa peevishly. He had never liked it less, and the Aphrodite bedroom was repellent. Was all this frou-frou and expense really necessary, as Sonia said it was, for love? She was always talking about love and sending in bills. He went out onto a balcony to get another glimpse of the mounted beauty, but the fellow looked in every direction but upwards, most exasperating, and the President dared not cough. Would Madame la Baronne desire the dining-room suite re-upholstered in banana beige? Yes, if he knew her, she would. Then he said he must reexamine the hydrangeas in the porch. The gendarme kept absolutely still, a model of Pottibakian manhood, not winking now, all glorious in plum-gray. How grandly he sat his horse! Cheerful chatter, meant to embrace him, brought no smile to the strong lips. Alarmed by the fluting quality in his own voice, Dr Schpiltz withdrew, sharper set than ever. Now he would never know what happens when two men . . . and it might have been such a lesson with such a teacher. . . . Well, well, he must just have his bathe and go, perhaps all's for the best.

Now the bathing-room at the Villa Lago is a veritable triumph of Lido art. Divans and gymnastic apparatus mingle inseparably. It is accessible from the house and also on the lake side, where great sliding doors give access to marble steps leading down to Mme Rodoconduco's private beach. The view is beyond all description —poets have hymned it: rhododendrons, azaleas, bougainvillaeas, the blue waters of the lake, and on the further side of it, just visible through the summer haze, the great rock of Praz, where the Pottibakians used to sacrifice their domestic animals before the introduction of Christianity. But the prospect gave the President no pleasure, not even when an aeroplane passed over it. Everything seemed worth just nothing at all. Holding up his swimming-suit he prepared to step into it, when there was the sound of crunched pebbles, and the gendarme rode round the corner of the little bay, dismounted, strode clanging up the steps, took a gauntlet off, and shook hands.

The President frowned—often a sign of joy in the middle-aged, and it was thus understood. "Your Excellency—at your service. Now. . . . My inspector has gone back to the city: he is a fool." He pulled the sliding doors together and latched them. "Excuse me. . . ." He hung up his spiked helmet next to Mme Rodoconduco's hat. "Excuse me again. . . ." He unbuckled his holster. Sitting down on a settee, which was so soft it made him laugh, he took his gaiters and boots off. "Oh,

I say, what a lovely room—better than the Victory Park."

Dr. Schpiltz could not speak. His mouth opened and shut like a bird's.

"Have you thought of me since?"

"Ye . . . yes."

"I don't believe you. What is my name?"

The President could not remember.

"Mirko. Mirko Bolnovitch. Oh, I say!" He had noticed the parallel bars. "That shall be my horse in here. Oh, I say!" He had seen the trapeze. Dr Schpiltz locked the door leading into the house. "I'll do that, Your Excellency, don't you trouble." And with a movement too rapid to follow he unlocked it. "Now I'm in your power."

"I think I'm in yours," said the President, admiring him more boldly.

"I'm only eighteen. Shall we see?"

"You come from beyond Praz, don't you, Mirko?"

"Yes. How did you know? By my speech? Or by something else?" He continued to undress. The uniform lay neatly folded, official property. "My singlet." He drew it over his head. "My shorts . . ."

"Well?"

"Well? Never content?" He stepped out of them smiling and sprang onto the trapeze. "Do you like me up here?"

"You are much too far off!"

"Oh, but come up here, Your Excellency, join me!"

"No, thank you, Mirko, not at my age!"

"See, it's so easy, catch hold of whatever you like, only swinging." The light filtered through high orange curtains onto loins and back. "It is cooler with no clothes on," he said. It did not seem to be. "Now I have exercised all my muscles except . . ." He was sitting astride the parallel bars.

The President of the Republic approached his doom. Deftly, as he did so, was his pince-nez twitched off his nose. "Now you can't see how ugly I am."

"Mirko, you ugly . . ." He tottered into the trap and it closed on him.

"Aie, you're in too much of a hurry," laughed the young man. "Come up and do exercises with me first. Business before pleasure."

"I'd rather not, I shall fall, my dear boy."

"Oh no you won't, dearest boyest."

Contrary to his better judgement, Dr Schpiltz now ascended the parallel bars. He became more and more involved. Heaven knew what he had to pass through, how he was twisted about and pinched. He felt like a baby monkey, scratched and mismanaged on the top of a lofty tree. The science of the barrackroom, the passions of the stables, the primitive instincts of the peasantry, the accident of the parallel bars and Dr Schpiltz's quaint physique—all combined into something quite out of the way, and as it did so the door opened and Mme Rodoconduco came into the room, followed by the Bessarabian Minister.

"We have here . . ." she was saying.

Neither of them heard her.

"We have here . . . we have . . ."

The Bessarabian Minister withdrew. Mirko, alerted, relaxed a grip and they fell off the bars onto a mattress. Mme Rodoconduco was so thunderstruck that she could not even scream. She remained in a sort of frenzied equilibrium, and when she did speak it was in ordinary tones. She said, "Bopp, oh Bopp, Bopp!"

He heard that, and raised a lamentable goatee. "You Jezebel! Why aren't you at the funeral?" he hissed.

"Whose funeral?" cried she in flame-coloured taffeta, Titian-cut.

"Your brother's."

"Alekko's? He's alive."

"How dare you contradict me? He's dead. Oh, oh. . . . You've written to me about his funeral twice."

"I never did, Bopp, never." Distracted, she picked up a bath-towel and threw it over the pair. They looked better as a heap.

"Disgraceful! Incredible! And I wrote back and sent you a cheque for the mourning."

"I have received no cheque," she cried. "Here's something gravely amiss."

"Yes, all you think of is cheques! What are you here for now?"

"Why, your telephone call," she replied with tears in her eyes. "You rang me up this morning to be here at 3.30 in case the Bessarabian Minister called."

"I never rang you up. More lies."

"You did, dear, you did really, I answered the call myself, and the Minister said you had rung him up also."

"The Minister? Good God! When is he coming?"

"He has come and has gone."

"Not—oh Sonia, not—"

"Yes, and his wife was with him, to see the view, and this is the view they saw. My villa. My Villa Lago. Well, this is the end of my career, such as it is. I can never go back to the stage."

"I am likely never to leave it," said Dr. Schpiltz slowly. "I shall go down to history as the president who—oh, what can even the historians say? I shall resign tomorrow, but that will be the beginning, not the end. Could I get over the frontier? Would an aeroplane . . . ? How ever did you open the door?"

"It was unlocked."

"Unlocked? I locked it myself!"

"I think we must both be bewitched," she said, shading her eyes. She was behaving wonderfully well, she was one of those women who behave alternately well and badly. The President began to be convinced of her sincerity and to feel ashamed.

"I know that *I* have been. What ever has possessed me? When I look round"—and he thrust his head out of the towel—"when I think what I was an hour ago, I begin to wonder, Sonia, whether those old fairytales you used to recite may not be true, whether men cannot be changed into beasts. . . ."

"Ah!" she interrupted, catching sight of the spiked

helmet hanging beside her hat, "I've seen the whole thing! We've got Waghaghren here!"

"Well, hardly," he demurred.

"It's one of his traps."

"Trap? But how should he set one?"

"Who knows how or why the Count does things? We only know he does them. Now are you absolutely sure you locked the door into the villa?"

"Absolutely, because this lad—because he—" He broke off and cried, "Mirko! You're not here under orders, are you?"

Mirko lay on the mattress half a-dreaming, drowsy with delight. He had carried out the instructions of his superior officer, gratified a nice old gentleman and had a lovely time himself. He could not understand why, when the President's question was repeated, he should get a kick. He laughed and made the reply on which the whole history of Pottibakia turns. If he had said "Yes, I am here under orders," or if, acting under orders, he had said "No," his country would still be part of the Comity of Nations. But he made the reply which is now engraved on his statue. He said: "What does it matter?"

"You will soon learn whether it matters," said the President. "Sonia, please ring the bell." Mme Rodo-conduco stopped him: "No, do not ring. We suffer too much from distant communications. I must question him myself, I see." She raised her eyes to the trapeze. "You! You down on the floor, you have admitted to His Excellency that you are an *agent provocateur?*"

Propping his chin on his fists, Mirko answered: "Gracious lady, I am. But His Excellency acts provokingly too. When I netted him in the park I thought to myself, 'This will mean fun.' And I am a peasant, and we peasants never think a little fun matters. You and His Excellency and the head of the police know better, but we peasants have a proverb: 'Poking doesn't count.' "

"And pray what does that mean?"

"Oh, never mind, Sonia, don't question him. You belong to such different worlds."

"You should know what poking means, lady, if half the tales about you are true. Anyhow, it is a religious story. It is about the Last Judgement."

"We are freethinkers, religion means nothing to us," said the President, but Mirko continued:

"At the Last Judgement the Pottibakians were in a terrible fright, because they had all done something which all three of us have done and hope to do again. There they were going up in a long line, the nobility like you going first, the people of my sort waiting far behind. We waited and waited and presently heard a loud cheering up at the Gate. So we sent a messenger to find out what had happened, and he came back shouting all down the line, "Hooray! Hooray! Poking doesn't count.' And why should it? Do you understand now?"

"I understand that you are the lowest of the low, or the Count would not employ you," said she. "Will you be so good as to insert that remark of mine into your report?"

"No need, gracious lady, a microphone is already installed."

"Where?" gasped the President.

"These new servants would know. That major-domo is a government electrician."

"Then has all I said been heard?"

"Yes, and all the strange noises you made. Still, what does it matter? It was fun. Oh, some things matter, of course, the crops, and the vintage matters very much, and our glorious Army, Navy, and Air Force, and fighting for our friends, and baiting the Jews, but isn't that all? Why, in my village where everyone knows one another and the priest is worst. . . . Why, when my uncle needed a goat . . ."

But here the door opened again and Mme Schpiltz entered the room. Dressed in alpaca and a home-made toque, she presented an equal contrast to her husband's bath-towel, to Mme Rodoconduco's Venetian splendours, and to the naked gendarme. As on her previous visit, she was greeted with torrents of talk and knew not how to reply. "Madame, madame," wailed her hostess, "we are ruined," and beneath her full-bosomed lamentations could be heard the President's plaintive pipe: "Oh Charlotte, I have been fatally in-discreet. Why did you come?"

"Because you telephoned to me."

"I telephoned to you? Never!"

"But what has happened? You have only been bath-ing."

"Madame, madame, do not ask him further, it is something too awful, something he could never explain, something which even I . . . and which you with your fine old-world outlook, your nobility, your strictness of standard. . . . Oh madame . . . and in my villa too, after all your previous goodness to me . . . my Villa Lago. . . . But you have influence in high financial circles, use it at once before it is too late, let us fly to a cottage *à trois* before the Count—what am I saying? The Count not only heard but he hears! Count Waghaghren!" She whirled her arms in every direction. "Somewhere, a microphone!"

"But I like the wireless so much as long as I have something to do at the same time," said Mme Schpiltz.

"Charlotte! We have reason to believe that a micro-phone has been secretly installed here, and that the Count can hear everything in his private cabinet."

"But why shouldn't he hear everything? I think that's such a nice idea. He is such a clever man, I knew his poor grandmother well. I remember him saying when he was quite a tiny tot, 'Me want to hear evvyfing,' and we saying 'No, baby dear, baby can't ever do that,' but he knew and we didn't, for thanks to this wonderful invention he can. How like him!"

"He has probably installed television too."

"How like him again! He always used to say, 'Me

peepy-weep,' and now he can. Really I do think science. . . . But can no one tell me what has happened?"

"I could," said Mirko.

"Charlotte, don't speak to that man! I forbid it!"

"Excuse me, Bopp, I shall speak to him; besides, judging by those clothes over on the divan, he seems to be a policeman, and so the proper person. Well, my man?"

"Lady, do you in God's name know what poking is?"

"But of course. There would be no babies without it. But naturally."

"Thank heaven for that! Well, His Excellency wanted to poke me but did not know how, so I showed him."

"And is that the whole story?"

"Yes."

"Young man, you didn't hurt my husband with rough jokes, I hope?"

"Only in ways he enjoyed."

"And are you yourself satisfied?"

"Not yet. I want to show him again."

"For that you will have to wait. Thank you." She dismissed him and turned to the others. "Well, there we are at last. I thought that someone had been hurt, and it's simply that two people—yes, one doesn't talk about these things of course, but really—what do they matter?"

"Ah!" cried Mirko, "here is someone at last who says what I do. What does it matter?" And he shouted out the cry which was soon to rend the nation asunder, shouted it with such force and, as it happened, so close to the microphone that Count Waghaghren fell senseless.

"What does it matter? Well, that's one way of looking at it, I suppose," said Mme Rodoconduco, examining her fingernails.

"It's the only way," pronounced the President. "It's essential to a stable society. But no government has ever thought of it, and we've learned it too late."

They were not too late, because the Count remained unconscious for the rest of the day. A master plotter, he left no one to carry on his plans, and by the time he came to himself the famous Manifesto had been drafted and affixed to the principal public buildings in the capital. Its wording was as follows:

Fellow Citizens! Since all of you are interested in the private lives of the great, we desire to inform you that we have all three of us had carnal intercourse with the President of the Republic, and are hoping to repeat it.

> Charlotte Schpiltz (housewife)
> Sonia Rodoconduco (artiste)
> Mirko Bolnovitch (gendarme)

There was some discussion as to the wording of the Manifesto. Mme Rodoconduco wanted some reference to the overmastering and ennobling power of love, Mirko something more popular. Both were overruled. The Manifesto appeared in the evening papers, and led to questions both in the Senate and the Chamber of Deputies. The Ministry could not answer the questions and resigned. The President then drove down in state and addressed both houses. He began by paying a glowing tribute to Count Waghaghren, whose organization had now reached such a pitch that not only the private actions of each citizen but even his or her thoughts would soon be recorded automatically. "I intend therefore," he went on, "to form a Ministry of all the Morals, which can alone survive such scrutiny, and as soon as it is in office its first duty will be to depose me. Once deposed, I shall be liable to arrest and to prosecution under our Criminal Code, the most admirable, as we often agreed, in Eastern Europe. Or it may be that I shall not be prosecuted at all, but dealt with summarily, like one of the signatories to the Manifesto, who has been sent for six years to the mines, on the charge of deserting his horse. The other two signatories are at large for the moment, but should not long remain so."

The scenes at the conclusion of his speech were indescribable, particularly in the Senate, where old men got up and poured out their confessions for hours, and could not be stopped. The Chamber of Deputies kept a stiffer upper lip, and there were cries of "Flogging's too good!" and faint counter-cries of "Flog me!" No one dared to take office, owing to the President's unmeasured eulogy of the police, and he continued to govern as dictator until the outbreak of the civil war.

He is now dictator again, but since all the states, led by Bessarabia, have broken off diplomatic relations it is extremely difficult to get Pottibakian news. Visas are refused, and the international express traverses the territory behind frosted glass. Now and then a postcard of the Bolnovitch Monument falls out of an aeroplane, but unlike most patriotic people the Pottibakians appear to be self-contained. They till the earth and have become artistic, and are said to have developed a fine literature which deals very little with sex. This is puzzling, as is the indissolubility of marriage—a measure for which the Church has vainly striven elsewhere. Gratified by her triumph, she is now heart and soul with the nation, and the Archimandrite of Praz has reinterpreted certain passages of scripture, or has pronounced them corrupt. Much here is obscure, links in the argument have been denied to us, nor, since we cannot have access to the novels of Alekko, can we trace the steps by which natural impulses were converted into national assets. There seem, however, to have been three stages: first the Pottibakians were ashamed of doing what they liked, then they were aggressive over it, and now they do as they like. There I must leave them. We shall hear little of them in the future, for the surrounding powers dare not make war. They hold—and perhaps rightly—that the country has become so infectious that if it were annexed it would merely get larger.

And what of the Count? Some rumours have come through. He fought in the civil war, was taken prisoner, and his punishment had to be decided. Mirko wanted him sent to the mines, Sonia flogged, the President banished, but Mme Schpiltz was the cruellest of all. "Poor man, I can't see what he has done," she said. "Do let him keep on doing it." Her advice was taken, and the Count was reinstated in his former office, which has been renamed the Lunatic Asylum, and of which he is the sole inmate. Here he sits all alone amid the latest apparatus, hearing, seeing, tasting and smelling through his fellow citizens, and indexing the results. On public holidays his private cabinet (now his cell) is thrown open, and is visited by an endless queue of smiling Pottibakians, who try to imagine the old days when that sort of thing mattered, and emerge laughing.

The Classical Annex

The Municipal Museum at Bigglesmouth was badly off for Greek and Roman stuff, and the Curator rather neglected what was known as the Classical Annex. So imagine his guilty conscience when one dark afternoon, just as the museum was closing, the custodian came to his office with news of a breakage there. It was like hearing of the death of a worthy but tedious relative. "Not the Early Christian sarcophagus?" he inquired, secretly hoping that it might be.

No, not the sarcophagus nor the nude neither, no, only minor objects.

"Objects? What? More than one breakage?"

"Well, sir, to be quite frank it's a couple of terracotta items in Wall Case A."

"Not the Tanagra statuette?" he cried with increasing emotion.

The custodian hastened to assure him that one of the items was not the Tanagra—everyone knew how valuable she was. The other, on the other hand, was.

"The best thing in the room—the only good thing in it. How on earth did it happen? Were you leaning on the case? Were you pointing her out to the public?"

The custodian waxed indignant. Most certainly he had not been pointing her out to the public. There never was any public in the Classical Annex.

"When did the accident happen?"

"I couldn't say, sir."

"Oh, couldn't you? That means you haven't been going your rounds properly."

Having silenced all criticism, except what came from his own conscience, the Curator snatched up his keys

154

and went to inspect. Crossing the entrance hall of the museum, with frieze entitled Motherly Love, he passed the unique series of wooden churns discovered in the bed of the Biggle, and the reconstruction of the Town Pump. Modern Art opened behind that. Beyond Modern Art was the Classical Annex. It was by far the least attractive room in the museum—stuffy, badly lit, and not too clean. He unlocked Wall Case A. Alas and alas! The Tanagra, a charming little girl, had fallen, pedestal and all, and chipped her pretty hat. The other statuette —a bearded Etruscan thing—had suffered even more, but this did not signify, as the City Council had been told that he was bad.

"You can go now, I will let myself out," he told the custodian, "and you had better think over what you propose to say to the Committee on Thursday. See! There is dust on the arm of the male statuette. He must have been broken for days."

Alone in the museum, he examined the wall case carefully, and discovered several further breakages. A small plaque representing a nymph had cracked, and an Apis bull had slid towards it, toppling onto its nose. Misfortunes tended to come in pairs—and as for the two terracottas it was almost as if they had picked their way to their common doom. With delicate fingers he tidied up the shelves, and was about to take the damaged objects to his office, and consider how best they might be repaired, when there was a tinkle behind him. The fig-leaf attached to the nude in the centre of the room had fallen onto the floor.

"Really, the things might be alive," he grumbled, picking it up. It was a veritable giant among fig-leaves, the work of a local ironmonger. He did not like to leave it for the charwoman to find it in the morning— employees at Bigglesmouth were easily upset. Owing to its weight, it had chafed through the suspending circlet of string.

The nude, now wholly so for the first time, was a worthless late Roman work, and represented an athlete or gladiator of the non-intellectual type. He had never liked it, and had reported strongly against purchasing it, and he liked it less than ever in the twilight that began to invade the dingy museum. The City Fathers had wanted something life-sized and cheap, "and they've got 'em both, by gad," he murmured, climbing fastidiously upon a chair, with the fig-leaf swinging from a new piece of string, and thinking how much more personable was his own son Denis than this classical lout.

"Scrap-heap's the place for you," he said, as he embraced the stone buttocks and fastened the string above them. "Broken up for road metal—that's all you're worth." Stepping down, he gazed at his handiwork. The fig-leaf didn't hang right—tilted out unsuitably. He quite lost his temper. Why should his time be wasted over all this rubbish? And clenching his fist he hit it hard. It fell into position with a ping. Dusting his hands against one another, he went back to the two statuettes.

He had put them for safety on the plush couch, at least a foot apart. Now they lay together, and, queerer still, appeared to have stuck. He had never known terracottas stick before—probably the result of the damp Bigglesmouth climate—and he felt quite despairful—everything he turned his back on seemed to go wrong. Would he never get home to his tea? As he bent down to separate them, he heard a string snap, and the fig-leaf whizzed across the room. It might have killed him. "Damn and blast you, that's too much," he cried, then shrieked, and leapt into the Early Christian sarcophagus. He was not an instant too soon. The nude had cracked off its pedestal and was swaying to fall on him.

With rare presence of mind, the Curator made the sign of the Cross, and the Classical Annex and all its contents became instantly still. It might have been a dream but for an obscene change in the statue's physique. He gazed from his asylum in horror. He glanced at the fig-leaf, now all too small. He backed away from it, crossing himself constantly, he could still see it from Modern Art, it was even prominent from among the oaken churns, he did not lose sight of it until he sidled under Motherly Love. Then he ran—yes, he did run. He let himself out of the museum, not forgetting to lock it carefully behind him as you may well imagine, then he rushed over Coronation Square and down Bonfire Street, where he boarded a municipal tram.

The Curator was no materialist, like too many savants of the nineteenth century. Oxford had taught him to admit the supernatural willingly, and he wasted no time in indignation or brooding. As soon as his natural terror subsided and one particular apparition ceased to threaten him, he began to think what should be done. Clearly something was loose in the Classical Annex, some obscene breath from the past, and it might not be impossible to convince the City Fathers of this, for they were God-fearing men. They did not really care for Greek and Roman stuff, and had only been tempted to the nude by its cheapness. "You never know where young people may not pick up dirty thoughts," Councillor Bodkin had said, when they sent the order to the ironmonger. Once get them impressed and all would be easy. His best plan, he decided, would be to close the museum on his own authority, and wire for one or two friends of his, eminent experts, whose names would intimidate the Mayor. Sir Newton Surtees the great speleologist, Canon Bootle Anderson who exposed the behaviourists, Dame Lucy Ironside, president of the Self-Health Association and organizer of the World Retention Movement—these were not inconsiderable figures, and their outlook was his own. In their presence the museum should be unsealed. If nothing was found—and he was well aware how impish the powers of darkness can be—he would resign his post and they would find him a new one. If anything was found, steps should be taken to exorcise the town and to dispose of the nude as a Priapus to some connoisseur.

It was night when he left the tram, but the walk down Michaelmas Avenue held no terrors for him. He had thought the thing out, with a mind both powerful and modern, and wiping his spectacles he looked calmly into the lighted doorway of his residence, and into the pale blue eyes of his wife.

"Hullo, dear, where's Denis?" she said.

"Denis? I don't know."

"He went to meet you."

"Did he? I must have passed him in the tram."

"You don't usually take the tram. What a nuisance, now he will probably rush all the way down, foolish boy, and he's practically nothing on but his football shorts. They've won that match and he wanted to tell you."

"Well, when he's rushed down he'll rush back."

"Unless he looks for you in the museum."

"He can scarcely do that," said the Curator quietly. "The museum is locked up."

"Oh yes he can, dear. He snatched up your duplicate keys. I couldn't stop him. He's getting awfully head-strong and excitable—dear, whatever's the matter?"

"Nothing." He rang the museum up and got Number Unobtainable. While his wife was preparing tea, he slipped out of the house. He reminded himself that it was only a statue, and a debased one right away in the Classical Annex, where Denis was unlikely to go. He compelled himself to keep calm, while running at full speed up Michaelmas Avenue and down Bonfire Street, until he was again in Coronation Square.

The museum squatted on the margin like a toad. He inserted a key into its skin, oilily, and it received him. None of the lights were on, which gave him hope. Then far away he heard a familiar, an adorable sound: a giggle. Denis was laughing at something. He dared not call out or give any sign, and crept forward cautiously, guiding himself by well-known objects, like the oaken churns, until he heard his son say, "Aren't you awful?" and there was the sound of a kiss. Gladiatorial feints, post-classical suctions, a brute planning its revenge. There was not a moment to lose, and as the giggling started again and soared up into hysterics against a ground-bass of grunts the Curator stepped into the

Christian sarcophagus and made the sign of the Cross. Again it worked. Once more the Classical Annex and all its contents became still.

Then he switched on the light.

And in after years a Hellenistic group called The Wrestling Lesson became quite a feature at Bigglesmouth, though it was not exhibited until the Curator and the circumstances of his retirement were forgotten. "Very nice piece, very decent" was Councillor Bodkin's opinion. "Look 'ow the elder brother's got the little chappie down. Look 'ow well the little chappie's taking it."

The Torque

The little basilica was crammed. Perpetua sąt to the left of the altar, robed in white. Through a thin veil her commanding nose and fastidious mouth could be clearly seen. She never moved, her eyes fixed ecstatically upon the godhead. Below her, on plainer chairs, sat her father and mother, Justus and Lucilla, landowners of substance, her young brother Marcian, and her little sisters, Galla and Justa. To the right of the altar, over-balancing the domestic group, towered the ecclesiastics: the Bishop of the district, the lesser clergy, the father confessors, and several solitaries who had been attracted by the strangeness and special sanctity of the event. The body of the church was filled with neigh-bours, the faithful and the curious. It was richly dec-orated in a rustic fashion, and above the altar, like a trophy, hung a barbaric torque of gold. Through the open western door Justus's farmyard could be seen. It too was full of people—slaves, husbandmen, soldiers. These last were all baptized Christians and particularly devout. They had been drafted in to protect the sacred ceremony from interference. The district was not as settled as it had been. Deceitfully now did it sleep in the autumn sunlight—the vineyards, the cornlands, the olive yards, the low ridges of the hills. The soldiers glanced occasionally at the hills.

Mass had been said. Lucilla, a little drowsy, awoke with a start. The great ceremony of her daughter's dedi-cation was to begin. Perpetua Virgo, perpetual virginity. She nudged her husband and he awoke frowning. For he had promised the Bishop to build a bigger, better basilica as a thank-offering, also Perpetua's dowry had to be surrendered to the Heavenly Bridegroom, and Marcian's heritage impaired, and the little girls go almost unportioned. He had not expected all this. He had hoped to marry his eldest daughter to some substantial farmer. There had been little talk of dedicated virgins when he was young, and he had never expected to rear one in the family. The animals mated—he could hear them at it when the chanting ceased—and are we not like them in that? Still frowning, he took his wife's hand ritually, then dropped it, for the Bishop had begun his address.

Standing beside the altar, the Bishop reminded his congregation that this dedication would in any case have taken place and been blessed, but it was now signalized by a miracle which would live in the annals of the Church for ever. Five days ago, as they all knew, the virgin Perpetua had set forth on a journey, not from idleness, not from wantonness, not from a desire to see the world (which she already too well knew), but to confer with a holy matron of her acquaintance upon religious matters. She travelled in all seemliness, with her brother as escort and a suitable retinue of slaves. Edifying was the meeting between the two devout females, long did they converse, many were the pious propositions they exchanged. Presently came the hour for her return to her parents' abode. She mounted her mule, her brother rode somewhat behind as was suitable, her retinue followed on foot. The evening was calm, the air balmy, no danger seemed to menace. But these are the moments when the Adversary is most active. She turns a corner of the road and—

"Oh my brethren oh my sisters, what did our virgin then see? Horsemen. What horsemen? Goths. She shrieks, she trembles, they bear down on her, Goths, Goths, hideous of form and of face, they are here. They lay hold of Perpetua and hale her off her mule, they clasp her, my brethren my sisters, she is lost. Is she not lost? It seems so. Her brother is overpowered, for he is but a stripling, her retinue scattered. With their booty

the Goths, yes the Goths I again say, ride onward into
the hills. They have captured that which is more precious
than gold or jewels, namely a virgin, Perpetua the virgin
whom the whole world could not ransom.

"What are they going to do to her, oh my brethren
oh my sisters, what?

"Night falls, they come to a miserable hut. Wine is
offered to Perpetua which she spurns and they drink and
there is an orgy. She is thrown to the ground. And one
of them—he who once wore this golden circlet above
our altar and now wears it no longer—nay nay I cannot continue—"

He paused, and there was silence in the basilica except for sore swallowings in throats. Using the frank
language of his age, the language of St Augustine and
St Jerome, he continued as follows:

"—and loosens his own. To lose her virginity to the
husband for whom she was once destined would be for
Perpetua defilement enough, but this! The ravisher cov-
ers her, his hot breath beats back her prayers, and his
member—and they are membered like horses . . ."

He paused again and somebody laughed. He started
with anger and amazement, and the congregation trembled. Who had laughed? They looked right and left, and
lo! the face of Marcian the virgin's young brother was
crimson.

For a few moments the service of dedication stopped.
Marcian gulped and gasped, and his features returned
towards their former colour. His parents bent over him,
his mother asked him whether he was ill. He shook his
head. He was a modest boy, in awe of his sister as they
all were, and his conduct was inexplicable. He now sat
with his head bowed and his thick lips closed—there
was a strain of African blood in the family and it had
come out in Marcian.

The Bishop looked at him and hesitated. He suspected diabolical possession, and the lower clergy were
crossing themselves right and left. Perpetua alone was
undisturbed. Her eyes remained fixed on the altar ec-

statically. She was far away from such trifles. And taking his cue from her he decided to resume his homily as if nothing had happened.

Let them note (he said) that at that supreme moment when all seemed lost the virgin's prayer was heard. There was a lightning flash, the Goth staggered back and fell as though struck to the ground. Nay more, he was visited with repentance and followed her humbly when she departed, and offered her as atonement that great golden torque that lay against the altar now. She returned home unscathed and triumphant, *virgo victrix*. She had done what the might of men cannot. And in due time, he doubted not, she would subdue all around her to her holy purpose, and the foul engendering which is Adam's curse would cease.

He looked at Justus and Lucilla as he spoke these last words, and they looked away. It was in sin that they had engendered Perpetua, and in sin—greater sin —Marcian. Much pleasure had gone to the making of Marcian. This, they now learned, is wrong. All fruitfulness and warmth are wrong. They tried to understand this and looked humbly at their formidable daughter, who alone could save them from eternal punishment. When the dedication was over they asked Marcian what had made him laugh. "I do not know, something I was not thinking of made me laugh," was his reply.

"It may harm us, that laugh of yours."

"I am sorry, dear father, I will try to laugh no more. But the cattle need driving in. The country is unsafe with Goths about. May I now go and help the herdsmen?"

"No, for there now has to be Holy Converse in the barn," said Lucilla with a sigh. "All must repair there."

They did so. The barn resembled the basilica, except that Perpetua now spoke. She exhorted all present to follow her example, the females particularly, and fixed her beady eyes upon her sisters, Galla and Justa, merry little maidens. Males, she explained, were of coarser clay, hewers of wood and drawers of water, and could achieve less. The Bishop took her up a little here. Males, he asserted, could also achieve virginity and must be encouraged to do so. The involuntary pollutions which sometimes overcame them were from the Devil certainly, but not fatal. He appealed—and here his eye fixed Marcian—to men and particularly to youths in the first tumult of their ripeness.

"He is a good boy," said his father.

"He is the comfort of our old age," said his mother. And little Galla and Justa piped up: "We like Marcian. Oh, we like Marcian much better than Perpetua. He makes us toys."

The Bishop threw up his hands in annoyance. "Toys? Toys? O generation of vipers, who will save you from the wrath to come? It is she, she alone, that virgin who consents to sojourn amongst you, she alone averts the merited thunderbolt." These were strong words, but he had been disturbed by the unseemly interruption in the basilica and was half-minded to pronounce an exorcism now. But there seemed insufficient evidence, so he terminated the Converse and proceeded to his bullock-cart. All accompanied him with the exception of Marcian, who exploded once more into laughter. For he, and he alone, knew how Perpetua's virginity had been preserved.

It had been preserved as follows.

That day, five days ago, when they met the Goths, he had set forth without forebodings. Attendance on Perpetua was part of his duty, he was humble and loyal and ready to die for her if necessary. She spoke little to him on the journey out; if she did so he rode forward to receive her orders and fell back to transmit them to the slaves. He did not ask himself whether he liked her—it would have been an unseemly question—but he knew that he lay under her continuous and permanent displeasure. For some years ago he had been guilty of impurity. One of his mother's house-girls had given him a thrill which he still remembered. His mother had beaten the girl, his father had laughed, all was passing off normally when Perpetua had a sort of fit. She called them all to her couch, and made him promise he would never be unchaste again. It was easy to promise, for he was thoroughly frightened, and being only thirteen assumed that his carnal impulses would weaken. She knew better. She had been waiting for such an opportunity as this, and she began to organize a holy spy-system with the help of the monks who began to haunt the farm. All was done in the name of his parents, and they were watched too, and gradually the ease went out of life. It was the price they paid for rearing a saint.

Brother and sister made a striking pair as they rode into the entangling hills—she severe, ascetic, veiled, he open to all the winds and suns of heaven, his knees and neck bare until she reminded him to cover them. Once he started a countrified song which the retinue took up, but she stopped that and substituted a psalm. When they reached their destination he had to remain outside it, for so holy was the matron that no male creature was suffered to enter her abode. Even male mosquitoes were prohibited, the slaves said. They became ribald on the subject, and he had to check them while not wanting to do so. "Tell your mistress that it is time we left, for the sun falls towards the hills," he told them presently. A slave passed the message through a grille to an aged woman, and after further delay Perpetua appeared.

She was even graver than before, but more disposed to talk. When they had started for home she summoned him and told him that she was now decided on perpetual virginity.

"It is God's will, sister."

"I shall not retire to the desert. The matron has counselled me otherwise. I shall make my abode amongst you."

"It is evidently God's will—sister, look at that hawk."

"What of it?"

"Someone has disturbed him."

"Marcian, when will you learn seemliness?"

"Have I not? I do try."

"I was about to speak to your edification, but you are diverted by the passing flight of a bird."

At this moment the Goths appeared. There were only three of them, and had Perpetua kept quiet the two parties might have ridden past each other with friendly salutation. But she lifted up her voice and prayed. "O Lord God of Hosts O God of Abraham Isaac and Jacob deliver us out of the hands of our enemies," she cried. Her prayer was heard by the slaves and they started to run away. The Goths chased the slaves. One of them, pressing by Marcian, nicked his horse on the rump with a knife. The horse reared and he fell off. Seeing him tumble, another Goth haled Perpetua off her mule. The disaster was immediate and complete. Brother and sister bit the dust while the squeals of their retinue grew fainter and the sun dropped towards the hills with a jerk.

Further indignities followed. His ankles were bound, he was made to hop so that he fell down again amidst loud laughter, a barbarian spat in his face, another threw an overripe fig, he was flung crossways on his mount, Perpetua replaced on hers, getting pinched in the process, and then they all rode deeper into the hills. They came to a hut, a sort of storehouse, for plunder lay about, including a barrel of wine. The captives were dismounted and Marcian's ankles freed. He began to look around him. One of them appeared to be the leader, for he gave orders and wore a magnificent torque of gold. Perpetua was engaged in prayer. He tried to comfort her, but could not gain her attention.

"Sister, I do not think we are in great danger. They seem to mean us no harm, though I cannot follow their speech. They want our mounts perhaps, not ourselves. I do not think they want us at all. They are only wild boys who do not know their own wishes or what is in their hearts."

"O God of Abraham Isaac and Jacob deliver us."

"Amen and I am sure he will. They are forgetting us, and soon we shall be able to walk away. I may even untether your mule so that you can escape in comfort."

"O God . . ."

"And look, they are preparing food."

"Food, brother?" The suggestion outraged her. "Unholy food."

"It has been stolen from holy people by the look of it."

"It is the fouler for that."

"Sister, I must confess I am hungry." For an animal had broken loose inside him. "You had delicate refreshment at the matron's, I was offered nothing. With respect I must eat." And walking boldly to the trestle where the Goths were at work he pointed to himself and said "Marcian", and pointed to the man with the torque, who said "Euric", and everyone laughed. The faces of the barbarians were frank, childish and powerful. Emotions passed over them like clouds. No one, not even themselves, knew what they would do next. Having given him their best, they drank to him and to each other and to the Majesty of Rome. And they drank to Perpetua and explored her contours with bold blue eyes. She fell on her knees, not the safest of positions. One of them licked his lips, another fingered his breeks, and suddenly all five were struggling on the floor. All five, for Marcian had intervened to save her. The confusion was terrible. Ten arms, five heads and ten legs got mixed into a revolving ball when the shrieks of the virgin and the howls of her ravishers floated out into the night. "Sister, escape," Marcian repeated. "I will hold them off from you. Escape." She escaped and he got raped.

The surprise exceeded the pain. "Not me, this can't be for me" was his thought as the notorious Gothic embrace penetrated. Women died from it, the story went. That seed was said to breed devils. "Well, scarcely in my case." The idea made him laugh, and he heard Euric laugh. For it had been Euric.

So like these Goths! Food and drink, lechery, sleep, fighting, food, mirth, drink, boy, girl, no difference. Euric rolled off him when satisfied and could easily have been killed. But one does not kill beasts or babies. And the other two were no longer dangerous. The force of example had proved too strong for them. Call themselves devils, did they? He knew better. What had happened was not serious. The discomfort was already passing off and no one need know.

He hurried after his sister, found her at prayer, set her on her mule and tried to bestride his horse. A warning twinge deterred him, so he walked instead and led his precious charge down the mountain. The moon had risen and revealed landmarks he recognized. For a time she was well content and sang psalms of deliverance, but when her heart was emptied she addressed him with asperity and chid him for his ill-handling of the expedition. He did not defend himself—he had scarcely reached the age of defence—and certainly he ought not to have fallen off his horse when the Goths arrived. Still, he felt he had made reparation of a sort and intercepted much that must have been intended for her.

"At what are you laughing?"

"I was not laughing, my sister."

"I saw your face in the moonlight. Why tell me a lie?"

"I am not lying."

"Marcian! Marcian! Have you even after this warning no fear of eternal damnation?" She would have said more but was checked by the sound of hoofs. She was being pursued.

Marcian led the mule into the shadow of a rock, and Euric thundered past them. He looked magnificent suddenly, the torque sparkled, his face was set in a dream. Gallop of witchcraft and vengeance. He was calling to some fiend of the night. Twisted in the rocks, it sounded to Marcian like his own name.

She began to rejoice.

"Yes, sister, he has again missed you, and I know the

path down into the plain, and there you will be safe. But sister, please refrain from singing. Your voice rings too sharp through the night and may lose you your virginity yet."

She opened her mouth to rebuke him but fell silent. The reappearance of the Goth had frightened her, and for the first time in her life she did as she was told. With bowed head, meditating on the universe whose earthly centre she supposed herself to be, she suffered her unworthy brother to guide her. He sought for patches of sand where the mule's feet fell softly, he extricated her chastity from the treacherous mountain curves, night lightened, olives and vineyards crept around them at last, dawn would soon break over their father's farm, when Euric reappeared, riding towards them, furiously.

Someone had to die this time and Marcian assumed it must be himself, and sprang into the middle of the path, ready to grapple, to be trampled on, he knew not what so long as it was his duty. But Euric swerved as they met, and bent sideways, and with both hands and terrific force crashed the torque round the boy's neck. "Marcian!" he shouted, and this time the word rang clear. There was no doubt about it. He vanished into its echoes, leaving nothing behind him but a snake of dust.

Marcian picked himself up, bewildered. The torque fitted him and almost seemed part of him. He touched its roughness and discovered that they were precious stones. Why had he been given it? And so skilfully? One of those stunning feats of horsemanship which were part of the barbarian legend. And were the Goths just warriors? Could they be warlocks as well?

He took hold of the mule and led it on, and they reached the farm without further adventure, and found there confusion of another sort. For some of the slaves in their retinue had found their way back during the night, and to cover their cowardice had spread tales of a great Gothic host which had carried the young

master and mistress into captivity. Lucilla and the
little girls were weeping, Justus was closeted with his
bailiff to discuss the best method of ransom, the neigh-
bours had been warned, the local legion, or what remained of it, was sending troops, and the Bishop had
readily pronounced an anathema. And just as the confusion was at its height the sun rose, there were Marcian
and Perpetua, she praising God as usual and he holding
his head high and necklaced with gold.

Oh, then was sorrow turned into joy, as a resident
catechist remarked, then was captivity led captive, and
Marcian smothered in kisses. Perpetua declined any
caress, for she now reserved herself for the Celestial
Bridegroom, and it was not until she had changed her
raiment and accepted refreshment that she consented
to speak. She then related her adventures as she believed them to have occurred, and without the embellish-
ments subsequently added to them by the Bishop. Her
homily was dry and her sanctity so overwhelming that
every word fell dead. "And after that I had escaped
from that Den of Lions," she concluded, "there was
pursuit, but I erred as to its nature, for which no one
can justly blame me. I supposed that that Son of Belial
was renewing his assault, but his intention was otherwise. He pursued me to ask my pardon."

"But how did you understand what he said, Perpetua?" interrupted one of the little girls. "I did not
know that Goths could speak." She entertained extreme
ideas about the Goths.

"I should like to know what he said, however dreadful it was," said the other little girl. "Did he ask you
to lie down?"

"Silence, Galla, silence, Justa," their parents cried.
"Here are no matters for you." But Perpetua responded
not unbenignly. Looking at them and at Marcian against
whom they were nestling, she explained the situation
further: the Goth had not spoken, only meaningless
shouts, but had done better than speech and offered

all he possessed as a tribute to her virginity: he had given her that golden torque.

"He didn't," cried Marcian before he could stop himself.

"He did, brother, and as an atonement for his sin. In the hope of escaping eternal punishment he cast it down at my feet."

"He didn't. He cast it round my neck."

She was too secure in her sanctity to take grave offence, and all that she said was: "Brother, I am well aware of that. When I said he cast it down at my feet I spoke as David might have, poetically. It is sometimes permissible to be poetic and you would do well to study the Psalms more. Your Father Confessor shall be informed of this. He cast it round your neck because you were in attendance on me."

"I wasn't." The remark was childish, yet it caused his family to stir delightedly. It was the first time she had been gainsaid for years. She ignored him, clapped her hands, and ordered the slaves to place the torque in the basilica, where it would be dedicated to God. "Father, are these your orders?" the boy cried.

Justus, still titular head of the house, looked annoyed. Lucilla ventured to say: "Daughter, we know that the ornament is yours, but our son looks so manly in it, it so suits the coming pride of his race. Daughter, could he not be allowed to display it up to the day of your own dedication?" She rejected this compromise and instructed the slaves to remove it by force. He was outraged and struggled and spat. "It is mine," he cried, "he gave it me, and before the gods die I'll give something to him." No one knew what he meant, and he did not yet know himself. "Before the gods die" was a rustic oath which he ought not to have used. His parents smiled at hearing it on his lips, and it reminded them of older, easier days. "Before the gods die I'll smack your bottom," a peasant woman would say to her child. The torque kissed him goodbye as he blasphemed, and left upon each of his shoulders a small

scarlet scar, which soon faded. Calm at once, he looked
about him in a dazed fashion. "What has happened?"
he asked.

His sister then arranged for him to undergo a penance. The penances were not severe. It was their fre-
quency that enfeebled.

During the five days before the dedication he became humble and helpful, busied himself on pious little
errands and duly revered Perpetua. Their joint adventure grew dim, nothing confirmed it, and it might have
faded away but for the Bishop's comparison of Euric
to a horse. "What about me?" he thought, and exploded
with laughter. For he was not ill-equipped, the slave-
girl had known as much four years ago. And he longed
to meet the Goth in the hills again and bring him to his
knees, and since that could not be he longed for the
unholiness of night.

The night came, stormy and dark after the pageantry
of the day. Everyone was tired, sanctity had not brought
peace. The children were excited and had fits of scream-
feared that the torque might be stolen from the altar.
Lucilla argued that no spirit, however evil, would go
to such lengths. Marcian took his father's side, and undertook to set a guard. He then persuaded them to go
to bed, went to his own chamber to find a cloak against
the rain, and before he could put it on fell asleep.

He woke with a start, convinced that something had
happened. As it had. He had forgotten to set the guard
for the basilica, and if there had been a theft—the
gods help him! He sprang up and went to inspect—it
was only across the courtyard. The door was ajar, but
when he looked in he could see, in the faint light of
candles, that nothing had been disturbed. The torque
stood in its usual position.

But lovelier than usual. He had forgotten how large
it was, how it glowed and curved like a snake, how its
roughnesses intoxicated. He was alone with it at last

and for the last time. It had been round his lover's neck once. The recollection made him go all faint. He swayed against it and found himself in his lover's arms. And he knew, without being told, that Euric, Euric the trickster, had lurked about the farm all day and hidden in the shadows to take him just like this, and he prepared to meet his former fate.

But things did not go as before. Euric was somehow different. He missed opportunities and failed to strike, and presently with an impatient grunt he flung himself face downwards on the basilica floor. The caprices of the barbarians are infinite, and this time he wanted to be raped.

Well, he should be and it wouldn't take long. The boy flung his garment off and mounted. Heaven opened and he rode like a devil, his head down, his heels in the air. *Itque reditque viam totiens,* as a pagan poet puts it, *destillat ab inguine virus,* and as it did so they fused. They had fused into a single monster such as trouble the vigils of saints. He would have withdrawn now but it was too late. Clamped by his lust, he was already half Goth, he felt heavings of laughter which became his own, they could talk without speaking, they never stopped loving, and presently they started to fly. They flew round and round the basilica and defiled it, they shot through its roof into the storm-torn night. There was a blinding lightning flash, and for one delirious moment he saw the farmyard beneath him and all the animals looking up. Then he fell through his own ceiling into his bed and awoke.

It had been a dream, and one for which he would have to do penance. But a dream so violent and warm that it must have been shared.

He sat up and reflected. After all, Goths do sometimes fly. That much is common knowledge. Only last year one of them had haled up an old woman who was hoeing turnips and dropped her into a muck-heap. They cannot fly far—the inscrutable decrees of Providence prevent them. Still, the basilica could not be called far. He got out of his bed to look at it and so discovered that it was on fire.

The alarm had already been given. Slaves shouted, children screamed, a monk pulled a bell, his mother had been hit by the bough of a falling tree. A tempest was abroad, alternating thunder with spouts of rain, and someone had unfastened the gate of the farmyard, and the horses had got out and were going wild. He found his father and they tried to establish order. The basilica, they noted, was not exactly burning, it was flickering with intense luminosity. What really mattered was the increasing panic, which they had not the skill to control.

It was stilled by the arrival of Perpetua.

Clad all in white, she issued from her apartment, advanced majestically and said, "My people, what is amiss?" It was the first time she had called everyone her people. And when she saw the quivering basilica she exclaimed: "It is the Enemy, it is the unhallowed one. By what means he entered I know not, but I will destroy him."

"Save us," all the people cried.

"With God's help I will do so."

It was at this point that Marcian flung himself across her path and said, "Sister, desist." She heard him but did not reply. He was beneath her attention. "Sister, do not, oh I implore you do not," he went on. "I do not, I cannot speak but oh keep away from the place. It may be that seeds of devils—it cannot be, but do not risk it. I think I have dreamed, yet I may dream that I dreamt, in which case the white-hot droppings—" As he said this the basilica's doors opened, and far within on the altar the torque showed scarlet. He cried: "Yes, there he is, there. We have been saved from him once— that is to say, you have and I do not signify. Let me save you again."

She paid no heed to such childishness, but his last

words annoyed her, and she permitted herself to say
scornfully, "Save me, brother? You save *me?*" and went
out intrepidly into the storm. There was a miraculous
lull, and all could see her in the plenitude of her sancti-
tude and power. *Virgo victrix,* she continued her ad-
vance. She entered the basilica, and as she did so a thunderbolt fell and reduced it and her to ashes.

It was the end of the world, or so they all thought,
and so the Bishop thought as soon as the state of the
roads permitted him to return and investigate. He had
always been suspicious of this farm and its inmates and
now he ordered exorcism, but it came too late. There
was nothing to exorcise. The place seemed equally dis-
possessed of good and of evil. He departed disconso-
late, and a number of the religious followed him, leaving a spiritual void.

Only the animals remained unaffected by the catastrophe. They clucked and copulated as usual. And the fields
revived after the rain and promised bumper crops. Marcian had to see to this. There was so much work to do
that he had not the time to repent. He duly recognized
in his spare moments that his impiety and lechery were
to blame and might damn him eternally, and he duly
mourned his distinguished sister and collected what
could be found of her into an urn. But what a relief not
to have her about! And what an economy to be free of
her hangers-on! A few hermits remained, a few shrines
of an earlier religion returned, no one disputed, no
one denounced, and the farm began to prosper. Fortunately it lay out of the route of the barbarian invasions
that devastated the rest of the province. It became a
charmed spot, and Marcian became gay and happy as
well as energetic, and no longer yearned nostalgically for
the hills. Home sweet home was enough. His parents
adored him, and he procured them a comfortable and
amusing old age. His little sisters adored him, and in
due time he took their virginities. He never saw Euric
again but could always send him messages—any young
Goth would accept one. And he gave the name of Euric

to his favourite mare, whose stable he shared on dark nights, and upon whom at the heroic moment he could be seen thundering across the sky, clamped, necklaced in gold.

The Other Boat

1

"Cocoanut, come and play at soldiers."

"I cannot, I am beesy."

"But you must, Lion wants you."

"Yes, come along, man," said Lionel, running up with some paper cocked hats and a sash. It was long long ago, and little boys still went to their deaths stiffly, and dressed in as many clothes as they could find.

"I cannot, I am beesy," repeated Cocoanut.

"But man, what are you busy about?"

"I have soh many things to arrange, man."

"Let's leave him and play by ourselves," said Olive. "We've Joan and Noel and Baby and Lieutenant Bodkin. Who wants Cocoanut?"

"Oh, shut up! *I* want him. We must have him. He's the only one who falls down when he's killed. All you others go on fighting long too long. The battle this morning was a perfect fast. Mother said so."

"Well, I'll die."

"So you say beforehand, but when it comes to the point you won't. Noel won't. Joan won't. Baby doesn't do anything properly—of course he's too little—and you can't expect Lieutenant Bodkin to fall down. Cocoanut, man, do."

"I—weel—not."

"Cocoanut cocoanut cocoanut cocoanut cocoanut cocoanut," said Baby.

The little boy rolled on the deck screaming happily. He liked to be pressed by these handsome good-natured

children. "I must go and see the m'm m'm m'm," he
said.

"The what?"

"The m'm m'm m'm. They live—oh, so many of them
—in the thin part of the ship."

"He means in the bow," said Olive. "Oh, come along,
Lion. He's hopeless."

"What are m'm m'm m'm?"

"M'm." He whirled his arms about, and chalked some
marks on the planks.

"What are those?"

"M'm."

"What's their name?"

"They have no name."

"What do they do?"

"They just go so and oh! and so—ever—always—"

"Flying fish? . . . Fairies? . . . Noughts and crosses?"

"They have no name."

"Mother!" said Olive to a lady who was promenad-
ing with a gentleman, "hasn't everything a name?"

"I suppose so."

"Who's this?" asked the lady's companion.

"He's always hanging on to my children. I don't
know."

"Touch of the tar-brush, eh?"

"Yes, but it doesn't matter on a voyage home. I would
never allow it going to India." They passed on, Mrs
March calling back, "Shout as much as you like, boys,
but don't scream, don't scream."

"They must have a name," said Lionel, recollecting,
"because Adam named all the animals when the Bible
was beginning."

"They weren't in the Bible, m'm m'm m'm; they were
all the time up in the thin part of the sheep, and when
you pop out they pop in, so how could Adam have?"

"Noah's ark is what he's got to now."

Baby said "Noah's ark, Noah's ark, Noah's ark," and
they all bounced up and down and roared. Then, without any compact, they drifted from the saloon deck onto

the lower, and from the lower down the staircase that led to the forecastle, much as the weeds and jellies were drifting about outside in the tropical sea. Soldiering was forgotten, though Lionel said, "We may as well wear our cocked hats." They played with a fox-terrier, who was in the charge of a sailor, and asked the sailor himself if a roving life was a happy one. Then, drifting forward again, they climbed into the bows, where the m'm m'm m'm were said to be.

Here opened a glorious country, much the best in the boat. None of the March children had explored there before, but Cocoanut, having few domesticities, knew it well. That bell that hung on the very peak—it was the ship's bell and if you rang it the ship would stop. Those big ropes were tied into knots—twelve knots an hour. This paint was wet, but only as far as there. Up that hole was coming a Lascar. But of the m'm m'm he said nothing until asked. Then he explained in offhand tones that if you popped out they popped in, so that you couldn't expect to see them.

What treachery! How disappointing! Yet so ill-balanced were the children's minds that they never complained. Olive, in whom the instincts of a lady were already awaking, might have said a few well-chosen words, but when she saw her brothers happy she forgot too, and lifted Baby up onto a bollard because he asked her to. They all screamed. Into their midst came the Lascar and laid down a mat for his three-o'clock prayer. He prayed as if he was still in India, facing westward, not knowing that the ship had rounded Arabia so that his holy places now lay behind him. They continued to scream.

Mrs March and her escort remained on the saloon deck, inspecting the approach to Suez. Two continents were converging with great magnificence of mountains and plain. At their junction, nobly placed, could be seen the smoke and the trees of the town. In addition to her more personal problems, she had become anxious about Pharaoh. "Where exactly was Pharaoh drowned?" she asked Captain Armstrong. "I shall have to show my boys." Captain Armstrong did not know, but he offered to ask Mr Hotblack, the Moravian missionary. Mr Hotblack knew—in fact he knew too much. Somewhat snubbed by the military element in the earlier part of the voyage, he now bounced to the surface, became authoritative and officious, and undertook to wake Mrs March's little ones when they were passing the exact spot. He spoke of the origins of Christianity in a way that made her look down her nose, saying that the Canal was one long genuine Bible picture gallery, that donkeys could still be seen going down into Egypt carrying Holy Families, and naked Arabs wading into the water to fish; "Peter and Andrew by Galilee's shore, why, it hits the truth plumb." A clergyman's daughter and a soldier's wife, she could not admit that Christianity had ever been oriental. What good thing can come out of the Levant, and is it likely that the apostles ever had a touch of the tar-brush? Still, she thanked Mr Hotblack (for, having asked a favour of him, she had contracted an obligation toward him), and she resigned herself to greeting him daily until Southampton, when their paths would part.

Then she observed, against the advancing land, her children playing in the bows without their topis on. The sun in those far-off days was a mighty power and hostile to the Ruling Race. Officers staggered at a touch of it, Tommies collapsed. When the regiment was under canvas, it wore helmets at tiffin, lest the rays penetrated the tent. She shouted at her doomed offspring, she gesticulated, Captain Armstrong and Mr Hotback shouted, but the wind blew their cries backwards. Refusing company, she hurried forward alone; the children were far too excited and covered with paint.

"Lionel! Olive! Olive! What are you doing?"

"M'm m'm m'm, mummy—it's a new game."

"Go back and play properly under the awning at once —it's far too hot. You'll have sunstroke every one of you. Come, Baby!"

"M'm m'm m'm."

"Now, you won't want me to carry a great boy like you, surely."

Baby flung himself round the bollard and burst into tears.

"It always ends like this," said Mrs March as she detached him. "You all behave foolishly and selfishly and then Baby cries. No, Olive—don't help me. Mother would rather do everything herself."

"Sorry," said Lionel gruffly. Baby's shrieks rent the air. Thoroughly naughty, he remained clasping an invisible bollard. As she bent him into a portable shape, another mishap occurred. A sailor—an Englishman—leapt out of the hatchway with a piece of chalk and drew a little circle round her where she stood. Cocoanut screamed, "He's caught you. He's come."

"You're on dangerous ground, lady," said the sailor respectfully. "Men's quarters. Of course we leave it to your generosity."

Tired with the voyage and the noise of the children, worried by what she had left in India and might find in England, Mrs March fell into a sort of trance. She stared at the circle stupidly, unable to move out of it, while Cocoanut danced round her and gibbered.

"Men's quarters—just to keep up the old custom."

"I don't understand."

"Passengers are often kind enough to pay their footing," he said, feeling awkward; though rapacious he was independent. "But of course there's no compulsion, lady. Ladies and gentlemen do as they feel."

"I will certainly do what is customary—Baby, *be* quiet."

"Thank you, lady. We divide whatever you give among the crew. Of course not those chaps." He indicated the Lascar.

"The money shall be sent to you. I have no purse."

He touched his forelock cynically. He did not believe her. She stepped out of the circle and as she did so Cocoanut sprang into it and squatted grinning.

"You're a silly little boy and I shall complain to the

stewardess about you," she told him with unusual heat.
"You never will play any game properly and you stop
the others. You're a silly idle useless unmanly little boy."

2

S.S. Normannia
Red Sea
October, 191–

Hullo the Mater!

You may be thinking it is about time I wrote you
a line, so here goes, however you should have got
my wire sent before leaving Tilbury with the glad
news that I got a last minute passage on this boat
when it seemed quite impossible I should do so.
The Arbuthnots are on it too all right, so is a Lady
Manning who claims acquaintance with Olive, not
to mention several remarkably cheery subalterns,
poor devils, don't know what they are in for in the
tropics. We make up two Bridge tables every night
besides hanging together at other times, and get
called the Big Eight, which I suppose must be regarded as a compliment. How I got my passage is
curious. I was coming away from the S.S. office
after my final try in absolute despair when I ran
into an individual whom you may or may not remember—he was a kid on that other boat when we
cleared all out of India on that unlikely occasion
over ten years ago—got called Cocoanut because
of his peculiar shaped head. He has now turned
into an equally weird youth, who has however
managed to become influential in shipping circles,
I can't think how some people manage to do things.
He duly recognized me—dagoes sometimes have
marvellous memories—and on learning my sad
plight fixed me up with a (single berth) cabin, so
all is well. He is on board too, but our paths seldom cross. He has more than a touch of the tar

brush, so consorts with his own dusky fraternity,
no doubt to their mutual satisfaction.

The heat is awful and I fear this is but a dull
letter in consequence. Bridge I have already mentioned, and there are the usual deck games, betting
on the ship's log, etc., still I think everyone will be
glad to reach Bombay and get into harness. Colonel and Mrs. Arbuthnot are very friendly, and
speaking confidentially I don't think it will do my
prospects any harm having got to know them better. Well I will now conclude this screed and I will
write again when I have rejoined the regiment and
contacted Isabel. Best love to all which naturally
includes yourself from

Your affectionate first born,
Lionel March.

P.S. Lady Manning asks to be remembered to
Olive, nearly forgot.

When Captain March had posted the epistle he rejoined the Big Eight. Although he had spent the entire
day with them they were happy to see him, for he exactly suited them. He was what any rising young officer
ought to be—clean-cut, athletic, good-looking without
being conspicuous. He had had wonderful professional
luck, which no one grudged him: he had got into one of
the little desert wars that were becoming too rare, had
displayed dash and decision, had been wounded, and
had been mentioned in despatches and got his captaincy
early. Success had not spoiled him, nor was he vain of
his personal appearance, although he must have known
that thick fairish hair, blue eyes, glowing cheeks and
strong white teeth constitute, when broad shoulders support them, a combination irresistible to the fair sex. His
hands were clumsier than the rest of him, but bespoke
hard honest work, and the springy gleaming hairs on
them suggested virility. His voice was quiet, his demeanour assured, his temper equable. Like his brother
officers he wore a mess uniform slightly too small for

him, which accentuated his physique—the ladies accen-
tuating theirs by wearing their second best frocks and
reserving their best ones for India.

Bridge proceeded without a hitch, as his mother had
been given to understand it might. She had not been
told that on either side of the players, violet darkening
into black, rushed the sea, nor would she have been
interested. Her son gazed at it occasionally, his forehead furrowed. For despite his outstanding advantages
he was a miserable cardplayer, and he was having
wretched luck. As soon as the Normannia entered the
Mediterranean he had begun to lose, and the "better
luck after Port Said, always the case" that had been
humorously promised him had never arrived. Here in
the Red Sea he had lost the maximum the Big Eight's
moderate stakes allowed. He couldn't afford it, he had
no private means and he ought to be saving up for the
future, also it was humiliating to let down his partner:
Lady Manning herself. So he was thankful when play
terminated and the usual drinks circulated. They sipped
and gulped while the lighthouses on the Arabian coast
winked at them and slid northwards. "Bedfordshire!"
fell pregnantly from the lips of Mrs Arbuthnot. And
they dispersed, with the certainty that the day which was
approaching would exactly resemble the one that had
died.

In this they were wrong.

Captain March waited until all was quiet, still frowning at the sea. Then with something alert and predatory
about him, something disturbing and disturbed, he went
down to his cabin.

"Come een," said a sing-song voice.

For it was not a single cabin, as he had given his
mother to understand. There were two berths, and the
lower one contained Cocoanut. Who was naked. A
brightly coloured scarf lay across him and contrasted
with his blackish-grayish skin, and an aromatic smell
came off him, not at all unpleasant. In ten years he had
developed into a personable adolescent, but still had

the same funny-shaped head. He had been doing his accounts and now he laid them down and gazed at the British officer adoringly.

"Man, I thought you was never coming," he said, and his eyes filled with tears.

"It's only those bloody Arbuthnots and their blasted bridge," replied Lionel and closed the cabin door.

"I thought you was dead."

"Well, I'm not."

"I thought I should die."

"So you will." He sat down on the berth, heavily and with deliberate heaviness. The end of the chase was in sight. It had not been a long one. He had always liked the kid, even on that other boat, and now he liked him more than ever. Champagne in an ice-bucket too. An excellent kid. They couldn't associate on deck with that touch of the tar-brush, but it was a very different business down here, or soon would be. Lowering his voice, he said: "The trouble is we're not supposed to do this sort of thing under any circumstances whatsoever, which you never seem to understand. If we got caught there'd be absolute bloody hell to pay, yourself as well as me, so for God's sake don't make a noise."

"Lionel, O Lion of the Night, love me."

"All right. Stay where you are." Then he confronted the magic that had been worrying him on and off the whole evening and had made him inattentive at cards. A tang of sweat spread as he stripped and a muscle thickened up out of gold. When he was ready he shook off old Cocoanut, who was now climbing about like a monkey, and put him where he had to be, and man-handled him, gently, for he feared his own strength and was always gentle, and closed on him, and they did what they both wanted to do.

Wonderful, wonderful....

They lay entwined, Nordic warrior and subtle supple boy, who belonged to no race and always got what he wanted. All his life he had wanted a toy that would not break, and now he was planning how he would play with Lionel for ever. He had longed for him ever since their first meeting, embraced him in dreams when only that was possible, met him again as the omens foretold, and marked him down, spent money to catch him and lime him, and here he lay, caught, and did not know it.

There they lay caught, both of them, and did not know it, while the ship carried them inexorably towards Bombay.

3

It had not always been so wonderful, wonderful. Indeed the start of the affair had been grotesque and nearly catastrophic. Lionel had stepped on board at Tilbury entirely the simple soldier man, without an inkling of his fate. He had thought it decent of a youth whom he had only known as a child to fix him up with a cabin, but had not expected to find the fellow on board too— still less to have to share the cabin with him. This gave him a nasty shock. British officers are never stabled with dagoes, never, it was too damn awkward for words. However, he could not very well protest under the circumstances, nor did he in his heart want to, for his colour-prejudices were tribal rather than personal, and only worked when an observer was present. The first half-hour together went most pleasantly, they were unpacking and sorting things out before the ship started, he found his childhood's acquaintance friendly and quaint, exchanged reminiscences, and even started teasing and bossing him as in the old days, and got him giggling delightedly. He sprang up to his berth and sat on its edge, swinging his legs. A hand touched them, and he thought no harm until it approached their junction. Then he became puzzled, scared and disgusted in quick succession, leapt down with a coarse barrack-room oath and a brow of thunder and went straight to the Master at Arms to report an offence against decency. Here he showed the dash and decision that had so ad-

vantaged him in desert warfare: in other words he did
not know what he was doing.

The Master at Arms could not be found, and during
the delay Lionel's rage abated somewhat, and he reflected that if he lodged a formal complaint he would
have to prove it, which he could not do, and might have
to answer questions, at which he was never good. So he
went to the Purser instead, and he demanded to be given
alternative accommodation, without stating any reason
for the change. The Purser stared: the boat was chocka-
block full already, as Captain March must have known.
"Don't speak to me like that," Lionel stormed, and
shouldered his way to the gunwale to see England
recede. Here was the worst thing in the world, the
thing for which Tommies got given the maximum, and
here was he bottled up with it for a fortnight. What the
hell was he to do? Go forward with the charge or blow
his own brains out or what?

Onto him thus desperately situated the Arbuthnots
descended. They were slight acquaintances, their presence calmed him, and before long his light military
guffaw rang out as if nothing had happened. They were
pleased to see him, for they were hurriedly forming a
group of sahibs who would hang together during the
voyage and exclude outsiders. With his help the Big
Eight came into being, soon to be the envy of less happy
passengers; introductions; drinks; jokes; difficulties of
securing a berth. At this point Lionel made a shrewd
move: everything gets known on a boat and he had
better anticipate discovery. "I got a passage all right,"
he brayed, "but at the cost of sharing my cabin with a
wog." All condoled, and Colonel Arbuthnot in the
merriest of moods exclaimed, "Let's hope the blacks
don't come off on the sheets," and Mrs Arbuthnot,
wittier still, cried, "Of course they won't, dear, if it's a
wog it'll be the coffees." Everyone shouted with laughter,
the good lady basked in the applause, and Lionel could
not understand why he suddenly wanted to throw himself into the sea. It was so unfair, he was the aggrieved

party, yet he felt himself in the wrong and almost a cad. If only he had found out the fellow's tastes in England he would never have touched him, no, not with tongs. But could he have found out? You couldn't tell by just looking. Or could you? Dimly, after ten years' forgetfulness, something stirred in that faraway boat of his childhood and he saw his mother. . . . Well, she was always objecting to something or other, the poor Mater. No, he couldn't possibly have known.

The Big Eight promptly reserved tables for lunch and all future meals, and Cocoanut and his set were relegated to a second sitting—for it became evident that he too was in a set: the tagrag and coloured bobtail stuff that accumulates in corners and titters and whispers, and may well be influential, but who cares? Lionel regarded it with distaste and looked for a touch of the hangdog in his unspeakable cabinmate, but he was skipping and gibbering on the promenade deck as if nothing had occurred. He himself was safe for the moment, eating curry by the side of Lady Manning, and amusing her by his joke about the various names which the cook would give the same curry on successive days. Again something stabbed him and he thought: "But what shall I do, *do,* when night comes? There will have to be some sort of showdown." After lunch the weather deteriorated. England said farewell to her children with her choppiest seas, her gustiest winds, and the banging of invisible pots and pans in the empyrean. Lady Manning thought she might do better in a deckchair. He squired her to it and then collapsed and re-entered his cabin as rapidly as he had left it a couple of hours earlier.

It now seemed full of darkies, who rose to their feet as he retched, assisted him up to his berth and loosened his collar, after which the gong summoned them to their lunch. Presently Cocoanut and his elderly Parsee secretary looked in to inquire and were civil and helpful and he could not but thank them. The showdown must be postponed. Later in the day he felt better and less inclined for it, and the night did not bring its dreaded perils or indeed anything at all. It was almost as if nothing had happened—almost but not quite. Master Cocoanut had learned his lesson, for he pestered no more, yet he skilfully implied that the lesson was an unimportant one. He was like someone who has been refused a loan and indicates that he will not apply again. He seemed positively not to mind his disgrace—incomprehensibly to Lionel, who expected either repentance or terror. Could it be that he himself had made too much fuss?

In this uneventful atmosphere the voyage across the Bay of Biscay proceeded. It was clear that his favours would not again be asked, and he could not help wondering what would have happened if he had granted them. Propriety was re-established, almost monotonously; if he and Cocoanut ever overlapped in the cabin and had to settle (for instance) who should wash first, they solved the problem with mutual tact.

And then the ship entered the Mediterranean.

Resistance weakened under the balmier sky, curiosity increased. It was an exquisite afternoon—their first decent weather. Cocoanut was leaning out of the porthole to see the sunlit rock of Gibraltar. Lionel leant against him to look too and permitted a slight, a very slight familiarity with his person. The ship did not sink nor did the heavens fall. The contact started something whirling about inside his head and all over him, he could not concentrate on after-dinner bridge, he felt excited, frightened and powerful all at once and kept looking at the stars. Cocoa, who said weird things sometimes, declared that the stars were moving into a good place and could be kept there.

That night champagne appeared in the cabin, and he was seduced. He never could resist champagne. Curse, oh curse! How on earth had it happened? Never again. More happened off the coast of Sicily, more, much more at Port Said, and here in the Red Sea they slept together as a matter of course.

4

And this particular night they lay motionless for longer than usual, as though something in the fall of their bodies had enchanted them. They had never been so content with each other before, and only one of them realized that nothing lasts, that they might be more happy or less happy in the future, but would never again be exactly thus. He tried not to stir, not to breathe, not to live even, but life was too strong for him and he sighed.

"All right?" whispered Lionel.

"Yes."

"Did I hurt?"

"Yes."

"Sorry."

"Why?"

"Can I have a drink?"

"You can have the whole world."

"Lie still and I'll get you one too, not that you deserve it after making such a noise."

"Was I again a noise?"

"You were indeed. Never mind, you shall have a nice drink." Half Ganymede, half Goth, he jerked a bottle out of the ice-bucket. Pop went a cork and hit the partition wall. Sounds of feminine protest became audible, and they both laughed. "Here, hurry up, scuttle up and drink." He offered the goblet, received it back, drained it, refilled. His eyes shone, any depths through which he might have passed were forgotten. "Let's make a night of it," he suggested. For he was of the conventional type who once the conventions are broken breaks them into little pieces, and for an hour or two there was nothing he wouldn't say or do.

Meanwhile the other one, the deep one, watched. To him the moment of ecstasy was sometimes the moment of vision, and his cry of delight when they closed had wavered into fear. The fear passed before he could understand what it meant or against what it warned him, against nothing perhaps. Still, it seemed wiser to watch. As in business, so in love, precautions are desirable, insurances must be effected. "Man, shall we now perhaps have our cigarette?" he asked.

This was an established ritual, an assertion deeper than speech that they belonged to each other and in their own way. Lionel assented and lit the thing, pushed it between dusky lips, pulled it out, pulled at it, replaced it, and they smoked it alternately with their faces touching. When it was finished Cocoa refused to extinguish the butt in an ashtray but consigned it through the porthole into the flying waters with incomprehensible words. He thought the words might protect them, though he could not explain how, or what they were.

"That reminds me . . ." said Lionel, and stopped. He had been reminded, and for no reason, of his mother. He did not want to mention her in his present state, the poor old Mater, especially after all the lies she had been told.

"Yes, of what did it remind you, our cigarette? Yes and please? I should know."

"Nothing." And he stretched himself, flawless except for a scar down in the groin.

"Who gave you that?"

"One of your fuzzy-wuzzy cousins."

"Does it hurt?"

"No." It was a trophy from the little desert war. An assegai had nearly unmanned him, nearly but not quite, which Cocoa said was a good thing. A dervish, a very holy man, had once told him that what nearly destroys may bring strength and can be summoned in the hour of revenge. "I've no use for revenge," Lionel said.

"Oh Lion, why not when it can be so sweet?"

He shook his head and reached up for his pyjamas, a sultan's gift. It was presents all the time in these days. His gambling debts were settled through the secretary, and if he needed anything, or was thought to need it, something or other appeared. He had ceased to protest and now accepted indiscriminately. He could trade away the worst of the junk later on—some impossible jewelry for instance which one couldn't be seen dead in. He did wish, though, that he could have given presents in return, for he was anything but a sponger. He had made an attempt two nights previously, with dubious results. "I seem always taking and never giving," he had said. "Is there nothing of mine you'd fancy? I'd be so glad if there was." To receive the reply: "Yes. Your hairbrush"—"My *hairbrush?*"—and he was not keen on parting with this particular object, for it had been a coming-of-age gift from Isabel. His hesitation brought tears to the eyes, so he had to give in. "You're welcome to my humble brush if you want it, of course. I'll just comb it out for you first"—"No, no, as it is uncombed," and it was snatched away fanatically. Almost like a vulture snatching. Odd little things like this did happen occasionally, m'm m'm m'ms he called them, for they reminded him of oddities on the other boat. They did no one any harm, so why worry? Enjoy yourself while you can. He lolled at his ease and let the gifts rain on him as they would—a Viking at a Byzantine court, spoiled, adored and not yet bored.

This was certainly the life, and sitting on one chair with his feet on another he prepared for their usual talk, which might be long or short but was certainly the life. When Cocoanut got going it was fascinating. For all the day he had slipped around the ship, discovering people's weaknesses. More than that, he and his cronies were cognizant of financial possibilities that do not appear in the City columns, and could teach one how to get rich if one thought it worth while. More than that, he had a vein of fantasy. In the midst of something ribald and scandalous—the discovery of Lady Manning, for instance: Lady Manning of all people in the cabin of the Second Engineer—he imagined the discovery being made by a flying fish who had popped through the Engineer's porthole, and he indicated the expression on the fish's face.

Yes, this was the life, and one that he had never experienced in his austere apprenticeship: luxury, gaiety, kindness, unusualness, and delicacy that did not exclude brutal pleasure. Hitherto he had been ashamed of being built like a brute: his preceptors had condemned carnality or had dismissed it as a waste of time, and his mother had ignored its existence in him and all her children; being hers, they had to be pure.

What to talk about this pleasurable evening? How about the passport scandal? For Cocoanut possessed two passports, not one like most people, and they confirmed a growing suspicion that he might not be altogether straight. In England Lionel would have sheered off at once from such a subject, but since Gibraltar they had become so intimate and morally so relaxed that he experienced nothing but friendly curiosity. The information on the passports was conflicting, so that it was impossible to tell the twister's age, or where he had been born or indeed what his name was. "You could get into serious trouble over this," Lionel had warned him, to be answered by irresponsible giggles. "You could, you know. However, you're no better than a monkey, and I suppose a monkey can't be expected to know its own name." To which the reply had been "Lion, he don't know nothing at all. Monkey's got to come along to tell a Lion he's alive." It was never easy to score. He had picked up his education, if that was the word for it, in London, and his financial beginnings in Amsterdam, one of the passports was Portuguese, the other Danish, and half the blood must be Asiatic, unless a drop was Negro.

"Now come along, tell me the truth and nothing but the truth for a change," he began. "Ah, that reminds me I've at last got off that letter to the Mater. She adores news. It was a bit difficult to think of anything to interest her, however I filled it up with tripe about the Arbuthnots, and threw you in at the end as a sort of makeweight."

"To make what sort of weight?"

"Well, naturally I didn't say what we do. I'm not stark staring raving mad. I merely mentioned I'd run into you in the London office, and got a cabin through you, that is to say single-berth one. I threw dust in her eyes all right."

"Dear Lionel, you don't know how to throw dust or even where it is. Of mud you know a little, good, but not dust. Why bring me into the matter at all?"

"Oh, for the sake of something to say."

"Did you say I too was on board?"

"I did in passing," he said irritably, for he now realized he had better not have. "I was writing that damned epistle, not you, and I had to fill it up. Don't worry—she's forgotten your very existence by this time."

The other was certain she hadn't. If he had foreseen this meeting and had worked towards it through dreams, why should not an anxious parent have foreseen it too? She had valid reasons for anxiety, for things had actually started on that other boat. A trivial collision between children had alerted them towards each other as men. Thence had their present happiness sprung, thither might it wither, for the children had been disturbed. That vengeful onswishing of skirts . . . ! "What trick can I think of this time that will keep him from her? I love him, I am clever, I have money. I will try." The first step was to contrive his exit from the Army. The second step was to dispose of that English girl in India, called Isabel, about whom too little was known. Marriage or virginity or concubinage for Isabel? He had no scruples at perverting Lionel's instincts in order to gratify his own, or at endangering his prospects of paternity. All that mattered was their happiness, and he thought he knew what that was. Much depended on the next few days: he had to work hard and to work with the stars. His mind played round approaching problems, combining them, retreating from them, and aware all the time of a further problem, of something in the beloved which he did not understand. He half-closed his eyes and watched, and listened through half-closed ears. By not being too much on the spot and sacrificing shrewdness to vision he sometimes opened a door. And sure enough Lionel said, "As a matter of fact the Mater never liked you," and a door opened, slowly.

"Man, how should she? Oh, when the chalk went from the hand of the sailor round the feet of the lady and she could not move and we all knew it, and oh man how we mocked her."

"I don't remember—well, I do a little. It begins to come back to me and does sound like the sort of thing that would put her off. She certainly went on about you after we landed, and complained that you made things interesting when they weren't, funny thing to say, still the Mater is pretty funny. So we put our heads together as children sometimes do—"

"Do they? Oh yes."

"—and Olive who's pretty bossy herself decreed we shouldn't mention you again as it seemed to worry her extra and she had just had a lot of worry. He actually— I hadn't meant to tell you this, it's a dead secret."

"It shall be. I swear. By all that is without me and within me I swear." He became incomprehensible in his excitement and uttered words in that unknown tongue. Nearly all tongues were unknown to Lionel, and he was impressed.

"Well, he actually—"

"Man, of whom do you now speak?"

"Oh yes, the Mater's husband, my Dad. He was in the Army too, in fact he attained the rank of major, but a quite unspeakable thing happened—he went native somewhere out East and got cashiered—deserted his wife and left her with five young children to bring up, and no money. She was taking us all away from him when you met us and still had a faint hope that he might pull himself together and follow her. Not he. He never even wrote—remember, this is absolutely secret."

"Yes, yes," but he thought the secret a very tame one: how else should a middle-aged husband behave? "But,

Lionel, one question to you the more. For whom did the Major desert the Mater?"

"He went native."

"With a girl or with a boy?"

"A boy? Good God! Well, I mean to say, with a girl, naturally—I mean, it was somewhere right away in the depths of Burma."

"Even in Burma there are boys. At least I once heard so. But the Dad went native with a girl. Ver' well. Might not therefore there be offspring?"

"If there were, they'd be half-castes. Pretty depressing prospect. Well, you know what I mean. My family— Dad's, that's to say—can trace itself back nearly two hundred years, and the Mater's goes back to the War of the Roses. It's really pretty awful, Cocoa."

The half-caste smiled as the warrior floundered. Indeed he valued him most when he fell full length. And the whole conversation—so unimportant in itself—gave him a sense of approaching victory which he had not so far entertained. He had a feeling that Lionel knew that he was in the net or almost in it, and did not mind. Cross-question him further! Quick! Rattle him! "Is Dad dead?" he snapped.

"I couldn't very well come East if he wasn't. He has made our name stink in these parts. As it is I've had to change my name, or rather drop half of it. He called himself Major Corrie March. We were all proud of the 'Corrie' and had reason to be. Try saying 'Corrie March' to the Big Eight here, and watch the effect."

"You must get two passports, must you not, one with and one without a 'Corrie' on it. I will fix it, yes? At Bombay?"

"So as I can cheat like you? No, thank you. My name is Lionel March and that's my name." He poured out some more champagne.

"Are you like him?"

"I should hope not. I hope I'm not cruel and remorseless and selfish and self-indulgent and a liar as he was."

"I don't mean unimportant things like that. I mean are you like him to look at?"

"You have the strangest ideas of what is important."

"Was his body like yours?"

"How should I know?"—and he was suddenly shy. "I was only a kid and the Mater's torn up every photograph of him she could lay her hands on. He was a hundred per cent Aryan all right, and there was plenty of him as there certainly is of me—indeed there'll be too much of me if I continue swilling at this rate. Suppose we talk about your passports for a change."

"Was he one in whom those who sought rest found fire, and fire rest?"

"I've not the least idea what you're talking about. Do you mean I'm such a one myself?"

"I do."

"I've not the least idea—" Then he hesitated. "Unless . . . no, you're daft as usual, and in any case we've spent more than enough time in dissecting my unfortunate parent. I brought him up to show you how much the Mater has to put up with, one has to make endless allowances for her and you mustn't take it amiss if she's unreasonable about you. She'd probably like you if she got the chance. There was something else that upset her at the time. . . . I seem bringing out all the family skeletons in a bunch, still they won't go any further, and I feel like chattering to someone about everything, once in a way. I've never had anyone to talk to like you. Never, and don't suppose I ever shall. Do you happen to remember the youngest of us all, the one we called Baby?"

"Ah, that pretty Baby!"

"Well, a fortnight after we landed and while we were up at my grandfather's looking for a house, that poor kid died."

"Die what of?" he exclaimed, suddenly agitated. He raised his knees and rested his chin on them. With his nudity and his polished duskiness and his strange-shaped head, he suggested an image crouched outside a tomb.

"Influenza, quite straightforward. It was going through the parish and he caught it. But the worst of it was the Mater wouldn't be reasonable. She would insist that it was sunstroke, and that he got it running about with no topi on when she wasn't looking after him properly in this very same Red Sea."

"Her poor pretty Baby. So I killed him for her."

"Cocoa! How ever did you guess that? It's exactly what she twisted it round to. We had quite a time with her. Olive argued, grandfather prayed . . . and I could only hang around and do the wrong thing, as I generally do."

"But she—she saw me only, running in the sun with my devil's head, and m'm m'm m'm all you follow me till the last one the tiny one dies, and she, she talking to an officer, a handsome one, oh to sleep in his arms as I shall in yours, so she forgets the sun and it strikes the tiny one. I see."

"Yes, you see in a wrong sort of way"; every now and then came these outbursts which ought to be rubbish yet weren't. Wrong of course about his mother, who was the very soul of purity, and over Captain Armstrong, who had become their valued family adviser. But right over Baby's death: she actually had declared that the idle unmanly imp had killed him, and designedly. Of recent years she had not referred to the disaster, and might have forgotten it. He was more than ever vexed with himself for mentioning Cocoanut in the letter he had recently posted to her.

"Did I kill him for you also?"

"For me? Of course not. I know the difference between influenza and sunstroke, and you don't develop the last-named after a three weeks' interval."

"Did I kill him for anyone—or for anything?"

Lionel gazed into eyes that gazed through him and through cabin walls into the sea. A few days ago he would have ridiculed the question, but tonight he was respectful. This was because his affection, having struck earthward, was just trying to flower. "Something's worrying you? Why not tell me about it?" he said.

"Did you love pretty Baby?"

"No, I was accustomed to see him around but he was too small to get interested in and I haven't given him a thought for years. So all's well."

"There is nothing between us then?"

"Why should there be?"

"Lionel—dare I ask you one more question?"

"Yes, of course."

"It is about blood. It is the last of all the questions. Have you ever shed blood?"

"No—oh, sorry, I should have said yes. I forgot that little war of mine. It goes clean out of my head between times. A battle's such a mess-up, you wouldn't believe, and this one had a miniature sandstorm raging to make confusion more confounded. Yes, I shed blood all right, or so the official report says. I didn't know at the time." He was suddenly silent. Vividly and unexpectedly the desert surged up, and he saw it as a cameo, from outside. The central figure—a grotesque one—was himself going berserk, and close to him was a dying savage who had managed to wound him and was trying to speak.

"I hope I never shed blood," the other said. "I do not blame others, but for me never."

"I don't expect you ever will. You're not exactly cut out for a man of war. All the same, I've fallen for you."

He had not expected to say this, and it was the unexpectedness that so delighted the boy. He turned away his face. It was distorted with joy and suffused with the odd purplish tint that denoted violent emotion. Everything had gone fairly right for a long time. Each step in the stumbling confession had brought him nearer to knowing what the beloved was like. But an open avowal —he had not hoped for so much. "Before morning I shall have enslaved him," he thought, "and he will begin doing whatever I put into his mind." Even now he did not exult, for he knew by experience that though he always got what he wanted he seldom kept it, also that too much adoration can develop a flaw in the jewel. He remained impassive, crouched like a statue, chin on knees, hands round ankles, waiting for words to which he could safely reply.

"It seemed just a bit of foolery at first," he went on. "I woke up properly ashamed of myself after Gib, I don't mind telling you. Since then it's been getting so different, and now it's nothing but us. I tell you one thing though, one silly mistake I've made. I ought never to have mentioned you in that letter to the Mater. There's no advantage in putting her on the scent of something she can't understand; it's all right what we do, I don't mean that."

"So you want the letter back?"

"But it's posted! Not much use wanting it."

"Posted?" He was back to his normal and laughed gaily, his sharp teeth gleaming. "What is posting? Nothing at all, even in a red English pillar-box. Even thence you can get most things out, and here is a boat. No! My secretary comes to you tomorrow morning: 'Excuse me, Captain March, sir, did you perhaps drop this unposted letter upon the deck?' You thank secretary, you take letter, you write Mater a better letter. Does anything trouble you now?"

"Not really. Except—"

"Except what?"

"Except I'm—I don't know. I'm fonder of you than I know how to say."

"Should that trouble you?"

O calm mutual night, to one of them triumphant and promising both of them peace! O silence except for the boat throbbing gently! Lionel sighed, with a happiness he couldn't understand. "You ought to have someone to look after you," he said tenderly. Had he said this before to a woman and had she responded? No such recollection disturbed him, he did not even know that he was falling in love. "I wish I could stay with you myself, but of course that's out of the question. If only things

were a little different I—Come along, let's get our
sleep."

"You shall sleep and you shall awake." For the moment was upon them at last, the flower opened to
receive them, the appointed star mounted the sky, the
beloved leaned against him to switch off the light over
by the door. He closed his eyes to anticipate divine
darkness. He was going to win. All was happening as he
had planned, and when morning came and practical life
had to be re-entered he would have won.

"Damn!"

The ugly stupid little word rattled out. "Damn and
blast," Lionel muttered. As he stretched towards the
switch, he had noticed the bolt close to it, and he discovered that he had left the door unbolted. The consequences could have been awkward. "Pretty careless of
me," he reflected, suddenly wide awake. He looked
round the cabin as a general might at a battlefield nearly
lost by his own folly. The crouched figure was only a
unit in it, and no longer the centre of desire. "Cocoa,
I'm awfully sorry," he went on. "As a rule it's you who
take the risks, this time it's me. I apologize."

The other roused himself from the twilight where he
had hoped to be joined, and tried to follow the meaningless words. Something must have miscarried, but
what? The sound of an apology was odious. He had
always loathed the English trick of saying "It's all my
fault"; and if he encountered it in business it provided
an extra incentive to cheat, and it was contemptible on
the lips of a hero. When he grasped what the little trouble was and what the empty "damns" signified, he closed
his eyes again and said, "Bolt the door therefore."

"I have."

"Turn out the light therefore."

"I will. But a mistake like this makes one feel all insecure. It could have meant a courtmartial."

"Could it, man?" he said sadly—sad because the
moment towards which they were moving might be passing, because the chances of their convergence might be

lost. What could he safely say? "You was not to blame over the door, dear Lion," he said. "I mean we was both to blame. I knew it was unlocked all the time." He said this hoping to console the beloved and to recall him to the entrance of night. He could not have made a more disastrous remark.

"You knew. But why didn't you say?"

"I had not the time."

"Not the time to say 'Bolt the door'?"

"No, I had not the time. I did not speak because there was no moment for such a speech."

"No moment when I've been here for ages?"

"And when in that hour? When you come in first? Then? When you embrace me and summon my heart's blood. Is that the moment to speak? When I rest in your arms and you in mine, when our cigarette burns us, when we drink from one glass? When you are smiling? Do I interrupt then? Do I then say, 'Captain March, sir, you have however forgotten to bolt the cabin door?' And when we talk of our faraway boat and of poor pretty Baby whom I never killed and I did not want to kill, and I never dreamt to kill—of what should we talk but of things far away? Lionel, no, no. Lion of the Night, come back to me before our hearts cool. Here is our place and we have so far no other and only we can guard each other. The door shut, the door unshut, is nothing, and is the same."

"It wouldn't be nothing if the steward had come in," said Lionel grimly.

"What harm if he did come in?"

"Give him the shock of his life, to say the least of it."

"No shock at all. Such men are accustomed to far worse. He would be sure of a larger tip and therefore pleased. 'Excuse me, gentlemen. . . .' Then he goes and tomorrow my secretary tips him."

"Cocoa, for God's sake, the things you sometimes say . . ." The cynicism repelled him. He noticed that it sometimes came after a bout of high faluting. It was a sort of backwash. "You never seem to realize the risks we run, either. Suppose I got fired from the Army through this."

"Yes, suppose?"

"Well, what else could I do?"

"You could be my assistant manager at Basra."

"Not a very attractive alternative." He was not sure whether he was being laughed at or not, which always rattled him, and the incident of the unbolted door increased in importance. He apologized again "for my share in it" and added, "You've not told that scruffy Parsee of yours about us, I do trust."

"No. Oh no no no no and oh no. Satisfied?"

"Nor the Goanese steward?"

"Not told. Only tipped. Tip all. Of what other use is money?"

"I shall think you've tipped me next."

"So I have."

"That's not a pretty thing to say."

"I am not pretty. I am not like you." And he burst into tears. Lionel knew that nerves were on edge, but the suggestion that he was a hireling hurt him badly. He whose pride and duty it was to be independent and command! Had he been regarded as a male prostitute? "What's upset you?" he said as kindly as possible. "Don't take on so, Cocoa, there's no occasion for it."

The sobs continued. He was weeping because he had planned wrongly. Rage rather than grief convulsed him. The bolt unbolted, the little snake not driven back into its hole—he had foreseen everything else and ignored the enemy at the gate. Bolt and double-bolt now—they would never complete the movement of love. As sometimes happened to him when he was unhinged, he could foretell the immediate future, and he knew before Lionel spoke exactly what he was going to say.

"I think I'll go on deck for a smoke."

"Go."

"I've a bit of a headache with this stupid misunderstanding, plus too much booze. I want a breath of fresh air. Then I'll come back."

"When you come back you will not be you. And I may not be I."

Further tears. Snivellings. "We're both to blame," said Lionel patiently, taking up the cigarette-case. "I'm not letting myself off. I was careless. But why you didn't tell me at once I shall never understand, not if you talk till you're blue. I've explained to you repeatedly that this game we've been playing's a risky one, and honestly I think we'd better never have started it. However, we'll talk about that when you're not so upset." Here he remembered that the cigarette-case was one of his patron's presents to him, so he substituted for it a favourite old pipe. The change was observed and it caused a fresh paroxysm. Like many men of the warm-blooded type, he was sympathetic to a few tears but exasperated when they persisted. Fellow crying and not trying to stop. Fellow crying as if he had the right to cry. Repeating "I'll come back" as cordially as he could, he went up on deck to think the whole situation over. For there were several things about it he didn't like at all.

Cocoanut stopped weeping as soon as he was alone. Tears were a method of appeal which had failed, and he must seek comfort for his misery and desolation elsewhere. What he longed to do was to climb up into Lionel's berth above him and snuggle down there and dream that he might be joined. He dared not. Whatever else he ventured, it must not be that. It was forbidden to him, although nothing had ever been said. It was the secret place, the sacred place whence strength issued, as he had learned during the first half-hour of the voyage. It was the lair of a beast who might retaliate. So he remained down in his own berth, the safe one, where his lover would certainly never return. It was wiser to work and make money, and he did so for a time. It was still wiser to sleep, and presently he put his ledger aside and lay motionless. His eyes closed. His nostrils occasionally twitched as if responding to something which the rest of his body ignored. The scarf covered him. For it was one of his many superstitions that it is dangerous to lie unclad when alone. Jealous of what she sees, the hag comes with her scimitar, and she. . . . Or she lifts up a man when he feels lighter than air.

5

Up on deck, alone with his pipe, Lionel began to recover his poise and his sense of leadership. Not that he and his pipe were really alone, for the deck was covered with passengers who had had their bedding carried up and now slept under the stars. They lay prone in every direction, and he had to step carefully between them on his way to the railing. He had forgotten that this migration happened nightly as soon as a boat entered the Red Sea; his nights had passed otherwise and elsewhere. Here lay a guileless subaltern, cherry-cheeked; there lay Colonel Arbuthnot, his bottom turned. Mrs Arbuthnot lay parted from her lord in the ladies' section. In the morning, very early, the Goanese stewards would awake the sahibs and carry their bedding back to their cabins. It was an old ritual—not practised in the English Channel or the Bay of Biscay or even in the Mediterranean —and on previous voyages he had taken part in it.

How decent and reliable they looked, the folk to whom he belonged! He had been born one of them, he had his work with them, he meant to marry into their caste. If he forfeited their companionship he would become nobody and nothing. The widened expanse of the sea, the winking lighthouse, helped to compose him, but what really recalled him to sanity was this quiet sleeping company of his peers. He liked his profession, and was rising in it thanks to that little war; it would be mad to jeopardize it, which he had been doing ever since he drank too much champagne at Gibraltar.

Not that he had ever been a saint. No—he had occasionally joined a brothel expedition, so as not to seem better than his fellow officers. But he had not been so much bothered by sex as were some of them. He hadn't had the time, what with his soldiering duties and his obligations at home as eldest son, and the doc said an occasional wet dream was nothing to worry about. Don't sleep on your back, though. On this simple routine he had proceeded since puberty. And during the past few months he had proceeded even further. Learning that he was to be posted to India, where he would contact Isabel, he had disciplined himself more severely and practised chastity even in thought. It was the least he could do for the girl he hoped to marry. Sex had entirely receded—only to come charging back like a bull. That infernal Cocoa—the mischief he had done. He had woken up so much that might have slept.

For Isabel's sake, as for his profession's, their foolish relationship must stop at once. He could not think how he had yielded to it, or why it had involved him so deeply. It would have ended at Bombay, it would have to end now, and Cocoanut must cry his eyes out if he thought it worth while. So far all was clear. But behind Isabel, behind the Army, was another power, whom he could not consider calmly: his mother, blind-eyed in the midst of the enormous web she had spun—filaments drifting everywhere, strands catching. There was no reasoning with her or about her, she understood nothing and controlled everything. She had suffered too much and was too high-minded to be judged like other people, she was outside carnality and incapable of pardoning it. Earlier in the evening, when Cocoa mentioned her, he had tried to imagine her with his father, enjoying the sensations he was beginning to find so pleasant, but the attempt was sacrilegious and he was shocked at himself. From the great blank country she inhabited came a voice condemning him and all her children for sin, but condemning him most. There was no parleying with her—she was a voice. God had not granted her ears— nor could she see, mercifully: the sight of him stripping[1] would have killed her. He, her first-born, set apart for

---

[1] stripping: *Forster's substitution for* topping a dago.

the redemption of the family name. His surviving brother was too much a bookworm to be of any use, and the other two were girls.

He spat into the sea. He promised her "Never again". The words went out into the night like other enchantments. He said them aloud, and Colonel Arbuthnot, who was a light sleeper, woke up and switched on his torch.

"Hullo, who's that, what's there?"

"March, sir, Lionel March. I'm afraid I've disturbed you."

"No, no, Lionel, that's all right, I wasn't asleep. Ye gods, what gorgeous pyjamas the fellow's wearing. What's he going about like a lone wolf for? Eh?"

"Too hot in my cabin, sir. Nothing sinister."

"How goes the resident wog?"

"The resident wog he sleeps."

"By the way, what's his name?"

"Moraes, I believe."

"Exactly. Mr Moraes is in for trouble."

"Oh. What for, sir?"

"For being on board. Lady Manning has just heard the story. It turns out that he gave someone in the London office a fat bribe to get him a passage though the boat was full, and as an easy way out they put him into your cabin. I don't care who gives or takes bribes. Doesn't interest me. But if the Company thinks it can treat a British officer like that it's very much mistaken. I'm going to raise hell at Bombay."

"He's not been any particular nuisance," said Lionel after a pause.

"I daresay not. It's the question of our prestige in the East, and it is also very hard luck on you, very hard. Why don't you come and sleep on deck like the rest of the gang?"

"Sound idea, I will."

"We've managed to cordon off this section of the deck, and woe betide anything black that walks this way, if it's only a beetle. Good night."

"Good night, sir." Then something snapped and he heard himself shouting, "Bloody rubbish, leave the kid alone."

"Wh—what's that, didn't catch," said the puzzled Colonel.

"Nothing sir, sorry sir." And he was back in the cabin.

Why on earth had he nearly betrayed himself just as everything was going right? There seemed a sort of devil around. At the beginning of the voyage he had tempted him to throw himself overboard for no reason, but this was something more serious. "When you come back to the cabin you will not be you," Cocoa had said; and was it so?

However, the lower berth was empty, that was something, the boy must have gone to the lav, and he slipped out of his effeminate pyjamas and prepared to finish the night where he belonged—a good sleep there would steady him. His forearm was already along the rail, his foot poised for the upspring, when he saw what had happened.

"Hullo, Cocoanut, up in my berth for a change?" he said in clipped officer-tones, for it was dangerous to get angry. "Stay there if you want to, I've just decided to sleep on deck." There was no reply, but his own remarks pleased him and he decided to go further. "As a matter of fact I shan't be using our cabin again except when it is absolutely necessary," he continued. "It's scarcely three days to Bombay, so I can easily manage, and I shan't, we shan't be meeting again after disembarkation. As I said earlier on, the whole thing has been a bit of a mistake. I wish we . . ." He stopped. If only it wasn't so difficult to be kind! But his talk with the Colonel and his communion with the Mater prevented it. He must keep with his own people, or he would perish. He added, "Sorry to have to say all this."

"Kiss me."

The words fell quietly after his brassiness and vulgarity and he could not answer them. The face was close to his now, the body curved away seductively into darkness.

"Kiss me."

"No."

"Noah? No? Then I kiss you." And he lowered his mouth onto the muscular forearm and bit it.

Lionel yelped with the pain.

"Bloody bitch, wait till I . . ." Blood oozed between the gold-bright hairs. "You wait. . . ." And the scar in his groin reopened. The cabin vanished. He was back in a desert fighting savages. One of them asked for mercy, stumbled, and found none.

The sweet act of vengeance followed, sweeter than ever for both of them, and as ecstasy hardened into agony his hands twisted the throat. Neither of them knew when the end came, and he when he realized it felt no sadness, no remorse. It was part of a curve that had long been declining, and had nothing to do with death. He covered again with his warmth and kissed the closed eyelids tenderly and spread the bright-coloured scarf. Then he burst out of the stupid cabin onto the deck, and naked and with the seeds of love on him he dived into the sea.

The scandal was appalling. The Big Eight did their best, but it was soon all over the boat that a British officer had committed suicide after murdering a half-caste. Some of the passengers recoiled from such news. Others snuffled for more. The secretary of Moraes was induced to gossip and hint at proclivities, the cabin steward proved to have been over-tipped, the Master at Arms had had complaints which he had managed to stifle, the Purser had been suspicious throughout, and the doctor who examined the injuries divulged that strangulation was only one of them, and that March had been a monster in human form, of whom the earth was well rid. The cabin was sealed up for further examination later, and the place where the two boys had made love and the tokens they had exchanged in their love went on without them to Bombay. For Lionel had been only a boy.

His body was never recovered—the blood on it quickly attracted the sharks. The body of his victim was consigned to the deep with all possible speed. There was a slight disturbance at the funeral. The native crew had become interested in it, no one understood why, and when the corpse was lowered were heard betting which way it would float. It moved northwards—contrary to the prevailing current—and there were clappings of hands and some smiles.

Finally Mrs March had to be informed. Colonel Arbuthnot and Lady Manning were deputed for the thankless task. Colonel Arbuthnot assured her that her son's death had been accidental, whatever she heard to the contrary; that he had stumbled overboard in the darkness during a friendly talk they had had together on deck. Lady Manning spoke with warmth and affection of his good looks and good manners and his patience "with us old fogies at our Bridge". Mrs March thanked them for writing but made no comment. She also received a letter from Lionel himself—the one that should have been intercepted in the post—and she never mentioned his name again.

Three Courses and a Dessert

being a new and gastronomic version of the old game of "consequences"

The first course by Christopher Dilke

Out of the bright sunshine of July, Captain Jervis stepped in one pace into the restful obscurity of the hotel. He stopped, hoping to hear some sound which would indicate the whereabouts of the person left in charge. There was silence. His arrival had occasioned no curiosity or even notice. He walked through the hall and found himself in a cocktail bar of which the bar was closed and locked. Further still, he emerged onto a covered terrace with glass panes overlooking the harbour.

It was disappointing to find no one about the place. He had had on the tip of his tongue the phrases, a little grandiose, in which he would have ordered dinner for five. Four of the five, after all, were persons of some importance, the chief actors in a drama of war and treachery. The fact that he, the fifth, had so minor a part in the affair—little more than the ordering of dinner —was what inspired his desire to seem important. He knew well that once the others arrived he would be unimportant enough, a person to make a note, to hurry up the dinner, or to answer the telephone. He was intelligent, the Brigadier thought a great deal of him, he had not done at all badly in the Army, but he was still only the Staff Captain. His job was to keep quiet and obey orders.

Through the large windows he could see out over the harbour and away beyond the headland to where a smudge of smoke announced the return of the little expeditionary force. That meant that three of the diners were on their way. It confirmed the news which had reached Jervis earlier through the hands of the cipher staff. Acting on his orders, he had at once called the Foreign Office on the telephone. A Mr Fitzwilliam was apparently not much excited, but signified his readiness to catch the 4.42 from London. Mr Fitzwilliam was presumably now not much more than a hundred miles away and this distance was rapidly decreasing.

The Brigade Major, it had been decided, would look after the disembarkation. The Brigadier, the lady, Mr Fitzwilliam and of course himself would have the honour of dining with the gentleman who had put them all to so much trouble. It was strange, thought Jervis, that his government should spend thousands, perhaps millions, of pounds for the purpose of capturing one person. And no doubt they would put this person, who had killed many innocent civilians, into a comfortable prison for a number of years.

But the Silver Fish Hotel remained empty of any sign of life. Captain Jervis glanced at his watch. In ten minutes it would be opening-time. He walked back into the hall. Under a quiff of fair hair his blue eyes were bright and watchful. He was convinced that someone must be in the hotel.

From the hall, swing doors opened into a long diningroom. Small tables were neatly arranged for four and two diners. A conically folded napkin and a fingerbowl awaited each client. Above the mantelpiece was a picture representing the Silver Fish in days gone by. An old salt, charmingly posed in the foreground, lent colour to the idea that it was some old fisherman's inn. Jervis made for a screen, which blocked one corner of the room. Behind this screen were more swing doors, the type of doors which in all well-conducted restaurants lead to the kitchen. And at this time of day, thought

Jervis, there must be someone in the kitchen. But it was a scullery which he entered next. On the table stood a can of cream. He stopped and dipped his finger. The cream formed a smooth film. He licked it off and turned to the baize door in front of him.

When he pushed this open, here at last there was someone. John Jervis, aged twenty-four, and having spent his whole adult life as an Army officer in wartime, was neither experienced nor *blasé*. Now he felt as tongue-tied and ingenuous as he had ever been. He might have been back at the Eureka tennis club, five years ago, watching the nymphs who played patball on summer evenings.

It was a young girl with dark red hair and a pale, creamy complexion whom he saw. Her eyes had very long lashes and her hair was dark where it clustered against her neck. She wore a pale green summer dress, and since she was leaning back this did not conceal the lines of her body. The unusual length of leg might have appealed to a connoisseur. By Jervis it passed almost unnoticed in the general impression. She had perhaps been shelling peas, for a heap of pods was on the table beside her. She was leaning against the encircling arm of a man in the uniform of a chef. This man was of generous stature and had a fair beard nearly a foot in length. He looked the kind of person whom one should know by sight. The girl had been looking up into the chef's face, but as Jervis entered she turned her greenish-blue eyes towards him with a look of inquiry. At the same time she disengaged herself from the chef's arm and came a step forward from the table. She fumbled with the knot of her apron behind her waist.

"You want the bar?" she asked. "I shan't be many minutes opening up. Sit down on the terrace a minute while I get ready."

Her voice was musical and held a trace of country accent. Jervis could not help but notice that it contained no particular friendship for him.

"I want to order dinner," he said, "for five." He made little attempt, now, to claim any special importance for this dinner. It might have been any friendly or sporting occasion rather than the historic happening that it was in fact.

"Five," the girl repeated after him. "I don't know that we can manage five." She looked inquiringly at the chef, who shook his big head and his cascading beard.

Forced to declare himself, Jervis spoke humbly rather than peremptorily, and without taking his eyes from the girl:

"I'm a staff officer. I've been ordered to make arrangements for this dinner. It is for a high-ranking officer and his guests. We shall need a private room in view of the importance of one of the party. I hope you'll be able to manage the affair for me without making any difficulties."

"So? I thought so," said the chef, and turned from the range. "All right, certainly we cook for five. We give you the St Germain of the new peas made with stock from the ham bone and finished with farmhouse cream. After that, we give you . . ."

The girl broke in, watching with amusement the chef's enthusiasm for his own cooking: "You'll enjoy your meal. He was at the Lombardy until it was bombed."

"Why did you leave the West End?" Jervis asked. "I should have thought a chef was safe enough in a basement kitchen."

Whilst he was speaking the girl had left the room, presumably to open up the bar. The chef did not answer at once. He picked up a long wafer-thin carving-knife with a concave blade and began to sharpen it with a stone.

"I cook when bombs fall on the Hotel Lombardy," he said, never looking at the flashing knife. "One bomb has fallen through nine floors onto my sauce cook. Dinner for five hundred peoples was all wasted. I could not sleep for one week with thinking of my poor sauce cook and all the other cooks who are dead. I escape because I fall on my face behind the *bain-marie*. After that I cook where there are no bombs. If there will come bombs here I will go to America."

The chef's hand flickered to and fro with amazing speed. His eyes were clouded with memories above the large nose and sardonic lips half concealed in his beard. His pronunciation was pure French in sound and Jervis could follow him only with an effort.

Presently the chef laid his knife down and said: "We drink a glass together."

From a little cupboard he took a bottle and two glasses, which he filled carefully with a bright yellow wine.

"A la victoire," he said, as they touched glasses. A look of cunning flitted momentarily across his face. It was difficult to know what he understood by victory. Perhaps, thought Jervis, it was not especially an English victory that he meant, but any victory so that he might cook again in peace with the materials which a cook requires. A few drops of wine lodged like crystals in the chef's beard. He wiped his lips with the back of his hand.

"Victory," Jervis said confidently as he drank. He had never tasted anything quite like this wine, and the colour gave him no clue to its identity. "This is good," he added. "I don't suppose you have a bottle you could spare? My chief has quite a palate."

Abruptly, from a certain distance, a woman's scream was heard. The sound was lightly pitched and in no way frightened or anguished. It had, indeed, a note almost of pleasure. Jervis had the strange sensation that he had been waiting for this sound, and he ran his tongue apprehensively over his lips.

The chef, at the moment of opening his mouth to speak, had stiffened with the sudden strain of listening. Then he took the knife from the table and, moving with extraordinary speed and silence for so big a man, went out through the green baize and the swing-doors into the dining-room. Captain Jervis followed blindly. Each door in turn slammed against him in the wake of the chef. Once in the dining-room, anxiety overtook him that he might be too late, and he began to run. Distinctly he heard a voice say: "I hate you. You never think of anything else." The door into the bar was open.

Whether he actually paused or not, Jervis was able to take in the scene as a single picture, every detail of which was clear to him. The red-haired girl, her figure showing again to glorious advantage, was bent back over the chromium rail of the bar. The chef appeared to have forgotten his knife, which hung loosely in his left hand. He was swearing in a furious mumble as he advanced upon the girl and the man who held her pinned against the bar. This man, since Jervis had not seen him before, at once fixed his attention. At first sight he appeared like one of those obscure film heroes whose name no one knows. Small, smartly dressed in blue, with a military moustache and neatly brushed hair graying above the ears, he had the ruthless expression of a small-town man of the world. His complexion was drab and unhealthy, though, and he looked frightened under the camouflage of his dapper turn-out. It occurred to Jervis at once, through some association of ideas, that this man was the manager of the Silver Fish.

Jervis jumped forward and struck the knife out of the chef's left hand just as the manager released the girl, raised the hinged end of the bar and darted behind its cover.

"Back, Quimerle. I order you," he said.

The chef had rounded on Jervis in fury and thrust him back against the opposite wall of the room. Jervis, half the breath knocked out of him, came forward uncertainly again to try and retrieve the knife from where it lay at the foot of one of the bar stools. But the manager reached his hand under the bar and now a bell began to sound insistently in the hall of the hotel. The manager seized with his right hand one of the squat bottles of liqueur on the shelf behind him. The chef was on his knees grovelling for the carving-knife.

A waiter, evidently he for whom the bell had been rung, came quickly through the hall. His tailcoat was half on and half off and he had no tie. It was apparent that he was no stranger to this kind of action, for without any hesitation he trod on Quimerle's hand and kicked the knife into the corner of the bar.

Then Jervis made up his mind. It was almost as if his part had been written for him and he had only to take his cue. He reached forward, caught hold of the girl's hand, and drew her away through the hall and out of the hotel. She gave no sign of resistance. As they turned onto the cobblestones of the pavement Jervis's ear caught the sound of splintering glass.

The sun still shone. Its evening light spread a patina of quiet beauty over the harbour. The broken pier, the half-sunken ammunition ship and the shattered submarine on the rocks assumed old-established and friendly shapes. Far out at sea, ships' hulls were now visible under the pall of smoke from the tunnels.

Jervis took the girl's arm and steered her down a flight of steep steps towards the beach. In a few seconds they were hidden from sight by semi-tropical shrubs and trees.

"This is lovely," the girl said, "running away like this. Let them manage their own silly bar. They're always fighting, and anyone can tell you that's no good for trade."

"Who are you?" asked Jervis humbly. "And who are they, and what's all the trouble about?"

A deep vibrant hum filled the air and reverberated above the cliffs and buildings. Miles overhead, so high that the eye could only distinguish them because of their number, fighters were flying out to sea. Jervis glanced at his watch, and the position of the hands told him that the planes, otherwise scarcely identifiable, were Spitfires from Tetlow airfield. Three squadrons of them were on their way out to maintain the air umbrella over Brigadier Miles and his men.

"My name is Belle," the girl said. "I don't like the manager much. You can't help admiring him, though, in some ways. He certainly knows the world."

"What about Monsieur Quimerle?" asked Jervis. His heart almost stopped beating as he waited for the answer.

"He may be a Frenchman," said Belle, "but he's clever all right, and you'd be surprised how strong."

Gloom fell on Captain Jervis. The conversation was disagreeable to him. Why he had expected anything better he no longer knew. But Belle's hand fell on his arm, and he turned to see her looking at him with parted lips.

Once more they were startled by a sound. A hundred feet below them, where a small jetty ran out to sea, a powerful marine engine roared into life. Manned by naval ratings, a motorboat purred away from the wharf and accelerated quickly, steering out to sea towards the approaching ships. Soon only the streaming wake was visible against the blue of the deep sea.

The Prisoner of State came ashore first. The collar of his coat was turned up to conceal the lower part of his face, and his hat pulled down to conceal the upper. Mr Fitzwilliam of the Foreign Office was waiting with Jervis on the jetty. He shook hands with the prisoner, murmured a few words to introduce himself, and at once led him away. He had no wish to be involved with "that military lunatic," as he styled Brigadier Miles.

The Brigadier was in great form. He tripped neatly out of the motorboat onto the jetty and extended a hand to the lady. "Come now, a little courage," he said. "Only one step and you're on dry land."

The lady jumped with a great swaying of bust and hips and landed successfully on the jetty. She was a beauty of the old school, an Edwardian demi-mondaine brought up to date. She wore a full-length fur coat of extravagant value and a circular fur cap in the Russian style. The Brigadier introduced her.

"Hullo, John. This is Captain Jervis, my Staff Captain; Miss Lily Latour. Run on, John, and see that fellow doesn't escape. We've been in enough trouble getting hold of him."

The Brigadier had discarded his tin hat to come ashore. He wore a red-banded peaked hat with his battledress. On his upper arm was the title of a Guards Regiment and the badge of the Airborne. He was just five feet two inches, bald and volatile. He had jet eyebrows and moustache. A volcanic energy was concealed in his small frame.

As soon as Jervis had gone ahead of them, Lily Latour said: "He knows I betrayed him. Or if he doesn't know he suspects so strongly that nothing would persuade him of the contrary."

The Brigadier took her arm. "You've done a good job," he said. "I know it's all a bit unpleasant, but you've been a good girl and everyone's pleased with you."

No one but this "military lunatic" would have dared to treat so famous a woman like a small child. But his flippant manner consoled Miss Latour. Even a little gaiety came over her features as she walked with him up the steep steps to the Silver Fish Hotel.

"I hope that young puppy has managed to order a good dinner," the Brigadier said. "This Foreign Office fellow can look after His Excellency, and you and I will have a good chat over our bite of food. Then I must go down and see my men ashore."

At the top of the steps they turned and looked back. Against a red-streaked sky the fleet was now approaching harbour. The leading vessels were only three miles from shore. Transports, landing-craft and escort vessels in their dapper camouflage dotted the sea for miles. High overhead the fighter cover was still maintained. The destroyers, their work done, lay ten miles off the harbour, ready to proceed back to their home port as soon as all the craft were within the protection of the shore batteries.

The hotel was busier than when Captain Jervis had first called there. The manager, his weaselly face wreathed in smiles, was waiting at the door.

"Show this lady upstairs," said the Brigadier. "I'll go in the bar for a minute. Where are the others of my party?"

"In the private room, sir. You'll excuse my asking, but is the gentleman in the gray coat—"

"Which way to the bar?" snapped the Brigadier. "The party has been booked in the name of my Staff Captain, Captain Jervis. I want no discussion at all about my guests."

Lily Latour smiled as she allowed the manager to shepherd her upstairs. Ten years as the toast of three or four capital cities had not damped her appreciation of a man. Most of all she liked powerful men. Perhaps it was only the most powerful man of all who could have persuaded her to carry out today's job. It was six weeks since a Daimler had turned the wide corner from Downing Street into Whitehall and carried her to a secret embarkation point on the coast. Six weeks in which to persuade His Excellency to revive the joys of the past in a small seaside resort where the facilities for guarding him were none too adequate. The rest of the story was a little distasteful to her. She felt, not without reason, that her part in it had been contemptible. But that did not affect her admiration for the Brigadier.

In the private room, Mr Fitzwilliam was having the time of his life. The conversation, he felt, was historic. It would be many years, at least in Foreign Office circles, before it was forgotten. The first step, naturally, was to get rid of the Staff Captain. The Army was useful as an instrument of policy, but not to be trusted when any degree of tact was required. Captain Jervis was sent to inform the Brigadier that an interval of half an hour before dinner would be appreciated, to give him time to carry out a preliminary interrogation. That killed two birds with one stone. It got rid of Jervis and it stalled off the "military lunatic".

"You may remember," said Mr Fitzwilliam, "that when we were both staying at Fouracres"—this was the house of a well-known political hostess—"I gave it as my opinion that you were closer to Great Britain in thought and feeling than any of your countrymen. As Ambassador to the Court of St James you were in a position to appreciate our determination to oppose the domination of the Continent by any single power."

His Excellency hardly listened. He wished to talk, but not along the lines suggested by Mr Fitzwilliam. He drank a glass of the yellow wine provided by the good offices of Monsieur Quimerle.

"From the Jura!" he commented. "It must be rare to find in your country now any wine that a man of discrimination can drink. By occupying the French vineyards, the Führer dealt a shrewder blow to your ruling class than any invasion of Poland or Greece."

Mr Fitzwilliam was scarcely perturbed by the change of subject. Bland and elegant, he adapted himself at once to the new topic.

"I remember a delightful place in the Jura," he said reminiscently: "a place named St Amour. In point of fact I spent my honeymoon there in '33."

"And if," said the Prisoner of State, "you had the chance to go back now to St Amour, would you be disappointed, do you think, or would you find something which for ten years has been lost?" He showed surprising animation. His heavy-lidded eyes for once lost their weariness. It seemed as if he really required an answer. Then he fell back in his chair and turned the glass in his hand. "I went back to Grivenchy," he said, "because that is the only place where I have been happy in all my life. What I wanted was to be lovers again with Lily, who spent a week there with me many years ago. In those days she was an unknown dancer at the Bal Tabarin. I was a secretary in the Paris Embassy. It was a week of exquisite pleasure. On my return I said nothing to my colleagues. I kept the memory to myself. I married, had children, but always I remembered that week at Grivenchy."

"And then?" asked Mr Fitzwilliam, hardly daring to breathe in case he should interrupt this flow of reminiscence. "What happened when you did go back?" He refilled the glasses to soften the impact of his question.

The Prisoner of State was staring into space with the expression of a prophet. He twirled the glass unceasingly in his hand.

"We were lovers again," he said, and there was a trace of Germanic coarseness in his tone. Even the German accent had crept back into his voice, which was ordinarily that of a native, whether of England or France. "It is all that I wanted. When the parachute troops came I was not even surprised. I had no wish to escape or to return to my post in the Reich. I was only" —he hesitated—"a little jealous perhaps that someone else had persuaded Lily to do this to me."

Mr Fitzwilliam intervened promptly, as was only his duty. "I hope no one, Your Excellency, has given you the impression that Miss Latour was concerned in the raid on Grivenchy."

The Prisoner of State smiled sadly. "You English," he said, "have an apt expression in such cases. You say, 'Let's play silly beggars!'"

For once in his life Mr Fitzwilliam was a little taken aback.

Jervis, meanwhile, had made the journey out to the kitchen again, and was trying unsuccessfully to pump Quimerle about the details of his quarrel with the manager. He had gone to find the Brigadier to deliver Mr Fitzwilliam's message. He had found him heavily preoccupied. In the bar, the Brigadier had succeeded in capturing Belle's interest. From his pocket he had produced a card bearing a geometrical design which you had to look at for exactly two minutes. The Brigadier's half-hunter was open on the counter and Belle was giggling as she concentrated her attention on the card.

It appeared to Jervis highly improbable that Mr Fitzwilliam would be troubled within half an hour, so he left the message undelivered.

Quimerle lifted a saucepan from the fire, and with an abrupt change of subject inquired:

"Now you've got him, what you do to him?"

"I can't talk about that, I'm afraid. I'm not allowed to discuss the matter at all."

Quimerle was undisturbed. "I tell you," he said. "You put him in nice quiet country house with officer to look after him, wine and chicken for dinner, and if he want what you call bit of fun you wink the eye to oblige him."

"After the war," said Jervis, "he will be brought to trial in an international court for the crimes he's committed."

"And the charges they are dropped as it happened last time. But what I would do," Quimerle continued, "I would cut his throat so, quickly, while I serve him his dinner."

A little pale at the thought of this dreadful scene, Jervis went back to the hall to wait for Miss Latour to come down. He was forestalled by Brigadier Miles.

"Go down," said the Brigadier, "and have a look at the hotel air-raid shelter in the basement. See that it's open and make sure you know the way. I have a feeling the Hun may still start something. Also get hold of the Gun Operations Room and tell them to give us a warning over the G.P.O. line if there's any hostile activity at all. We don't want to rely on the sirens."

"Will they do that, sir?"

"If I say so they will. I'm going to get Miss Latour now and we'll have dinner in five minutes."

Brigadier Miles took the head of the table. On his right sat the Prisoner of State and on his left Miss Lily Latour. Mr Fitzwilliam sat at present alone at the foot of the table, for Jervis had not returned from his mission. Halfway up the cellar steps, Belle was telling him:

"The manager's frightened of Quimerle, but he doesn't dare to sack him or he'd lose half the trade."

"Do they know about us?" Jervis asked.

"Not a thing. The manager thinks I went up to my room."

"You must go back to the bar, Belle, or someone will start breaking the place up."

Jervis went straight to the telephone. It was a public box just inside the entrance. He made the call the Brigadier had ordered and then left the box. On the point of entering the private dining-room he decided to telephone Port Control. It was advisable to leave a message for the Brigade Major that the Brigadier would be seeing the men before they dismissed. When he re-entered the telephone box the line was dead. He could get neither the number he wanted nor the exchange. He returned to the dining-room.

Soup was being served. He slid into his place as the silver tureen came round. A small bowl containing dice of fried bread accompanied it. He gave himself a generous helping and stirred the smooth green fluid with his spoon. He promised himself to try the telephone again in ten minutes' time.

Meanwhile life was very pleasant. In the private dining-room the theme of a silver fish was constantly repeated. On the undrawn curtains, the napkins, the crockery and the spoons the same fish leapt and curved over before falling back into a sea conventionalized in one curling wave. Jervis allowed his gaze to play round the room. Four spoons were already dipping in the soup, but a number of mirrors, inset in the furniture, reflected a whole company of spoons which rose and fell rhythmically. As Jervis began his meal he saw out of the corner of his eye a fresh platoon of spoons join the main body.

His Excellency, crumbling a piece of bread in his left hand, said:

"Crème St Germain. One might never have crossed

the Channel. There is nothing better than the taste of the young peas."

"I must apologize," said the Brigadier, "for the lack of wine. With the exception of a rare bottle one is condemned nowadays to the products of a number of British firms. What raw materials are used, and who decides whether the concoction is port or sherry, I have not discovered. I prefer to drink whisky and soda unless I have good reason to do otherwise."

"At the best hotels," asked Lily Latour, "can one still get good wine?"

"At three pounds a bottle one can get a sugary liquid, I understand," Jervis put in.

"I thought," said the Prisoner of State, "that the centre of London would have been destroyed by air-raids."

A dead silence followed on this remark. Everyone was perhaps following some train of thought private to himself, some recollection of death or disaster. Jervis, gazing at his wineglass, became conscious that, ever so slightly, it was vibrating. He looked up and met the Brigadier's eye. Faintly but unmistakably the hetero-dyned note of heavy bombers could be heard. And before either could make any movement a siren very close to the Silver Fish began its wavering, alternating note of impersonal alarm.

The second course by E. M. Forster

"The fish will be sherved in the selter," announced Brigadier Miles, when the siren had completed its third ululation. "Hullo, a spoonerism! Don't often achieve a spoonerism." Rising leisurely, he gave his arm to Lily Latour. "John, lead on. You know the way. Mr Fitzwilliam, will you safeguard our guest, also that decanter? I don't know which of them is the more precious."

"I used to be terrible at spoonerisms," prattled Miss Latour as she swept off. "I never could say—let's see—

what was it I never could say?—I know—I never could say, 'She stood at the door of the fish-sauce shop, beckoning him in."

"Beckoning him in, excellent."

They reached the lounge, and there mingled with the guests who were issuing from the public dining-room. Mr Fitzwilliam surveyed the situation with distaste. "You have, I think, no parallel to the spoonerism in your language," he remarked to the Prisoner of State. "You are fortunate."

"No. The Reich presents few parallels. Though there was, if I recollect, a fish-sauce shop (do I phrase this epigram correctly?) at Grivenchy. Lily will bear me out."

"What is that, Henning?" She half turned with a smile. Belle, who was locking up the bar, watched them.

"That fish-sauce shop of Grivenchy, where she stood in the door beckoning him in."

"I—I don't quite follow you."

"You did not. I followed you. I am here."

Miss Latour's smile became more rigid, and she touched it at either end with her hand as though to keep it in position. "Never mind, good girl, well done," said the Brigadier.

Jervis, down the cellar stairs, received the effusive apologies of the manager, who seemed to regard himself as personally responsible for the raid. He replied, "Oh, that's all right, this'll do, I've already had a look. We want somewhere to sit, and if possible to eat, until the All Clear sounds." And indeed the cellar might have been worse. It was warm and well-lit, and there was a big table of the school-feast type with forms along it. An occasional silver fish was stencilled on the cellar's rough-cast walls, to indicate that there would be no reduction in the bill.

"You shall certainly sit, sir, you shall certainly eat, but I am mortified that I cannot provide better privacy for your party."

"Have you no second shelter where these other good people could go?" inquired Mr Fitzwilliam from the rear.

"No, sir, nothing, this is the only accommodation either for visitors or staff. We applied for a permit to construct an additional refuge, but were refused on the ground that the work was of insufficient national importance."

"A regrettable refusal." The other good people, looking none too good, incommoded him and made him feel that he did not want to be buried with them. He was as brave as any Landseer lion, but he did stipulate that death should find him among his official equals, and here was the Army, blundering as usual, and threatening him with an all-too-common grave.

"Fortunately there are two staircases, sir, so if you will kindly sort yourselves out we will start serving the fish."

Jervis felt uneasy and a little guilty at this. He hadn't, in his preliminary survey, spotted the second staircase. He had been too busy with Belle. Yes, there it was, curving up into the darkness from a recess, and, as far as he could calculate, communicating directly with Quimerle's kitchen.

"Yes, sir, that is the so-called Smuggler's Stairway. Yes, madam, many strange things went up it in the old days, and came down too, I expect. And there was a continuation of it (now cemented up of course) which led right beneath us under the tropical garden onto the beach. Will you sort yourselves, please"—advancing and retreating and rubbing his hands, and trying to combine, with his obsequiousness and showmanship, the air of a man about town.

"But I cannot endorse this arrangement," Mr Fitzwilliam protested; he foresaw correspondence between the Foreign Office, the War Office and the Ministry of Home Security in the event of a direct hit; and he wanted it to be known that his own attitude had been, from the first, indubitable.

"Do these damned people think they've bought the bloody place?" called an angry voice behind him—a woman's voice. "Blocking up the stairs—it's disgraceful. Hi you, young man, you get a move on, you." And she pushed the representative of the Foreign Office with her handbag. There was a tiny tinkling sound. The knell of a vintage. An ambrosial ghost. The decanter had smashed against the cellar wall.

"Butterfingers!" cried Brigadier Miles, for though he appreciated wine his first impulse was to be facetious.

"Really, it is scarcely my fault when a member of the public loses self-control."

The woman, still in a fury, shouted: "Give them another bottle of the same, waiter, and put it on my bill. Lady Dawes' bill. There's more from where that comes from, I suppose."

"Madame, that came from the Jura," said the Prisoner of State in tones of exasperation. The English under danger were more than he could bear.

"It can come from the judge for all I care."

"Ah. Another epigram!"

Brigadier Miles clapped his hands. He must rally his flock before it was contaminated by backchat. He descended the wine-wet stairs, advanced to the table, and reconstructed the amenities of the private room, so far as possible, by seating himself at the head upon an empty cider-cask. On his right, as before, sat the Prisoner of State, on his left Miss Latour. They were flanked by Mr Fitzwilliam and by Captain Jervis respectively. Beyond Fitzwilliam and Jervis were two butler's trays, laid along the wooden forms at Jervis's orders, and serving a little to protect the flock from the common herd. It was not much of a barrier, and the voice of Lady Dawes could be heard clearly across it. She spoke, among other topics, of the vulgarity of luxury in wartime, of the sufferings of dogs and cats, and of staff-officer mentality. She pleaded, always at the top of her voice, for a jollier and a simpler world with less red tape and red tabs. She had odious confederates who said to one another in her pauses, "Isn't May marvellous, isn't May unique? She doesn't care. It does people like that good to hear that sort of thing once in a way. What do they want to be down here for? Why weren't they seeing to things upstairs?"

Meanwhile the semblances of the second course began to arrive. Knives and forks came down the Smugglers' Stairway, and were clattered in heaps. Bread was dumped. Glasses. Belle made herself useful. As she gave Jervis a napkin, she whispered to him, "You won't enjoy your fish."

"Why not?"

"Ah!"

Realizing that she wanted to speak to him, he got up under the pretext of choosing Miss Latour a piece of bread. "Why not?" he repeated.

"Quimerle's gone."

"Quimerle's gone? When did he go?" He thought quickly, remembering the dead telephone, and the instant of its death.

"After he'd sent in the soup. You never saw such a mess in the kitchen in your life. Shirley—she's the vegetable cook, or supposed to be—is doing the whole dinner with the bootboy to help. They don't know where anything is, they've dropped paraffin into the sauce instead of salad-oil, they've—well, you'll see. The manager's furious. This is the third time Quimerle's let him down. He's temperamental, of course. They say all geniuses are. Quimerle's a marvel, I must say. It's too funny seeing the manager smirking down here and then skipping up the stairs to swear. He's taken the whole of the keys. What upset him, heaven above knows, but he's gone. Who's that fat woman you're sitting next?"

Heaven above did know perhaps, thought John, his mind on the advancing bombers. He didn't like the way things were turning out, at all, and must report to the Brigadier. "I can't answer questions," he said to Belle, "and I shouldn't have called Miss Latour fat."

"You can't answer questions but you don't mind ask-

ing them. Anyhow, I don't like her, and I bet she's got
something on her mind. I wouldn't like to have *her* conscience. And I don't like the man she's with. Nor the
fool from London. And I'll tell you something else,
John. That other woman who calls herself Lady Dawes
and tries to be rude—"

"Tries? I should have said she succeeded."

"Well, I've seen more rude people than you have in
my job, and I don't think she's natural. She's too thick
with the manager, too. Do you know she's got a room
here, and when he's tired of me, which mercifully he is
occasionally—and the drink that goes up to them, and
then all this talk of luxury! Lady Dawes is a very good
judge of wine indeed. I've heard Quimerle say so, and
he ought to know. She's looking at us now. Don't turn
around. Anyhow I don't like her."

"Is there anyone whom you do like?"

"Your Brigadier."

"Anyone else?"

"Don't be silly. This bit of bread looks like an antique. Take it back to your Lily, and let me get to
my work. If I get any news of Quimerle I'll tell you,
and meantime you can take it from me that the next
course'll be muck."

Too true were Belle's words. Down the Smugglers'
Stairway descended slabs of sole, pallid, veined, looking as if they had come down in the train from Whitehall with Mr Fitzwilliam, and not unlike him in texture. Quimerle had had some dreadful retrospective effect. The Brigadier apologized. "You know England,
Your Excellency, and so you won't expect fish to be
fresh on the seacoast. We always send it to mature in
London when we can."

"Exactly. Round your Empire; like East Indian sherry, when your Empire included India."

"Still, it is not altogether our fault this time. I'm sorry we have to continue our meal under such uncomfortable circumstances."

"Oh, it is nothing, nothing. Yes, I know England and

how you are situated. You are used to it. You seldom digest a meal without interruptions, and I shall soon accommodate myself too. You have astonished me with excellent soup and a memorable wine. I could not expect fish to be achieved as well. For this is not fish. No, we will agree not to call this fish."

"Where's the sauce, John?"

"I'm afraid there won't be any sauce, sir."

"Any hope of another bottle of that wine?"

"I'm afraid not. I believe there's to be some Algerian with the entrée."

"There would be."

"It amazes me to hear wine mentioned at all in England," said the Prisoner of State, who now that his compatriots were above him had become subtly insolent. "As Balzac remarks: 'Partout où la chimie est pratiquée, on ne boit plus de vin,' and yours is a great industrial country."

"Ah, Balzac!" said Miss Latour, preparing to be cosmopolitan.

"Yes, I was sure you would recognize the quotation, Lily. For it comes from his *Splendeurs et Misères des Courtisanes.*"

"I haven't read that particular Balzac, as a matter of fact," said she, laying down her fork and staring at her bread with distaste.

"No? I thought I remembered us reading it together in your Bal Tabarin days. You began it and did not finish it perhaps. You should read it to the end. It is a most illuminating Balzac for you. *Splendeurs . . . et Misères des Courtisanes.*" His voice became brutal and mystic. "Read it to the last line, my dear Lily. Learn what such women are reduced to, however splendidly they start. Learn how they end."

Miss Latour got up. She was outraged. She would have swept from the cellar. The wooden form caught her at the back of her substantial knees and prevented her from moving, and the Brigadier pulled her back into her seat. He never spoke, for which she was grateful.

She looked across him at her former lover, she readjusted her smile. "All men insult one sooner or later unless they are really strong," she was thinking. Then she blew her nose and found herself crying. It was so unfair, when she had spent her life trying to make men happy. Of course, she was open to criticism over Grivenchy, but she had hoped that Henning would never suspect her, and, now that he did suspect her, he really should have showed some largeness of mind instead of . . . catching one out . . . humiliating one over fish-sauce shops . . . Balzac. . . . To her horror, the tears were now streaming. Belle watched her again, this time more gently. An unexpected chord of sympathy had been touched. Lady Dawes, her tongue wagging, watched too.

As if irritated beyond bearing by the whole damned business, Brigadier Miles now jumped off his cask, and called upon Jervis to report. They stood with their backs to the cellar wall, where they could command the entrances of both staircases. The guests had now received their portions of naked sole, and were washing them down with water or beer. The electric light beat upon them unkindly from the low ceiling, picking out their tonsures and the tops of their ears, and the scraggy or fluffy napes of their necks. The excitement of entry was over. The conversation was about raids, past, present and future, varied by a little grumbling, and by intimate inside knowledge of the mentality of Hitler. That is to say, it was shelter-conversation, and it could be trusted not to alter until the All Clear or the Last Trump sounded.

When John had finished: "Of course the line's been cut," the Brigadier snapped. "By the cook or by someone. By your barmaid, perhaps. Of course we're surrounded by spies. Go and have a look out of doors and try to ring the Brigade Major again. When you've failed to get him, come back here and stay here. Our job is to stick to our man till he's in the jug. Nothing else."

"No bombs yet, sir, that's coming."

"You think so?" He bounced back to his perch. With vigour and fierceness, he flung himself into social small-talk. At the bottom of the stairs John paused for a moment and watched him. He had quelled Mr Fitzwilliam and the Prisoner of State, he was increasing the intervals between the sniffs of Lily Latour. A remarkable man. The whole scene—the long low intensely lit cellar, the smugglers' old halfway house—seemed to vibrate with his energy. Looking at him, John thought for an instant of Quimerle. Strong—both of them strong. What women wanted, what men somehow didn't equally admire, was strength. John wondered for a moment whether he himself was adequately strong, but he couldn't be bothered to worry, the situation was too exciting.

The telephone was still dead, so he pushed open the door of the hotel and looked out at the night. No bombs had fallen, but the night was not calm. From the port came sounds of confusion. The Commando had apparently been disbanded, and he got the impression that more communications than his own had been cut. False orders issued, perhaps? The Prisoner was of such immense value, the very course of the war might turn on his custody, and even during his spree at Grivenchy plans must have been laid by his friends to cover every contingency. Even now—even down in the cellar—he must be surrounded by friends.

Then the bombing started, but some way off. They had gone for the Tetlow airfield. Tiresome for Tetlow, but not John's concern. Relieved, he looked up at the stars, and tried to remember that they are other worlds, also perhaps the producers of life. But this is an old-fashioned thought, dearer to the nineteenth century than to the twentieth, and it did not interest the young man much. He was more thrilled by the discovery that one of the stars had disappeared. There it was again, though . . . but now another one had vanished. He tumbled to it now. Parachutists! The attack on Tetlow was a blind. The heavens were crawling with them, and some of them must already have touched the earth.

Here was something further to report, and he hurried back to the cellar. It was a relief to find it exactly as he had left it—the diners still exchanging the low-down on Hitler, the fish still on their plates, Lady Dawes showing off, the manager hovering equivocal, Belle lovelier than ever, and, dominating them all and holding them together as in some modern Last Supper, the virile Brigadier. He advanced, and, as if he had stepped upon a spring, the lights fused.

The darkness only lasted for a moment. Torches were soon flashed, matches struck. The cellar still looked the same. But the Brigadier no longer occupied his little perch. He lay bleeding on the floor behind it, his throat cut.

The third course by A. E. Coppard

You would be inclined to think, would you not, that Fate has some inkling of individual limitations and would therefore be enjoying a good snigger at the problem she had thus posed for a young and untried Army officer. There he was, in an underground cellar half full of frightened people struggling in darkness, a murderer among them, a State Prisoner of vast importance unguarded there, and upon the world outside hell itself dropping demons from the sky.

The sudden plunge into darkness had forced shrieks from the women and curses from the men, forms clashed over as all sprang to their feet and collided and scrambled in panic.

"Switch on the light, blast it!" Lady Dawes yelled. "Switch it on, somebody, can't you! Switch it on!"

A couple of torches peered magically, spasms of light came from matches, and amid the crowd huddling round him Captain Jervis was confronted, for the first time in his life, by the Real Thing, though it was in a form to which his military training provided no immediate reaction and his genius, such as it was, afforded no response. The body of the Brigadier was making faint staccato twitchings such as might be made by a mechanism of springs from which the steely virtue had been suddenly withdrawn.

Lily Latour gasped, "Oh, Henning!" His Excellency, stern and unperturbed, was at her side, and she clung to him.

Brigadier Miles was dead, or as good as dead. Someone with the velvet tread of a fox had sneaked up on him, had "done him in"—and was still there among them? Jervis felt horribly baffled, all the responsibility now crashed upon him, the paramount importance of delivering the State Prisoner to the authorities was now his charge, as well as the task of grabbing the foul murderer who had killed his chief, and he had no aid, no resources, no men to issue commands to. A colloquialism from a recent film was chattering "Who done it? Who done it?" in his half-stunned mind when his arm was clutched and shaken by Mr Fitzwilliam who growled: "Take charge, for God's sake! Do something, man! Get us out quick!"

So Captain Jervis drew his revolver and, still dithered by the shock of the drama, gasped out: "Who done it?"

Naturally enough there was no answer, but above the silence that had fallen as he swung menacingly round there arose from without the noise of spasmodic but incessant machine-gunning.

What do I do now, he wondered, I must do something, but what the hell can I? Boldly he called out: "Somebody in the room must have done this."

The challenge merely evoked whispers and gasps of denial. Mr Fitzwilliam impatiently asked: "What did you expect? Do something, man." The young captain thereupon bent over the body whose gashed neck leaked so bloodily; although without previous experience of such things he was sure the Brigadier was stone dead.

He fumbled at the Brigadier's holster and collected his revolver. Then, hesitating with a weapon in each hand, he could only wonder again: "What do I do now?" A feeling of absurdity struck him. He restored his own revolver to its holster.

"Manager! Manager!" he called. "Where's the manager?"

There was no answer.

"Is there a doctor here, or a nurse?"

There was neither.

Snatching a torch from the nearest hand, Jervis waved its beam along the row of peering horrified faces and around the cellar. Sternly he called out: "No one leaves this cellar, understand! That's an order. You're all in a spot. I'm a dead shot."

There were some murmurs from the unofficial group, swelling into protests until Jervis swung his revolver at them.

"Back to the wall, backs against that wall, damn you!" he yelled fiercely.

They mutely obeyed. His Excellency, with Lily Latour and Mr Fitzwilliam, got behind him. The others were now all corralled in a sort of way and this somewhat elated him—but only for a moment. What now? What the devil was he to do with them now? He dared not leave the Prisoner of State—the unknown murderer too was there, lurking for a dig at Jervis perhaps.

"Mr Fitzwilliam," the Captain at length said, "take my gun, will you?" He held it out behind him without turning and Mr Fitzwilliam took it.

"Shoot anybody who tries to make a getaway. Anybody. And shoot to kill. Mind now, it's cocked. Stand by those stairs; the other stairs lead to the kitchen. I've got to go there to have a look around. Keep everybody here till I get back. Got the idea?"

Mr Fitzwilliam inquired timidly: "Suppose you don't get back?"

"That," replied the Captain airily, "is your funeral."

Mr Fitzwilliam thought he understood. Taking his

position at the foot of the dining-room stairs he waved His Excellency and Lily Latour into the corner facing him.

"You others," the Captain cried, "hands up, all of you, and no funny business."

Flashing his torch upon the parties ranged along the wall and with his revolver at the ready he strode to the recess at the far end of the cellar where steps led up to the kitchen. He ascended the steps backwards. There were half a dozen and they slewed round in the ascent until he was unsighted. He pushed the door half open and warily entered the kitchen. The full light there was restorative, though the smell of recently cooked fish was unpleasant. Belle was there, alone, standing on a chair, apparently searching for something on a high shelf. He called to her brusquely.

"Hullo," she answered.

"Where's everybody?"

She explained that they had all dashed off to the domestic dugout, expecting bombs to fall.

Jervis stood with his elbow propped against the half-open door.

"Come here!" he commanded.

The long-legged creature stepped down and advanced nonchalantly.

"Quick!" he yelled, angered by her attitude.

"Johnny!" she pouted coyly.

"Stow that, and don't ask questions. This is serious. Do exactly as I tell you. No, no, don't ask questions," he repeated. "Run around and lock the other door to this cellar. Go on, quick." He stamped his foot. "I'm waiting for you to come back. Don't ask questions now."

"D'you mean the door from the dining-room?"

"That's the door, that's the one."

"It *is* locked," she said. "I locked it myself as soon as you were all down there."

"Why did you do that?"

"It's the rule whenever there's an alert, to keep 'em in till the All Clear."

A horrid suspicion then made a dive at him. "How did you get up here? You were down in the cellar when the lights went out, I saw you."

"Yes, I came up to get some candles while Oscar mended the fuse. But there isn't a damn candle in the place. It's only the cellar circuit fused and he's at the meter board mending it now, it won't be a minute."

"Oscar? Who's Oscar?"

"The manager, all the others have bolted."

"The manager! How did *he* leave the cellar?"

"Same as me," she replied flippantly.

Jervis surveyed her with such contempt that she asked: "What's all the fuss about?"

"You came up together! You and the manager?"

"Ah. We twined our arms and knees and rolled up."

"Go and fetch him to me, fetch him here," he barked savagely, waving his arm. It was only then that she observed the pistol. Realizing that something unusual was afoot, she exclaimed "Oh!" rather forlornly.

"Fetch him! D'you hear!"

Belle turned and fled away, and for the life of him he could not help admiring the grace of the creature. She returned almost immediately with the manager, who advanced brushing his hands to rid them of dust.

"Sorry about that, sir," he said, "but it's O.K. now. Only the fuse."

Jervis was baffled again. The manager looked so spick and span, so unruffled and benignant, that it was hard to associate him with the murder. But if it wasn't him—who else could it be?

"While the light was out," Jervis said, "my chief, the Brigadier, was killed."

"Killed!" the manager gasped. "What . . . how . . . but no, you are joking, eh?"

"Somebody in that cellar," Jervis savagely intoned, "caught him from behind and cut his throat, and nobody heard a sound of it."

"Dead?" whispered the manager.

"God, yes! His head's half off."

The man and Belle were apparently stricken with horror. "But who did it?" both asked.

"I don't know yet. No time. I'm in a horrible spot. Have you any idea?"

They gazed at each other, shook their heads slowly. Their distress was fairly persuasive. Yes, they had rushed up out of the cellar together directly the lights went out. It sounded genuine. Jervis realized that up to now he had been suspecting three people—the manager, Quimerle, and His Excellency himself. Quimerle seemed out of it altogether, and the manager, although he inspired little liking or trust, certainly had no guilty appearance, so the Prisoner . . . ?

"Whoever did it," Jervis said, "is going to hang for it, and hang good. He *must* be still in the cellar. I'll keep that crowd down there, but I've got to get my party out of it. There's this raid on, all the phones are dead, we are cut off, and I don't know a thing about what's happening anywhere yet. I'm going to get that murderer, but my first job is to hand my party into safe custody. You needn't fear bombs, they won't drop anything, this is a parachute raid. I want help."

The manager and Belle took the matter courageously enough, but none of their suggestions seemed useful to the Captain. He alone knew what the raiding party were after, and he couldn't reveal it to this couple.

"I want to get off the land. Can you find a boat? Not a motorboat, that's noisy and they've got the harbour taped for sure. A sculling boat, so I could slip them somewhere. Anywhere away from the land."

Strange—there seemed to be no boats within reach.

"But a harbour—and no boats!" exclaimed Jervis.

"Yes!" Belle suddenly remembered. "There ought to be one in the creek below the plantation—Johnson's boat! Yes, yes, I'll get it, I'll take you. I can scull and I know the harbour fairly well."

"Oh, but . . ." the manager demurred.

"That'll do," Jervis gruffly said. "You push off, Belle, and get it ready." He was sweating with anxiety. "Wait there till I bring the party down. You're an angel, Belle."

"And dinner?" the manager feebly suggested.

"Aw, to hell with that," Jervis said.

"It's washed out, anyway," Belle added. "Quimerle's hopped it, the girls have gone, there's nothing I could cook, I never could cook, and besides—I've been conscripted now!"

There was no more to be said about it, and she hurried off to fetch a jacket.

"You now, Mr Oscar . . . what *is* your name?" Jervis contrived to waggle his revolver in a mildly significant way.

"Watson. Oscar Watson."

"You'll come with me back to the cellar. Does this door lock—is there a key?"

"Yes, yes, it hangs there." The manager wiped his damp hands on his hips. "And bolts, too, see!"

"Good. Now then." Jervis pulled the door open. "After you. No, you go first, please."

In that order they descended the steps to the cellar, now well lit again.

"Over there, Oscar," Jervis grimly indicated the wall where the unofficial group was still lined up.

Oscar Watson obeyed. Then, with his revolver trained at a threatening angle upon that group, Jervis called out: "You will all be kept here for the present. Don't try any funny business and you'll be O.K. Mr Fitzwilliam, bring our friend this way, please, and follow me."

Jervis preceded them up the steps, followed by Lily Latour weeping, His Excellency majestic, and Mr Fitzwilliam strangely composed now. When all were in the kitchen Jervis locked the door, slipped the bolts, and pocketed the key. While he was outlining the new proposal to Mr Fitzwilliam, Belle burst in upon them, all wide-eyed and panting.

"The boat's not there, John!"

"Where is it, then?"

"It's not there," she repeated, shrugging her shoulders. "Gone."

"Oh God!" Jervis groaned, "That's that! Where do we go from here?" "And there are some men," she added breathlessly, "soldiers, I think, lots of 'em, bobbing about; they are up to something."

"What! Where?"

"Down by the trees."

"Are they our men?"

"I couldn't tell, it's dark down there, I couldn't make out."

"Many of 'em?"

"Well—plenty."

"Did you hear them talking?"

"No, not a sound. I heard one or two whistles, signals I should think, but that's all."

Detonations sounded close now, and the spasmodic blur of rapid fire.

"Guns," Belle remarked.

Nothing more was said, and it seemed that nothing could be done. The party lounged against the big kitchen table while Jervis stalked about in perplexity until His Excellency suavely asked: "Would you care for me to go out and do a little snooping?"

Jervis scowled at him, vouchsafing no other answer. The Prisoner then airily lamented the loss of their dinner.

"Don't!" Lily Latour shuddered. "I couldn't touch a thing."

"I have no wish for anything more," Mr Fitzwilliam said deprecatingly.

"And who the blazes wants to eat now?" Belle asked indignantly.

"Why," His Excellency said slowly and imperturbably, "I should like to. Do you know, Lily, I recall a meal I once took with a most amiable gentleman in Marlow on my very first visit to this admirable country. For that, too, suffered from an interruption. My host was noted for his fondness for what he called Old

English Fare, strange dishes, very bucolic. But a most admirable old fellow, rich and wise and courtly and kind. He regaled me with boiled pig's head, pease pudding, and a prostrating liquid called cider. And then we were interrupted, my dear. The chimney catches fire. The fire brigade comes. They were somewhat drastic, but they made a good job."

At this point the Captain raised his hand warningly and whispered "Hush!" There was a shuffle of feet at the outer door. The door opened and a man looked in inquiringly, a man with a long fair beard—Quimerle.

The dessert by James Laver

The smart little touring car came to a halt in the cobbled market square. The dust of what had evidently been a long and rapid journey had dimmed its shining surface, but could not conceal the elegance of its line. Both doors opened simultaneously and the occupants climbed out, on the right of the car a young man in the middle twenties in carefully negligent tweeds, and with a short-clipped moustache; obviously an Englishman and almost certainly, as the observant onlooker would have remarked, an Army man. On the other side of the car stood for a moment, looking about her with wide-eyed delight, a girl, or rather a young woman, slim, long-legged and with the most remarkable coppery hair. The two met in front of the bonnet of the car, and the man took her arm with a proprietary air, the somewhat self-conscious proprietary air of one whose proprietorship is not, perhaps, of very long date. They looked like two young people on honeymoon, which is not surprising, for that is precisely what they were.

"Where are we, John?" said the girl.

"Douarnenez, I think, if my map-reading is up to standard."

"As if you could ever make a mistake!"

Yes, it was obvious that they were very newly married indeed.

"The first thing to do," said the young man, "is to find ourselves a billet. There must be plenty of hotels. I vote we leave the car here and wander round for a bit. It's still quite early."

It was indeed barely six o'clock, but the little cafés round the square were already fairly full. A narrow but animated street debouched into it from the opposite corner. There seemed to be several hotel signs.

"Come along," said the young man, still grasping his wife's arm, and guiding her over the cobbles. Suddenly he gave a startled exclamation and stopped dead.

"What is it?" she asked anxiously. "Aren't you well?"

"Look at that;" and he pointed to the sign over the door of a little hotel.

"What?"

"Poisson d'Argent."

"What of it? What does it mean?"

"Poisson d'Argent," he explained, "is French for the Silver Fish."

"Well!"

"That is where we must stay," he announced with conviction, "unless it's too disgusting."

It was not too disgusting. In fact it seemed a very charming little hotel; and they were received by a neat and not at all bad-looking maid who said But yes a room was available and would they have the goodness to wait a small moment and she would fetch the proprietor. "He is in the kitchen," she explained, "for he is also the chef. Like that, one eats well, is it not?" And she vanished into the inner recesses, while the two travellers looked into one another's eyes and their thoughts became strangely reminiscent.

"Fancy another Silver Fish," said the girl, "and here —in Brittany."

But she had scarcely time to finish the sentence before heavy footsteps were heard on the stone flags of the passage and the manager stood before them. He was a big, stout man and as he moved into the patch of sunlight from the door both the visitors gave a cry of recognition.

"Quimerle!"

"The same," said that individual, throwing his head back so that his magnificent beard stuck straight out in front of him. "But may I ask—?"

Then he too gave a cry of astonishment.

"Why, it is Captain Jervis and—and Belle!"

"Major Jervis," the girl corrected, "and Mrs Jervis."

"Mrs Jervis! Ah! I begin to understand. But how did you find me? What led you to—?"

"It was the name of the hotel," explained the Major.

"Ah yes. Le Poisson d'Argent. I chose the name myself. A touch of sentiment. Not that I had any reason to think kindly of the old Silver Fish—"

His manner changed abruptly, became suddenly professional. Did they wish to stay for a night or two? A double room of course (and he smiled slightly). And they would no doubt be dining at the hotel.

"If you can promise us a better meal than the last one we ate, or did not eat, at the Silver Fish," said Jervis.

The proprietor of Le Poisson d'Argent laid his forefinger against his nose and then wagged it slowly in front of them. "That at least I can promise." And he led the way to the little office where they were to register their names.

"And what would you like for dinner?" he asked when these formalities had been concluded.

"Anything at all," said Mrs Jervis. "We know you cook so well." But her husband was more exigent.

"I should like," he said, "the meal which we should have eaten that night at the Silver Fish, if there had been—fewer interruptions."

"Fewer interruptions!" cried Quimerle. "That is good —and so English. If I remember rightly, the interruptions, as you term them, included an air-raid, an invasion by German parachutists and a murder! But we will not speak of those things now. We began, if I remember rightly, with a Crème St Germain?"

"Yes, that was it."

"And then there was a sole. Terrible! But I had nothing to do with it. And the other dishes did not appear at all."

"Too true," murmured the Major.

"This time it will be different. Leave it to me, Monsieur and Madame." His professional manner was once more dominant. "And meanwhile I will tell Marie to show you your room."

Two hours later they were seated in the neat little dining-room. They had been given the place of honour, the table in the embrasure of the window, from which they could look out over the square and catch a glimpse, beyond it, of tall masts in the harbour.

"This soup," said the Major, "is even better than the last. Don't you think so, Belle?"

His wife raised her eyebrows slightly and tossed a shining curl back from her white forehead.

"You forget," she answered, "that I was not sitting down with the company. I was waiting at table. And Crème St Germain was not provided for the staff supper."

The Major looked slightly pained and for a moment devoted his attention to the wine which Marie had just poured into their glasses. It was a light white wine, fresh and clean to the palate, but there was no label on the bottle and Jervis could not put a name to it.

"Now for the sole," he said.

It was delicious, cooked in the simplest way, *légèrement dorée*, the firm white flesh melting in the mouth. They ate it in silence. It was not that they did not appreciate it, but their thoughts were elsewhere, at another dinner in another country, in the third year of the Second World War. Unconsciously they were waiting for someone—for Quimerle. Doubtless he was still busy in the kitchen.

Jervis was gazing absently at the little desk at the far end of the room, the desk at which "Madame" sits enthroned in so many French restaurants. But Madame, if there was a Madame, had not yet appeared. He took another sip of his wine, and when he looked again, behold, the seat behind the desk was no longer empty. A large lady in a black silk dress had taken her place there and was busy with her papers and her small change.

"Belle," he said softly.

"What is it, John dear?"

"Do you see what I see?"

The girl's eyes followed his in the direction of the desk.

"But—but she was with you that night," she stammered; "the lady who—I don't know her name."

"Lily Latour."

"Lily Latour! But what is she doing here?" And her lids narrowed as if she suddenly remembered, only too clearly, the terrors and the mysteries of "that night".

"It looks," said her husband smiling, "as if more than one wedding resulted from our little dinner party at the Silver Fish."

"I see. But it's all a bit uncanny, isn't it?"

"Unexpected anyway. I wish Quimerle would come. There is so much I want to ask him. After all, I had my duty to do, and when the troops approaching the hotel turned out to be English, who had mopped up the German parachutists without difficulty, I collected the Prisoner of State and that Foreign Office fellow, commandeered a car and took them both back to London. I left all the other complications—"

"Including me," pouted Belle.

"I came back for you. But I never saw any of the others again, except of course the Brigadier, or rather his coffin. He was given a military funeral."

Belle shuddered slightly.

"And then, as you know, I was sent overseas, and we couldn't even get married until, until—"

"Last Friday," said Belle.

He smiled at her and raised his glass.

"But I wish Quimerle would come."

It was not, however, until they had passed from the sole to the saddle of lamb and from the white wine to Pommard '34, and from all these to a memorable cheese, it was not until the dessert plates had been set before them, that the proprietor appeared. He had taken off his white cap and apron and was dressed once more as they had first seen him. He entered quietly, watchful and collected, conferred a moment with Madame at the little desk, and then passed between the tables, bowing to his guests, joking with some and conversing gravely with others. Belle became quite flustered as she watched him. John Jervis peeled a pear with pretended nonchalance. He knew that Quimerle would finally come to sit at their table.

If Lily Latour had seen them she gave no sign. She was busy with her dockets and her calculations. Still Quimerle's slow progress continued until at last, when Jervis had eaten the last of his pear, the big bearded man came to the table in the window.

"Well," he said, still in his professional manner, "you have dined well, I hope." Then, relaxing a little, he added: "At least as well as on the last occasion."

Belle could contain herself no longer. "Oh, Monsieur Quimerle," she said, "there is so much we want to ask you."

The big man's manner changed again. He glanced rapidly round the room to see that nothing needed his attention, then sat down calmly at their table. Then he turned round and beckoned Marie to him.

"Une bouteille d'Armagnac," he said, "et trois verres." It was not until the pale straw-coloured liquid gleamed in their glasses, until he had raised his own and bowed over it, first in the direction of Belle and then in that of Jervis, that he spoke again.

"Eh bien!" he murmured, "you wish to ask me many things?"

"But of course," cried Jervis. "How you came here and—and everything."

"It is very simple," answered Quimerle. "It so happens that Douarnenez is my native place, and besides, I was tired of working for others. I had accumulated a little capital. What more natural than that I should return here and set up for myself, modestly, I confess, but not, I think, without a certain distinction."

Before his hearers could frame the compliment which seemed expected he went on:

"You wonder, no doubt, about Lily, but she also is part of my past."

"Part of your—?"

"I knew her when she was a dancer at the Bal Tabarin and I—I was in the kitchen of Foyot's. You see, the wheel has come full circle. It is true that Madame no longer dances—"

He paused to take another nip of brandy.

"I lost sight of her for many years. We parted, I fear, in anger. I am by nature a rather jealous man."

"I know," whispered Belle softly, a remark which caused something almost like anger to pass over her husband's face.

"Do not distress yourself, Monsieur le Commandant," said Quimerle smoothly. "If I resented the advances of Oscar Watson it was (how do you say it?) in an avuncular capacity."

Belle giggled slightly and once more Jervis glanced at her. He wished the conversation would take another turn.

"You were jealous about Lily Latour," he prompted.

Quimerle spread his hands in a deprecatory gesture. "I was jealous," he said, "but I was also sensible. Lily went her own way, and I could not blame her. But I did not like to meet her men friends. In fact there were only two of them I ever did meet: the Prisoner of State, as you so humorously called him, and Brigadier Miles. Fortunately they are both dead."

Jervis started a little at this cold-blooded announcement.

"Both dead!" he muttered.

"But yes! The Prisoner of State, as the world knows, was condemned by the International Court and duly executed, and the Brigadier, as you also know, was murdered."

Quimerle laughed at the horrified silence which had fallen upon them.

"Perhaps you think I murdered him?"

"Of course not."

"But the idea had crossed your mind?"

Jervis shook his head in what he hoped was a convincing manner. Belle said nothing.

"The strange thing," said Quimerle, "is that the murder of Brigadier Miles had nothing to do with either jealousy or with affairs of state. It was, as you might say, a completely meaningless murder."

"But who did it?"

"You remember Lady Dawes?"

"The loud-voiced woman at the next table?"

"Yes. I suppose you did not notice the people she had with her?"

"No, I can't say I did, particularly. They were a pretty nondescript lot, I thought."

"Among them was a sort of novelist—"

"A writing fellow!" cried Major Jervis with some disgust. "Who was he?"

"His name," said Quimerle, "was E. M. Forster. Ever heard of him?"

They both shook their heads.

"But why—?" asked Jervis.

"He didn't like soldiers."

"Didn't like soldiers! Why not?" cried Belle.

Quimerle smiled at her indignation. "Perhaps," he said, "his nurse was frightened by a soldier when she was pushing him in his perambulator. It is called, I think, a complex. Anyway, the sight of Brigadier Miles with his medals and his tabs, his assurance and his efficiency, his obvious command of the situation, was too much for him. When the lights went out he seized his opportunity and cut the Brigadier's throat."

There were exclamations of horror.

"Has he been hanged?" asked Belle.

"Not yet," said Quimerle with a touch of regret.

"But he will be, surely?"

"I don't know. I don't know. These writing fellows, as you call them, can get away with anything."

NOTES

ANSELL

At one point the manuscript is unclear: "scraped" (page 2, line 14) could be "scooped". On page 5, lines 13-14, the manuscript has "reason of", probably a slip of the pen for "reason for". On page 6, line 9 from bottom, "ones" is not in the manuscript.

The Boy's Own Book (page 2) supplies not only a recipe for bird-lime but an account of "bat, trap and ball", a game of ancient origin usually known as trap, bat and ball (or trap-ball), and "by many considered to rank next to cricket". In commending it to his son the narrator's father was echoing Lord Chesterfield: "You will desire to excell all boys of your age at trap-ball, as well as in learning."

The *Libro del Consolato del Mare* (page 5; known in English as the Book of the Consulate) was a fourteenth-century codification of customs followed by Mediterranean countries with regard to war contraband.

ALBERGO EMPEDOCLE

Three departures have been made from the text of the story published in *Temple Bar*: on page 13, line 17 from bottom, "effort" replaces the latter's "effect"—a very plausible misreading of Forster's hand; on page 15, line 19, "woken" has been substituted for the presumed misprint "woke"; and on page 29, line 17, "he should forgive"—not "she . . ."—must surely be correct.

Girgenti is the pre-1927 name of the Sicilian town known to the Greeks as Acragas, to the Romans as Agrigentum, and to the modern world as Agrigento. It is interesting, and possibly significant, that the "two fallen columns" of the ruined Temple of Zeus between which Harold falls asleep and dreams of a previous life when he "lived better . . .

loved better" are clearly the legs of a gigantic male figure, one of a series of *Atlantes*, alternately bearded and beardless, which originally supported the entablature; during the nineteenth century one of these was reconstructed, recumbent, and would have been seen by Forster during his visit to Girgenti in April 1902.

The Hôtel des Temples (page 17) was the name of an actual hotel at Girgenti, but a 1900 Baedeker shows no Albergo Empedocle; Forster and his mother stayed briefly at the Albergo Belvedere—which his mother considered dirty. The name he chose is peculiarly appropriate: the philosopher Empedocles (*c.* 493–433 B.C.) was not only the town's most famous citizen, and commemorated as such in many local names, but a believer in reincarnation who himself claimed to be a fallen divinity.

THE PURPLE ENVELOPE

The text incorporates three editorial emendations to the typescript: the insertion of "a" before "gray tangle" (page 38, line 6 from bottom) and before "horizontal bar" (page 47, line 6 from bottom), and (page 50, line 6 from bottom) the substitution of "when" for "which".

"In Tune with the Infinite by Mr Trine" (page 39) is not an invention of Forster's, but the most popular, in its day, of many high-selling books with high-sounding titles by Ralph Waldo Trine (1866–1958). First published in 1897, it ran into countless editions and translations, including a version in Esperanto. In 1917, however, it provoked an irreverent retort, *Harmony or Humbug?*, by one George Bedborough, who had earlier achieved some notoriety for his part in the publication of Havelock Ellis's *Studies in the Psychology of Sex*.

THE HELPING HAND

On page 63, line 4, "it" is not in the manuscript.

Whether or not "Lady Anstey"—who reappears in "The Eternal Moment" as a painter of water-colours—was based in any way on Maud Cruttwell (see page xii), her "little apple-green book, four shillings net, being one of Messrs Angerstein's series of Pocket Painters" was probably suggested by a Bell series, Great Masters in Painting and Sculpture, which were priced at five shillings and in their unfaded state could no doubt have been described as "apple-green". Maud Cruttwell contributed volumes on Luca Signorelli (1899) and Andrea Mantegna (1901).

THE LIFE TO COME

Of two typed versions, one has numerous autograph corrections (and one whole manuscript page, apparently a reconstruction of a missing one), while the other is a fair copy which introduces errors as well as correcting them. Editorial emendations of both typescripts are: "lay" for "laid" (page 70, line 15 from bottom); "root" for "roots" (page 71, line 14 from bottom); the interpolation of "a" before "painful effort" (page 83, line 5 from bottom); and (page 85, line 6 from bottom) the omission of "as he bent back" after "as he embraced". In this last instance, the insertion of a comma would produce a possible reading ("as he embraced, as he bent back his friend"); but it seems more likely that one phrase represents an interlinear or marginal correction of the other, and that Forster failed, as he sometimes did, to delete the superseded words before having the manuscript typed.

In a letter to Siegfried Sassoon dated 21 July 1923 Forster wrote:

> I wish the story could have another ending, but however much skill and passion I put into it, it would never have satisfied you. I tried another chapter, it is true, in the forests of the Underworld "where all the trees that have been cut down on earth take root again and grow for ever" and the hut has been rebuilt on an enormous scale. The dead come crashing down through the foliage in an infernal embrace. Pinmay prays to his God who appears on high through a rift in the leaves and pities him but can do nothing. "It is very unfortunate," says God: "if he had died first you would have taken him to your heaven, but he has taken you to his instead. I am very sorry, oh good and faithful servant, but I cannot do anything." The leaves close, and Pinmay enters Eternity as a slave while Vithobai reigns with his peers. I hear rejoicing inside the hut, to which occasionally the slaves are summoned, I see them come [sic] out again broken in

spirit and crowd outside the entrance or lie like logs under the ice-cold flow of the stream. A gloomy prospect you see—except for Vithobai, who has won the odd trick.

DR WOOLACOTT

On page 88, line 21, "was" is not in the typescript.

ARTHUR SNATCHFOLD

The opening words perhaps reflect a sequence of events similar to that postulated for page 85 (see above): Forster may have written "Sir Richard Conway" above the original "Conway", the typist may have expected Forster to choose between the first and the parenthesized words, and Forster may not have noticed what has happened—or he may have been amused by the result. That the typist ran into trouble later in the story is evident from a one-line gap in the typescript after "failed to do this" (page 111, line 12 from bottom); the first eight words of the next paragraph are an editorial conjecture.

On page 102, line 8, the "a" before "moment" is not in the typescript. On page 108, line 3 from bottom, and page 109, line 16, "had" and "praised" are editorial emendations of "has" and "praise" respectively, as is (page 116, line 11 from bottom) "Women's" of "Village"; such a slip (compare page 112) is much more likely to be Forster's than Donaldson's.

THE OBELISK

The source for this story is a very heavily, and often hastily, corrected typescript. The following words have been inserted by the editor: on page 122, line 9, "why"; on page 129, line 8, the second "her"; on page 130, line 14 from bottom, "it"; on page 132, lines 18 and 29, "you"; on page 135, line 6, "and". Conversely, on page 126, line 12, a superfluous "the" has been omitted before "Tiny's"; and on page 133, between lines 19 and 20, the following paragraph should clearly have been (but was not) deleted by Forster in the course of rewriting:

"The word means a needle, and it is not ob, but obelisk, obelisk" said Ernest, who even at moments of stress demanded accuracy, as well she remembered.

At one point in the typescript the sense appears to have become inverted: on page 129, line 12, "her hand" must surely be correct—the typescript has "his hand". However, the typescript's "nothing Tiny wouldn't say no to" (page 123, line 6 from bottom) probably reflects the speaker's, rather than the author's, confusion between two ways of saying the same thing, and has therefore been retained. If, finally, "happy tears of happiness" (page 131, line 15) reflected unmistakably a similar confusion—or rather, in this case, an imperfectly executed change of intention —"happy" would have to be omitted; but it seems possible that the tautology is meant to match the banal, cliché-ridden quality of Hilda's thoughts in this paragraph.

WHAT DOES IT MATTER?

The problem of determining the relationship between various typescript and manuscript versions and fragments is here particularly acute. The text given is based on the later of the two typescript versions, but incorporates one manuscript fragment which was apparently intended to replace the corresponding passage in the typescript. Three small pencilled corrections to the typescript, however, have not been incorporated, since they appear to be the work of another hand—perhaps J. R. Ackerley's.

On page 143, line 13, "Lido art" is an editorial emendation of "the Lido art", the reading of the text favoured at this point; a version believed to be earlier reads "the Lido style", and it seems likely that Forster changed "style" to "art", but forgot to make the necessary contingent deletion of "the". On page 151, line 6, "capital" is an editorial emendation of "capitol"—which, since "principal" in the same line has been spelled "principle", seems likely to be another spelling mistake. On page 152, line 16, "glass" is an editorial emendation of "glasses".

THE CLASSICAL ANNEX

Two words have been interpolated editorially: "her" (page 154, line 8 from bottom) and "been" (page 157, line 17). In alternative manuscript fragments—the main version begins in typescript and ends in manuscript—the wife goes into somewhat implausible detail about the football match, gives her husband a mild rebuke for leaving his keys lying

about, and remains unaware of his agitation as she goes
off "to decide between toast and crumpets". Back at the
museum, the Curator "knew what he had to do"—presumably, get into the Christian sarcophagus and make the
sign of the Cross—but the fragment peters out amid "laughter of a sort long exorcised" and inconsequential, partly
obscene chatter from the boy.

The Hellenistic statuettes found in graves at Tanagra
(page 154), in eastern Boeotia, are exceptionally lively and
attractive, and the amusingly devious manner in which the
custodian reports the breakage of one is easy to understand.

THE TORQUE

Another messy story from the textual point of view. About
three-quarters of the way through, the manuscript (echoed
so far by a typescript) splinters into a number of overlap-
ping fragments. A continuous narrative can be pieced together in more ways than one, and the arguments in favour
of the version given here are far from conclusive.

On page 165, line 17, "he", is "she" in both the manuscript—surely a slip of the pen—and the typescript. On
page 172, lines 11–12, the manuscript has been altered by
Forster from "Euric's member to a horse's. 'What about
mine?' " to "Euric to a horse's. 'What about me?' " The
intention is clear, and there seems no alternative but (re-
luctantly) to carry it through by emending "horse's" to
"horse", and ignoring the pencilled reinsertion of "member" in another hand. On page 174, line 6 from bottom,
"this" is not in the manuscript.

Perpetua owes only her name to the third-century saint.
The quotation from the "pagan poet" on page 173 is something of a cheat. On metrical grounds it is clearly not continuous, but one might have expected it to come from a
single passage in a single poem. In point of fact, though
both phrases are from Virgil, the first is from the *Aeneid*
(VI. 122; "again and again he journeys back and forth"—
with no sexual connotation), the second from the *Georgics*
(III. 281; "the slimy fluid oozes from his groin").

THE OTHER BOAT

The nature of the textual problem has been outlined in the
Introduction (page xxiv). Though the arguments are in-

volved, the conclusion is fairly clear: that the manuscript fragments (as distinct from the typescript or published ones) were intended by Forster to replace the corresponding passages in the complete typescript.

On page 177, line 17, "fast" is presumably Lionel's childish mistake for "farce". On page 184, line 2, "wearing" is not in the typescript. On page 175, "happy" (line 26) and "moods" (line 33) are editorial emendations of "happier" and "mood" respectively. On page 190, line 6, "or" is not in the typescript.

On page 191, line 8 from bottom, the manuscript fragment which represents the text at this point had, originally, "may bring strength and be useful". This has been "corrected" by Forster to "may bring strength and be could be [sic] summoned". The phrase "could be summoned" occurs also in the typescript ("its strength survived and could be summoned"); in transferring it from the old version to the new, Forster seems not to have noticed the resultant clash of tenses, which has been eliminated by the emendation of "could" to "can".

On page 200, lines 25–26 are an editorial interpolation; something of the kind seems needed, and there is independent evidence to suggest that two lines were inadvertently omitted at this point during retyping. On page 203, line 8, the second "the" is not in the typescript. On the same page, line 8 from bottom, "could" is an editorial emendation of "would"; in Forster's handwriting the two are easily confused. Finally, on page 205, line 15, "lay" is not in the typescript.

THREE COURSES AND A DESSERT

The quotation on page 231 from *Splendeurs et Misères des Courtisanes* occurs in volume I, chapter 36.

BARD BOOKS

the classics, poetry, drama and
distinguished modern fiction

FICTION

ANAIS NIN READER Ed., Philip K. Jason	49890	2.95
THE AWAKENING Kate Chopin	45666	2.25
THE BENEFACTOR Susan Sontag	11221	1.45
BETRAYED BY RITA HAYWORTH Manuel Puig	36020	2.25
BEYOND THE BEDROOM WALL Larry Woiwode	47670	2.95
BILLIARDS AT HALF-PAST NINE Heinrich Böll	47860	2.75
CALL IT SLEEP Henry Roth	49304	2.50
A SINGLE MAN Christopher Isherwood	37689	1.95
CATALOGUE George Milburn	33084	1.95
THE CLOWN Heinrich Böll	37523	2.25
A COOL MILLION and THE DREAM LIFE OF BALSO SNELL Nathanael West	15115	1.65
DANGLING MAN Saul Bellow	24463	1.65
EDWIN MULLHOUSE Steven Millhauser	37952	2.50
THE EYE OF THE HEART Barbara Howes, Ed.	47787	2.95
THE FAMILY OF PASCUAL DUARTE Camilo José Cela	11247	1.45
GABRIELA, CLOVE AND CINNAMON Jorge Amado	18275	1.95
THE GALLERY John Horne Burns	33357	2.25
A GENEROUS MAN Reynolds Price	15123	1.65
GOING NOWHERE Alvin Greenberg	15081	1.65
THE GREEN HOUSE Mario Vargas Liosa	15099	1.65
GROUP PORTRAIT WITH LADY Heinrich Böll	48637	2.50
HERMAPHRODEITY Alan Friedman	16865	2.45
HOPSCOTCH Julio Cortázar	36731	2.95
HUNGER Knut Hamsun	42028	2.25
HOUSE OF ALL NATIONS Christina Stead	18895	2.45

SUN CITY Tove Jansson	32318	1.95
THE LANGUAGE OF CATS AND OTHER STORIES Spencer Hoist	14381	1.65
THE LAST DAYS OF LOUISIANA RED Ishmael Reed	35451	2.25
LEAF STORM AND OTHER STORIES Gabriel García Márquez	36816	1.95
LESBIAN BODY Monique Wittig	31062	1.75
LES GUERILLERES Monique Wittig	14373	1.65
THE LITTLE HOTEL Christina Stead	48389	2.50
A LONG AND HAPPY LIFE Reynolds Price	48132	2.25
LUCIFER WITH A BOOK John Horne Burns	33340	2.25
THE MAGNIFICENT AMBERSONS Booth Tarkington	17236	1.50
THE MAN WHO LOVED CHILDREN Christina Stead	40618	2.50
THE MAN WHO WAS NOT WITH IT Herbert Gold	19356	1.65
THE MAZE MAKER Michael Ayrton	23648	1.65
A MEETING BY THE RIVER Christopher Isherwood	37945	1.95
MYSTERIES Knut Hamsun	25221	1.95
NABOKOV'S DOZEN Vladimir Nabokov	15354	1.65
NO ONE WRITES TO THE COLONEL AND OTHER STORIES Gabriel García Márquez	32748	1.75
ONE HUNDRED YEARS OF SOLITUDE Gabriel García Márquez	45278	2.95
TENT OF MIRACLES Jorge Amado	41020	2.75
PNIN Vladimir Nabokov	40600	1.95
PRATER VIOLET Christopher Isherwood	36269	1.95
REAL PEOPLE Alison Lurie	23747	1.65
THE RECOGNITIONS William Gaddis	49544	3.95
SLAVE Isaac Singer	26377	1.95
A SMUGGLER'S BIBLE Joseph McElroy	33589	2.50
STUDS LONIGAN TRILOGY James T. Farrell	31955	2.75
SUMMERING Joanne Greenberg	17798	1.65
SWEET ADVERSITY Donald Newlove	38364	2.95
62: A MODEL KIT Julio Cortázar	17558	1.65
THREE BY HANDKE Peter Handke	32458	2.25

Where better paperbacks are sold, or directly from the publisher. Include 50¢ per copy for postage and handling, allow 4-6 weeks for delivery.

Avon Books, Mail Order Dept.
224 West 57th Street, New York, N.Y. 10019

BD (2) 2-80

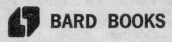 **BARD BOOKS**

DISTINGUISHED FICTION

The Novels of Thornton Wilder
America's Most Honored Writer

THE CABALA	24653	1.75
HEAVEN'S MY DESTINATION	23416	1.65
THE IDES OF MARCH	25213	1.75
THEOPHILUS NORTH	19059	1.75
THE WOMAN OF ANDROS	49460	2.25
THE EIGHTH DAY	44149	2.95
THE BRIDGE OVER SAN LUIS REY	45245	2.25